SHADOW *of* DESCENT

Robert Joseph

HH

HUGO HOUSE PUBLISHERS, LTD.

Shadow of Descent

This is a work of fiction. Names, characters, businesses, places, events, locales, and incidents are either the products of the author's imagination or used in a fictitious manner. Any resemblance to actual persons, living or dead, or actual events is purely coincidental.

ISBN: 978-1-948261-25-8

Library of Congress Control Number: 2019916631

Second Edition

Cover design and interior layout: Ronda Taylor, www.heartworkcreative.com

Hugo House Publishers, Ltd.

Austin, TX • Denver, CO
www.hugohousepublishers.com

DEDICATION

To my mother, a voracious reader with unconditional love for her children.

BOOK ONE

Chapter One

Munich, Germany

CYNTHIA FELT THE SUN BREAK THROUGH THE GRAY DOME OF CLOUDS covering Munich's English Garden. The warm afternoon sun was a gift that lifted her spirits.

She braced herself with one hand on a park bench as her children trotted off to play on the park lawn.

Marta, their au pair, held Cynthia's other arm as she eased down onto the wooden bench. Marta asked, "Are you sure you're strong enough for this outing?"

"I'll be fine. Max and Anna need some time outside. It's such a nice day today."

"Max's birthday party took a lot out of you. I think you need more rest."

They had celebrated Max's third birthday the day before. It was one of the few times her husband had spent a full day with them since they moved to Munich.

Would Max and Anna even remember the birthday party? Would they remember me? Cynthia knew the answer. *They wouldn't.*

She had researched the latest scientific findings on childhood memories. Max and Anna were too young. She lied to herself, hoping for a chance that her children would be the exception.

A breath of summer air slid through her thin hair, an innocent sensation but a harsh reminder of what little time she had left.

She felt some discomfort from sitting on the wood bench, and crossed her legs to search for relief. She tugged the hem of her blue summer dress down to her knees as she watched her children play.

This is all I ever wanted. Maybe the breach in the clouds was a sign. The sun's bright rays a message that my prayers have been heard.

Then, a flutter confirmed the life growing inside of her.

"Marta, promise me again that you will stay on after I'm gone, and take care of them."

"I promise," she replied, "but Mr. Tobin is a good man. He'll slow down."

Jeff Tobin hadn't accepted his wife's illness. They had more money than many third-world countries, and he had proven himself over and over with unparalleled success. But, his work had taken over his life and there was no room left for his family. She worried about who would be there for her children when she was gone. *They need a parent, not a caregiver.*

It was hopeless to keep stewing about the same concerns. She tried not to agonize over things she couldn't control.

What goes on in my Max and Anna's minds? Is their behavior normal? Will their personalities be the same when they are adults?

Even though Anna was younger, she was clearly the leader. Max followed his sister on the paths she created, as though she was the general and he was her soldier.

Cynthia asked, "Your children are grown. Did their personalities change much from when they were Max and Anna's age?"

"Seems like a long time ago. Not much. I'd say they're basically the same. Your children are so happy and healthy. They will grow up to be beautiful, loving adults, just like their mother and father."

Cynthia noticed a dirty-looking vagrant across the lawn looking at her children. She asked, "Who or what is that over there? He looks so young. Do we need to move on?"

"Looks like one of the homeless beggars we have scattered around the city. Don't worry; he's just looking for food."

She turned her attention back to her children. Max's curly brown hair and Anna's blonde, nearly white, locks were a beautiful contrast. They shared the small part of the park with students throwing a Frisbee, families enjoying a picnic lunch, retirees walking their white schnauzers, and young lovers snuggling on out-of-the-way benches. Every few minutes a group of tourists rode by on one of the many bike tours roaming around Munich.

Anna, the general, had her soldier marching all over the open expanse of the lawn, and the children's play caught the attention of a young couple sitting on a bench. The couple was a fresh, romantic sight, and the splendor of their youth radiated all around them. The natural beauty of the young lady's body and face caught Cynthia's attention. *I remember those days.*

The young lady wore short shorts, revealing long, tan crossed legs. Every detail under her thin top stood out. Her light brown hair was pulled back away from the soft features of her face. Her dress and attitude were similar to the way Cynthia remembered herself when she was that age. *Not that long ago.*

The girl was tangled up with a young man with bushy dark hair who was a little too tall for his weight. He had the usual gangly, lanky body of a boy transforming into a man, and he couldn't sit close enough to his girlfriend. They sat, as one, enjoying their time in the sun.

Their affection reminded Cynthia of the time when she and Jeff had met on the first day of class their freshman year at the University of Iowa. Cynthia's face flushed as her tardy entrance interrupted the professor. She found an open seat in the front of the class that was next to a handsome young man with a welcoming smile. Jeff Tobin was that man, and it wasn't long before they would be spending all their time together.

Cynthia nodded at Marta to call her attention to the young couple. "Believe it or not, Jeff and I used to sit like that when we were younger. Not that long ago."

The sight of the two lovebirds brought back nostalgic feelings she hadn't thought of in a while. She wanted to tell the young couple that today may be the best time of their life. She wanted to tell them that time is a precious commodity. No person can capture or stop time from moving too fast. They should know the important things in life and not get caught up in anything that took time away from each other or their family.

We used to sit as one. We were just as inseparable. Maybe it's just impossible to hold on to those feelings, just as it's impossible for children to remain children. I have to appreciate the time I have and remember when we had our time in the sun.

Here I am, in Germany, sitting in a public park, unable to fight a horrible disease, unable to turn back the clock to our life in California or back to our days in Iowa City. I'm completely powerless to exert any control over my own destiny.

We thought it would be a quick trip over here, and then we'd move back to our house in California. The doctor had assured us that the treatments would give me a chance and that I was getting the very best of care. But I still wish we were home.

Anna ordered her big brother around without any of the usual sibling bickering. She was creating a unique structure with sticks and branches that Max retrieved from the trees bordering the lawn. Max needed to enlarge his radius of operation to keep his general happy. He ran over to the edge of the lawn and peered into the trees on the other side of the bike path, braving the foreign territory.

He ran back to his sister with his arms full. Along the way a short, crooked stick fell from his grasp onto the pathway.

Max stopped, and looked back at the stick in the middle of the path. His sister was running toward him. Maybe because of what he perceived to be a dangerous commotion on the path coming their way he left the lone stick on the pathway and ran to Anna, where he dropped his bundle. He used his hands to guide her behind him. Both of his arms extended back behind him to corral and protect Anna while they watched the disturbance play out in front of them.

Cynthia saw what concerned Max. A tour guide, leading a pack of twenty tourists on bicycles, was rushing their way.

The guide looked over his shoulder to get the attention of his group and said, "Just around the corner is the second-largest beer garden in Munich. It's also the second-largest in the world—"

At that moment the front wheel of his bike slipped on the stick that Max had dropped onto the path. The guide desperately tried to keep his bike upright, but because of his awkward position, he had no chance. His fall created a chain reaction that ended up with the group of tourists in a tangled pile of wheels, arms, and legs. There were screams, skinned knees, and hurt pride.

The guide picked himself up and looked back in disbelief. He snatched up the wicked little stick that had caused all the commotion. He could only shake his head as he tossed the stick back into the bushes.

Anna went back to creating a masterpiece of assembled tree branches, while giving specific commands to her older brother.

A sharp pain shot through Cynthia's spine—another reminder of her health's continuous descent. She felt another flutter from her unborn baby, who probably felt the same pain and was fighting for its life.

Marta said, "I think that I felt that one. Are you okay? I wish you would take the medicine they gave you. You know it would help."

"I won't do that to the baby. I'll be fine."

Cynthia placed both hands on her swollen belly to comfort and encourage the life inside. She looked at Max and Anna as she caressed her stomach.

Her somber mood lifted when she heard Max and Anna laughing about something they were doing and again when she saw the young couple wave to her children when they stood to walk away.

Her contented moment was interrupted when the homeless child walked from the other side of the lawn to where the young couple had been sitting. The boy snatched up a brown bag that they had left on the park bench. He looked thrilled when he pulled a fat, half-eaten pretzel from the bag and began to devourer the treasure.

That disturbing scene shocked Cynthia. She had never considered the possibility of a child having to scavenge for food.

Cynthia asked, "Where are his parents? How could a child find himself in this dreadful position? Promise me again you'll watch over them for me."

"I will. Don't worry."

Cynthia felt weaker after that last shot of pain, but was able to return her attention to Max and Anna as they continued their happy, carefree child's play. She hoped Anna would retain her creativity and strong will. She trusted Max would always be there to support and protect his little sister.

The lovebirds walked away on another one of the paths. The group of bruised bikers silently walked their bicycles down the path, away from the accident site, and the young vagrant slipped away in a different direction, eating the prized pretzel.

Cynthia took in all of this beautiful, imperfect life.

A gap opened again in the blanket of clouds. Once again she enjoyed the sun's warm rays on her face.

Then, like a light switch flipping off, her world went black.

Chapter Two

San Francisco

(Seventeen years later)

Richard Holmes sat alone, behind the walnut desk at one end of his office on the 39th floor of the Addison Building in downtown San Francisco, waiting for a 10:00 a.m. appointment with his nephew. He contemplated his upcoming retirement.

He reviewed the rationalizations that justified his unethical career and wondered about how to pass a burden of guilt heavier than his half-ton desk on to his nephew, Anthony Holmes.

If the interview went as expected, young Anthony would be asked to take his place in this chair and his place as patriarch of the family business.

On paper this was the best job a trust officer could hope for—one account, no competitive pressure, no one looking over your shoulder. Do anything—at any cost, at any time. Just do not lose the Tobin Family Trust account.

The hundred-year-old desk was as pristine today as it was when Richard Holmes first moved into this office seventeen years ago. His office was the biggest in the building, signifying his ownership interest and his value to Addison National Bank and Trust.

His broad back and shoulders settled into the indentation he'd molded in the cushions of the leather chair. His gaze took a reminiscent inventory of the office. On his right were two giant wooden bird's-eye maple doors that were the entry point for the office. To his left was a large triple door ensemble. The door in the middle opened onto a large balcony overlooking Golden Gate Park and the Pacific Ocean.

The four walls of the room rose above the walnut wainscoting to the coffered ceiling. A large, hand-cut crystal chandelier hung in the center of the room.

I was forced to take the reins, and I've been the one who's had to shoulder the responsibility for keeping this damn bank afloat. I accepted the burden of trying to keep our family together like Dad wanted. I was the one who negotiated the buyout and gave my idiot siblings what they wanted. I was the one responsible for paying off that debt, and I'm still the one obligated to keep the rest of my family living their life of leisure.

The Tobin children want for nothing, unlike the 1,580 employees who depend on Addison National. Those employees and my family have relied on my ability to make the hard decisions and to keep the doors of this institution open. I had no choice. I have no choice. I've done my best.

Richard shook his head and looked again at the closed bird's-eye maple doors that formed what he imagined was a large, peering eyeball. It seemed to be looking directly back at him, witnessing his dishonesty. Those doors were one thing from his office he wouldn't miss at all. As much as Holmes wanted his privacy, he usually left one of the doors open to keep the eyeball from forming.

At 9:59 Anthony Holmes stepped off the elevator onto the 39th floor, the most coveted office space in the building. Anthony had been on this floor only one other time, when the president of the bank had an important delivery stalled down in the main bank. Someone yelled for Anthony to run the package up to the 39th floor, and he did so with great haste. The delivery was anticlimactic, because the president's office was right next to the elevator doors, and his secretary was there waiting.

Anthony had gotten only one foot off the elevator before she stopped him, grabbed the package, and hurried away. At least he had a chance to sneak a peek at her lovely cleavage. Then he looked down the long, wide corridor to his uncle's office and the majestic doors he had heard so much about.

Anthony had waited a long time for an invitation from his uncle. While he had no clue about why his uncle had asked for this meeting, he was excited to be on the 39th floor.

The elevator doors closed behind him, he turned to his left and started the long trek to the end of the hall. He walked on the dark green carpet, past reception areas with receptionists who looked as if they had just stepped off the front page of a *Cosmopolitan* magazine. He walked past doors with bronze nameplates; engraved with names of men he had never met, knowing they were the very top executives of the bank. The closer he moved to his uncle's office, the bigger the offices became.

He heard the fabric of his pants rubbing together with every step. *Damn …* His hands started to perspire.

That's the last thing I need right now, thinking about the big introductory handshake. He wiped his hands on the back of his pants and kept walking.

When he arrived at the reception area outside his uncle's office, he found the most strikingly beautiful woman he'd ever seen. When he looked down to greet her, he felt a little unsettled. But he managed to say, "Anthony Holmes, here to see Mr. Richard Holmes." The young lady smiled.

Wow.

"Well, hello Mr. Holmes. Mr. Holmes is waiting for you. You can go right in."

At precisely ten o'clock Anthony Holmes pulled open the heavy door of Uncle Richard's office, not knowing what to expect from this meeting. He only knew he was on the 39th floor, where he belonged, where he would do anything to stay.

As Anthony walked through the doors, Uncle Richard stood up from his desk chair with a smile on his face. He met Anthony in the middle of the room and extended his hand. Anthony noticed for the first time that he looked almost exactly like his uncle, but quite a bit smaller.

If my father were in the room, he would look like an exact replica, only he was a much bigger man than Uncle Richard. The three of us would look like stair-step triplets.

Anthony followed his uncle to the conference table. He sat down at the same time as his uncle, and in the same manner. He crossed his hands on the big table; the same as his uncle did, and waited patiently, trying to hide his excitement.

"Anthony, Addison National needs your help. The honor of this bank and the honor of your heritage rest on your ability to understand and execute the duties of my job, your possible new position in the bank. I want you to understand that what I'm about to tell you is confidential. The reason you are sitting here in front of me today is because I trust you. Your father and I have been the very best partners since we were children, and now it is your time.

It's your time to take the baton as the Holmes family patriarch. We have faith that you are the right man for the job, and you can handle this important obligation. Please understand that the faith we place in you will result in many rewards, but it will also require discrete responsibilities."

Anthony replied, "I understand."

"Twenty-five years ago I met a very impressive man who came to the bank in need of financial assistance for his new company. That man was Jeff Tobin. In those days I worked in the commercial loan department and was interested in what he had to say. He gave me a remarkable, but very technical, business plan detailing his company's innovative products. For some reason I clearly and completely understood everything he said and wanted to offer the bank's support. With much tribulation, we were able to persuade the ultraconservative board of directors to take a chance with this man and his company. He and his business partner, Allen Woods, used incredible intelligence and a strong work ethic to take their landmark invention and their company into the core of the computer revolution. Their invention allowed computers to talk to one another faster and more efficiently. It had none of the hype or the glamour that Intel, Microsoft, or Apple Computer had with their products. But all of those companies eventually came to rely on Tobin's creation to run their computers. Their router was an integral piece in nearly every computer, and the need for their product grew exponentially as the computer age took over.

"Jeff Tobin was a friend of mine from the start. He was a very charming, charismatic gentlemen and an unusual engineer. He could speak in a way anyone could understand, even when describing the technical details of why their start-up company was on the cusp of greatness.

"The same product with the same business plan never would have gotten past the stodgy old board of directors we had at the time. But Jeff Tobin had a way about him that made everyone he met want to be part of his future.

"Their invention started gaining acceptance all over the world. With the U.S. operation running smoothly, Tobin decided to move his family to Munich, Germany, to start the European subsidiary. Within a year of moving there, his wife, Cynthia, died of a prolonged illness, leaving him alone with his children. Just a month after his wife died, Jeff was in London on business with his children and their nanny.

"One afternoon he uncharacteristically canceled an important meeting and went back to their villa early. His secretary told me the last words she heard from him —"Anna's smile is haunting me. Do you mind if I go back and spend some extra time with my children?"

"My friend, Jeff Tobin, was playing ball with Max and Anna in the front yard of their rented villa when Max accidentally kicked the ball into the street. Jeff looked to his left for traffic as he dashed into the street to retrieve the ball. That instinct cost him his life. In England traffic comes from the right. Jeff stepped off the curb into the path of a delivery truck.

"Jeff and Cynthia Tobin named me and our bank as executor and trustee of their estate. They also named me as guardian of their children. Because of my relationship with the Tobin family, I was put in charge of the account, and I gave up my additional duties in the commercial loan department. They had no relatives on either side of their families. Jeff's parents had both died of natural causes seven or eight years before. Cynthia's parents, unfortunately, had died in a tragic auto accident when she was just sixteen years old. Both Jeff and Cynthia were only children.

"The Tobin children were so young, and with such a tragedy in their lives I decided to bring Max and Anna back to the States. I was able to find a convent in dire need of funding, and they agreed to take on one of the children until the child was old enough to attend boarding school. The convent, not far from here, had a group of sisters who loved and looked after Anna during those early years. I found a similar solution for Max in a Catholic convent located in Boston. As years went by the children grew up in these schools, and I looked after them to make sure their needs were met. During this time the Internet revolution took over. The stock price of Jeff Tobin's company just kept going up and up. His share of the company grew into tens of billions of dollars. Luckily, I sold all his common stock before the big crash, and the proceeds have been invested in Addison National's Certificates of Deposit. We retain the Tobin Family Trust assets in our bank, and our bank needs to continue to hold onto this account.

"You probably know that your father, your aunt, Joni Linn, and I bought out your other aunts' and uncles' interests in the bank. For the last ten years, Addison National's profits were used to pay off the debt that funded the buyout.

"That debt is now behind us, but Addison National has not put much money back into the business. To right the ship, we have brought in a Wall Street consulting firm to help guide the bank through the twenty-first century, but the transition will be a slow one. We are a long way behind our competitors.

It will take a lot of time, and possibly a small miracle to get us caught up with the rest of the industry. We are living on borrowed time here. The only thing keeping this bank afloat is the assets of the Tobin Family Trust.

"I want to make this crystal clear and make sure you completely understand that your future, the livelihood of your family, and my family rely on the profits of this bank. And, I have to say it again. This bank needs the Tobin Family Trust to stay alive.

"Because this one account is so important to our family, I've had to—and you will have to—accept some challenging responsibilities."

What's he leading up to? Anthony thought. *What's going on here?*

"The most important part of this job, the one that requires the utmost attention, is keeping the trust money in this bank. Technically, Max and Anna could move their money. They are now adults and have the power to do whatever they want. However, my interpretation of the trust's intention is to continue to manage Max and Anna's accounts for their benefit. While both Max and Anna have had the very best education available, neither of them have the specific kind of financial education to manage their own affairs. Addison National has a commitment; an obligation to stand behind the Tobin children, to help them through the uncertainties life may throw at them. Do you understand what I am telling you, Anthony?"

"I understand," Anthony replied, and he understood there was more going on regarding these children.

Richard continued, "I made a decision years ago not to expose Max and Anna to the tragic details of their past. I have intentionally withheld the details of their trust fund from them for fear the information may fall into the wrong hands. There are tens of billions of dollars in the Tobin Family Trust. Can you imagine if either one of the children were drawn into a friendship with the wrong kind of people? Those people could take advantage of Max's or Anna's kind nature and swindle them out of their assets. There is good reason to believe any details from their past would be an obstacle to their schooling and a healthy, productive life. They have adapted very nicely over the years and are happy with their lives. The funds from their trust will afford them every possible luxury this world has to offer, but the shock of knowing the truth could jeopardize their well-being.

"Our job as their trust officers appointed by their father, I remind you, is to protect these children. Any deviation from the course that has been laid out for them over the last almost two decades would put their lives in unnecessary turmoil. I consider myself their protector. If we don't look after these children, who will?" Richard paused, then looked directly into his nephew's eyes and said, "Anthony, do you understand what I am telling you?"

Anthony saw the whole picture laid out in front of him. He understood that his uncle had intentionally kept these young children separated and ignorant of their trust fund for fear they would put the pieces together, take over control of their own money, and possibly move their money out of Addison National. It was clear Uncle Richard had developed this scheme of isolating the children because he knew there was strength in numbers. Keeping them away from each other would keep them in place, so they would not question his actions.

Anthony realized the immense importance of the proper execution of this job, of keeping the Tobin children blind to what was rightfully theirs, and how significant those ramifications were to Addison National and his family. He understood there was some unethical behavior going on here and knew that whoever took over for his uncle would be forced to take on the same responsibilities. That kind of confidentiality and unique relationship with the bank demanded a compensation package equivalent to the associated risk. His uncle had enjoyed the benefits. He had been able to rationalize how the end result justified his means.

Anthony thought, *He would not have asked me to this meeting if he didn't think I was capable of filling his shoes.*

Anthony understood that this was a dream come true. He could hardly hold back his enthusiasm at the thought of being considered for this position. He thought of the power and wealth this would mean. He would finally be able to lure and support a beautiful trophy wife.

He thought about the new lifestyle they would enjoy. They would be members of the yacht club and travel all over the world. They would probably own a second home in Aspen or possibly Tuscany. He thought about the pleasant sights he would see just walking down the hallway of the 39th floor every day to this office, *his* office.

Could I have the same dazzling receptionist?

He pictured himself sitting in the leather chair behind the big walnut desk, and he gave the exact response his uncle waited to hear. "Uncle Richard, I completely understand."

His uncle smiled and said, "When the children were in school I had complete control of their actions. Max has graduated from college, and Anna is in her second year at Pepperdine University. Basically, they are both on their own. I communicate with them via phone and email. They both have a no-limit debit card with a green light for unlimited spending. At this point, it is our job to give them whatever they want. There are no constraints. They could never even put a dent in just the interest their fortune earns."

"They both believe that the trust states that the bank has one hundred percent control of their funds until they are thirty years old. At that time, I told them that the trust specifies a release of up to ten percent of their funds if certain conditions are met. I have cautioned them that we monitor their spending and have the legal power to curtail any overly frivolous lifestyles."

Uncle Richard continued, "Max is very accommodating, even docile. On the other hand, Anna is a problem that we will have to continually fight. That girl has a very strong will. Once, she went on a spending spree and then started asking too many questions. I had to shoot one across her bow, so to speak, and I temporarily canceled her card after she single-handedly put on the biggest party Pepperdine University had ever seen. The all-night party included two rock bands and a stage set up on the beach.

"When she learned I had cut off her credit card, she turned that shot of mine around and came right back at me with all guns blazing. I settled her down with some thoughtful paternal concern, but learned not to turn over that rock again. I decided to just give her what she wanted. She is convinced of the details I outlined just now regarding the trust, and there is no way she could possibly spend enough money to have any impact on the balance of the trust. So I think it's best to just let her do what she wants, pay her bills, and don't go borrowing trouble.

"Their complete biography is documented in an encrypted file that will be made available to you. For the next month, I'll show you how our twenty-four-seven worldwide surveillance operation works. You and I will become one in the way we monitor and protect our clients. I will remain in the loop, but gradually you will make the decisions about how best to serve your clients."

Anthony wanted to let his uncle know that they were on the same page. He said again, "Uncle Richard, I completely understand."

Richard Holmes stood up from the table, walked across the back of the office to a large armoire, and pulled open two doors, revealing a neatly appointed bar. He chose two large brandy snifters and raised them up to the light for inspection. He found a bottle of what was sure to be a rare brandy and then walked back to the conference table. He placed the snifters on the table and said, "I don't usually do this, but I feel a celebration is in order. Your understanding of this matter has lifted a large burden from me. I have complete confidence in your ability to stay the course with this very important matter."

Richard slowly poured a few ounces of the valuable liquid into the snifters. "Do you have any questions for me?"

Still trying to withhold his exuberance, Anthony stood up and said, "I look forward to following in your footsteps. I will continue to protect the Tobin Family Trust."

Anthony's uncle replied with a conspiratorial smile.

He mimicked the way his uncle held the brandy snifter and swirled the golden-brown liquid. They clinked glasses, with a toast to the future.

Chapter Three

San Francisco

(Two weeks later)

ANTHONY HOLMES WAS ALONE, SITTING BEHIND THE BIG WALNUT DESK in his uncle's office. He liked it. He felt he deserved it. His body was a little too small for the chair, though. His feet dangled above the floor, his glossy black shoes swaying back and forth. This was a problem. *Soon I can get my own chair, a chair with a seat I can lower. Hold it; wouldn't the top of the desk be too high then? Yes, it would. If my feet were on the floor, then the top of the desk would be almost shoulder height. That will never work. I could get another, smaller desk, but this is the best desk in the bank, by far.* He leaned back and stared at the ceiling as he pondered the problem further.

Maybe I could find a box or a stool to rest my feet on while I sit. I would feel comfortable, no one would be able to see the box, and that way I can keep the big desk and look bigger than I really am. That's it, that's a good idea. We'll go with that one.

At the same time, crammed into row 38, seat B, of the airliner, Max Tobin was reading a sports novel. The book was well written, but he was restless, and his thoughts kept wandering. He thought about why he was going back to Carnoustie, Scotland, the only place in the world where he felt he belonged.

Also at the same time, Anna Tobin was in row three, seat C, first-class, and she was on her fourth gin and tonic. She looked at her little pink slippers sticking up in the air and wondered how Mr. Holmes would react when he saw the charge for this first-class ticket to Huatulco, Mexico. She hadn't decided what she was going to do when she got there, but she knew for sure what she was not going to do. She was not going to class or worry about what some middle-aged arrogant professor thought about the work she turned in. Anna was officially starting her permanent spring break—the start of her new life—and it was off to a good start.

———

Max sat in a near fetal position in the coach section of the airplane. The young mother sitting on his left was desperately trying to comfort her crying child, and a snoring, overweight man sat on his right. A pretty flight attendant gave him a flirty smile. It had been five hours since he had sat down in the seat, and he wanted to get up and stretch his legs. Max interrupted the busy mother next to him and squeezed past her to the aisle.

This plane was huge, and before he could figure out which way to walk, the smiling flight attendant appeared. She looked up at Max and said, "This way, Mr. Tobin." Max wondered how she knew his name as he followed her to the back of the plane, where she opened the door of the restroom and then followed him into the tight quarters.

While Max had never had this exact thing happen in the past, he did find himself in similar situations often.

The stewardess pressed herself tightly against him, and he looked down to see her big blue eyes and mischievous smile. She placed the palms of her hands on his chest and slowly slid them up to his shoulders. While she massaged his chest and shoulders, the young lady said, "Do you mind?"

Who am I to say no? Max thought as she carried on.

About ten minutes later Max made his way back to his seat.

The frazzled mother stood, holding her wailing infant, to let Max slide by. Suddenly, she thrust the baby into Max's arms, and he heard the same words again—"Do you mind?" Max had never even thought about holding a baby, especially one as upset as this little one. The sobbing baby looked at him for the first time and, unexpectedly, finally stopped crying. Max cradled the child in his arms as the mother opened the overhead luggage compartment, pulled out a bag, and retrieved a full bottle and a clean diaper. She replaced the bag and dropped back into her seat.

The young mother looked at Max and reached for her baby, who was now asleep. The words, *I'll hold her for a while* unexpectedly escaped from Max's mouth. The mother and the other passengers sighed in relief.

In just a few minutes the mother fell asleep, as well. Max looked down at the peaceful baby and felt a twinge of tenderness that he had never experienced before. Comforting the infant gave him hope that it was possible for him to find love and family somewhere in this world. It allowed him to be cautiously optimistic about going back to Carnoustie to find something he couldn't define, something that may not exist, but something he had been in search of his entire life.

Max sat with the baby in his arms and thought back to when he traveled to Carnoustie with his college golf team and played golf through the wind, past the pot bunkers, and on the lightning-fast greens. The tournament ended with his match against Scotland's best, Ian McDowall, on the twelfth hole. Max rolled in an easy ten-footer for another birdie to end the match. The gallery respectfully applauded both players and started to make their way back to the clubhouse. Max shook McDowall's hand, but before he could let go, he heard McDowall say, "I'll tote yer bag the rest of the way, if you'll play on."

The rest of the crowd caught wind of what was happening, and they watched as Max played on alone. He finished the last six holes four under par. The tournament was match play, and on number two and number seven, tap-in putts were conceded, so there was no official score. Max's score would have broken the course record. Everyone in the small town was wild with excitement. That was one tournament where his coach or teammates couldn't hold him down. The people of Carnoustie knew what they saw. They toasted Max all night. For one of the few times in his life, Max felt at home, as if he were one of them.

⚬

Anna had had too much to drink. She sat halfway back in her first-class seat, enjoying some ridiculous movie she had seen many times before.

She felt a tap on her shoulder and turned around to see a man looking at her. He said something that Anna couldn't hear because of the headphones she wore. To rectify the situation she removed the headphones and attempted to stand up. But her elbow slipped off the leather armrest, she lost her balance and spilled some of her drink. Anna sprang from her seat to minimize the damage, and then she turned around to see a middle-aged man gaping at her. She couldn't help but chuckle when she saw the look on his face. She smiled at him and said, "Hello." The man didn't move. He just looked at her with his mouth slightly open. He didn't speak. He took a step backward and hurried away. Still smiling, Anna looked around at the other passengers, hoping for an explanation. All she received were blank stares. She shrugged, dropped back into her seat, put the headphones back on, and giggled her way through the rest of the movie.

Anthony Holmes was still pondering his future when the door opened and his uncle walked into the office. Anthony stood up and said, "I thought you were planning to take the afternoon off today. Sorry ... I didn't mean to sit—"

"Don't worry about it, Anthony. Sit down. There are some things I want to go over with you before I leave. You should know that Max is on his way to Carnoustie, Scotland, and Anna is on her way to Huatulco, Mexico. I want you to dig into their records from The Agency and try to figure out why they're going there and what they're planning to do when they get there. But first I want to go over the details of our relationship with The Agency and how they support our mission of protection for the Tobin children."

Uncle Richard went on, "The Agency is responsible for knowing exactly where the Tobin children are and what they're doing at all times. They should be able to offer a prediction of what they will be doing next. I have a direct line to Reed Jackson, the owner and the man in charge of The Agency, to discuss any unusual activity that may be observed. Over the last fifteen years, the twenty-four-hour surveillance operation was mundane duty for these professionals. The children were basically locked away in boarding schools and college without many options or maybe better said, without many possibilities for independent decision making. Because of their ages, the children were compliant subjects. College life changed that behavior somewhat over the last couple of years, but nothing a little more money and manpower couldn't easily handle. Clearly, as Max and Anna get older, additional challenges to the covert operation will be introduced, but there is unlimited funding available. In a perfect world, Max and Anna will soon get married and settle down into normal American family lifestyles.

"The Agency has a dual mandate in their job description: number one, to monitor and report on the Tobin children's daily activities; number two, to protect the children from dangers from the outside world. Protection is equally important because the Tobin Family Trust documents specifically state that if one of the children dies, their share of the trust will automatically be given to a group of charities.

"The biographical files for the children are set up as individual records for each of them, and the software programs hosting these files offer powerful search engines and sorting capacities.

"From Max's files, you could choose the word *Carnoustie* and watch as the software lists all the possible information in order of probable relevance. You can read about the Crown Cup matches from last year and see the newspaper articles describing how 'Brau Iceman' humbled the competition and how Max became a cult hero to the residents of Carnoustie."

Uncle Richard went on, "Max is the easy one. As for Anna in Huatulco, Mexico, I don't have the slightest idea as to what that girl is up to. You probably should give Reed Jackson a call and ask him about what's going on there. I've told him that you are gradually taking over my duties here, so he's expecting your call. That's about it for me today."

Richard took out his cell phone and said, "If you need anything, just give me a call. And don't hesitate to ask Michelle for some help. Just push that button on the phone and she'll pop in here to see what you need."

"Thanks. I'll get to work."

After Uncle Richard left the office, Anthony turned on his computer and typed the word *golf* as a keyword for finding Max's files. The information came up, telling me about how Max learned to play the game at an early age. During the summers of his grade school years, when all the other children went home to their family, Max stayed in the empty dormitory of his school. He was allowed off campus to play golf a few blocks away at a nine-hole municipal golf course and driving range. During the week Max was welcome on the golf course, and he spent nearly every day roaming the small golf course on his own, practicing, playing golf, and sometimes hanging out with the groundskeeper and his staff. Eventually, he naturally fit into the daily life of all the workers at the course. Nick was the head groundskeeper, and he was also a very good player. He taught Max the basics, but let him find his own game on the driving range and let him play round after round on that old golf course.

21

In the afternoon and on weekends the small nine-hole municipal course was crowded with golf leagues and weekend players. Young Max did not belong on the golf course alone with that motley crew, so he had to find another way to occupy his time. Staying at the boarding school was one option, but being alone in his dormitory room really wasn't a very good choice.

A short bike ride across the tracks were public basketball courts occupied by inner-city, black juveniles who took the game of basketball very seriously. When the golf course was full, Max went to those courts and fought like hell for a chance to play. His continuous attendance, his fight for a spot on the court, and the fact that he went there at such a young age eventually paid off, and he was adopted and protected by this group of athletes. As the years went by, he developed unique friendships with all of the players. The gangbangers who didn't play basketball didn't like having this punk white kid invading their turf, but Max was a protected guy on the streets of this neighborhood. Everyone knew and respected this unwritten law.

The Agency's notes said that Max was a natural basketball player, and because of his size and the street smarts he learned in those tough games, he turned into a terror on the court. He played street ball with and against groups of tough characters. As Max got older and stronger, he spent most of his time on the "A" court, playing with current and past college players. It was a great learning experience in many ways but a big disappointment in many more. Max's style of streetball was too primitive for his small school and the schools they competed against. Max was unstoppable on the court by any of his teammates, and that drove his coach crazy. The coach was more interested in having the boys run offensive plays and stick to the strict regimen he had developed. No team had an answer for this six-foot, six-inch maniac, who was strong as an ox and could jump out of the gym. He made everyone else on the court look like sissies, which didn't sit well with the parents who were paying a lot of money for their sons to get the attention they felt they deserved. Their pressure on the administration at his school was even greater than that from the other teams in the conference. They wanted Max off the court. Eventually they all got what they wanted. Max quit the team.

Anthony finished the section about Max's golf experience by reading how Max never played anywhere but on that one small nine-hole municipal golf course until he tried out for the golf team his last year in college. He was one of the best players on the team, but rarely was allowed to play because the team was already set, so there was no way for Max to break into the starting lineup. The college was primarily concerned with building resumes and appeasing the parents who were paying the overpriced Ivy League tuition—the same way Max was held back in high school on the basketball court because he had no one pulling strings for him. There was no one in Max's corner except for the brothers across the tracks.

Anthony read a letter from Reed Jackson to his uncle regarding some concerns he had. From Reed Jackson:

"Max has a few good friends, but something is missing. His classmates have expectations from their parents and hope from their grandparents. Those subtle, yet firmly understood expectations guide the young men as they slowly develop into men. Max has no expectations. He has no role models or family history to guide him in any direction. Like a rudderless boat struggling against the current, Max fights hard for something he can't define or imagine. He's drifting through the important years of his life, just going through the motions without guidance. He has no purpose in his life. I'm not sure what the solution is, Mr. Holmes. You should know Max is a good young man, but he needs some direction."

Anthony went into Anna's file and typed in the keyword *Huatulco*. Nothing came up. He typed the word *Mexico*, and there were still no hits. He thought it was time to give Reed Jackson a call to find out what he knew.

"Hello, this is Jackson."

"Hello Mr. Jackson, this is Anthony Holmes, Richard Holmes's nephew. I will be your new contact regarding the Tobin children."

"Yes, Mr. Holmes. Your uncle has given me the green light to start working with you. What can I do for you?"

"I'm curious about why Anna is going to Mexico."

"She took us by surprise when she made the arrangements to travel to Huatulco, Mexico. Huatulco is a quaint town on the pacific side of Mexico, way south, almost to Central America. There are a few small resorts there and a couple of towns where native Mexicans live. There is no industry there. The Mexican government decided about thirty years ago to build an infrastructure to support the resorts. The area is very safe compared to other places in Mexico. It's basically an area where Mexicans go on vacation instead of Americans."

Holmes said, "Can we assume she's going there on spring break? I'm looking at photos of her in the file. Is that the way she really looks?"

"Yes, unfortunately, that's the way she looks. A typical college spring break is our assumption. She has just one bag with her and a return flight booked for next week. We have three men on her flight who will keep their eye on her.

"Okay. Let me know right away if you have any concerns." Holmes hung up before Jackson could respond. Holmes thought about the call. He thought he had demonstrated enough authority to make Jackson understand who was in charge.

Chapter Four

Huatulco, Mexico

(Same day)

ANNA FELT A WARM BREEZE WHEN SHE STEPPED OUT OF THE AIRPLANE. Palm trees swayed in the wind, and she could smell the fresh ocean air. *Nice, I must be in the right place.* Her hair blew back as she glided down the portable stairway that had been rolled up to the aircraft. She stopped at the bottom of the steps and tilted her head back to accept Mexico's warm afternoon sun. She held that pose for a moment, as if being touched from above by the sun's rays. She stretched her legs as she strode across the tarmac toward the terminal. She couldn't help but smile as each brisk stride put a little more distance between her and her school, between her and everything she wanted to forget, and closer to the start of her new life.

Several minutes later, all the passengers were queued up in the narrow roped aisles behind Anna, waiting for the Mexican customs officials. Anna's first-class ticket put her at front of the line where she felt the typical, lingering stares that always came her way for no reason. She heard whispers from the other passengers behind her as she wondered again about her encounter with the odd man on the plane.

She refused to look at the other passengers, refused to acknowledge their presence or to let them think she gave one little shit about any of them. Anna stood up straighter, withdrew more, and put her headphones back on as she waited impatiently.

Come on, let's get going, Anna thought as she witnessed the lack of activity around the passport booths. She half expected something to go wrong with her escape plan. *Could Mr. Holmes have rescinded her passport from the bank in San Francisco?* If he had, would that be because he somehow knew her intentions? Or was he upset about the expense of the first-class plane ticket and the suite she had booked at the beach resort? She was certain all her documents were in order. *Just play it cool. I'll find out soon enough.*

While the heat and humidity were a welcome change from the plane ride and the west coast spring weather, she started to feel a little uncomfortable, a little claustrophobic, with all the people in such a small space.

Her fears proved to be unfounded when she breezed through customs with only a few terse questions from the agents. Anna proceeded to baggage claim and watched the conveyor belt for her luggage. Again she felt the stares of the other passengers, who scanned her up and down. She hated to be around other people, and she assumed that everyone could see she was alone, that she was the one who didn't belong there. She had been an outcast her whole life, the girl with no family, with no friends, with no love. She had learned a long time ago from the isolation inflicted on her by her pompous classmates to take those looks and turn them around, to stand up straighter, and to hold her head higher. She had turned the emptiness in her heart into her own kind of fury, and that fury had made her strong and confident.

Anna positioned herself on one side of the baggage claim turnstile, with her small backpack slung over one shoulder. There, she was out of sight and away from the passengers crowding around the baggage carousel. Now she felt content, safe, and peaceful, with no eyes on her or snickers behind her back.

The crowd grew restless because the conveyor belt wasn't moving. Passengers huddled close together, blankly looking at the motionless conveyor belt. The bored, impatient people once again turned their attention to her.

A middle-aged couple was standing just on the outside of the fray, looking directly at her. The man said something to his wife, and Anna wondered if they had been in the first-class seating area on the plane.

A young family of five huddled near them. Their youngest daughter looked right at Anna and then said something to her mother. The mother glanced at Anna and then whispered something to the little girl. The rest of the family eyed her and then quickly turned away. Anna stood up straighter and looked away.

Beep, beep, beep. A red light flashed, and mercifully the baggage conveyor belt started moving. When Anna saw her bag, she shouldered her way through the crowd, grabbed it, and hurried away. Outside, she spoke fluent Spanish to a cab driver waiting at the curb.

Five hours after leaving the airport, Anna's cab drove up the hill to the Camino Real Resort. When she opened the front passenger door, several empty cans of Tecate beer fell out.

Anna had persuaded the cab driver to stop on the way from the airport for some cold refreshments. He turned off the main highway and drove down a dirt road to a small cantina, which was busy with all kinds of activities. Children played soccer in the parking lot, and a steady stream of locals came and went at the small store. The driver asked Anna if she would wait a few minutes while he went inside to talk to his brother. Anna sat on a picnic table and watched the children play soccer. She felt at ease, a little out of place, but she was excited about her new independence.

Ten minutes later the cab driver walked out of the cantina carrying a cooler. Anna saw him from the middle of the soccer game, with all the children around her. She reluctantly bid adios to the children and returned to the cab.

Several stops later, they finally arrived at the Tangaluna Bay resort area. Anna had enjoyed the trip. She loved meeting all new people and conversing with them in their native language. *Maybe some of that bullshit schooling actually paid off.*

Checking in to the resort was another adventure. She shelled out five-dollar tips like breadcrumbs to seagulls, enjoying every minute of it. Eventually, she found her suite and quickly unpacked her things. She thought about going out and getting crazy at one of the bars in the neighboring town of La Crucecita. But the day was mostly behind her, and she'd had enough alcohol already, so she decided to stay in for the night.

She had dreamed about this day for a long time, a day when she was on her own, a day when all the decisions that were made were hers. She felt as if she'd pulled off an escape from a maximum-security prison, and now she was free.

Anna didn't know when the fun would stop, when her credit card would be maxed out, or when Mr. Holmes would send for her. She predicted that it would be at least a few weeks before he pulled on the reins. That was one of the things she didn't know. What she did know was that until that time came, she would take advantage of every minute. She wondered what was in store for her tomorrow. There were so many options. She smiled just thinking about the possibilities. She decided to start the morning out with a nice long run. She knew a good run would clear the alcohol from her system. She had already mapped out a route from one the tourist maps she'd snagged at the front desk. She thought about going on the advertised "Snorkeling Adventure," on a shopping spree, or just lounging around the pool. *I can do whatever I want.*

Tiredness settled in, and Anna prepared for bed in the huge suite. The bed was big enough for four people. She tossed her only real friend, a threadbare, faded pink bunny rabbit, onto the middle of the king-sized bed and followed it there. With her bunny snuggled under her chin, she struggled to find the perfect arrangement of pillows and her headphones.

Anna always wore headphones when she slept. She needed the constant noise to quiet her thoughts, to occupy her mind so she wouldn't think about her futile situation. As a child, she had cried herself to sleep nearly every night. She was forced to learn how to be strong during the day, but even now she couldn't fight the night. At night her mind wandered, allowing sadness and loneliness to fill her thoughts.

She reviewed the events of the day. How different her life could have been if she'd had someone in her heart. She didn't have a single memory of her parents or a picture she could use to conjure a fantasy. Deep down she knew her mother was loving. She was certain her mother looked down from heaven to give her strength for the next day. She was sure her father was proud of her, and if he was there, he would protect her and take away all this pain. Night after night her hopes and prayers were never answered. Anna dealt with the emptiness of night by filling her mind with anything else. She learned to never, ever, sink into the torture of hope.

Spanish gibberish flowed through the headphones, into her ears, and her mind. Anna closed her eyes. Tonight she wouldn't let her thoughts wander around in the past. She forced herself to listen to the sounds coming through her headphones. She smiled as she reviewed the events of her happy day, and how … then she caught herself and concentrated on the gibberish.

Chapter Five

Carnoustie, Scotland

(The next day)

Tom Riley was one of the professional master caddies at Carnoustie Golf Club. He had just finished playing his morning game. From the members' tees, he was out with a thirty-five and back in with a thirty-eight, which was good enough to win both his Nassau bets. He and seven of his mates had two standing tee times at 7:38 and 7:50 each morning. They played a big skin game, a team best-ball, and whatever individual games they could muster up within the group. The betting didn't amount to much, but whenever Tom could snag a few quid off his friends, it usually meant he played well. Five of the eight players of his group caddied for tourists in the afternoon to earn some extra money.

Tom and his good friend Michael drew a 1:30 tee time for their caddying duties, and the time had come to finish up their pies, their pints, and their stories. From the starter's window, Tom and Michael had their foursome pointed out, and with a keen eye they tried to predict the better players. The better the player—the easier the afternoon. After introductions, Tom picked out a bag and carried it to the driving range, where he stood it up and inspected the clubs. He took a small towel from his back pocket and pulled out the sand wedge to clean it. Tom could tell a lot about a player just by looking at his clubs. The bag was a walking bag, but it looked as though it had never been off a cart. Tom was glad he didn't have to lug around one of the big leather bags so many of the Yanks brought over, because they felt the need to look like one of the touring pros. All in all, it looked as if this would be a good afternoon, and if his player didn't get totally humiliated by the course, there should be a nice tip.

Tom looked up and down the range while he waited for his player to finish his lunch. Michael had picked out a spot downrange and was going through the same motions. Something at the far end of the range caught Tom's attention. He squinted a little and noticed a big man with hands in the perfect position at the top of his backswing. The shoulder turn was powerful, and the sound of the impact was substantial, but Tom couldn't see the ball in flight. The man teed up again and duplicated the exact same swing. This time he found the ball in flight. *Could that be Max Tobin, the young man I caddied for last year in the Crown Cup matches?* Tom left his bag and started walking downrange, and without looking at Michael as he walked by, said, "Will you watch me bag for me, Michael?"

Soon he got close enough to recognize "Brau Iceman." Tom walked up right behind Max when he was in his pre-shot routine. With perfect balance and a force like no other, Max ripped another one high, long, and straight. Max seemed unfazed by Tom's presence behind him. He was reaching for another ball when Tom said, "What brings you back, Mr. Tobin?"

Max looked up and smiled when he recognized Tom—a grin as big as his tee shot. "I came back to play the course, Tom." Max extended his big paw and gave Tom's hand a good shake.

Tom said, "What are your plans for your stay?"

"I was just hoping to see you and the other guys and hopefully play the course, but the starter said the course is booked all week."

Tom told him how the members had the course in the morning, and the tour groups had the afternoons. As Tom explained this to Max, he felt puzzled by Max's blank reaction. Tom thought for a second and said, "I tell you what, you can have my time in the morn and play in my group. I have to get back to me bag now, but I'll see you here tomorrow morn at seven."

"Thanks, Tom. I'll be here."

As Tom walked back down the range he couldn't help but wonder what Max Tobin's story was. He hated to give up his spot in the morning because of how well he played earlier in the day, but he couldn't leave Brau Iceman hanging.

When Tom got back to the bag, his player was already hitting some half-swing wedges to get warmed up, and after about half an hour on the range the foursome headed to the first tee. The four players were friends from Chicago, and they had spent over a year preparing for this trip. Tom listened as the four of them talked about each other's game, made some small bets, and predicted each other's score. Tom's player said he was an eight on his home course, and he let it be known that his course was one of the best—the US Open had been played there. Tom could tell he had a pretty good game. His compact swing would help when the wind got up later in the day. Tom also knew this guy wouldn't break a hundred.

Five hours later, Tom's player walked up the 18th fairway. He had already breezed past a hundred on his scorecard. Tom watched as he hacked the ball out of the gorse into the water and thought, *It will be nice to see Rose and tell her about my day. I bet she's made a good supper.* The guy took a drop and hit what he thought was a nice shot, but the wind grabbed it and threw it into one of the large pot bunkers protecting the 18th green. Tom watched the man blast out of the bunker and thought, *My Lazy-Boy is going to feel good tonight. I wonder what Max ended up doing all afternoon.*

Tom played his role pretty well all afternoon, and he felt good about the big tip he received. He had a lot to tell Rose about his day. As he walked up the hill away from the course, he looked back to see Max in the same place on the range, still hitting balls. Tom shook his head and continued home.

The next morning everyone was excited because word had gotten out that Brau Iceman was back in town. Tom arrived at the course a little early, and sure enough, Max was already there, practicing his chipping. Max was by himself, and he looked out of place to Tom, partly because of his size and partly because of the feeling Tom had the day before. Max played the pro tees, and Tom's buddies played the members' tees, as always. All the guys were in awe of what they saw in Max's game. Max played with rented clubs, wore tennis shoes, and still played the course under par. It was great to watch, but they all felt the same way—it wasn't their regular game.

After they were done playing, the group sat together for a lunch of pies and cold beer. The conversation revolved around Max. Tom asked Max what his plans were.

Max said, "I just graduated from college and really don't have anywhere to go. I've never really had a home. The only places I've ever known are the schools I attended. I don't have any specific plans. I came back here because of how well I played in last year's tournament and how Carnoustie felt as much like home to me as anywhere else."

After some head scratching by the men in the group, they all agreed to meet at O'Malley's for supper after the afternoon rounds.

When Max walked into O'Malley's, he spotted Tom with a big group of people in the corner. Tom waved him over and introduced him to all the guy's wives. For a short time Max felt as if he was part of something, but one by one the couples eventually all went home. Max was left alone. He didn't know anyone else in the pub, so he soon felt out of place. Max could tell the other patrons at the bar knew who he was, but it was clear to Max that he was an outsider.

The next morning Max went back to the course, but no one offered to give up his spot for him to play. Max stayed on the range by himself and hit balls all morning. He was able to fit into an afternoon cancellation with one of the tour groups. He played with some hacks from New Jersey who didn't respect the game of golf, didn't respect Max's game, and didn't respect one another. Max played well, but no one cared. He didn't care.

<hr />

From a distance, Tom watched Max two-putt for an easy par on the 18th hole.

As predicted, Max started walking back to the hotel, and Tom watched him approach. Max walked with his head down, looking at the ground just in front of his feet. As he came closer, Tom broke his concentration, saying, "How'd ya play today, Max?" Max raised his head, looking surprised, but when he recognized Tom, he straightened up and flashed his patented big-dimpled smile.

"Hi, Tom, nice to see you. What are you doing up here?"

"I was waiting for you to finish up and wanted to see if you'd like to grab a pint or two with me before I go home for supper."

"Sure, Tom, of course I would. Should we go back to O'Malley's?"

"Nah, let's just walk over here to Shivas'. He has a small place close by, and he's been a friend of mine since we were in school."

Tom chose a small table out of the way, where they rested their pints of cold Guinness.

Tom wasn't sure how to begin the conversation, and he didn't have any idea where it would lead, but there was something in the back of his mind gnawing at him. He knew he had to see if he could help Max. Tom said, "I asked you to come and sit with me because I wanted to find out what your plans are, and if there is any way I can help you sort things out. It seems to me you are a little lost and are looking for some direction. You told me you graduated from college, but you don't have any specific plans in your life right now. I was wondering if you have any family that you keep in touch with or if you have looked at getting a job."

Tom listened as Max explained how he had lost his parents early on, had absolutely no other family, how he grew up in boarding schools, and basically had been alone his whole life. He explained how there was a trust fund set up for his benefit, and the assets in the fund were controlled and administered by a bank in San Francisco. Max told Tom about how his contact at the bank paid his bills, and this man had assured him that there was enough money in the trust to cover his expenses, so he didn't have to work.

Max said, "When I finished my finals a couple of weeks ago, the lease was also up on my apartment. I didn't see any reason to stay in Providence, so I contacted Mr. Holmes from the bank to see if I could come back here. For whatever reason, Tom, this place has felt like home to me more than any other place I've lived. But after today I'm not sure I belong here either. I guess I was just hoping to find the same feeling I had when I was here last year."

Tom leaned back a little in his chair, took a big drink of beer, set his glass back down, and said, "I can tell you've had a tough start in life, but you are a young, strong man with endless opportunities. I can understand why you came back here, and the boys and I are all pleased to see you again. But I have to tell you—Carnoustie is not a place for you. Carnoustie is a place for a man like me—a man without a lot of options. I'm okay with that, because it's been my life from the beginning, and it's where I belong. Carnoustie isn't the kind of place an outsider can come to and make their home. Everyone here has deep roots, with generations of families who have lived here and who have all grown up together. I hate to tell you this because I consider you a friend, but you have to figure out something else."

It was clear to Tom that Max was hearing something he already knew, but saying those words to a person he regarded as his friend was tough. Max slumped in his chair, and Tom could see his eyes swell.

Tom went on, "My wife and I were never fortunate enough to have children, so I'm no expert on giving you advice about how you should live your life, but if I did have a son, this is the conversation I hope I would have had with him."

"Thank you. This means a great deal to me."

"At the end of the day, it is your life and you have to decide how you want to live it. My father told me when I was young, to define what kind of man I wanted to be and then make certain my actions lined up with my definition. I would say the same to you. Define what kind of man you want to be and then wake up each morning and be that man.

"You have a purpose in this life. While we can't see what it is now, someday, if you stay humble, everything will become apparent. You have to be patient, though. Even though it doesn't seem like it now, time goes very fast. When you get to be my age you'll look back at this time in your life and remember how it all went by in an instant—an instant, Max. Every day is one less day in your life, so make sure you treat it as a new experience, a new opportunity to be more humble and to better define yourself.

"That's about all I have for you, my friend. I just gave you all I know about living a happy life. Seems like pretty simple things, I know, but you will be tested by people who are not your real friends or by forgetting that your athleticism, good looks, and financial position are all things you didn't earn. You are a fortunate man, and I have faith you will find your way. As time goes by, remember our conversation, and remember you always have a good friend right here."

They looked at each other, eye to eye, and Tom could see Max's eyes change again.

Max noticed a silence had covered Tom's presence, and it was clear he was pondering something very important. He pretended not to notice by casting his gaze around the pub. A few other men sat together at similar tables. Max recognized the faces of some of them, and he could see they were all interested in him and Tom and probably wondered what we were up to. Max brought his attention back to the still-pensive Tom and waited to see what would happen next.

Tom said, "I've decided I want to try to give you a gift. This gift is something very few people in the history of the world have ever known. I am breaking centuries of unwritten laws by even mentioning this to you. But I think it's important, and I think you deserve a piece of our life—the men of Carnoustie."

Max didn't know what to say. "I don't need a gift. Sitting here talking with you is the best present I could hope for."

"It's not that kind of gift, and there's further proof you deserve it. What I want you to have has no weight or volume. It's more of a state of mind. A fable was written a long time ago that Scottish men all over our country hold in secrecy. No ears but Scottish ears have ever heard the verses, and it's sacrilegious to even tell an outsider of its existence, least of all suggest they may take part in the ritual.

Only specific, sanctioned Scottish tavern owners are allowed to keep a copy of the revered manuscript titled "Toil and Time" behind the bar. They have a responsibility to protect the document, to never let it escape the tavern's confines. For over two hundred years this tradition has held. Now as a gift to you, I'm going to ask Shivas and the rest of the men in this pub to make an exception and allow you to hear the mystical words. Let's see if we can find consensus here, among my friends."

"Shivas!" Tom cried loud enough to catch everyone's attention. "Would you please set up the bar and yourself with a nice pour of the eighteen-year-old Oban Scotch whisky and hand me your copy of 'Toil and Time'?"

A hush blanketed the room. Shivas looked at Tom and shook his head no.

Tom stood up and said, "Gentlemen, I ask that today we make an exception and offer Brau Iceman this gift as our appreciation of the respect he has shown the men and the links of Carnoustie."

The pub grew quiet again as the men looked at one another, seeming to consider Tom's bold request. Tom was one of the most respected citizens of Carnoustie, and it was clear the men valued his words. They talked quietly among themselves, occasionally glancing at Max. Finally, they all rapped their beer mug on the wooden tabletops and gave Shivas looks of approval. Max could see Shivas pondering this important decision, and then he gave his good friend Tom a big smile, with all five of his teeth.

Shivas turned and opened the crooked doors of an antique cabinet behind the bar. He took out his sparkling crystal tumblers. All the men applauded him, and one man cried, "Here, here!" Shivas slowly and carefully poured the single malt Scotch whisky into the heavy glassware. Tom distributed the drinks to everyone.

As the others looked on, he said to Max, "You hold in your hand proof that God loves man. The story of how this fine Scotch whisky was made will be told to you in a few minutes, but it is important that you understand the beauty of this creation and consider the respect all the men in this room have for you by giving you this gift. Everyone in this room expects the words you are about to hear to guide you through your life, much the same as the words have guided all of us."

Max sat up straight and looked around the room with an acknowledgment of understanding and appreciation, but he still had no idea what would happen next.

Tom looked across the room at a young lad sitting by himself and said, "Dylan, the door."

Max had met Dylan Raymond at the caddie shack last year. He was a local boy, coming of age, who wanted to be part of the scratch golfing group, and he wanted to be part of the Carnoustie lore. He was a good player, and he fit into some of the good golf matches when there was an odd number. He sat with boys at the caddie shack for lunch, and he spent a little time in Shivas' pub. But he was on the fringe of the "good guys" only because of his age. Max could tell that the old-timers really liked Dylan, but he still had to pay his dues. They all had.

Dylan had disappointment written all over his face. He walked to the door and opened it to leave.

Tom said, "Dylan, no. Lock the door and please join us."

An ear-to-ear smile bloomed on Dylan's face. Tom handed Dylan one of the crystal tumblers partially filled with the smooth, sienna-colored scotch. The smile on his face hadn't dimmed in the least as he accepted the glass. Dylan sat down at his table again and leaned back against the brightly painted sky-blue wall, carefully clutching his priceless drink. His thick, curly brown hair escaped the confines of his golf cap and covered most of his face. Dylan placed his new best friend, the beautiful sienna colored single-malt on the table next to a small vase, holding what could be best described as a young smiling flower, a soft fresh lily. The contrast of these colors, the symbolism of Dylan's inclusion linked with Max's suspect invitation, and the grin that may never leave his young face was one more element of this exclusive soiree that Max would never forget.

With everyone in place, Tom slowly walked to the end of the bar and turned as though on a stage in front of his now captive audience. He picked up the faded leather portfolio that Shivas had placed on that end of the bar and opened it.

Toil and Time

Picture a majestic oak tree created from a tiny acorn. Envision a million years of transformation the soil needed to act as an agent to sustain life. Imagine the trial and error of skilled craftsmen passing on their discoveries and talents to future generations.

A hundred years of strong, powerful growth could offer no defense when the crash of that mighty oak startled its neighboring creatures.

Stout men dissected the mammoth beast. The wood was measured, was cut, was pieced inside forged metal rings, then pounded, cut again, tested, charred, and filled with the pride of human labor no machine could replicate.

The dormant barley seeds laid naked and vulnerable in the warm, moist, black earth. A series of random, uncontrollable events including the sun, the clouds, the Man, and the seasons, allowed the plants to grow strong. The only certainty was those variables would always be different, but every year, nature found a way.

The finished produce had no value— without the secret recipe, without proper methodology, without the master's touch.

Thousand-year-old peat bogs were forced to awake, to finally come to life, and asked to participate.

Centuries-old copper stills witnessed natural distillation where science reacts exactly the same when heat and liquids fuse.

Day after day, night after night, for the next eighteen years the cunning spirits comfortably hid in closed, dark confines, slowly sapping, thieving the oak's last bit of strength.

As I sit here tonight pondering many of life's mysteries, the fine crystal recedes, and the unique taste of these cool spirits come back to life one last time, arousing my anticipating palate. I consider the toil and time sacrificed for my benefit. I am a Scot who acknowledges and accepts this sublime gift as a reward, as an invitation to find more humility in my life-—very single day.

Tom read the title out loud.

"Toil and Time"

He then looked back up at his audience and recited the first paragraph from memory in a mesmerizing, slow, even tone:

"Picture a majestic oak tree created from a tiny acorn. Envision a million years of transformation the soil needed to act as an agent to sustain life. Imagine the trial and error of skilled craftsmen passing on their discoveries and talents to future generations."

Tom's head leaned forward to find his place on the printed pages and continued in a noticeably bolder tone:

"A hundred years of strong, powerful growth could offer no defense when the crash of that mighty oak startled its neighboring creatures."

Tom let his hand drop, giving visual life to the falling tree while he read on:

"Stout men dissected the mammoth beast. The wood was measured, was cut, was pieced inside forged metal rings, then pounded, cut again, tested, charred, and filled with the pride of human labor no machine could replicate."

In a quieter, more deliberate tone he continued:

The dormant barley seeds laid naked and vulnerable in the warm, moist, black earth. A series of random, uncontrollable events including the sun, the clouds—" He pointed up at the heavens—*"the Man, and the seasons, allowed the plants to grow strong. The only certainty was those variables would always be different, but every year, nature found a way."*

The tone of Tom's voice changed again, this time to that of a scholarly teaching voice with a specific rhythm and cadence. He used his hands and arms in a way that complimented his smooth, deep voice, giving the words a spirit and soul.

"The finished product had no value— without the secret recipe, without proper methodology, without the master's touch."

Tom pointed in the known direction of the peat bogs. *"Thousand-year-old peat bogs were forced to awake, to finally come to life, and asked to participate.*

"Centuries-old copper stills witnessed natural distillation where science reacts exactly the same when heat and liquids fuse."

He paused and looked at the men in the pub, then continued slowly in the low whisper. *"Day after day, night after night, for the next eighteen years the cunning spirits comfortably hid in closed, dark confines, slowly sapping, thieving the oak's last bit of strength."*

Chapter Five

Tom stopped and nodded to his audience, giving the signal that it was time—permitting them to join in. The men stood and held out their heavy, hand-blown crystal vessels filled with one of Scotland's best single malt whisky, and they all followed Tom's lead as they recited the last paragraph in unison, together with the pride of camaraderie, the pride of their heritage, the pride of their line of descent. The men knew these words by heart and were prepared to finish this story with a restrained force that properly polished their shared experience.

All the men recited together, *"As I sit here tonight pondering many of life's mysteries, the fine crystal recedes, and the unique taste of these cool spirits come back to life one last time, arousing my anticipating palate. I consider the toil and time sacrificed for my benefit. I am a Scot who acknowledges and accepts this sublime gift as a reward, as an invitation to find more humility in my life ... every single day."*

With that, the men all had big smiles on their face. They took a sip of their whisky and then clinked each other's tumbler with a toasting gesture. Tom walked back to the group, and Max touched Tom's tumbler with his, then turned to toast with his compatriots.

One by one the men came by to shake Max's hand and at the same time congratulating Tom for the fine job he had done reciting the verses. Throughout the room you could hear, "Well done, Tom" and "Congratulations, Max."

Eventually things settled down. Dylan unlocked the door and everyone returned to his seat.

Tom said to Max, "Let's ask Shivas to give us a topper on our Guinness. We can sit here, enjoy this scotch, and talk about the Open three weeks from today on the Old Course. I have to get home soon, though. Rose will be expecting me." Max nodded in agreement and raised his hand to get Shivas' attention as if he belonged, as if he'd done this a thousand times before.

Later that night Max went back to O'Malley's and sat alone at a table to have dinner. Different groups of friends came and went. He was jealous of those people, and he wondered about how good it must feel to belong. He also felt eyes all over him from everyone there. Max was used to strangers staring. He thought people could tell just by the way he looked that he was alone and he had no family.

Max sat alone in the middle of O'Malley's localism. He thought back to his conversation with Tom, and he agreed with Tom's paternal advice. *Carnoustie isn't where I belong.* Max wondered about what he should do. He thought, *Tomorrow I will call Mr. Holmes and see if he has any suggestions.*

At times like this Max tried not to think about how things would be if he had a home, if he had a family or a father like Tom. He had learned a long time ago not to let his mind slip into that void. As a child, he would dream about how things would be if he had a mother to hold him and a father to nurture him. Thoughts like those were always present, always torture, and always his last thoughts of the day.

As a child, Max's tears put him to sleep nearly every night, but they never helped. Nothing ever changed. The new day brought the same pain. As he grew older he came up with different ways to shut those thoughts out of his mind. Playing golf and basketball were the only times his thoughts weren't allowed to wander back into the void of loneliness, but the nights were still a problem. He knew he didn't fit into this society, but after talking with Tom, he hoped there was a place for him somewhere.

Max walked back to the hotel alone, under the black night sky, and did what he could to not let himself sink into the darkness of hope.

Chapter Six

San Francisco

(Two years later)

ALLEN WOODS SAT ALONE WITH HIS ELBOWS ON HIS DESK AND HIS FACE buried in his hands. His desk was complete chaos. Books, stacks of reports, and handwritten notes were scattered everywhere. It was ten o'clock in the evening. He thought about the last few years—where and when everything had gone wrong. He reviewed every different scenario, none of which would help now. He was so close, but needed one last cash infusion to keep everything up and running.

He looked up and gazed around the room as if he was seeing the mess for the first time. The state of his office confirmed the certainty—organization was not his strength. His strength was the genius of creativity. He had proven himself time and again in the past. But what he had then and needed now was the ability to get the job done. He needed his rock—his old partner, Jeff Tobin.

He knew if Tobin were there, they would not be in this mess. CTAG Pharmaceuticals, his promising company, would be on the verge of one of the best success stories ever known to mankind. Instead, he found himself spending most of his time scrambling to find additional investment funds. The promise was there, but the competence to manage the business was not. Tobin would have been able to figure out the insane FDA clinical trials, the production problems, and the finances. Woods knew he needed Tobin all along, but thought he could find someone else or that he could handle the day-to-day activities. He found that creativity was nothing without organization.

Those thoughts reminded Woods of Cynthia Tobin, how her life was taken by cancer and how he had dedicated his life, and most of his fortune, to finding a cure. *Tobin and I decided to work together and use our profits to find a cure, but it's clear, I needed him from the start.*

Woods thought again about those days with Tobin and how they felt when their success began. He recalled his time together with Jeff, Cynthia, young Max, and baby Anna. He remembered Tobin's work ethic, how his mind never shut down, how he would stay so completely focused until he went through every possible scenario, and he always came up with the best answer.

Then, probably from reminiscing about the good old days, from out of the blue, as though touched by an unexplained force, the answer came to him. He stood up with new vigor and said out loud, "Mr. Holmes."

Woods remembered how Tobin had persuaded this stuffy banker to take a chance with a loan from the bank in the early days of their start-up computer company. Woods had never met Mr. Holmes, but remembered how elated Tobin was when he came back from the bank with the good news. He also remembered how Tobin told him that they paid that bank many times over what they owed and how Holmes would always be there if they needed him. Standing more erect than he had in the last year, Allen Woods walked out of his office with a feeling hope.

———⊰◦◦◦⊱———

A few days later in his cab ride across San Francisco, Woods practiced what he was going to say, reviewing all the bullet points on how to make the bankers understand the situation. He tried to predict what questions would be asked. He knew he would have to explain it in layman's terms, and he wished Tobin were there. Tobin knew how to talk to these people. He always knew exactly what to say.

Woods didn't speak directly to Mr. Holmes when he called the bank, and he was surprised that he was able to get an appointment on such short notice. He thought that was a good sign. Obviously, Mr. Holmes remembered him and was eager to meet with him.

Allen Woods walked through the big, bronze metal doors of Addison National Bank & Trust, on time and prepared. He crossed the worn but extremely clean and shiny marble floor of the lobby to the receptionist, who was sitting at her large cherry wood desk, perched on an oval pedestal. She looked just like the floor and the rest of the lobby, as if she had been there a hundred years and was barely kicking.

Woods said, "I have an eleven o'clock appointment with Mr. Holmes. Can you point me in the right direction?" The receptionist looked up at him, and without changing her skeptical expression, looked back down at her paperwork and said, "His office is on the thirty-ninth floor." Without looking up, she pointed a crooked finger and said, "You may use those elevators over there." Woods looked at where she pointed and, without a word, crossed the shiny floor to the elevators.

When he stepped off the elevator on the thirty-ninth floor, another receptionist greeted him. She was much younger and more helpful. She directed him to Mr. Holmes's office at the end of the hall. Woods walked past a host of closed doors with what seemed to be important bronze nameplates identifying the occupants. He passed several other smiling receptionists before reaching the end of the hall, where he met what seemed to be a very pleasant young lady. "I'm Allen Woods, and I have an eleven o'clock appointment with Mr. Holmes."

"Hello, Mr. Woods. You can go right in. Mr. Holmes is expecting you."

Woods walked into the huge office and saw a short, stout young man standing in the middle of the room. Woods said, "I have an appointment with Mr. Holmes."

The young man said, "I am Mr. Holmes."

Feeling confused, Woods replied, "Oh, excuse me. I was expecting a much older man."

"I'm sorry for the confusion. My uncle retired two years ago. I'm Anthony Holmes. I've taken over all of my Uncle's accounts." With that, Holmes offered his hand and said, "It is a pleasure to meet you, Mr. Woods. My uncle has told me a great deal about you, and it is a true honor to finally meet you."

"Thank you," Woods said, smiling and shaking his hand. "How is your uncle?"

"He is getting along very well. I wanted him to be here today, but he's out of the country."

"I'm sorry I missed him. The last time I talked with him was just after my partner, Jeff Tobin, died, and I was unable to attend the services. Your uncle and I had a good conversation over the phone. It was good of him to step in and take care of everything for the Tobin family."

Holmes gestured to the big conference table at the side of the room. "Please sit with me and tell me what I can do for you."

They sat down. Woods handed Holmes a folder with "CTAG Pharmaceuticals, Inc." written on the front cover.

Holmes took the folder and put it aside. "I'd like to hear the story from you, if you don't mind."

"All right, as you know, Jeff Tobin and I were pioneers of the computer revolution. Together we were able to invent, develop, and mass-produce computer components that allowed electronic information to completely change our society. After Cynthia Tobin died, Jeff and I decided to create a new business to find a cure for cancer. Unfortunately, as you might know, Jeff Tobin died shortly after Cynthia's passing. I'm a medical scientist by nature, and I had an idea about how to change the way medical science looks at cancers and a host of other diseases. Jeff agreed that this idea was worth investing our money and talents. Together, we decided to fill the hole Cynthia left in our lives with a commitment to find, develop, and make available cures for some of mankind's worst diseases. Our mission was to use our wealth to honor Cynthia's life by funding this project. Tragically and unexpectedly, Jeff also died, but I would not let my idea or my promise for Cynthia's memory die with him.

"For the last twenty years, a dedicated staff and I have built CTAG Pharmaceuticals. Wall Street press reporters pronounced CTAG as 'See Tag.' The new company was created to develop and manufacture medicines based on antisense technology. Drugs made by using this technology work at the genetic level to interrupt the process by which disease-causing proteins are produced. Almost all human diseases are the result of inappropriate protein production. This is true of both host diseases such as cancer and infectious diseases like AIDS. Traditional drugs are designed to kill the bad proteins. Antisense drugs are designed to inhibit the production of the disease-causing proteins."

Woods went on, "Information necessary to produce proteins is contained in the genes. Specific genes contain information for producing specific proteins. Genes are made up of DNA, which contains information about how much of which proteins are to be produced. The DNA molecule is a 'double helix,' which has messenger RNA—mRNA—that carries information necessary for the cell to produce a specific protein. During the transcription from DNA to mRNA, the two complementary strands of the DNA partly uncoil. The 'sense' strand separates from the 'antisense' strand. Antisense drugs contain complementary strands of small segments of mRNA. Each antisense drug is designed to bind to a specific sequence of its mRNA target and inhibit production of the protein — essentially starving the cancer or AIDS virus. Traditional drugs try to kill the proteins after they are already created. Antisense drugs have the potential to be more specific, less complex, more rapid, and more efficient, with fewer side effects than traditional drugs."

Fearing he was losing Mr. Holmes, Woods stopped and looked at him.

"All right," Holmes said. "Go on."

"There is no question to anyone in the field that antisense technology has the promise to change the world. There is also no question that given enough time there would be a cure for cancer, AIDS, and the other horrible diseases in the world. Unfortunately, I feel alone in this struggle. Over the last twenty years, much of my personal fortune has been depleted. The capital from the IPO and subsequent secondary offerings is declining. I was able to convince two major pharmaceutical companies to share some of the patents in exchange for grants about ten years ago. But as soon as these competitors saw the potential for this low-cost cure for all of society's ills, they not only withdrew their support, they spread negative propaganda to undermine the whole concept. CTAG already has over six hundred patents, twelve antisense compounds in clinical trials, and a rich pipeline of preclinical compounds. The laborious task of satisfying the FDA through animal and human clinical trials is almost complete."

Woods then reminded the young Mr. Holmes about the relationship he had with the bank in the past and how the bank had prospered from their very successful business relationship. He thought he had done a very good job of explaining his breakthrough and showing Holmes the success he had achieved to this point, along with the promise of success in the future. He had laid out every detail of what was needed and explained how and when the bank's loan would be paid back. He could back his request with exact dates. Phase III clinical trials were nearly finished, all with successful outcomes, and the production side of the business was ready to go.

The entire time Woods went through his presentation, Holmes listened closely and scratched out a few notes, but he didn't seem genuinely interested. Woods finished the presentation with a request for the capital needed to keep the business afloat until the clinical trials were complete.

After Woods finished, he waited for a response. Holmes looked at him with a smug look on his face and said, "You have an interesting concept here, and I'm sure you have put a lot of time and effort into this project, but without some kind of revenue stream, it would be very unlikely I would be able to convince the loan committee to take on this big of a risk." Holmes paused for a while, and then said, "I'll tell you what I'll do, I'll ..."

In the middle of that sentence, Woods knew he had failed. He thought again about Jeff Tobin and what he would have done differently, but he came up with nothing.

Holmes stood up and said, "I'll take your presentation to the loan committee and do everything I can for you. But I don't want you to get your hopes up."

Dumbfounded, Woods replied, "I think it would be better if I made the presentation directly to the committee."

Starting toward the door, Holmes said, "That's a good idea, but it's not possible at this time. Let me get the ball rolling first, and when the time is right, I'll bring you in. The committee is a very conservative group. They want things done a certain way." He still had that smug look on his face. "The committee meets next week. I'll put this on the docket and get back to you as soon as I can."

Woods didn't know what to do or say. It seemed his whole life was resting on this little shit who was rudely dismissing him, ushering him out of the office. As Woods was literally being pushed through the doorway, he again tried to think about what Jeff Tobin would have done differently. When he couldn't think of anything, and before he walked out the door, he turned back to Holmes and said, "How have Max and Anna gotten along through the years?"

The expression on Holmes's face changed in an instant. "The children—?" He looked both surprised and wary. Then he composed himself. "From what I understand they are— they are — fine. We are not in contact with them in any way, and we haven't been for a number of years."

Holmes shook his hand and then tipped his head at his secretary. "Leave your number with Michelle. I'll get back to you next week. This has really been a pleasure, Mr. Woods." Anthony Holmes turned his back on Woods, walked into his office, and shut the door behind him.

Woods made the long walk back to the elevator, feeling deflated. At the same time, he thought something was wrong with the way Holmes had reacted to his inquiry about Max and Anna. *He's hiding something ... .*

—————◦◦◦————

Holmes went back to his desk and sat on the front edge of his uncle's big leather chair. He couldn't sit all the way back in the chair, because even with the block in position, his feet still dangled. He sat forward with his feet resting on the block of wood under his desk and reviewed the conversation he just had with Allen Woods. He thought about some of the other problems he had to deal with and realized this job had been impossible to do from the start. *It's much clearer now.* His uncle had taken care of the Tobin account for over seventeen years without any problems. It was easier for him. The children were children then, and they were safely stowed away in their boarding schools. The job only required renewing the CDs and paying for the children's expenses. Every day over the last two years had been worse than the previous day. *Anna was completely out of control ninety percent of the time, Max couldn't do a damn thing by himself, and the board of directors of the bank kept increasing the stakes and the pressure.*

Now I've got Allen Woods asking questions about the Tobin children. I have to figure out a way to keep Woods out of the picture or else this whole thing could blow up in my face. This office, my income, and my slush fund are all at risk.

Holmes picked up the phone and touched the speed-dial button for The Agency. The call went straight through to Reed Jackson. Holmes told Jackson about the Allen Woods situation. Jackson assured Holmes that he would get started on that complication right away. Holmes then asked Jackson, "Where are we on the problem in Mexico?" Jackson replied, "Tomorrow it will be done." Jackson went on to assure Holmes that his best men were on the job and that the plan would go off as expected, with no surprises. Holmes hung up the phone and thought about what he had ordered Reed Jackson to do about the boy in Mexico and about what decision he'd be forced to make regarding Allen Woods.

Anthony Holmes sat uncomfortably in silence, contemplating the life he had chosen. He felt the burden of his decision to end the life of the young Mexican man, the burden of his expanding unethical business decisions and, more recently, his dishonorable personal behavior.

He looked at the massive doors protecting him from the outside world. Then he saw the shadow of the eye in the bird's-eye maple looking directly at him, judging him. He felt the shadow and knew it had witnessed his descent from moral decency. Holmes snatched up his phone and buzzed Michelle outside his office. She picked up the phone and said, "Yes, Mr. Holmes?"

"Is he gone?" he whispered.

"Yes, Mr. Holmes."

"Then open that damn door!"

Chapter Seven

Munich, Germany

(Same day)

STEFAN JAEGER OPENED THE WIDE, HEAVY DOOR OF THE HILLTOP TAP with a smile on his face, expecting to see a few of his high school friends and coworkers from the police department. It was his birthday. Thirty-three is a great age for a man. He felt stronger, faster, and could handle his liquor better than he ever could in his past.

That night was his first night out with the guys in months, maybe years, and he had been looking forward to it for a long time. Most of his friends were single. They lived a carefree life that Stefan heard about every morning at work. Tonight was his night. He wanted to be included in the stories at work for a change.

Even though he had missed out on the late-night partying, Stefan wouldn't change one thing about his life. He had married the most beautiful girl he'd ever seen. She was his best friend and the envy of all his friends. Their active, strapping son worshipped the ground he walked on. All day, every single day, he counted down the minutes to the end of the shift so he could run home and be back where he belonged—home with one arm around his wife and one arm around his boy.

Stefan was a fit man, five feet, ten inches tall, 185 pounds. He worked out to stay in shape for his police duties and still played a little football on weekends. His thick crop of dark hair was cut short and tight, like a military recruit's. He was proud to represent the Munich police department. His father was still on the force, his father's brother worked for Germany's BKA (the equivalent of the FBI in the U.S.), and his older brother was a firefighter. The Jaeger stable of men had proudly been connected to Germany's law enforcement departments for several generations.

49

With just one foot through the door, he saw most of his old high school friends at the back of the bar. He casually strolled right into the middle of the group and accepted a pint of cold beer in one hand and a double shot of schnapps in the other. He downed the schnapps in a heartbeat and followed it with a big gulp of cold beer. His friends cheered and slapped him on the back. .

A few shots of schnapps had never been a problem for Stefan. He could hold his booze, so he wasn't concerned when one of his best friends from high school handed him another shot and said, "Nice to see you Bull, and even better to hear you're getting on so well."

"Hubie," Stefan said, "you have no idea how good it is to see you. What's it been, ten or twelve years? I heard you're a big shot up in Berlin now. Never a doubt in my mind you'd be running the world. I couldn't pick a better man for the job. Everything good? How are your parents and your sister?" Hubie didn't have a chance to answer.

One of Stefan's coworkers interrupted them and thrust another shot at him. "We finally get this guy to come out and have some fun with us. Happy birthday!" Steffen threw back the shot and chased it with another big drink of cold beer. This went on for a couple of hours. Stefan was having fun. He thought about leaving a couple of times but put it off, thinking, *"This is my neighborhood pub— I walked here, and I can walk home. It's not really that late anyway".*

Nine o'clock to midnight went by in what seemed like twenty minutes. Stefan was still on his feet, but only barely. When all of his friends went home, he joined some people at the bar who were really friendly—a guy and two girls. They carried on talking, laughing, and even flirting harmlessly. More drinks, more shots, and Stefan excused himself to go to the restroom. Before the door closed one of the girls followed him into the small room. He tried to tell her that the ladies' restroom was one door down. *Wasn't it?*

She crushed herself against him. She looked good, felt good. "No one's in here," she said, slurring her words. "No one will know." She grabbed Stefan's hands and worked them all over her breasts. Somehow, she undid his pants. He resisted, but couldn't find a way to stop her. *This is wrong. I have to get out of here!* Then the door flew open and one of his new friends lifted his phone and took a few pictures.

What the f...? This isn't what I signed up for. Stefan pushed the girl away, shouldered his new friend aside, and stumbled out of the bar. He lurched his way home and plopped onto the couch so his drunken state wouldn't offend his sleeping wife. His last thought of the night was, *Man, I'm glad I don't have to go to work tomorrow.*

Chapter Eight

Playa del Carmen, Mexico
(The next morning)

WIDE OPEN DOORS INVITED THE MORNING SUN THROUGH THE SHEER curtains and onto the curves of Anna Tobin. Feeling the sunshine blanket her body, she woke to Armando's presence. She hugged her worn pink bunny rabbit and fondly remembered how the night before had ended.

Silently, she poured her thin, flexible body off the big bed, not wanting to wake Armando on his day off, and prepared for the eight-mile run by stretching as she dressed. She eased the door shut behind her, walked to the end of the hall, bounced down the stairs, and stepped into the fresh new morning.

The sun seemed to be suspended in midair, hanging just over the horizon. Anna loved this time of day with the sun's softer light, the sky's darker shade of blue, and the empty brick-paved streets. Quickly finding a good rhythm, she set a brisk pace. The wind was calm, the air was cool, and the thoughts of the afternoon's exciting surprise for Armando allowed her mind to wander into a place that had been off limits for years—a place of love and hope.

The last two years had been unbelievable for Anna, and today marked the start of a new chapter for her and Armando. Her surprise for him was the boldest display of arrogance yet for Mr. Holmes. It had arrived yesterday. Her pace and her heart rate increased as the excitement grew.

She thought about the time two years ago when she had escaped to Huatulco, Mexico, to find a new life. The town of La Crucecita was where she spent most of her time, and soon she was very well known by the locals. Her typical day consisted of a morning run from her resort to Santa Cruz and back again for fresh fruit by the pool of the resort. After breakfast she would go to Parroquia de Nuestra Señora de Guadalupe, the quaint and beautiful Catholic church located at one end of the town square in La Crucecita. The citizens of La Crucecita were rightfully proud of their church. Anna was directly in the middle of many of the church's outreach programs and was personally responsible for funding many of those activities.

Her evenings started with dinner at one of the many local restaurants and then off to her favorite nightspot, "La Crema." It was a small second-floor bar overlooking the active town square of La Crucecita. A widow owned the bar, and her sons managed the day-to-day operations. It was truly an authentic Mexican setting, although it had some American capitalistic flavor with its pizza and signature T-shirts. Le Crema had live music Wednesday through Saturday, and it was the place to get dressed up, boozed up, and dance. The crowd was usually a mix of local young people and Mexico City vacationers. Anna usually sat at a table on the balcony overlooking the town square. The owners appreciated the money she spent and her lively personality.

One night, while on the dance floor, she noticed a young man who was taller than the others, clearly of Spanish descent, and probably vacationing from Mexico City. The beat of the drums and the bass kept up a loud, pounding rhythm, and soon Anna and this mystery man were dancing together. She felt a chemistry with him that she had never felt before. Anna thought he was the most handsome thing she had ever seen, but it was clear to her that he did not think of himself that way. She also noticed a difference in the way he reacted to her. She didn't get the usual up-and-down stares she had grown accustomed to from other men. The longer they danced the closer they became. There were welcome soft touches as part of the natural dance movements, and they seemed to share a closeness with each other in spirit, as well. The young man had deep, dark eyes, smooth, brown skin, and thick, wavy, jet-black hair. He was slender, but he had broad, masculine shoulders, and when he touched her she felt a new sensation.

They danced for over an hour, until a young lady tapped the mystery man on his shoulder to summon him away. He smiled at Anna and lifted a hand into the air. She reached up and put her hand in his. They let their eyes say goodbye. Anna stayed on the dance floor and watched him follow the girl and some others out the door. The night went on as usual, but the cab ride home was different. Anna felt as though she had found and lost the best thing that had ever happened to her.

The next morning started the same as usual. Anna's run to Santa Cruz was like every other morning, with greetings from the street sweepers—"*Hola,*

Anna!"—and yells from the workers sitting in the back of pickup trucks driving by—"*Buenos días*, Anna!" The run was a good one because Anna had many thoughts from the night before. The steep hill on the way back to her resort was easy because her thoughts were centered on what may have been. It had been a long time since Anna had any thoughts of a romantic nature because of the work she was doing for the church and the fact that there weren't any good candidates in the places she went.

The dance floor was dark. Anna tried to remember the details of the man's face. She remembered a big, friendly smile and long, thick black hair, but had trouble visualizing many of the other details. She wondered who that girl was that interrupted their dancing. He was probably in trouble with his girlfriend. *He made no advances to me that should have caused a problem with his girlfriend.* Her thoughts kept churning, and what was an hour's run seemed to fly by in only a few minutes.

Anna had just settled down on one of the chaise lounge chairs for her fruit breakfast by the pool when, to her surprise, a deep voice interrupted her thoughts. "Do you mind if I join you?" She looked up to see that big smile from her mystery man. In daylight he looked even better than she remembered.

Anna sat up a little straighter in her chair and replied, "There you are. I wondered what happened to you after you left me all alone in the middle of the dance floor. I don't mind at all if you join me, as long as your girlfriend doesn't get mad at you again." She gave him a big smile.

He offered his hand as an introduction, with a broad smile of his own. "That was my little sister. I don't have a girlfriend. My name is Armando Ruiz, and I don't see how I can live another minute without you in my life." With that confident greeting, Anna couldn't help but extend her hand and say, "Then you better join me pronto, Mr. Armando Ruiz. I wouldn't want to be responsible for such a tragic end to your short life. My name is Anna."

Armando Ruiz sat down next to Anna and said, "Last night was really fun. I'm glad we have a chance to meet again. It must be real destiny." He flashed his big smile.

Anna didn't know what to think about this class A schmoozer, but she liked what she saw. "So what brings you and your family to Huatulco?"

"Just a quick holiday my mother and my sister set up to try to get my father and me back on speaking terms."

"You can't stop there, Mr. Ruiz. What's gotten between you and your father?"

"Let's just say he doesn't agree with my lifestyle. My father was hoping I would follow in his footsteps at the bank. He has done amazing things there, so I can understand how he feels, but it's just not the way I want to live my life. As a result we both continue to dig our heels in deeper. My poor mom and sister are caught in the middle." He shrugged.

Anna said, "Sorry to hear. Maybe you both just need a little more time and guidance from the women in your life." She smiled.

Armando smiled right back and said, "I can see my new friend is both beautiful and smart," as he snagged a strawberry off her plate. Then he said, "What are your plans for this fine day, Miss Anna?"

"As soon as I finish my breakfast, assuming there's any left"—she smiled—"I will do what I do every day. Go into La Crucecita to help Father Gomez and the nuns at the church. The church is very special."

Armando said, "What makes it so special?"

"For one thing, it has a unique bell tower that has not one but two large bells. One hangs over the other. Also, when you look up at the cupola inside the church, you'll see a twenty-five-foot-long mural of the Virgin of Guadalupe, which is said to be the largest one of its kind in the world. Also, it's the people that make it the most beautiful church in the whole world. Why don't you join me? We could use your help today moving some new furniture into the school."

The rest of that week they spent every second together, and with each tick of the clock, Anna fell further. It was easy for her to leave Huatulco and go with Armando across Mexico to Playa del Carmen, where she took a suite in the new Riu resort. She liked the area because of the European mix of tourists. Armando had a small apartment in Puerto Adventura, a small town about twenty miles south, where his day as a mate on a fishing boat for "Captain Rick" started six out of seven mornings each week at six o'clock.

As Anna approached the turn-around point of her morning run, all she could think about was how Armando would react when he saw his surprise.

She had secretly flown to Miami a couple of months before to shop for a new fishing boat. She found the perfect small yacht. With some stellar negotiation and a guarantee of payment from Addison National Bank, she bought the thirty-six-foot fishing boat for Armando. It had finally been delivered to the Marina in Puerto Adventura yesterday. She planned to take Armando to the marina that day and surprise him with what would be the start of the rest of their lives together.

The three men from The Agency had different plans for Armando. Anthony Holmes from Addison National had ordered them to take Armando Ruiz out of the picture.

The job was an easy one for the men of The Agency. Anna's long runs and Armando's work schedule were like clockwork. The Agency men had documented their lives for months. They were professionals. They left nothing to chance. As Anna made her turn for home, the men from The Agency saw Armando stir because of a manufactured noise. Armando got out of bed to investigate.

Anna's pace got faster as she turned for home with thoughts of Armando's surprise and of how he had changed her life. She never thought she could be so happy. She promised herself to never take one minute for granted, to always remember the loneliness and emptiness of her past. She thought about what a terrific mother and father they would be and about how they planned to give their children unconditional love and security. Her long, fast strides were quickly bringing her closer to home.

Feeling confused, Armando was sure Anna had left for her morning run. He had taken two steps away from the bed when a man rushed at him from the balcony. The intruder swung a metal pipe that landed on the side of his head. A horrific bolt of pain shot into his brain. He managed to remain standing, digging deep within himself to find the strength to fight back.

Anna felt her heart rate soar, and she realized that her pace had increased because of her excitement. She looked up at the bright blue sky and felt a rush of complete euphoria.

These men were professionals. They didn't care about young love or dreams of the future. They didn't care about Anna's hopes. This was just another job to them, another faceless entity to be discarded in the swamp fifty miles away.

Another man crashed the back of Armando's skull with a wooden bat, then used it on the rest of his body. The three assailants tucked Armando's lifeless body into a service cart, gathered all his belongings, and placed the prewritten note on the dresser.

They left the room and pushed the heavy cart down the hallway, taking all of Anna's dreams with them.

Anna finished her run with a sprint up the stairs. She jogged down the hall and opened the door to share her excitement and her surprise with Armando, but all she found was the note.

> *Anna, my angel, I cannot go on like this and lead you*
> *on for another day. My place is with my family, and*
> *this decision is out of my control. Please do not try to*
> *contact me. I am sorry.*
>
> *Armando*

Anna's heart stopped, and she crumpled onto the hard tile floor. She lay there curled up in a tight ball, whimpering, in her own sweat and tears.

Chapter Nine

Belfry Resort, England

(Same day)

M AX TOBIN WANTED TO OPEN HIS EYES BUT COULDN'T. *WHAT HAPPENED last night?* His forehead throbbed with pain. Memories of drinking one shot after another, along with gaps of lost time, amplified the pain. His throat hurt, probably from sleeping on his back with his mouth wide open in a drunken, unconscious state. The smell of cigarette smoke made him feel queasy. He hoped lying completely still would make his headache vanish. *I need to rethink my lifestyle. It's a complete disaster. Maybe,* he thought, *if I could just go back to sleep, I'll feel better.*

A smooth leg brushed against his and then quickly pulled away. With his eyes shut and his body paralyzed, he frantically scanned his memory again, trying to remember what had happened and who was in bed with him.

This is all Mr. Holmes's fault. He's the one that suggested the Belfry Resort after my trip to Carnoustie. He said The Belfry was one of the best in Europe, where I would fit in with the rich and famous rather than with the locals at Carnoustie.

The leg moved again. *I can't ignore this much longer.* He desperately tried to find a clue in his aching head about how the night had ended. *Hell, how did the night begin?*

This had happened to him once before. Last winter he and his group of so-called friends were in the Austrian Alps, skiing the slopes of Zugspitze. One night they met up with a large group from Norway. *It was probably the combination of a Jacuzzi and too much bourbon that were the culprits.*

The next morning he woke up to a pink-faced, yellow-haired girl from Oslo. He had a little help escaping because it was her snoring that woke him up. He was able to leave the room without notice and didn't go back for days.

This morning was different for two reasons. The first was a good thing—she wasn't snoring. The second wasn't so good—she was probably awake.

Just when Max was about to confront the situation, the door of his suite crashed open. Harry and Nick came flying in screaming, "Get the fuck out of bed Max, our plane leaves in a few minutes!"

Harry threw Max some clothes from the pile on the floor, and the three of them ran out of the room, leaving the door wide open. Max's head pounded, but he remembered their plan to go to Cozumel, Mexico. "What about my clothes? I haven't packed!"

"We don't have time, Max," Harry replied as they ran down the hall past the Riley bar. You can get what you need when we get there."

Max said, "What about the girl?"

When Nick heard that, he laughed so hard that he tripped over his own feet. "Max, ol' boy, let's just say Harry and I saved you from chewing your arm off." All three of them laughed as they jumped into the waiting cab.

The plane ride was a long one. Max was able to sleep and put most of the night before behind him. He didn't know anything about Cozumel, which wasn't unusual.

Nearly every day he thought back to the afternoon he had spent with Tom Riley in Carnoustie. He thought about Tom's advice about how to find true happiness. Every time he remembered that day, he felt more ashamed.

Define what kind of a man you want to be and then be that man.

Max had tried several times to cut his ties with these guys, but they always found a way to lure him into another adventure. Mr. Holmes kept the credit card bills paid and encouraged him to continue his life of nothingness.

This will be the last time.

I need to define what kind of man I want to be.

I'll call Mr. Homes when we get back.

Chapter Ten

Playa del Carmen

(Two days later)

ANNA WALKED ALONG THE BRICK-PAVED SIDEWALK FROM HER RESORT IN Playa del Carmen to a Señor Frog's bar, where she'd been before.

Still in shock from Armando's sudden decision to leave without a word, she had decided to leave the resort for the afternoon.

It's a nice day today. I have to put all this behind me.

She had repeatedly replayed every detail of the previous few weeks, looking for a clue, a reason he would do that to her. Do that to them.

Eventually, the immune system she had developed to protect herself from love and hope responded. *I'm never going to allow anyone to do that to me again. I trusted him. Nothing makes sense. I never should have let him get that close.*

With Armando's absence, it was even worse than before because she knew what was missing. Sleeping alone and remembering the past put a couple more layers on her already thick amour.

Señor Frog's was perched on concrete pylons above the beach and the crashing surf. The beach side of the building was open to the ocean, and there was a line of bar stools there that overlooked the cool blue of the ocean and sky.

Anna chose a stool, sat down with her back to the noisy crowd, and gazed at the horizon.

The late afternoon went just as expected. She brushed away would-be suitors and hoped the loud music would erase the thoughts of Armando. She watched the Cozumel ferry pull up to the dock, as it did every day. *This margarita isn't helping. I'll get a double shot in the next one.*

Anna watched the stream of people disembark. She picked out different people and watched them, trying to imagine their life story. Anna noticed a big, tall young man in the crowd. *There's a good one.*

He was interesting to her because of his size and how he seemed to be the center of attention for the rest of the group. The young man waited his turn to get off the narrow gangway.

Anna had ample time to observe him and create a story for his life. *Those are probably his fraternity brothers and sisters from college. I bet he's engaged to the one hanging all over him, and they'll probably be happy the rest of their damn lives.*

He was too far away to make out the details of his face, but she was sure his life had already been all planned for him, the same as Armando's. When the time came, his family would pull the right strings and force him to tow the line they had attached to him. Dreams and love were just talk. The reality of life is to never trust anyone and never let anyone get close.

Pissed again, she took another drink and forced her gaze back to the emptiness of the blurred horizon.

Max, the boys, and some newly acquainted young ladies had hopped onto the ferry that took them from Cozumel to Playa del Carmen. It was a short trip, and there was bar service. After the ferry arrived at the dock, they waited their turn getting off the ferry, and then disappeared into the tourist-filled streets.

Three men from The Agency who were assigned to Max covertly followed the group. Three different men assigned to Anna were positioned around Señor Frog's, prepared for the possibility of Max's arrival.

Outlaw, one of The Agency men, said to the man in charge, Reed Jackson, "You tell us what you want done, and we'll make sure it happens. There are six of us on top of the situation as we speak, and we're in constant contact with each other and both subjects."

Jackson replied, "Continue, observation only. Hopefully they won't get close to each other."

Max and his friends stopped at several bars and shops that bordered both sides of 5th Avenue. They bargained with the local craftsmen, but never made a purchase. The afternoon flew by, and a couple of hours before the ferry was scheduled to return, the group stumbled into Señor Frog's. The eight of them pulled a couple of tables together near the front door and settled in with tall half yards of strong margaritas. The place was packed. Everyone there was either well on their way or already there.

Outlaw said to Jackson, "They're on opposite sides of the room. Between the six of us, we'll be able to keep them away from each other."

Jackson replied, "Understand that they cannot meet, speak, or even look at each other. If there is even a remote possibility of that happening, take Max to the ground and then out the door."

With confirmations from all six men, they spread out across the big open room, trying to blend into the crowd. Max was seated with his back to the crowded dance floor, and Anna had her back to the whole world. The six men from The Agency had everything under control. Señor Frog's was wall-to-wall people, so it would be easy for The Agency men to steer either one of them away from the other. Max had a sweet thing sitting in his lap, and it didn't look as if he was going anywhere. The men responsible for Anna knew her well and knew there was no chance she would get out on the dance floor. As time went on, the party intensified with every hard-driving song and every tequila shot thrown down.

Anna stood up and headed to the restroom. The Agency men jockeyed into position. Outlaw yelled to the members of the other team, "Apache, she's on the move. Cochise, get ahead of her!"

She edged herself into the gyrating, shoulder-to-shoulder crowd on the dance floor. Her slender build and athleticism allowed her to weave through the crowd with ease while The Agency men got stuck in the frenzy. She walked right past them. Max was still sitting with the girl nestled in his lap. The men tried desperately to catch up to Anna, but the harder they tried the worse it became.

Anna walked closer to Max's table. Outlaw could see he was out of position, and he did what he could to get in the way. He was too late. He had to stand down. *She might walk right past Max.* All he could do was hope and watch what happened.

Harry stood up at the other end of the table. His hip caught the edge of their table and that rocked one of the tall margarita glasses. Nick tried to grab it, but he missed, knocking the glass over. The contents spilled into what little room was left in Max's lap. He jumped up, sending the girl in his lap onto the girl sitting next to them. They all laughed. Max tried to brush the liquid off his shorts, backing away as he did so. He accidentally bumped into Anna. Max turned to apologize.

The Agency men tried to intercede, but they were too late. All they could do was watch Max, who was looked completely dumbstruck when he saw Anna. He tried to stutter an apology. Everyone at the table saw the same thing that The Agency men had been forced to endure for years. Max waited for a response from her, but Anna just gave the stranger her mad-as-hell look.

Still desperate to break up this encounter, Apache pushed and shoved his way through the crowd. Someone pushed back, and a scuffle ensued. Two bouncers bulled their way through the crowd, toward the sound of breaking glass.

<hr />

Anna felt the big man who had bumped into her put a hand on her waist and he guided her behind him. He then extended both arms behind his back to corral and protect her while they watched the melee play out in front of them. She felt the man's strength and perceived his actions to be that of protection and not that of advantage.

After things settled down, Anna returned to her seat and stared at the horizon again. She thought about the tall stranger until a vision of Armando interrupted her thoughts.

Soon the ferry's horn blasted, a signal to its passengers that it was time to leave. The day-trippers walked, stumbled, and shuffled back onto the dock, laughing and roughhousing. The tall stranger was among them. He stopped and looked back at the bar. Anna could tell he was looking for something. When he spotted her, he grinned and raised his hand in the air to say goodbye. Anna acknowledged his gesture with a slight lift of her hand and tip of her chin. Then, she immediately turned away to the frenzy on the dance floor.

Chapter Eleven

San Francisco

(Next morning)

THE MORNING'S DOWNTOWN SAN FRANCISCO TRAFFIC WAS AT ITS USUAL standstill—a perfect opportunity for Allen Woods. He threw a twenty-dollar bill into the front seat of the cab and got out the back door. So far everything was on track.

The past few days he had had a feeling that someone was following him, and the feeling was later confirmed. That forced him to deal with the situation head-on and to figure out who and why. If he was correct, a man several vehicles back— also stuck in traffic—would get out of the passenger side of a black Escalade. There he was —the same man as yesterday.

Woods calmly walked through the knotted traffic and up a side street, heading for the back-alley entrance of his office building. Woods was sure the man had been hired by one of the giant pharmaceutical companies. They constantly kept tabs on him in the hope they could get out in front of and possibly sabotage any announcement regarding the results of the most recent, completely successful, phase III clinical trial, which had resulted in a cure for Crohn's disease. It wasn't the first time they had stooped to these drastic measures, and he was not at all surprised to know they were planning something. *Not sure who's following me or why, but I'll know soon enough.*

Woods walked past the dumpsters and the usual homeless vagrants milling around. He went to the back of his building and used his key to open the door, thinking, *This morning you're the one in for a big surprise.*

Woods shut the door behind him, then opened it a crack and looked out. A man dressed like one of the vagrants crept up behind the man and whacked him on the head with a club. The man dropped to his knees, then crumpled onto the pavement.

The attacker quickly lifted the man's watch, billfold, and small handgun. Then he pried off the back of the fallen man's phone, inserted something, and returned the phone to the same pocket. The process was completed in less than a minute. The attacker and all the vagrants scattered in different directions.

Woods went to his office and waited for the call. The security company in charge of managing his office building had taken the job to help Woods. The professionals had assured him the plan was sound, and the incident would be chalked up to one of the 1,027 muggings that occurred in this city every year.

Woods let out a deep breath as he sat behind his desk, surrounded by his usual mess. He looked at the new cell phone sitting in the middle of his desk and waited for the inanimate object to come to life. *Come on, what's taking so long?*

Woods thought about those faceless corporate powers that continuously created obstacles to interfere with his company's success. *Their single intent is to protect their corporate profits, with absolutely no regard for the suffering.*

Woods concluded,—*I must seem vulnerable because of my age. That's why they keep coming at me. When I see pictures of myself I can understand why. I may look old, but my race is not yet run!* He imagined all the things that could have gone wrong with the plan. One scenario after another played out in his mind, and none of them was good. He assumed that his office phones were tapped, so he had bought the cell phone specifically for this mission.

Woods couldn't wait any longer. He picked up the phone and hurried out of his office, out of the building, and into the crowd on the street. Paranoia was getting the better of him as he scanned the blank faces of strangers for some hint of danger. Then the vibration of the phone in his hand nearly scared the life out of him. He held his composure, though, and ducked into a men's clothing store. He pretended to look at the overpriced garments hanging on one of the racks as he opened the phone and said, "What happened?"

The voice from the phone said, "The plan for taking out the man who was following you went off as expected." Woods breathed a sigh of relief as he scanned the front door and windows for a sign of anyone trying to look like everyone else. The voice continued, "We don't have all you want yet, but within the next twenty-four hours our research report will be complete."

"Do you know who he was working for?"

"Give us a few hours to do a good job for you and figure all this out. Let's talk in the morning. We'll have all the answers by then. The most important thing right now is that we're certain they're convinced the attack was just a random mugging. The transmitter that was placed in his phone is working perfectly. We have a good recording of several conversations that you'll be able to hear for yourself. We have his ID, and we're working to find out which company employs him. All this will come together in time for our meeting tomorrow morning. It's very important for you to keep a typical schedule. Meet me at the café where we met yesterday, and I'll give you a full report."

"Okay, tomorrow morning will work. But call me before then if you find anything."

The next morning Allen Woods waited impatiently with an order of coffee and toast. He sat on a faded, red plastic bench seat in one of the eight booths that bordered the outside wall of the small cafe. He scanned the morning paper, looking for a story that matched the incident he was responsible for creating —*nothing*.

The paper was filled with stories of the world's plight, but Woods' main focus was centered on trying to figure out who the people were and what they wanted from him. Even though it was still too early to be concerned, he couldn't help but wonder where his contact was. Through the big windows, he could see all the people passing by. Soon he realized they could see him, as well. *They may be watching me right now.*

The door opened, and his contact walked straight to the small booth. He slid into the bench seat across from Woods and placed a file folder on the table between them. The waitress approached them, but his contact waved her away.

"The man following you took a good shot to the head, but refused medical treatment at the scene. The police were called, but no witnesses were found, so no official report was filed. We were able to identify the man. He works for a well-respected private security company called The Agency. After the cops left, the injured man placed a call. Here's a transcript of the conversation." He handed a stapled group of about five pages of paper to Woods. "You can see they're convinced the attack was a random assault with no indication of CTAG's involvement."

"Do you know who hired them?"

"We don't know who hired The Agency yet, but we've obtained a partial list of their clients." He slid another piece of paper across the linoleum tabletop.

Woods scanned the list of about twenty business names, but did not see any of the pharmaceutical companies he had expected.

"The transmitter in the phone will continue working for another seventy-two hours. My men are researching the companies on that list to find any connection to the large pharmaceutical companies you suspect. It's not unusual for organizations like these to create small, anonymous shell companies to try to disguise the larger corporation's intentions. We'll figure it all out, but this deeper research will take a little more time. The man pointed to one line on the transcript of the telephone conversation and said, "Look at this." He read aloud, "Holmes isn't going to be happy. He wanted Woods put down sooner, rather than later.' He looked at Woods and said, "That's straightforward enough. They want you dead." Woods was stunned. The name *Holmes* jumped out at him. That had to be Anthony Holmes at Addison National. Woods looked back at the client list, and there it was, staring back at him as though it were in bold letters, Addison National Bank & Trust. In that instant it became clear. *Just asking Anthony Holmes about the Tobin children had initiated this kind of response? What more is that toad capable of? What's he's hiding? What's he done to Max and Anna?*

Chapter Twelve

Peto, Mexico

(Same morning)

JUST OUTSIDE THE SMALL VILLAGE OF PETO, A TWELVE-YEAR-OLD BOY NAMED Javier tended to the needs of the family's mule. That was his job. The mule was more important to his family than he was. Javier was responsible for coaxing the mule to transport their valuable harvest to the village. They were in the middle of harvest season, which put some added pressure on Javier to partner with the big, stubborn animal.

Javier knew that by every modern-day standard the people of Peto lived in poverty. They had lived their lives nearly the same way for hundreds of years. The absence of electricity, modern communications, and contemporary transportation kept the so-called luxuries of modern life from spoiling their pristine community.

The families of Peto were just fine with their lives. They had seen some of what the modern world offered, and they didn't want any part of it. They preferred to be left alone. On three different occasions over the past twenty years, Peace Corps workers had come to establish a modern school in their community. The purpose was to bring the children into the twenty-first century. The Peace Corps workers couldn't accept the fact that the people of Peto didn't want to be brought into the twenty-first century. Children like Javier learned all they needed to know while they worked alongside their parents and other family members. That kind of education was essential to maintaining the village's fragile society. Each new generation was taught centuries of tried-and-true methods of farming, cooking, homebuilding, and medicine from their family. Putting them in school for eight hours a day was a sure way to destroy the little niche the families of Peto had carved out for themselves in the world.

They were descendants of the ancient Mayan Indians, who at one time had the most advanced civilization in the world. Centuries of European diseases and military invasions had wiped out the Mayan empire, except for a few pockets in the interior of Mexico. The Mexican government learned that interfering in the culture of villages like Peto eliminated a happy, self-sustaining society and changed it into a society of welfare and/or warfare. The Peace Corps and the Catholic Church hadn't accepted this truism or accepted the fact that there were people and places in the world that did not want what someone else deemed correct.

Their economy was built around farming and a barter system. Food and labor were the main sources of revenue. Each family unit had its own expertise that they'd learned through centuries of trial and error. Javier's family specialties were asparagus, corn, and chickens. Asparagus was a good crop for the Perez families because they were the only family that raised it. When their crop of asparagus ripened, it was a good bartering tool, because it was always in demand.

The two-and-a-half-mile trip to town could have been made in five minutes with a proper road and modern transportation. The Perez family had neither. Their road was a dirt path made more difficult to travel by its steep inclines and declines, ruts, and potholes. Their big mule pulled an ancient-looking, two-wheel cart, which was prone to tipping over. If that happened on the way to market, it was a disaster for the entire group of Perez families. The asparagus that fell into the dirt had to be washed with clean water and restacked. Getting clean water in the middle of nowhere wasted valuable time. That meant produce baked in the hot sun and wilted. It also meant that the trucks from the resorts had probably already left the village. If the Perez family lost out on even one day's sale, every member of the family would feel the financial loss.

The trip was one of constant risk and tension because of the variables and the importance of success. The best way to achieve success was to keep the mule walking at a steady pace with complete silence. The mule was easily distracted if all the attention wasn't centered on him. Experience had also shown that anytime the mule stopped, a tip-over was much more likely to happen, not only because of getting the mule started again but because of the effects on his psyche. If the pace of the mule remained uninterrupted, completing the trip was much more probable. The combination of Javier and his Uncle Augie had been a solid one for the last three years. Javier's job was to walk alongside the mule to comfort and steer him. Augie's job was to walk beside the cart to prevent its tipping over and to give the cart a push as circumstances required.

The fifth day of the harvest was a typical day on the Yucatan peninsula—just beautiful. The previous four trips had gone without incident. Augie and Javier were about halfway through the two-hour trip to the village and were getting close to the most hazardous part of the trip, where the dirt trail took them past an area that was on the edge of a marsh.

The trail was usually wet to some degree, depending on whether it had rained recently or had rained anywhere within the drainage area of the marsh. Javier saw the wet part ahead, and without a word he gave Augie a look that said, *let's take extra care.* Javier stroked the mule's neck and whispered in his ear. He surveyed the road as he slowly walked ahead. The left side of the trail looked better, so he steered the mule that way. Walking backward, Javier signaled for his uncle to sit in the rear of the cart in case he had to help push. They didn't want the mule to either stop or lunge forward. Javier thought it looked pretty good. When he took his first step into the mud, his bare foot found hard ground quickly. He sighed with relief.

The mule entered the mud as Javier stroked the side of his neck. Javier looked ahead to the right and the left to find the best path possible. His keen eyes picked out something on the right side of the path—something he couldn't believe, didn't want to believe. His sudden hesitation caused the mule to sense that something was wrong. The big animal raised his head. That was not a good sign. Javier reacted quickly by stroking the mule's neck and whispering again in his ear. Augie noticed the slight hitch and braced the cart.

The mule continued through the mud. Javier forced his gaze to the front. He didn't want a problem here, of all places. But he couldn't resist the temptation to look back. Javier remembered the words his father had said to him many times. They were words that Javier didn't totally understand and didn't believe were meant for him until now. *There will be a point in your life when you are forced to use what you've been taught and apply those teachings. Something will happen to you when you're alone and you will have to make your own decision. That decision will stay with you and define who you are.*

Should I just ignore what I saw? Javier thought, *does it even matter? Should I tell my uncle? No talking. Getting to town is too important. Should I ...* His mind raced, and so did his heart. He looked back, and he spotted it again. Then he saw something even more wrenching.

Javier turned his head and looked at the road ahead. It was flat and dry. He couldn't take it any longer. He pulled on the mule's reins, and the mule came to a halt. Augie gave him a questioning look from the side of the cart. They didn't say a word. Javier couldn't move.

Augie pulled on the brake handle and hurried to his nephew. Javier started to cry, and his uncle embraced him. Javier pointed back at the muddy stretch of the trail. His uncle looked that way, squinted, and searched for what had upset Javier. Just off the side of the trail was a human hand sticking out of the mud.

They had both seen dead people before. There were no hospitals or formal mortuaries where they lived. Part of living was dying. People got old or sick and died. It happened often.

Augie looked at Javier and said, "We could have dealt with this on the way back."

Wiping tears away from his eyes, Javier said, his voice cracking, "I ... I ... I saw it move."

Chapter Thirteen

San Francisco

(The same day)

TWO O'CLOCK THAT AFTERNOON, ANTHONY HOLMES'S DAY WAS DONE. The elevator doors opened to the lobby of Addison National. He stepped forward and walked across the marble floor. People watched him as he made his way across the lobby. He heard his thighs scratching together. He reached into his pocket and felt the remote key to his new Corvette.

Holmes had just bought the new sports car because he felt he was owed some extra comforts. To accommodate those needs, he had spent the last two years lying to the board of directors, his family, and to himself. He had known his job was impossible from the start because it was so morally wrong. His uncle had been able to justify what he created by believing that the lives of the Tobin children were not as important as the lives of his family and everyone working in his bank. *He wasn't keeping the Tobin children from their family—they had none. They had every benefit any child could want.*

Anthony Holmes continued the charade by using that same line of reasoning, but he had taken it one step further. He felt the importance of his job was not properly rewarded by his current six-figure salary, so he developed a scheme where he was able to siphon off part of the Tobin children's Trust money into his own pocket.

In addition to the "usual and customary" costs for monitoring and protecting the Tobin children, Anthony Holmes had created separate offshore accounts. The funds in those accounts could not be traced back to the bank. The purpose of the funds was to pay for any additional services that may rise from extraordinary circumstances. No one on the board of directors wanted to know about the illegal accounts.

With no paper trail, no auditors, and no oversight from the board, Holmes got away with siphoning money from the Tobin Family Trust for his own personal needs. Holmes knew the importance of his job at Addison National. He knew he was in a position of untouchable tenure.

Holmes was on his way to his lover's apartment for their three o'clock Thursday afternoon rendezvous.

He eased his new Corvette into the right lane on the freeway to avoid a quick lane change when he approached his exit a few miles away. His thoughts wandered. *What will Cecilia have in store for me today?*

He had fallen madly in love with Cecilia six months before, after a chance encounter at a downtown cocktail lounge one evening. Holmes was there with a few coworkers when he noticed a beautiful Hispanic woman smiling his way. He turned around to see whom this lovely creature was smiling at, but no one was behind him. When Holmes turned around again, she winked at him. Holmes nearly fell off his stool.

A few minutes later Cecilia joined him at the bar and said, "Would you allow me to buy you a drink? I had a terrible day today, and you're the only one in this place I'd like to talk with right now." She spoke in deep, sexy, accented voice. Holmes could feel the faucets under his arms turn on and wondered, *is the wetness visible through my suit coat?*

Holmes pushed his glasses up to get a better look at her. She said, "I see that all your friends have left. Would you mind if I sat here with you for a while to keep those men over there from bothering me? Is that a Citron and tonic?"

Holmes blurted out, "Yes, yes, it is."

Within a few minutes, Cecelia and Tony (she called him Tony because she felt Anthony was too formal for them) found that they had a lot in common. It was amazing to him how beautiful and intelligent this woman was and how they had nearly the same travel interests and political views. They were able to talk together so easily, as if they'd known each other for years. Holmes made her laugh often, and they both agreed they were very lucky to have run into each other. After having several drinks together, they decided to meet again the next week.

Cecelia told Holmes that she was in a very abusive relationship with someone she had known a long time, and she was afraid to even consider leaving him. Holmes admitted he was unhappy at home and had considered separating, especially after his big promotion at the bank.

Cecelia said, "I have a friend in the real estate business. He has a furnished apartment for rent. We could use the apartment as a place to meet more often. It's a much quieter setting than here in the bar."

Holmes didn't know what to say.

"If you think about that idea," she said, "it does make a lot of sense. I mean, Tony, with all these people around …" She placed her hand lightly on Holmes's thigh, several inches above his knee. With her big brown eyes, she looked deep into his eyes and said, "Tony, do you want to spend more time with me?" Her hand slid a little higher on his leg. She licked her bright red lips and leaned closer to him. "I can make you feel really good, Tony. You would want that, wouldn't you?"

Holmes broke his eyes away from Cecelia's tantalizing mouth, and down to her soft invitingly displayed cleavage. He looked back at the promise in her big brown eyes and said, "Set it up."

That was six months earlier, and every day since then they had fallen deeper and deeper in love. Holmes thought about her all day and couldn't wait for their scheduled times together. He found it interesting that Cecelia was so punctual. Cecelia explained, "A man in your position needs certainty in his life. A man in your position needs a proper schedule. A man of your position needs to be in charge."

Holmes took care of Cecelia by covering the high rental cost and giving her countless expensive gifts. Cecelia took care of Holmes.

Holmes's daydream was interrupted by a phone call. He found the Bluetooth button and answered, "Yes?"

"Mr. Holmes, this is Jackson from The Agency calling to bring you up to speed with a few matters of importance."

"Go ahead."

Jackson said, "Max is on his way back to England with the same group he traveled with to Cozumel. Anna went for a long run this morning, as usual, and then spent her day at the beach reading two large books. She's been alone. She hasn't made contact with anyone except a couple of employees at the resort."

"Has she started drinking yet?"

"Negative, Mr. Holmes—looks like she's content with staying at the resort with her nose in those books."

"Has anything come up about the missing Mexican man?"

"No, sir. There is no story there. No body, no story."

"What's the status of the Woods debacle?"

"No indication the incident in the alley is related to us. He's been all business. Hasn't had any unusual conversations or made any suspicious contacts. Our bugging devices are all working in both his home and his office. He is constantly in our sights. If he makes a move, we're prepared, and we know how to deal with him. I think our decision to let that sleeping dog lie was the right one. He seems to be no threat to us at this time, and the less activity around this whole case, the better. It would be nice to see things settle down for a while. We also have three men on Max's plane, but have no indication regarding his future plans."

"All right, Jackson. Just remember this is your call on Woods. You'll have to take full responsibility if any of this mess comes back to us. Don't bother me the rest of the day, but give me an update in the morning." He hung up without giving Jackson a chance to reply.

With the music turned off and only the sounds of his vehicle and traffic, Holmes's thoughts started to wander again. The conversation he just had with Jackson reminded him of the young Mexican man, Armando, he ordered to be killed. He tried to put those thoughts out of his mind but couldn't because the pictures he saw of Armando before the incident were pictures of a young man full of life. He compared those to the photos he had requested of Armando after the attack, as proof of death.

Armando's father was too connected in Mexico and in the U.S. with his own banking concerns. If Armando and Anna stayed together and continued down their current path, they would marry and have a family. From there it wouldn't be long before his father would start asking questions. Armando had to be taken out. It was unfortunate, but I had no other options.

Holmes pulled off the interstate at his exit and made a quick left turn. He scanned both sides of the street to find a parking spot, one where he wouldn't have to parallel-park. He also hoped that he didn't have to see another man leaving Cecelia's apartment as he had several times before. When he had confronted Cecelia about her visitors, she just said, "That's none of your business. It's your fault because you come too early." Holmes assumed she had other suitors, but didn't care. She said she loved him and only him.

It was his lucky day. A spot was open right on the corner and only a block away.

Chapter Thirteen

Holmes jumped out of the car, rushed across the street and into the apartment building. He gave his usual knock on the front door a few minutes after three o'clock. The door opened to the lovely Cecelia, beckoning him in, wearing little more than her big, bright smile. Holmes took one step into the apartment and fell a little further from the line of decency.

Chapter A

Munich, Germany

(Same day, late at night)

*T*HE GIRL COULDN'T, SHE WOULDN'T, LET HER YOUNG MIND OR BODY SLEEP BECAUSE *of what she feared. She knew he was coming.*

She was alone in the dark. Her heart stopped when she heard his footsteps. She could tell by their erratic sound that he'd binged again on cheap schnapps. The girl prayed that the chair wedged tightly against the door would hold. He is coming.

She was in bed, wearing her double-layered winter pajamas, with half of her face on her thin pillow. The old quilt and top sheet were pulled up tightly to her chin, and her knees were together and drawn up close to her elbows in a fetal, defensive position. She peered through the dark at the door, specifically the door-knob. Listening. Silence. Maybe he won't, maybe he already stumbled past and went to his own room. Shhhh. *Waiting. Then his diabolical attempt at a quiet turn of the doorknob broke the hopeful silence. All her senses were on their highest alert as she silently slid through the very small space between the side of her bed and the outside wall. Slowly she poured her thin, flexible body into the darkness under the bed. She was an expert at this move. Her well-practiced technique was executed flawlessly.* He won't give up without a much bigger fight.

From under the bed the girl could see a strip of light between the bottom of the bedroom door and the wood plank floor. She saw the silhouette of his dirty, oversized boots. He slammed his body against the door. The door bulged, the chair quivered, and she felt the intensity of his anger grow.

The chair had withstood his first attack. The girl was faint with terror. She fought back the tears welling in her eyes. If he breaks through, I won't be able to stop him this time. He's too heavy, too strong, and more furious because of my constant insubordination. *She could almost smell his putrid breath, and she cringed at the thought of his disgusting hands. Trembling with fear, she thought,*

I've fought him so long. I can't win. Does anyone know where the love of God goes when a child feels this kind of peril? Tonight, he is coming.

With his next attack the thin wooden chair legs splintered, and the door burst open. The beast's boots paced back and forth in front of her as he mumbled. She fought to remain completely still and silent. His boots walked ... away. Is he gone? Shhh, stay still, stay silent. He's gone?

Suddenly, the beast yanked her bed up and tossed it to the other side of the room. He stood over her, panting, and she screamed, but heard no sound. The beast grabbed her arms, and she tried to scream again, but couldn't. Panic threatened to paralyze her. Fearing for her life, she tried again to scream as loudly as she could. He clamped a filthy hand over her mouth. She clawed it away and screamed. This time she heard her scream.

She startled awake, quivering and gasping for air, and looked around. She tried to get her bearings. *Did anyone hear ... Has anyone spotted me? What time is it?* Then she remembered her horrible, reoccurring nightmare—the memory of her life and what she had barely escaped.

Chapter B
Munich, Germany
(Same night)

THE GIRL WAS WIDE AWAKE NOW, TIGHTLY WRAPPED IN A THICK, DARK blanket. The hood of her black sweatshirt covered the back of her head. She was hidden in the undergrowth, the strap of her backpack looped around her left hand and an open jackknife clutched in her right. She was prepared to protect her few possessions as well as herself. She listened with all her senses, trusting her instincts. She felt safe—for now.

She thought again about her recurring nightmare. She was the foster child, the baby her own mother didn't want and would not love. A family who received a monthly payment from the German government for providing her basic needs took her in. For seventeen years she perfected her camouflaged existence. But that wasn't enough. She learned how to show no feelings, to expect no comfort, and to never give them the ammunition they craved for their certain betrayal.

She was the outsider, which was continuously made clear. The mother of the family doted over her own daughter and daily confirmed the distinction between the two girls.

When her body started to change, so did the stares of the husband/father/ beast. His wandering hands would surprise and scare her. She could hear his sinister snicker as she struggled to get away. The mother was no help even though she knew exactly what was going on. The mother and daughter had been jealous from the start, and it was easy for them to look the other way. The girl had the starring role in a real-life horror story.

One night she woke with his hand over her mouth. She managed to get free and screamed loud enough and long enough to root him from her room. A few weeks later he surprised her in the kitchen before school.

The girl was dressed in her school uniform, and she sensed the danger when he appeared. He trapped her against the wall with his arm across her throat. The other hand went under her skirt. She smelled his foul breath when he said, "You live under my roof. Don't try to fight me. You won't win. You give me what I want, or I'll make it much worse."

With his arm across her throat, she couldn't catch her breath. She couldn't summon one of her loud screams. *What is he doing to me?* She tried again to get a breath, but couldn't. The mother surprised her husband when she came into the kitchen and interrupted his attack. He let her go, and she collapsed onto the floor, gasping for air. The mother yelled at her, "Get to school! Get out of this house!"

With the certainty of more brazen attacks, the girl slept on the floor in the daughter's bedroom for weeks, but the mother soon put an end to that. Seventeen years old and out of options, she had no choice but to escape the hell in that home and take her chances alone in the park.

Chapter Fourteen

San Francisco

(Next morning)

THE NEXT MORNING REED JACKSON PHONED HOLMES IN HIS OFFICE, AS requested, and gave him the morning update. "Hello, Mr. Holmes. This is Jackson."

Holmes started the conversation, "I've been thinking more about the Allen Woods problem. I don't want to take any chances with him. I have a bad feeling about this one, and I want something done about it soon. Try to make it look like an accident if you can, but get it done."

Jackson knew what he was asking and didn't like the request or his tone of voice. After a short pause, Jackson said, "Are you sure that's the direction you want to go? You pay me for advice, and I have to tell you this one will be a lot trickier than the man in Mexico. Woods is an American citizen, a good citizen. There will be a full investigation by very competent law enforcement agencies."

Holmes yelled, "That's what I pay you for! I pay you to take care of the shit I don't want to think about. I pay you very well. If you don't have the stomach for this one, I'll get someone else!"

No one talked to Jackson like that, but for the first time in his life, he sat there and took the abuse. He knew he was already in too deep with Addison National, so trying to jump out now would put a big hole in the revenue he needed to keep his business going. His men and their families all depended on him to keep the money coming in.

Every year Addison National's business represented more and more of The Agency's bottom line. Jackson now found himself overly reliant on Holmes. He didn't have any other options. *I guess there's no such thing as pride when you're trying to make a living.* He swallowed that pride and said, "You're the boss, Mr. Holmes. We'll get this done."

Chapter C
Munich, Germany
(Three weeks later)

THE GIRL SAT ALONE ON ONE OF THE THOUSANDS OF PICNIC TABLES SCAT-
tered throughout the vast expanse of the English Garden. She was reading
a book, trying to fit in, and trying to be invisible. She spotted two "others"
doing exactly the same thing—watching, waiting for an opportunity, hoping
someone would throw away part of a pretzel or sandwich. Then came the
challenge. Compete for the prize and get the food before one of the "others."
Do it in a way that doesn't attract attention, attract the eyes of the "un-others"
or the eyes of the law.

She and the "others" tried to go unnoticed all day, every day. The homeless,
the dredges of society, were recognizable to one another, but were invisible
to the swarms of people in the park. She knew the signs—always alone, eyes
scanning the crowd, wearing the same clothes every day with their unkempt
hair partly captured by a dirty hat, and the same gray complexions. They
were her competition. They were the enemy. They would steal her backpack,
her only possession, if they had the chance, and they would hurt her badly to
decrease the competition. This was the purest form of survival of the fittest.
She'd cut off her hair and found men's clothing to disguise herself. A woman,
a girl, was too vulnerable and more visible than a man.

Visibility meant capture, which meant a horror much worse than what she
had escaped. She learned, adapted, understood her position, and modified
her behavior in order to survive. She had grown smarter and learned to trust
her instincts.

The park was huge, and no one knew its paths, trails, roads, gardens,
meadows, forests, or attractions better than she did.

The girl had several resting or nesting areas throughout both ends of the
park. At night she had to become invisible to the "others," because they became

dangerous when no one was in sight. Her sleeping areas were well hidden and always had two escape routes that she could negotiate in the pitch-black night.

Before she settled into one of her dens at night, she took off on a brisk run through the park, always taking a different route and always running silently through the trees. Then she'd double back in quick and ingenious ways to be certain there were no followers. She had a stealth way of suddenly disappearing, lying in the brush, and listening for any unnatural noise. The girl could crawl on her stomach for hundreds of yards under and through the thick brush, something that no one else could emulate.

After she nestled into one of her dens, she could find comfort with her blanket and her pride. She slept, but was somehow alert, always listening, always on edge and waiting for intruders. She had learned from trying to fight off the hands of the beast that she was no match for a man's strength. She had to rely on her ability to anticipate, react quickly, and flee a dangerous encounter. With escape routes in different directions from all her dens, she knew she could outrun anyone through the park. She knew the park like the back of her hand and knew she could run for miles faster and longer than anyone.

Soon I'll be eighteen and able to get a job, earn some money, and start living a normal life—my life. For a short time she had worked in a restaurant, but it wasn't long before the authorities were notified, and she was sent back to the same foster home. She heard the lies and felt the scorn when the family tried to get their monthly payment again. Worse, she could feel the clock ticking inside the beast. She managed to escape from the home a few days later without incident.

The public library was her refuge during the day. She spent time inside to continue her schooling and to clean up in the public restrooms. The library was enormous, so she had no problem staying invisible. But there were no food opportunities in the library. She was forced to spend time in the park to find a meal.

The girl spotted a man across the open lawn. She had noticed him often over the past few weeks. *I bet he can see the invisible. I'm sure he's left me food before.*

He sat alone with a big sandwich, potato fries, and a stein of beer in front of him. Even with hundreds of people all around them, he saw her. He left the table with a feast of a meal unattended. The girl started her journey across the lawn, trying to remain invisible. But then she saw one of the "others" hurrying toward her prize. *He is much closer. He'll get there before me.*

To stay invisible she couldn't make sudden movements or create a scene. The police and the park rangers were everywhere, and they would not tolerate any disturbance.

She decided to back off and wait for another opportunity. She veered away. Then she noticed the man returning to his lunch. The "other" was forced to modify his plan. *I was right. He can see us. He must have lived this same life sometime in his past.*

The girl looked at him. He waved her over. Uncertain, she didn't move. He motioned again.

She walked his way. The girl arrived and stood on the opposite side of the large picnic table. The man pushed all the food toward her, and with a foreign accent he said, "Help yourself."

She sat down on the bench and tried to look like a man instead of a girl. She knew that her voice was a dead giveaway, so she didn't speak. She ate. *This sandwich is so fresh and so good.* There was a large stein of beer on the table. She looked up to get his permission. The man nodded, and she took a big drink of beer. Quietly, quickly, and politely she ate the food and drank the beer. *That was a great meal— a two-day meal.*

The man said, "My name is Silvio." He waited for her to respond. She didn't. "I see you in the park, and I feel bad about how you live. I know you must have a good reason to live this way, and know all you need is a little help. I want to help you. I want to take care of you. I want to be your friend and want you to be mine." Again he waited for a response. She looked away, away from those eyes. *Do not speak.*

After a while he said, "You can come with me now, away from here, to a home with new clothes and a warm shower. There are other girls for you to meet, and they will help you, too."

There was another long period of silence. "I do want to care for you." Silvio pushed fifty euros across the table. The girl looked at the money.

I've never seen that much money. I know what he wants. Without looking at him, she snatched up her backpack, left the money, and walked away.

<hr />

Silvio walked off in the opposite direction and approached two men waiting for him. Speaking in his native Chechen tongue, Silvio said, "We'll give her one more chance to come voluntarily. If she refuses, I want you to take her. Aslan and I will train this one. I know if we get her cleaned up and properly trained, she could end up being one of our best earners. We paid extra for her. You should see the pictures of her before she ended up here in the park. So don't hurt her. When we're done with her, I'll let you guys have a turn before we put her out."

Chapter Fifteen

Peto, Mexico
(The same day)

HALFWAY AROUND THE WORLD, THE EARLY MORNING SUNLIGHT STREAKED through small gaps of rough-cut wood that made up walls of a small hut. Armando lay there on a hard cot.

He slowly woke. A stretch of his lean limbs delivered a hellish reminder of excruciating pain from his head to his toes. In spite of the agony, he had a feeling of overwhelming joy as he remembered ... Today was the day.

Three weeks before, he was on the edge of a swamp fighting off creatures without shoulders. Against all odds, a boy had seen his hand reaching for life. With great sacrifice to themselves and their families, the boy and his uncle unloaded their valuable asparagus crop on the side of the road and loaded the stranger on their ancient two-wheel cart. Their mule carted him back to their homes, where everyone from all seven families had a hand in helping to nurse him back to health.

Armando sat on the edge of his cot. *How am I going to do this?* He assumed he looked grotesque. There were no mirrors in the village. No vanity among its citizens. Everyone here was accepted just the way they were. *I'm not even sure I want to see what I look like.*

Compared to the day they pulled him from the swamp, Armando looked much better. They had done a good job of cleaning him up, but his nose was still tender. He could tell there was something going on with his right eye because his right eyebrow was in his line of sight.

His hair was clean, but it was long, thick, and matted. It hid a dent on the back of his head that concerned him when he ran his fingers over the painful edges. He still had open wounds all over his body. His broken ribs had started their healing process, finally allowing him to catch a full breath, but something was still wrong with his left leg.

He had been alert for about a week and able to walk the past couple of days. All he could think about the entire time was, *Why? Was Anna in the same kind of danger? What happened to her?*

The families that helped him could not have been more welcoming. Their nourishing Mayan culture and ancient medical techniques had saved his life. Armando hoped the families knew how grateful he was for their kindness. Javier, the young boy who had spotted him, was especially helpful and protective.

They spoke a language he didn't understand. A few of the family members spoke a little Spanish, so they had some limited communication.

Armando limped out of his hut into the soft light of the morning and faced a smiling audience of thirty people. They were waiting for his farewell breakfast to begin. The adopted son stood tall, with a broad smile on his battered face. His smile was his only means of giving thanks, of showing his sincere appreciation.

After breakfast, Armando followed Javier and his best friend on the path to the village. Javier showed him where he had found him. Armando felt every bump on the rough road with a pain that seared through his body. He was not anywhere near full strength or completely healed, but couldn't wait any longer. *I may never get my strength back.*

They made it to the village in time to catch a ride from one of the trucks taking fresh produce to Playa de Carmen. Hopefully, he was going back to Anna and their life together. They arranged for the truck driver to stop inside the guarded front gate. This area of Playa de Carmen was gated for a reason. The golf course and the high-end resorts wanted to keep the locals and nonmembers out.

Armando would stand out in this immaculate country club setting. His hair was wild, and his clothes were tattered, making his overall appearance frightful. All this gave him the look of trouble in the eyes of a tourist or security guard.

The guard at the gate didn't detain them. About a quarter of a mile in, Armando slipped out of the truck and scurried away from the open street without incident. He knew that this area was on Anna's usual morning running route and that he was there early enough to catch her if she still lived here. He crouched out of sight in the lush greenery and waited,

He replayed the day the men had jumped him in Anna's room for what seemed to be the millionth time. He was still racking his brain for even a hint of a logical explanation for the violence. With only illogical reasons remaining, all potential scenarios meant danger for Anna, which was why he couldn't just go back to her room and knock on the door. It was better if the men who had done this to him to think he was dead.

There is no reason for Anna to stay in Playa. The only reason she came here was because I worked at the marina. What does she think happened to me? Where does she think I went? Every time he went there, the pain in his head spiked. *Was Anna hurt because of me?*

Squatting in the bushes reminded Armando of the swamp, where he was in and out of consciousness while he crawled through the mire and fought off the swamp creatures. A natural instinct of survival and thoughts of returning to Anna kept him alive. *Waiting here in these bug-infested bushes is a picnic compared to the swamp. My life has changed forever.*

He waited patiently for Anna. He waited for something that might not come. Even if Anna did turn that corner, there was no certainty things would ever be like they were before.

Armando recalled the muffled voices on the morning he was attacked, but could never make sense out of what he heard. He didn't get a good look at any of the attackers. He stayed on his feet after the first strike, but wasn't able to move or fight back. *From behind came another blow. They must have continued to beat me before they left me for dead. But, why?*

Armando thought about how bad he looked and about how Anna must have thought that he had abandoned her. *Why would she want a repulsive coward of a man back in her life?*

There she is! Her long, fluid stride, her posture, her golden hair, her face, and her grace were a stunning reminder of why he'd fought so hard to stay alive.

Anna neared him more quickly than he had anticipated, and he had trouble getting out of the bushes. His left leg didn't work very well. He stumbled out on to the sidewalk and then fell into the street. Anna stopped a short distance away, spun, and sprinted away.

He picked himself up and shouted, "Anna, stop! It's me, Armando!" She took a few more strides, then stopped, turned around, and stared at him, looking puzzled. He knew what she saw—a skinny, dirty man wearing ragged clothes, standing crookedly, with long, stringy hair covering most of his face.

"Anna, it's me!" he cried, then flashed his trademark smile. Anna timidly drew closer, still prepared to bolt. "Please, Anna, it's me, Armando."

She stepped a little closer. Still smiling at her, Armando raked back his scraggly hair so she could get a better look at his face. She inched closer.

Armando extended one hand to clasp the only hand that would ever hold his. Now she was close enough to inspect his face. She clapped both hands over her mouth and burst into tears. Then she swatted his hand away and threw herself into his arms. "My God!" she said between sobs. "What happened to you? Where have you been? What happened?"

Armando felt her true love with that hug. He wanted to stay there forever, but he knew they had to get away from there. "Anna, we have to go. We're in danger if they see us."

"If who sees us?"

"Please trust me." He led her back through the bushes and on to the golf course.

They found a secluded place where they couldn't be seen from the road. Armando told her everything that had happened to him since the morning they last saw each other. Anna listened intently to his story.

"They left a note that looked like your handwriting," she told him. "It said you went back to be with your family and you didn't want to see me ever again. I was running home to tell you about the fishing boat I bought for us, and you were gone. Let's get you back to my place and clean you up."

Armando replied, "We can't go back to your place. Everything has changed. We have to assume that whoever did this to me thinks I'm dead. We also have to assume the men who did this still want me dead. I don't have a clue why, but I'm worried about you, too. We know you're involved to some degree because of the note they left. Clearly they wanted me out of the way, and they didn't want you looking for me."

Anna agreed. They decided that she should continue her run just like always and continue her usual routine. They planned for her to gather their personal effects, including passports, cash, credit cards, and clothes. Then she would meet Armando on their boat.

They embraced and kissed, and Armando made his way off the grounds of the resort and headed to the main road, where he would catch a bus to La Aventura.

Anna had only two miles left on her run back home, but it seemed like twenty miles. Running at a normal pace seemed impossible. Several conflicting emotions swirled in her mind. She replayed Armando's story over and over, and while she was elated to have him back, now danger seemed to lurk around every corner.

They were in my room, they forged the note, and they knew Armando called me his angel. Who would do that to Armando? None of this makes sense.

Her adrenaline was flowing, and her heart raced. She slowed down and remembered their plan. If it all went as planned, they would be together soon. *Slow down, and look normal. Don't let them see what I'm feeling.*

Armando mingled with some tourists and a few locals at the closest bus stop, waiting for one of the many buses that traveled from Cancun to the ruins of Tulum.

He boarded the southbound bus for the thirty-minute ride to Puerto La Aventura. He sat in the back of the bus with his head down, trying not to attract attention. He had a lot on his mind as passengers around him came and went.

Anna told him where their boat was tied up. This was the perfect time of day for him to blend in with the rest of the crowd, because it was feeding time for the dolphins. The daily event attracted tourists who watched the feeding frenzy.

Armando easily walked through the crowd to Anna's boat. He couldn't help but walk a bit slower so he could admire the vessel's appearance as he approached. *Nice job, Anna.* He carefully climbed aboard and limped down the stairs to the landing area just outside the galley.

Anna felt as if she was being watched the whole time in her suite and she couldn't wait to get out of there. She quickly packed everything they needed and went downstairs to get a cab.

"*Hola, Ernesto. Buenos días!*" she said to her favorite driver. "*La Adventura por favor.*" A trip to the marina wasn't unusual for Anna, and she was well-known there. The regulars would not be surprised to see her that day.

Over the past few months, she had often made the trip to spend time on her yacht. Some of Armando's friends had given her basic instructions for handling the boat. She had spent lots of time on board to become more familiar with its operation.

Anna paid the driver and carved her way through the crowd. She tossed her backpack on the back deck. Armando was exactly where she hoped he would be. *Perfect.*

She gave him a sly smile. She was wearing tight, white shorts and a pink halter-top.

She hoped Armando liked what he saw.

Her hair waved in the breeze, and her flip-flops slapped the planks of the dock as she walked away. She took long, confident strides on the weather-beaten wood decking as she headed to the bait shop.

She returned with three bags of supplies. When she saw Armando again, hidden at the bottom of the stairs, she wanted to run to him, to make sure he was real.

Suddenly, Anna felt a pressure of hidden danger closing in. She wanted to scream! But, couldn't take a chance to even look into the shadows. She had to assume that they were there and could reach out to stop her. *Don't give them anything*, she told herself over and over. She stayed the course, untied the mariner knots, and hopped into the aft of the boat.

Anna went through the yacht's normal prestart routine and started the engine. Then she untied the last mooring line. She returned to the helm and slowly backed out of the slip. Once they were away from the crowded marina, she pushed the throttle forward and steered the boat toward the open water, taking herself, her Armando, and all their dreams with them.

Chapter Sixteen

Belfry Resort, England

(The same day)

THE DRIVE FROM THE AIRPORT IN MANCHESTER, ENGLAND, TO THE Belfry golf resort in West Midlands was one of complete chaos and horror. Driving on the opposite side of the road from the passenger seat in an unfamiliar car on narrow roads was a white-knuckle experience that Allen Woods was not prepared for.

Woods was relieved when his rental car rolled into the parking lot. He had been through a lot in his life, but the drive through the English countryside may have been his biggest challenge. The vagueness of the trip only amplified his state of bewilderment.

The discovery a few days before about Anthony Holmes's intentions to kill him forced a response. He had to find Max or Anna Tobin and explain the situation before it was too late. The PI firm he hired found Max quickly, but they were still working to locate Anna.

Woods felt as though he was grasping at straws. He didn't have much confidence in his ability to engage Max Tobin, explain his past relationship with his father, and educate him about Addison National's true intentions.

It all sounded simple enough, and Woods knew his strength was making a plan, but his weakness was in the execution. He knew he didn't have much to go on, but trusted Max was a responsible person who would give him a chance to tell the story. He hoped Max was looking for answers. Woods knew he would have only one shot. But for now, he just wanted to get out of the damn vehicle.

He checked into one of the guest rooms at the Belfry and opened the blinds. *What an amazing color of green, golf course green, the color of manicured perfection that highlights our selfish and wasteful civilization*, thought Woods.

The proud history of past Ryder Cup matches and the sheer beauty of the tree-lined vistas created an overwhelming aura that any golfer or sports enthusiast would marvel at. Woods was neither. He didn't understand the game of golf, and he felt just as uncomfortable in the emerald paradise as he had when he was driving on the wrong side of the road to get there.

Woods quickly found his way to the golf pro shop. He asked a very young-looking bag boy, "Is there any chance you know a man by the name of Max Tobin?" The young man, who had pink cheeks and an unfair thicket of blond hair, smiled at him but didn't respond.

The dapper lad stood behind a glass-topped counter that contained golf balls, golf gloves, and various other golf accessories. He looked down at a sheet of paper Woods saw was titled, "Tee Times." The boy then looked up at the big, round clock on the wall behind him, gazed through a large plate-glass window at the course, looked at the timesheet again, and then looked at Woods.

In an English accent he said politely, "His foursome is next off the last, but the group in front of his is known for their, let's say, somewhat deliberate play." The boy's eyebrows went up and down a few times. He had finished his sentence with a snicker in his eyes, as though Woods was now privy to an inside joke. Woods had no idea what most of that meant, so he didn't respond. He hoped there was more of an explanation with an actual answer in it.

"Looks like we have some open tables and chairs out on the veranda. You can wait there and watch them finish up their round. They should be done in about twenty minutes."

Woods understood the twenty minutes part. He walked out the big glass door to the patio and sat at an empty table.

Enjoying the warm sun and the solitude, he wondered if he would be able to recognize Max from his memory of Max's parents.

Woods tried to recall the image of his tall friend, Jeff Tobin, but then his mind wandered to the last conversation he had at the Addison National Bank with the smug Anthony Holmes. He remembered the look on Holmes's face when he asked about the Tobin children and how Holmes's reaction started a chain of obscure events that led him to this place.

The warm sun started to make him feel relaxed. He never had time for simple pleasures like this in his life. A gentle breeze cooled his face and skin.

A loud, obnoxious voice coming from the eighteenth green disturbed Woods's solitude. He looked that way and saw two young men chasing each other, brandishing their golf clubs and shouting a string of profanities. Then Woods spotted Max Tobin walking away from the commotion, heading toward him. His body and gait were identical to those of his father.

Woods rehearsed his scripted introduction. He remembered the reports from his private investigators. Max had lived here for the past couple of years with no apparent job or other means of support. Woods had learned that Max golfed all day, partied all night, ran with loose women, and generally had been living a life of decadence with a group of nitwit friends.

Was it possible that Max didn't care about his past, didn't care about this old man who was a friend of his father's, wanted this current lifestyle, and didn't want his carefree life to be disturbed? Max walked closer. *This is my chance. Time to stand and be recognized.*

Suddenly, one of the golfers from the group rushed up, jumped onto Max's back, and rode him like a horse, sidelining Woods' introduction. The motley crew pulled chairs around a table right next to Woods. He was close enough to hear every word of their conversation. It was clear they had been drinking most of the day. Max was quiet compared to the other three, who were exceptionally lewd. Two of the boys continued the bickering they had started on the green, with accusations flying both ways about some sort of cheating that went on during their play on the course.

"Harry, you lying son of a bitch, we all saw you move your ball clear of that tree on number fourteen!"

Their foul language and the way they talked about the waitress, the other people sitting on the patio, the friends they planned to meet up with that night, and even each other made Woods feel ill.

One of the boys said, "Max, we hear Maggie is bringing Beth with her to the club. Word is that the two of them want to do a double leg over with you in your suite tonight. Reliable reports are saying that you will be exceptionally busy all night long."

Woods thought this was just a group of losers. *Maybe Max had turned out to be nothing like his parents. Maybe he was the exact opposite of them.* Woods felt disappointed. Another round of drinks accompanied additional vulgarity and attention-seeking clamor.

Sitting in plain view but completely unnoticed, Woods was able to scrutinize this group closely.

Max was the quiet one, not really a participant in the spectacle. He looked more like a casual observer. Woods was especially pleased to see Max interrupt one of his friends when he started to berate the polite waitresses. "Harry, lay off. She's just doing her job, and trying to make you happy is impossible." With that, the whole group fell silent, and the young lady clearly appreciated Max's chivalry.

Max's quiet demeanor and his act of protection for the young lady gave Woods hope that he was different from the rest of the group. *Maybe the good traits of his parents are still inside Max Tobin, wanting to surface. Maybe there was still hope.*

Soon the entire patio was full of people, jabbering with one another. Woods tried to make out what they were saying but got a little confused. That wasn't unusual. Unfortunately, the feeling of confusion crept in too often. He sometimes felt as though he was behind, a little slow. He felt as if he was always trying to catch up when he walked down the sidewalk or drove down a street. He tried to fit into conversations and social engagements but always felt as though he was on the outside looking in. That bothered him. No one cared about him. There wasn't one person in his life that he had any connection with. No one had any empathy for how he felt or understood what these changes meant to him.

He looked at Max sitting quietly at the next table in the middle of all the commotion. He thought Max looked somewhat alone, a little behind, and on the outside looking in. He thought maybe that was exactly what Max felt. It was clear that Max didn't belong in this group or in this place. *Maybe Max was looking for a way out. Maybe he was looking for someone who really cared about him. Maybe he was waiting and hoping for a connection just as much as I am.*

After observing Max for a while, Woods felt more optimistic. He had a renewed fight inside, and he thought there might be a chance for a positive meeting with Max.

He overheard the boys' plan for the night. He knew they were planning to meet another group at the club later that night, and then Max's group would leave first thing in the morning to go to Amsterdam. Woods decided to confront Max later at the club, where he could isolate him from his friends. Feeling very much relieved after making this decision, Woods watched the waitress deliver another round of drinks to Max's table. He shook his head, stood up, and walked away.

<hr />

After a very late supper, Woods walked along the stone, dimly lit, outdoor walkway from the hotel to the nightclub. He assumed Max and his friends would be gathering there soon. Woods was surprised when he entered the club and found it empty of guests. Several staffers moved tables around and set up the bar for the night's festivities, but he was the only patron in the place. *It's nine o'clock at night. Where is everyone?*

Just as he sat down at a table, a young lady with pink hair, piercings in her lower lip, nose, and ears, and a dragonfly tattooed on the side of her neck walked up to him and curtly said, "What can I get you?"

Feeling a little stunned by her appearance, Woods said, "Uh, could I have a cup of coffee?"

The pink-haired, ring-nosed alien responded, "I'd have to go next door to get that."

Woods just looked at her and raised both his eyebrows as if to say, *That's your job, young lady.* She understood his look and stomped away.

An hour later the place was full. It was full of people, full of noise, full of smoke, and Woods was full of disgust. He could not understand how these people could live this way. He felt uncomfortable, completely out of place. But he had to wait for Max. He soon realized that this was the only time in the past thirty years when time actually moved slowly. He thought about how quickly those years had gotten behind him. He wrung his seventy-seven-year-old hands and tried to make sense of what he saw around him.

He spotted a couple of the boys in Max's group walk in. They were part of a larger group that included five or six young ladies, all of them dressed like strippers. They hovered around the front entrance, looking as if they were haggling with the doorman.

Then Max showed up with a shapely young lady on each arm. He paid no attention to the melee his friends had created. Woods couldn't wait. Now was his time.

Woods stood and called out, "Max Tobin!"

Max turned around to see who was calling his name. Woods raised his right arm to get his attention. Just then two of Max's friends stepped in front of him.

"What can I help you with, old man?" one of the men said.

Somewhat taken aback, Woods looked at him and said, "I need to talk with Max Tobin."

"What do you want with him?"

"Please," Woods said as he tried to walk around the young man. "I just need a minute of his time."

Woods spotted Max's broad back walking away. He saw Max's hands fall from the girl's shoulders inside the back of their low-cut slacks—into a place that Woods had never known.

One of the young men put the flat of his right hand on Woods's chest and pushed him back. "Take a hike, old man," he yelled over the noise. "Max doesn't want anything you're selling."

Upset and dumbfounded, Woods could see that his one opportunity was slipping away. Woods yelled back, "I have to talk with Max about his father."

The two young men laughed in his face. One of them said, "Get out! You don't belong here."

Woods didn't have the strength to fight off these two turds or the madness of the crowd. He watched Max and the girls disappear into the darkness. They were right. He didn't belong here. Woods didn't look at either of the rude young men in front of him. He admitted defeat to himself and headed for the door.

<hr />

Just as Woods turned to leave, Max turned his head and saw his white hair and hunched shoulders retreat out the door.

Nick and the others settled into a booth next to Max, who had a drink in one hand and a supple feel in the other. Still peering over the back of the booth, Max said, "Nick, "what's up with that old man?"

"No worries, old boy, Nick replied. "Harry thought he was the same guy who was bothering you last week about some investment deal. Harry took care of him for you. The old man said something about your father, though, before Harry sent him on his way."

Max turned to the beautiful Maggie, who had a shot glass filled with Grey Goose in both hands and the offer of a spectacularly sensual night in her eyes. Max accepted the shot. He knew that look. He smiled and winked at her. They clicked their shot glasses. Then a thought about his old friend Tom Riley from Carnoustie jumped into his mind.

Maybe it was the sight of the man's white hair, or maybe it was the word *father*, but for some reason, he'd had the same feeling when he sat with Tom in Shivas' pub. He heard Tom saying, *Define what kind of man you want to be, then be that man.*

Max turned to Maggie and whispered in her ear, "Save my place, love. I'll be right back." He kissed her soft cheek.

He pried her semi-good-looking friend's active hand from his crotch and left the booth, then bumped his way through the crowd to the front door.

He walked into the dark night and looked around, trying to find the man. At the end of the dimly lit walkway leading back to the resort, Max saw him struggling with someone.

Max yelled, "Hey!" and sprinted toward them. Just before he got there, the shadow released Woods.

"What's going on here?" Max cried.

Max felt something on his back. It felt as though someone had jumped on him trying to get a rebound in a basketball game. His natural basketball instinct kicked in. He did a slight reverse pivot and ducked his head to his right. At the same time, he quickly lifted his left elbow up strong and fast, catching the intruder just under his waist.

The man flipped over Max's head at the same time his partner moved forward to intercede. The flipping, turning motion of the man in the air increased in velocity and consequently the force of impact when the two assailant's heads collided and created an eerie sounding thud. The loud sound of the dull thump precluded the two of them lying on the ground unconscious.

Woods looked at Max with panic in his eyes and shouted, "We have to get out of here now, Max. I knew your parents, and I have a lot to tell you, but we have to move now. We're both in great danger. Please trust me. Let's go!" Woods tossed his keys to Max and said, "My car is right over there. You drive."

Max helped Woods jog across the parking lot. He took a quick look behind them. Both attackers lay still. As Max unlocked the car, Woods said, "This is worse than I thought. We need to get out of here and find your sister."

The tires of the rental car squealed as they roared out of the parking lot. Max glanced at Woods and yelled, "My *sister?*"

Max steered the racing rental car out the back entrance of the resort property and on to the highway. Woods looked back to see if any headlights were behind them. Both of them had caught their breath.

Max said, "What the hell was that all about back there? And what about my father and sister?"

Woods tried to remember his notes, and he searched for the best way to start the conversation. But it was hard to concentrate because of Max's erratic driving. Woods could tell that Max wasn't much better at driving on the British roads than he was. Woods said, "Do you know how to drive this car?"

"I really don't drive by myself very often, especially over here. Actually, I never drive over here. No one will let me."

"Oh, that's reassuring."

Just then the left side of the car clipped a rural signpost.

Woods cried out.

Max said, "Take it easy, I got this now. Where are we going anyway?"

"We need to go someplace where we can stop and talk. There's no way we can talk while you're driving."

"Kingsbury isn't far from here, and I know a couple of nightspots we can check out."

"No way. No more clubs, pubs, taverns, or anything remotely similar. I'm not going through that again. How about a café somewhere?"

"I know of one there, but I'm not sure if it's open yet."

"Yet? It's eleven at night. What time could it possibly be open?"

"I've only been there a few times at the bar's closing time, so I'm not sure of their hours. We can check it out," Max said as they got stuck in the inside lane of a roundabout—the wrong lane for them. Max jerked the steering wheel. A driver behind him laid on his horn. Somehow Max managed to bail them out of the intersection.

Max smiled at Woods. "Don't pay any attention to these Brits" as he looked in the rearview mirror. "They always seem to be pissed about something."

Soon they were on a straightaway. No oncoming headlights. No lights behind them. Woods let out a sigh of relief. They drove in silence for a while.

Somehow they managed to get through the outskirts of town and into the city. Max drove slowly, looking up and down the streets, trying to find the café. Finally, Max spotted a parking stall. He barely slowed down as he whipped the rental car into the tight spot, almost hitting a Mini Cooper on Woods's side of the car.

Feeling a little shaken up but happy the vehicle had finally stopped, Woods said, "Do you see the café?"

"No, but I know it's around here somewhere." He eyed a neon-splashed pub nearby.

"Don't even think about it," Woods said. "We're not going in there."

"Where?" Max smiled with a playful look in his eyes. "What's wrong with this place?"

"I don't think you understand the gravity of the dangerous situation we find ourselves in tonight."

"Ourselves? A few minutes ago I was sitting between two of the loveliest creatures on Earth. Now I'm in this car with somebody I don't know, and I don't know why."

"You're right. Let's just get out of here and go someplace where I can talk to you in a civilized manner. I'll explain everything to you then."

"Can you get your car door open far enough to get out of the car?" Max asked, looking at how closely they were parked to the car next to them.

"I think so, but I might need a hand. Would you mind coming around to my side and helping me up?"

Before he went for the door handle, Max looked back at Woods and asked, "By the way ... who are you?"

"Just get over here and help me out. I'll explain it all when we get settled."

They got out of the car and walked down the sidewalk. Limping a little, Woods hung on to one of Max Tobin's big arms.

"Did you get hurt by those men in that scuffle back there?"

"No, I don't think so. Just hang on. It just takes me a little while to get my legs underneath me after sitting in the car. It's hell getting old." Woods released Max's arm, and said, "Anyway, you owe me, because believe it or not, twenty-some years ago, I was the one helping you walk."

Max smiled and shook his head, then reached down to embrace the arm of his new mysterious friend.

Woods said, "I see there's a park bench over there. It's a nice night. Let's just sit there."

Woods started with how he met Max's parents in Iowa City when they were students attending the university there. He told Max about how brilliant his father was and how beautiful and loving his mother was.

"I had no idea," Max said. "I've never known anything about them. Not one single thing."

"What did they tell you?" Woods said. "Who raised you? Where did you grow up?"

Max explained his childhood and college experiences. He told Woods about the boarding schools he attended and how basketball and golf were a big part of his life growing up. He told him the story of Carnoustie and how he ended up here.

Woods said, "See, Max, this is the whole problem. Your parents both died at about the same time, leaving behind an unbelievable amount of wealth. I believe the bank has your inheritance tied up and has deliberately withheld the truth from you so they can maintain a grip on your money. There is a man named Holmes at the bank who—"

Max said, "I know the guy, Anthony Holmes. He's been really good to me. He's the one that takes care of my expenses, and he's never questioned my bills. He even made good suggestions about what I should do."

Woods said, "I know Anthony Holmes well. Please, let me keep going. Your parents and I moved from Iowa City to California and started a computer company. We revolutionized the digital world. Max, your parents and I were inseparable, the very best of friends, and we spent every day together. Your Dad and I worked during the day, and I would go home with him for dinner and more work. I was there when you were born. I held you in my arms. You recognized me as a family member back in those days. And when your sister was born, I helped your beautiful mother by tending to you while she—"

"My sister? I never knew I had a sister. What happened to her? Where is she?"

"I'll get to that. Our company grew out of control. We made so much money that we didn't know what to do with it. Your father was brilliant, and he knew how to run the business side of the company. He established a relationship with a big bank in San Francisco, and that's how Anthony Holmes entered the picture. Our business grew too fast overseas, so we decided it would be best if your father moved to Munich, Germany, for a couple of years to get the European operation running smoothly.

"Then your mother developed a horrible, untreatable cancer that took her life. Your father and I decided I should shift my attention to the medical field and use our wealth to find a cure for cancer and other dreadful diseases. Your mother's passing created a big hole in our lives. Everything we did seemed meaningless. Your mother was a very special person, so your dad and I decided to dedicate the rest of our lives to finding a cure for cancer as a way to honor your mother.

We began with setting up a pharmaceutical company. Our original plan was for me to get things started with the new company, and your father would finish what he had started in Munich. Then he was to join me in our quest.

"A few months after your mother died, your father was killed in a freak auto accident in England. After that, I made a big mistake by assuming you had family that would step in and take care of you and your sister. I don't know what happened, but it's clear no one stepped in, and the bank, Richard Holmes, and now his nephew Anthony Homes have intentionally kept you ignorant of your wealth and even kept your sister a secret from you. I'm sure the men back there are agents of the bank, and if you hadn't intervened like you did, I know they would have killed me to keep you from finding out the truth. I've been on the run from them for the last several days, trying to figure out a way to find you and tell you this story."

Max sat silently, trying to sort out all the new information.

Finally he said, "We have to find my sister. What's her name? I don't even know her name."

"Her name is Anna, and I don't know what's become of her. I hired private investigators to help find both of you. They were able to find you, but Anna, it seems, lives somewhere in Mexico. To find your sister, we have to go back and confront Anthony Holmes at the bank."

A black sedan crept down the street. Woods's justifiable paranoia flared up. He told Max to be ready to run at any moment. It turned out to be some locals, but even Max looked upset with the thought that those men would be back.

Max said, "What are we going to do? Why don't we just call the police and put an end to this right now?"

"We don't know those men back at the Belfry. We couldn't even pick them out of a lineup. You can be sure they can't be linked to the bank or to Anthony Homes.

"What should we do next?" Max said.

"We need to get out of here, go back to the States. Holmes is the key. We have to surprise him in his office, where he'll be forced to face our accusations, with witnesses, and without the danger of the men we escaped back there. Big money is involved here, Max, and there are people that will do anything to maintain control of it. The men we encountered tonight are just the beginning. We got lucky tonight. We won't get lucky again. We need to move while we're safe, while we're lost to them, while we're alive. First, we need to go back and get your passport. I have mine in the car."

Max said, "I have my passport on me. We're all planning to leave the country first thing in the morning. I've been caught with my pants down a time or two in the past, so I always keep my passport with me."

Woods said, "Then we leave tonight. Except how the hell are we going to drive anywhere? I'm not sure either one of us is capable of driving through the night to an airport."

"No worries, mate. I'll just call the Belfry. They pretty much do anything I ask. I can get a driver here, discretely, in a half hour."

Max pulled out his phone, and Woods grabbed his hand before he turned it on. "Max, if you turn that phone on, they may know where we are in an instant. As a matter of fact, you're going to have to get rid of it."

"Again, no worries. I can use your phone to make the call. I'll have Nick come with the driver and take your car back. I can tell him a small part of what's going on."

"That all sounds good. Let's get out of here."

A half-hour later, a big Mercedes pulled up with Nick in the passenger seat. Max told Nick to drive the rental car back to the Belfry and put his phone in his room. "I'll pick up a disposable phone and call you later with more details," Max told Nick to watch for any out-of-place, military-looking guys. And whatever you do, don't tell Harry one single bit of information about tonight. I mean it, Nick. You know he can't keep his damn mouth shut. Now listen,

I'm counting on you. If everything goes right I'll meet you in Amsterdam in a couple of days, and we'll celebrate. I'll explain everything then."

"But—"

"No buts, Nick. I need your help with this one."

With that, Allen Woods followed his new mate, Max Tobin, into the backseat of the big Mercedes, and they left for the international airport in Manchester. Woods and Max continued their discussion about Max's parents. Max took it all in like a big sponge, but the closer they got to Manchester, the heavier the reality of danger and the importance of their trip was. They had gotten a little head start, and if they could get a flight anywhere, they should be able to make a clean getaway. Then they would be able to construct a plan for finding Anna and confronting Holmes.

By the time they finished their conversation, Allen Woods felt for the first time in a long time that he had made a meaningful human connection. It felt good. He hoped Max felt the same way.

***

Several hours later they were sitting at a small table outside a coffee shop in the Charles De Gaulle airport in Paris, France. They had managed to buy tickets, get through security, and board a flight out of Manchester without delay. They both felt good about how things had gone but were still on guard.

Sitting across from each other, they were able to look over each other's shoulders to spot any threat around them. They were close to their gate, and they had about fifteen minutes before their flight from Paris to Boston would start to board. It was now almost ten in the morning. Woods had bought first-class tickets for them. They hadn't had a wink of sleep and were exhausted. Their flight time to Boston was eight hours. Woods just wanted to feel safe boarding the plane and then tuck himself into one of those first-class pods that he usually walked past on his way to an uncomfortable coach seat. Even though it was an eight-hour flight, they should arrive early in the afternoon because they'd gain six hours with the time change. They had a three-hour layover in Boston before boarding for the final leg to San Francisco. Woods wanted both of them to be refreshed when they walked off the plane there.

Woods said to Max, "Keep your eyes on the people behind me. If you see anything remotely out of place, don't panic—just bend down to tie your shoe and keep your head below the table. I'll get up and go into the diner and survey the situation. If I see anything, I'll do the same, and you go into the diner to have a look."

Max looked up from his five-egg omelet with his mouth full and said, "I got it, Mr. Woods. We've been over this a hundred times. I'm trying to act normal, and you should do the same."

"You're right, Max. There's no way they could be on to us."

Woods noticed Max smiling and paying a little too much attention to something behind him. Woods turned around to see a group of young ladies across in the cafe eyeing Max.

"Max, please try to stay focused. We only have a few more minutes here."

"I know, I know. They're just being young and having fun. It's the way, Mr. Woods."

"Let me ask you something, Max. How does it feel to wander through life with no worries except for when, how, and with whom you're going to get laid?"

Max stopped chewing his food while he thought about that question. Then he grinned and said, "It feels pretty fucking good."

Woods was taken aback by the language and the response. He couldn't help but laugh at the young man's answer. Max joined him in laughter.

Woods said, "Maybe you should concentrate on quality instead of quantity."

"Hey, now, that's a low blow, Mr. Woods. Most of the time I'm minding my own business, just like right now."

"Your father used to get those same looks all the time. You Tobin men really have a tough time of it. The difference is that your father was married to the prettiest and sweetest woman in the world. To your dad, there were no others."

"Good to know. I can't wait to see those pictures you were telling me about. It would be nice to get to know my parents any way I can. Is there a Mrs. Woods waiting for you back home?"

"No, I never had time for that. Your dad was lucky to find your mom before we started our company, because once things got rolling, neither one of us had time for any of the casual things in life. When I think about it now, I realize it must have been hell on your mother back then.

"For twenty-plus years, I've been working nonstop, trying to get CTAG Pharmaceuticals up and rolling, but without your dad's help, it has been a real struggle. Seems like the last thirty years of my life have gone by in an instant, and I'm really worried about how this will all end."

"You don't have to worry about a thing now." Max leaned back in his chair, laced his fingers behind his head, and let his stomach start digesting the pile of eggs, bacon, and cheese he had just eaten. With the confidence of a young man who didn't have a clue about life but had the very best intentions, he said, "We're going to sort this all out at the bank. Then you and I will go find my sister and make sure she's all right. Then, the way I see it, Anna and I are going to hang out with you just like family."

Chapter Seventeen

Paris, France
(The same morning)

COCHISE WATCHED MAX AND WOODS WAIT IN LINE TO BOARD THEIR plane. Speaking into a transmitter in his collar to Jackson, he said in a low voice, "I have a ten here." Geronimo said to Jackson, "It's a ten here," Renegade said, "Ten here." The three men stood in their assigned position, waiting for Jackson's orders. Thirty was a rare perfect score. Any combination of numbers that totaled twenty-eight and above was always a sure "go."

Normally, with a triple-ten confirmation, Jackson would reply immediately. He knew that there would never be a better time for mission success. However, a reminder of the triple-ten response jumped into Jackson's mind from the day before at the Belfry. Just thirty seconds after that triple-ten confirmation there, Max Tobin entered the picture, and the mission failed miserably. Maybe this was a sign. Maybe it was a good time to regroup.

The men from The Agency hadn't anticipated that Max would follow Woods out of the club. Neither did they anticipate that Max would knock out two decorated Navy SEALS.

The third man of the three-man team at the Belfry made the decision to stand down when he saw his team sprawled on the lawn. The third man was there to protect and save a fallen team member if the situation required that. It was not his job to try to complete the mission when the other two had failed. There was no threat beyond the attack on his partners, so he did his job and stayed hidden.

If he had seen anything else that would endanger his partners, he would have been forced to intercede. Their training had proven that there would always be another opportunity. So he stayed in the shadows, just as he was trained to do, and watched Max and Woods drive away. They had another opportunity when Max's and Woods's passports were checked through security at the Manchester airport. The Agency knew in an instant their plan to fly to San Francisco through Paris. They had their second chance.

Getting through security with their weapons was easy for these professionals. They were prepared for nearly any situation. Hidden inside the belt of all three of the men were ten-inch, extremely stiff strips of plastic. When the three strips were woven together, they created a rigid, sharp, and deadly weapon when in the right hands. With The Agency men, that weapon was in the right hands. One of The Agency men was in a position where he could bury the razor-sharp knife in Allen Woods's back, just under his shoulder and behind his armpit.

Before the strike, there would be an attention-grabbing commotion created by a second man—a diversion. The weapon was so thin and sharp that Woods would barely feel its penetration. After the downward push of the shaft deep into Woods' soft tissues, the weapon would simply be left in his body. The blunt end of the shaft would disappear underneath his clothing and into Woods' heart. No blood would escape from the victim for at least thirty seconds. Thirty seconds was enough time for the three of them to escape. The sight of an old man staggering and then falling onto the floor, although a concern, was not unusual. No one would instantly suspect an act of murder.

Woods stood behind Max in the first-class queue, waiting for their turn to board the plane. Renegade was in place fifty feet away, with a perfect line of sight to the scene. He had just finished blocking the vision of the last security camera.

Geronimo was eight feet to the side of Woods, standing in the middle of the gathering crowd, who were waiting for their group number to be called for boarding. He was there to create the diversion. He had a perfect opportunity to pinch a lady's butt. She would naturally turn around to confront the culprit. Geronimo would cover his mouth and scream in a high-pitched voice. Then everyone nearby would turn to watch the lady accost the innocent gentleman behind her.

Cochise was in an ideal position; his drawn weapon was covered by his jacket. The strike would be quick and easy. The choreographed maneuver was now set up perfectly. Jackson and the other three men had all heard the triple-ten confirmation in their earpieces.

Woods didn't usually splurge for first-class tickets, but he thought about what a good decision he'd made. Max was in front of him as they prepared to board the plane. The boarding process was going slowly. Woods looked around Max's broad back to see if he could identify the reason for the holdup. Just then he heard a loud, shrill scream come from a lady close by.

***

Jackson said, "Abort, repeat abort!" into his transmitter. Geronimo had acted prematurely when he heard the triple-ten confirmation and assumed the mission was a "go." He went ahead and pinched the woman and screamed his scream. The scream accidentally put the plan in motion. Cochise had heard the scream and was about to stab Woods when he received Jackson's abort order. It came just in time to stop the attack.

No questions asked. The three men casually broke away from the crowd and melted into the stream of passersby. They waited for further instructions. Just after Jackson's abort message, he said, "Are the carrots cooked?" All three of his associates quickly replied, "Negative." Jackson let out a deep sigh of relief. Thankfully, the lady with the sore bottom and the gentleman with a red face behind her were the only casualties.

Jackson knew he had done the right thing by aborting the kill. He was a good man, even if slightly tarnished, and a better man than those who would blindly follow a kill order from a slimy man like Anthony Holmes. Jackson hadn't signed up to do wet work but looked at where he was now.

Jackson knew Woods's story. Woods was a brilliant, selfless man who had done nothing but try to do the right thing every single day of his life. Taking the order from Holmes to have his men kill the young Mexican man, Armando was a horrible mistake. Killing Woods was just not right, no matter how much blood money Holmes paid The Agency. He would have to find a different way to handle all this, and the clock was ticking.

Chapter Eighteen

Tulum, Mexico

(Same morning)

ANNA WOKE. SHE FELT THE SWAY OF THE BOAT, HEARD ARMANDO'S breathing, and sensed a slight ache in her right shoulder. She wanted to change position, but decided against it because she didn't want to do anything that would ruin the moment. She opened her eyes to the morning's first light. The rocking of the boat was more noticeable with the sight of a small, white cloud appearing and disappearing in one of the teak-trimmed portholes of the small bedroom.

Armando's left arm lay across Anna's flat tummy with his hand between her breasts, and his right arm cradled her head. His chest and midsection were against her back. She wanted this moment to last forever. Waking up tangled in each other's limbs and each other's love was how she hoped every day of their life would begin.

Armando stirred. She could tell by the sound of his breathing that he was coming awake.

She felt him … and she responded. Armando's left hand moved and began to explore every inch of Anna's curves. Then his right hand came into play, participating with the same sensual intentions. After a few minutes, it became harder and harder for Anna to restrain herself from Armando's specialized attention to detail. She turned to him and kissed his lips while she gazed into his dark brown eyes. Their natural rhythm floated in harmony with the rocking of the boat, with their human desires, and with their hungry, rekindled love.

Afterward, they remained in each other's arms with soft kisses and whispered avowals of love confirming what they already knew to be true.

Grimacing, Armando tried to sit up. She could feel his agonizing pain. She helped position a pillow behind his back and then gently nuzzled against him.

"I never want to get up," she said.

"I know. Neither do I."

They looked out the small portholes as the morning light streamed into their nest. Their silence was crowded with thoughts and memories of how they had talked and made love throughout the night. It was nice to just lie together in silence, thinking about each other and their future.

Armando had scrubbed every inch of his body the night before in the yacht's small shower. Anna gave up on the job of fixing his hair and cut it all off. Then she went to work on the rest of him with the supplies she had brought, sterilizing and bandaging his wounds. Armando gave her more details about the horrors of the swamp and about how he was miraculously saved by a group of native Mexican families who nursed him back from the dead.

They still couldn't think of a reason why this had happened. Was it a revenge plot? Maybe. But who would want to take revenge on Armando? Was it a kidnapping scheme that went wrong because Armando's father was well connected, very wealthy, and a prominent businessman?

Armando said, "Kidnapping for ransom happens often in Mexico, and I'm definitely a prime target. It's also possible my father had a conflict with another business entity that has ties to one of the Mexican cartels. Revenge for my father's actions or lack of action may have brought on the violence."

They agreed that their next step was to contact Armando's family. Armando said, "Because I've pretty much cut ties with my family, they probably don't know about my absence. I guess I'll have to walk across that burning bridge and reach out to my father."

Armando shook his head and sighed. He brushed a wisp of Anna's hair off her face and said, "I feel like being here with you is just another one of my dreams, and I'll soon wake up alone again, in the swamp."

"Look at me," Anna said. "What we have is real, and we're never going to let anything come between us again. We're going to figure this out, get past this, and get on with our lives. Now let's go topside, have some breakfast, and get some fresh air, and you can tell me again how much you love me and how much you love our boat." As Anna slid away, she stopped on the edge of the bed, reached back, and put her hand on Armando's head. She giggled and said, "And you can get started on growing your hair back."

<hr />

Armando didn't move. He eyed the contrast of Anna's tan back with her white buttocks as she sashayed to one of the built-in wooden dressers that held some of her clothes. Anna's long, sculptured legs supported her feminine hourglass shape. Her blonde locks danced as she rummaged through one of the drawers.

Armando took in every inch of this beautiful creature and wondered—*why would she love me?* He was close to pulling her back into bed when she lifted a light green and blue bikini from a drawer. She turned around and said, "Is this okay?" She held up a postage-stamp-size piece of cloth in one hand and two bits of the same material with strings attached in the other. The colors of the suit accentuated the blue of her eyes.

He didn't care what she put on that picture-perfect body. He said, "Yes, that one will be perfect."

She pulled on her bikini bottom as she stepped through the doorway into the galley. She secured the top of her bikini with two unnaturally bent arms behind her back and then started up the stairs leading into the sunlight of the bright new day.

Anna turned back to him and said, "Let's go. We have a big day ahead of us." She ran up the stairs.

Her feet slapped the top deck, and then he heard the splash from her dive into waters of the Gulf of Mexico.

He slid out of bed, put on a pair of shorts, and followed his treasure's path at a much slower pace. Armando walked up a couple of the stairs and then stopped to admire the deep blue of the morning sky. When he got topside, he was equally amazed by the deep dark blue of the open ocean. He walked to the back of the boat.

Anna floated in the clear indigo water. She smiled when she saw him and splashed water his way.

"This water feels great," she said. "I wish you could jump in and join me."

"Next time—give me a few days, and I'll be all over that fine invitation."

Armando looked to his left at the unique sight of a sixty-foot wall of jagged, gray rock formations framing the long, white-sand beach that bordered the ruins of Tulum.

The sight reminded him where they had dropped anchor the night before. He took in every detail of the scene, reminding himself about what it meant to be free, alive, and back with Anna.

He scanned the beach and the rock wall, looking for any sign of danger. *I can't drop my guard and give them the upper hand. Can't assume our escape is final. Have to assume the monsters are preparing a response.* He had to assume they hadn't really escaped anything and that the next time they encountered those men, he wouldn't be as fortunate.

It was still early in the day before tourists poured into the park to roam the ruins, and to enjoy one of Mexico's most beautiful beaches.

The beach and surrounding areas were quiet and void of human life. Armando wondered, *what can't I see? Will they come at us from the shadows after we dock, or will they come at us by boat?* With that thought, he turned his attention back to the open ocean. He scanned the horizon again, this time with a different purpose.

Armando's thoughts were interrupted when Anna pulled herself onto the boat from the stern. Her wet hair was slicked back, away from her face. Her wet bikini clung to her every detail, and the sunlight shimmered off his beautiful reward.

He could only shake his head at the sight of splendor walking his way. Anna stopped a few paces in front of him. She smiled, tilted her head, and asked, "Are you ready for your breakfast?"

"Yes, I am." Armando reached out and pulled her close. He wrapped his arms around her and whispered, "I love you, Anna, and I love our boat."

Chapter Nineteen

Tulum, Mexico

(Same day)

FROM THE SHADOWS OF THE TULUM RUINS, APACHE REPORTED TO JACKSON, "We have eyes on her. There is an unidentified man on board who is … is very close to her. It's clear they slept together last night. She just returned to the boat after an early-morning swim and walked right into his arms."

Jackson replied, "That makes no sense. Who is he? Why don't we know about him?"

"Chirica has the scope on him to take an easy shot anytime you give the go.

Looking through the scope on his Barrett M82 sniper rifle, Chirica said, "This man's hair is cut short, and he looks pretty beat up, but from here, "I'm sure he's the Mexican man, Armando, who we killed."

Jackson's mind raced. *How could that be? Must be a mistake. Could this be another sign, a reprieve?* The silence lingered. Jackson considered this new information.

Jackson said, "Degree of certainty on ID?"

Chirica said, I'm over a half-mile away, but I'd say ninety percent certainty. Judging by the way the two of them are all over each other, I'd say ninety-nine percent."

"Is it possible that man is still alive? Jackson said.

Outlaw replied, "I carried him a good hundred yards into that swamp and dumped his body, a body that had no pulse. He was face down in the mud when I walked away. We all thought he was dead. There was no way he could've crawled outta there after the beating he took. Hell, I barely made it out of that swamp alive."

Chirica said, "It's him! I just saw his smile. I would, too, if I had that fine piece of ass walking my way."

Jackson said, "Put all the weapons away. The park is going to start filling up soon, and I don't want to take any chances with one of the park rangers. Keep your eyes on them, observation only, and no contact."

Apache said, "We have a boat available, and I could easily take them on the open water. The GPS location sensor we installed on her boat is working perfectly. We could get to them quickly."

"No, leave them alone for now. Apache, you and Outlaw go back and get the boat ready, but don't have any weapons on board. Chirica, monitor them on shore from your vehicle. If they haul anchor, stay close enough so you can be there when they dock. No contact, eyes only. Boys, we have to come up with a new plan."

Chapter Twenty

Tulum, Mexico
(Same day)

*A*GAIN.

What a nice way to start the day, thought Armando. *I could get used to this.* He made his way up the stairs for the second time that morning. Anna was preparing breakfast.

The back deck of the boat was big enough for a small table and chairs. Anna stood at the table, wearing a bright yellow bikini, slicing a ripe melon. Juice was poured, and she placed the melon on dishes she had bought weeks before.

She felt very pleased with herself as Armando walked up from the galley. "What's going on up here?"

Anna thought her man looked about twenty pounds under his normal weight, but he was already looking much better than he did just twenty-four hours before. His new short haircut and lean physique gave him a *GQ* look.

Anna felt the warm rays of the rising sun. *Armando can't have much sun exposure yet.* She slid the table and chairs forward into the shade of the captain's platform.

The morning was filled with the bright sun, the blues surrounding their boat, the sounds of water lapping against the sides of the yacht, and the screams of gulls wheeling about. This was the life Anna had hoped for, and now it was right there in front of her.

"This looks perfect, Anna. Thank you." He sat down in the shade and put on his sunglasses. Anna dragged her chair to Armando's side of the table so she could sit right next to him. She sat down and gave him a big smile. She was happy with this new arrangement and with their solitude.

They enjoyed the morning, the fresh food, and each other's company for a few minutes before Armando said, "We have to talk about what happens next concerning our situation. Why this happened to me. I can't stop thinking about that, and if I'm placing you in danger. This feels so good to be here with you now, but we have to start trying to find some answers."

"I know, I know. I'm not sure we're even safe out here on the boat. After hearing your story, I've felt like someone is watching us."

By the time they finished breakfast, they had decided what to do next. Armando went below deck and returned with a phone. He pushed some buttons, and they waited.

Armando said "Papa? It's me, Armando." He wore a pained expression while he listened. "Dad, I, we, are in some serious trouble here, and I'm calling to ask for your advice."

After a short silence, Armando started from the beginning telling his father about what had happened during the past several months. Anna stayed glued to his side and listened intently to every word. Armando's father asked a few very specific questions, trying to understand their situation. Armando answered each question as best he could, but he wasn't of much help. He and Anna simply didn't have the answers.

Then, in an authoritative voice, Armando's father began his appraisal of the situation. "I can understand why you think this violence was a result of a revenge-type hit from one of my enemies, but I don't have any associates who are connected in any way to cartel-type businesses. If this was a hit by such an organization, they would have just opened fire on you at the side of the road and left you there. They would not have tried to hide their actions, and they would not have failed.

"The facts don't support a kidnapping either, because there was no request for ransom. The kidnappers would have held you hostage at some unknown location and opened up a dialog with me in an attempt to secure the ransom. That never happened, so I think we can rule out kidnapping.

"If you are sure you haven't upset or created enemies on your own, then I think we need to look at Anna's side of the equation. This all points to a botched American hit, because Americans would typically try to cover their tracks. No one from Mexico would care about hiding that kind of crime.

"You tell me she has no family and that she has been living off a trust account. She recently bought a new, very expensive yacht using the trust account's funds. She has never met the trustee or even discussed the conditions of the trust or its holdings. Anna is past the legal age, so all that should have been spelled out to her a long time ago.

"There is something very wrong with her story. Either she isn't telling you the whole story, or there is someone behind this that is intentionally keeping her in the dark regarding her trust. It's possible the large disbursement for buying the boat created a big red flag for whoever is behind this. They may think you are a threat to them.

"My advice is to follow the money. Money is the root of most evil. You need to start at the bank with her trust officer, since he is your only known contact. Anna needs to understand the details of this trust. The trust officer has a fiduciary responsibility to disclose all the details of the trust and the investments made by the trust. It is very possible there are competing interests that Anna doesn't know about influencing the trustee. Such as unknown relatives who have an interest in getting her out of the picture. You and Anna will not be safe until you know what's going on at that bank.

"Every person in the world has family. Anna has to have a line of descent that she should at least know exists. Clearly she had a mother and a father, and there have to be records somewhere detailing her ancestry. The shadow hiding her line of descent is wrong and probably the reason you are in danger. There are just too many unanswered questions. She needs answers to these questions, and the bank is where you need to start. What is the name of the bank that holds her trust?"

"Addison National Bank & Trust in San Francisco."

"Okay. I could do some checking on the bank. Would you like me to do that?"

"Let me talk all this over with Anna. I'll get back to you soon. I can't thank you enough for your help."

"You are my son, Armando. I will do everything I can to help you through this."

"Thank you, Father. This means a lot to us."

"Armando, one more thing. Say hello to Anna for me. We can't wait to meet her."

Chapter D
Munich, Germany
(Same day)

A FEW DAYS HAD GONE BY SINCE THEIR ENCOUNTER. THE GIRL KNEW THAT Silvio had seen through her disguise, and she also knew what he wanted from her. She wanted to avoid any contact.

The girl thought about the emptiness and the struggles in her life. She'd hung on knowing she would be eighteen years old soon, and then she would have a chance at a real life. She wanted a life like all the people around her in the park—like the visible people. She wanted to be like people who had jobs, families, and futures. She would make the most of her chance to come out of the shadows when her time came. She just needed an opportunity, but she had no chance until her eighteenth birthday.

Then she contradicted her own thoughts by reversing the reasoning. *Why should I have to spend any more time sleeping in the park, afraid to sleep, afraid when I'm awake? It would be nice to start a new life now. Silvio seems genuine. He's the only person who has been nice to me. Let him take care of me. This may be my opportunity.* Then, the thought of men like the beast with their hands all over her jolted her back to reality.

She glanced up from a book she was reading and scanned the park for food opportunities. There was a group of families with children gathering for what looked like the start of a peachy family picnic. Usually this was a good opportunity. Family gatherings always involved good, wasted food. She scanned the perimeter and spotted three other scavengers sitting in their usual places, who were tuned in to the same event. She would probably have to move on and hope for a better opportunity somewhere else.

The girl spotted Silvio sitting by himself. He waved her over. She did not acknowledge him. He motioned to her again. She remained still. Silvio stood up. Even from a distance, she could see anger in his eyes—the same kind of anger she remembered from the beast.

She stood, snagged her backpack, and hustled away in the opposite direction.

———◊◊◊———

Silvio turned and walked to the nearest park exit. He approached two men. "Follow her," he said. "Take her. I'm through playing Mr. Nice Guy."

Chapter Twenty-One

Paris, Atlantic Ocean, Boston
(Next day)

WOODS WATCHED MAX SLEEPING IN AN AWKWARD POSITION. THE FIRST-class seat looked small. He made everything look small.

Woods closed his eyes, and he wanted more shut-eye on the long flight to Boston. Then—on to San Francisco, where they would confront Anthony Holmes.

At the same time, Anna and Armando rounded Key West on their way to Vero Beach, Florida. Armando calculated they were six hours away from their destination, and he was sure there was no way they could have been followed.

His father had a friend who owned a second home with a dock on the Intracoastal Waterway in Vero Beach. Their plan was to navigate around the tip of Florida, sail past Miami, and cruise up the Intracoastal. After a good night's rest in Vero Beach, they planned to fly to San Francisco the next day.

Holmes had a new plan of his own. He was not happy to learn that Armando Ruiz was alive after he was assured of the contrary. He did not appreciate Reed Jackson's council regarding Allen Woods's intentions only to have Woods show up a few days later and engage Max in England.

Holmes decided to take things into his own hands and bring in another group that could handle these more difficult assignments. He thought the new security company would be more likely to take any orders he gave them and then execute those orders proficiently. Holmes even asked Reed Jackson what he knew about this new group called "The Order."

Holmes had called Jackson and got directly to the point. "Based on recent failures regarding Ruiz and Woods, I've taken the liberty of hiring, shall we say, a subcontractor to finish these jobs. It is my understanding this group is more competent and specialized in this area. Your firm will still be responsible for the more mundane duties of monitoring the Tobin children and reporting back to me. But first I need to get this mess cleaned up, and then I'll bring you back in. What do you know about a group called The Order?"

⟹◦◦◦⟸

Jackson wanted to reach through the phone and strangle Anthony Holmes when he heard the words *The Order* and the word *competent*. He had to assume that Holmes had already hired them. So Jackson did what he'd always done—played it cool, not giving away any of his true feelings. He agreed with Holmes on the decision, but wanted to tell him that The Order were a group of psychopathic mercenary traitors who could not make it in the real U.S. military.

He had even fought against most of them on several different occasions. The men from The Order were soldiers of fortune who killed for the highest bidder, and they were responsible for the death of many U.S. troops.

He said to Holmes, "I've heard good things about those guys, but you may want to be careful because they're known as thugs with limited brains and conscience. I actually trained with a few of them."

Holmes seemed to like that answer.

Jackson said, "If that's the direction you want to go, I'll support you. I want you to know that Anna and Armando have just docked in the small community of Vero Beach, Florida. We don't know why they are there or what their plans are going forward. I'll have my men stand down until I hear from you.

"Also, Max and Woods should land at Logan International in Boston in four hours. They have a three-hour layover there. We will suspend our surveillance of those two until you contact me again. I understand your decision, and I want you to know we're available for any support services, as needed."

Holmes said, "Good. We'll take it from here. I'll be in touch when it's over." He ended the call before Jackson could respond.

After Jackson aborted the plan to kill Allen Woods in the Charles de Gaulle airport, after he learned that Armando was alive, and after he took the phone call from Anthony Holmes that included an inquiry about The Order, Reed

Jackson altered his mission from one of obeying Anthony Holmes's orders to a mission of protecting Max, Anna, Armando, and Allen Woods. This was now a personal issue—an important one, so important that he made a conference call to the six men who were involved with this case.

He gave them all the significant details of his talk with Holmes. "I'm changing our mission. From now on we're going to protect the Tobin group. You all know the men from The Order. When they show up anywhere near the Tobin family, we will neutralize them." Jackson knew that his men would be on board with this new mission. They all knew the degenerates from The Order, and they longed to take some overdue revenge on them.

"I intentionally gave up the location of Anna and Armando to Anthony Holmes," Jackson said, "because I believe Vero Beach is the best place that we can protect them. We'll have to figure out our plan in Boston on the fly. I'm going to allow you men to come up with your own plan of action at both locations. I trust your judgment. We will have the element of surprise on our side."

Chapter Twenty-Two

Vero Beach, Florida – Boston, Mass.

(Same day)

ANNA AND ARMANDO TIED UP THEIR BOAT TO THE DOCK AT ARMANDO'S father's friend's house and strolled through the city park to the Atlantic Ocean side of Vero Beach. The walk through the park was a short one. Armando thought they were safe.

They checked in to the Coste d'Este resort. They were exhausted. Before long they lay tangled in each other's limbs. Armando whispered to Anna, "This feels good, right now, right here with you. We made it through the dark night, past the pirates and drug smugglers, avoided the enemy's radar, and maintained our cloak of invisibility. We have succeeded against insurmountable odds for the first leg of our journey."

Anna laughed. "Were you reading spy novels when you were crawling around in the swamp?"

"No, I just feel like we're on this exciting, but dangerous, mission, and we're ahead of the bad guys— for now, at least."

"I agree, 007. Who am I, Miss Playmate?"

"Yes, you are." he pulled her close. "That reminds me, we still haven't named our top-secret stealth getaway yacht."

"Let's sleep on that one. It's time."

After a few hours of sleep, Armando woke to find Anna scrolling through her iPad. He said, "What are you up to now?"

"I've been checking out this Vero Beach place. It seems Vero Beach is split in half by that north/south Intracoastal waterway we sailed in on. The permanent residents live inland on the west side of the Intracoastal. On the east side, where we are, is a thin strip of land that has beach homes and luxury condominiums owned by wealthy snowbirds. There are some boutique shops, family-run restaurants, and a few small resorts like our lovely place. The locals don't want their community to become the next Miami Beach or Fort Lauderdale. So they passed laws that prohibit buildings from being built that are taller than six stories, and they created ordinances that outlaw large chain stores from coming in and ruining the small-town feeling."

Armando said, "Well done, Miss Playmate. I'd say this is a perfect place to start the next leg of our adventure. Let's go check this place out. I'm starving."

"I agree. I booked us on a flight tomorrow morning, so there's no reason not to relax a little tonight. Let's get cleaned up and change your bandages."

———⊷⊶⊷———

Woods and Max deplaned and slowly made their way through the masses to find their next gate at Logan International Airport in Boston. They were rested, but still a little groggy from the flight and the time change.

Woods said to Max, "Keep your eyes open. We have to stay vigilant and assume the worst. If you see anything out of place, tell me immediately."

"I'm on it, Mr. Woods. Let's get to our next gate so we can put our backs to a wall."

———⊷⊶⊷———

Renegade, Cochise, and Geronimo had already split up—one in front of, one behind, and one next to Max and Woods as they shuffled down the busy concourse to their next gate. Their primary mission was to find the men from The Order, which they didn't think would take long. The men from The Agency appreciated Jackson giving them the green light to create and execute their own plan.

When Max and Woods found a place to sit at their next gate, each of them took up a position where he could observe the whole area.

Renegade whispered into his collar, "Do you see them?"

Cochise replied, "I see one of them, and I know that son of a bitch." He paused, and then said, "There's another one in the Starbucks line."

Geronimo said, "Yeah, I got those two—any others?"

Before any of his associates could answer, he noticed that Max and Woods were staring at one of the men from The Order, who was holding up a large print photo of Max Tobin.

"Are you kidding me?" The Agency men all said at the same time.

———◦◦◦———

Max nodded at Woods and then toward the man scanning the crowd, holding a sheet of paper in his hand. Max said, "See that guy over there? He could be one of the men who are after us. He seems to be looking for something – probably us. Maybe now's the time to bring in the police, Mr. Woods. Who knows what that guy is capable of?"

"That would be a good idea if we had anything to tell the police. What are we going to say? We think that man jumped me a couple of days ago in England? But we're not sure. Besides, there's more to all this than you know. I hired some men to rough one of those guys to find out why they were following me. I could be in trouble with the law for doing that."

"How did they find us?"

"I don't have any idea."

Max turned back to Woods. "I have an idea. We might miss our flight, but I can guarantee we'll be rid of that guy and whoever else is with him."

"Let's hear it."

"Remember I told you that I grew up here in Boston and played basketball in a bad part of town? I was well known and protected there, but there's no way any other white man or someone dressed like that guy would make it out of there in one piece."

"Maybe you're protected, but what about me?"

"Don't worry, you're with me. We'll pretend we're going for a walk or to get a bite to eat, and then we'll take the escalator down to the baggage claim area and go outside and grab a cab. They won't be expecting us to make that move. If I'm right, they'll follow us into the projects. Then we'll just let nature take its course. If we miss our flight, we'll get the first flight out in the morning. If I'm wrong, we'll have plenty of time to go back through security and make our flight."

"Sounds like our best option. Let's go."

Max and Woods meandered down the concourse and rode the escalator down to the baggage area. When they got to the bottom, Max turned around, looked up, and saw the man at the top standing with another man, both looking at them. Max and Woods hurried outside and hopped into the backseat of a waiting taxi.

Woods told the driver, "Just drive away now, and fast! We'll give you further instructions in a minute."

They sped away. After about a minute the driver said, "I need to know where you guys want to go."

Max replied, "You know the basketball courts up in Roxbury?"

"Yeah—but I got to tell you guys, that's no place you want to go. I grew up there, and even I don't feel safe in that neighborhood."

Max said, "You grew up there? Did you ever play ball on those courts?"

"Yeah, I had a little game back in the day, and they're still banging around up there, but the rest of that place is really bad."

"What name did you have when you played?"

"They called me Peanut."

"Man, I know you, Peanut. Don't you recognize me? They called me Ivory."

The driver took a quick look over his shoulder. "Yeah, I do know you. You always played over on the A court. Brotha, you're a legend up there. Where you been?"

"I went away to college and then moved out of the country for a couple of years. Do you think I'll still know anyone up there on the courts?"

"I can guarantee you will. That place hasn't changed a bit. The same guys are still there mixing it up. I go up there every once in a while just to watch. Sometimes they want me to fill in, but my days with that game are behind me now."

"Here's the deal, Peanut. There are some dudes following us who want to do my friend here some serious harm. I'm hoping some of the brothers will help us out with these guys. Do you think I still have some pull up there?"

"Hell, yes. All those bangers loved you. They'll do anything for you. I'll stick around and lend a hand, too." Peanut adjusted his rearview mirror. "You're right. There's another cab following us right now." The driver glanced at them again. "Hey, you guys are gonna be able to pay the meter, right?'

"For sure, Peanut—we'll take good care of you."

Anna and Armando asked some of the locals about good places to eat. They took the advice of one of the bellmen and decided to walk through the village to a small place called The Tides Restaurant, just a few blocks away. The pleasant hostess asked them to wait at the bar while she got their table ready. The small bar at The Tides was just outside the restaurant on the patio, where they had additional seating.

A window above the middle of the bar opened into a small area where the adept bartender worked his magic. The bar top was about eight feet long, with room for four bar stools.

Feeling invigorated and wanting to take advantage of their free night, Anna asked the bartender for a Tito's vodka martini with two blue cheese olives. Armando's eyebrows went up when he heard Anna's request. "Make it two," he said.

Standing on the sidewalk in front of The Tides, Apache said to Outlaw and Chirica, "You guys look like a couple of real peckerheads." He laughed as he looked them up and down. They were dressed in Bermuda shorts, golf polos, and casual tennis shoes, as if they had just come from one of the local golf courses. Although dressed a little down for The Tides, they fit right in as golfing tourists.

Chirica laughed. "We know. Don't say another word or you'll be wearing these shorts around your neck."

Apache said, "You guys try to blend in here. I've got some real work to do." He walked away as Outlaw declined the hostess's invitation to wait at the bar.

It didn't take long for Anna and Armando to be led to their dinner table. Armando ordered the thin-sliced duck appetizer and fresh pompano for both of them. He allowed the waiter to suggest a bottle of DuMol Pinot Noir to pair with their meal. "This is my treat," he said to Anna. "The captain has to take good care of his crew."

"Aye, aye, captain. This better be good, though, if you want to take liberties with me later on tonight."

———◦◦◦———

Max, Mr. Woods, and Peanut crossed the tracks into the projects of Roxbury. They passed blocks of typical inner-city blight, with sketchy characters hanging around on street corners. The only color of contrast to the gray buildings and streets was green weeds growing up through the cracked concrete. Most of the buildings looked deserted and were boarded up.

Peanut pulled his cab up to the side of one of the four basketball courts that were in the middle of what looked like six vacant high-rise buildings. The buildings weren't vacant, but they had fallen into complete disrepair.

When they got out of the cab, everything around them stopped. Dogs stopped barking, birds found a perch, vehicles on the street slowed, characters on the street turned their way, and the basketballs on the courts were held.

Woods followed Max and Peanut into the hard looks of adult basketball players, who seemed to dare the three outsiders to take one more step. Peanut told Max and Woods to stay put while he walked ahead.

Max told Woods, "Keep your head down and stop gawking."

Woods did so and then asked, "Are you sure about this? It's not looking real promising here." Then he did the exact opposite of what Max had told him to do. He stared at Peanut talking to four or five large, strong young men.

A cab pulled up and parked on the street one block back. Woods figured it was the cab that had followed them.

Peanut and three of the basketball players walked toward them. Two other players peeled off and jogged away in a different direction.

Woods felt relieved when he could tell that Max recognized the men. Max said, "Eb-o-ny. I was hoping to see you here. You're looking fit, my man!"

The cool, hard-looking Ebony bumped fists with Max and then gave Max a big bear hug. "I been missin' you, man," he said to Max. "This place ain't the same without your lily-white ass chasing me all over the court."

The other two young men beamed at Max. He greeted them by name and pulled them into a man hug. Soon ten or fifteen other players surrounded Max, chattering away, all vying for Max's attention.

Woods felt relieved when it was clear that all parties involved were glad to be in each other's company.

Ebony stopped the chatter, saying, "I got to tell ya, Ivory, you look like shit, man. You been livin' the good life or what?"

"Yeah, and I've haven't played any ball, but I'm sure I got a little left in the tank if you guys have a spot for me."

Max walked with the group onto the court as one the older players signaled something to a kid watching from the sidelines. The kid nodded and sprinted away.

Woods and Peanut stood nearby, watching the players warm up and listening to the creative banter among the players. They chose sides—skins against shirts. Just as the game began, the kid who had run off came back holding a chair.

The boy walked up to Woods, wearing a big smile on his handsome, brown face, and said, "Here ya go, mister. This game could take a while." He scooted the flimsy white plastic chair behind Woods.

Woods accepted the chair and said, "Thank you very much, young man. What's your name?"

"My name is Milton Hyde. Do you mind if I get back to my game over there, mister?" He pointed to a different basketball court.

"Of course not, Milton."

The boy jogged away.

Woods carefully sat down in the wobbly chair and tried not to worry about the men who were chasing them.

<hr>

After dinner, Anna and Armando settled their bill with their new best friend, the charming maître d' and promised a return visit. The Tides Restaurant had turned out to be a welcoming place where they got to know many of the other diners. They even met the distinguished mayor and his elegant wife.

Feeling a pleasant buzz from the vodka and wine as they walked hand in hand back to their resort, Armando said, "This sands the edges off the last few hectic days."

Anna replied, "Yeah, I like this Vero Beach place. I could get used to this small-town feeling."

The soft light and empty streets seemed eerily quiet to the men from The Agency. They were invisible and in the best possible position for protecting Anna and Armando. But, the two of them were exceptionally vulnerable, even with the men from The Agency watching over them. A sniper with a high-powered rifle was all that was needed to take them out. Apache and his men knew that the hired guns from The Order had the equipment and the skills.

While Anna and Armando strolled down the middle of the wide, deserted street, a soft breeze rattled the palm fronds overhead. The men from The Agency were on their highest alert, watching, listening, and waiting.

The Agency men could sense the killers from The Order somewhere in the area, but where? They couldn't let this sleepy town lull them into dropping their guard. They wanted to sweep Anna and Armando away to a place where they weren't so vulnerable. It was nearly impossible to keep them out of harm's way, especially with them unaware of the danger. If they could find the men from The Order, they could then neutralize the threat.

When they were just a couple of blocks from the resort, Chirica and Outlaw used a side street to ease in behind Armando and Anna, who suddenly stopped in front of a bar/restaurant named Bobby's. They heard her say to Armando, "Let's pop in here for a nightcap. This place looks too old-school-cool to pass up."

Anna and Armando found a place at the far corner of the large, square bar and engaged in polite conversation with one of Bobby's several bartenders. As a bartender shook their vodka martinis, two men who looked out of place slithered in and sat at the opposite end of the bar. They looked like trouble, both of them muscle-bound, unshaven, and dirty. They ordered two straight bourbons and tried to fit in to the cozy bar.

Still dressed in their snappy golf attire, Chirica and Outlaw sat at the bar within earshot of the men from The Order. They overheard one of them mutter under his breath to the other, "This looks too easy. It's clear they don't have a clue what's about to happen to them. Are you sure the boss said to keep our hands off the girl? She looks like she'd be a lot of fun."

His partner replied, "Yeah, that's what he said, but how would he know? Her boyfriend is a dead man walking. We'll follow them out of here and then take them at gunpoint when they enter their room. I can already see your knife on his throat as I gag Goldilocks there. We'll have her for the whole night."

Anna and Armando were well-rested from their nap earlier in the day, and they were chatting with the locals sitting around them. The people at Bobby's were just as friendly as the ones they had met at dinner.

Outlaw and Chirica listened as the two thugs talked about Anna and watched them drink one bourbon after another.

Outlaw asked Chirica, "How do you think Apache is getting along?"

"I'm sure he didn't have a problem breaking into that pharmacy without tripping the alarm. He'll be ready for us, with everything tucked away and in a perfect spot. I can't wait until the rest of the men see what we're gonna do to these guys."

"Yeah, it will be sweet.

Anna and Armando said good-bye to their new friends at the bar and left out the front door.

The men from The Order saw their chance. They threw a few twenties onto the bar top and followed them out the door.

Anna and Armando walked hand in hand down Ocean Drive. The men from The Order were just a few steps behind them, with handguns bulging from under their shirt. The assassins probably thought their scheme was on schedule.

The men from The Agency had a different plan. The first step started when Anna and Armando turned off the sidewalk and walked into their resort property. Within seconds, Chirica and Outlaw grabbed their prey from behind. They cupped the men's faces with a cloth soaked in chloroform. The men struggled, but had no defense.

Apache suddenly appeared, steering the SUV up next to them. Chirica and Outlaw poured the limp bodies into the back of the SUV, and they sped away. The operation was executed in just a few seconds.

The Agency men considered putting a bullet into each man's head. But that was too easy. They decided on a different, more interesting experience for these Rambo wannabes.

Their SUV rolled into the driveway of a vacant home that Apache had scoped out earlier. They carried the unconscious mercenaries to the backyard, stripped them naked, and scattered their clothes, guns, and knives, all over the pool area. They kept their phones and IDs. Then they placed the naked men next to each other in one of the big lounge chairs with a half bottle of bourbon beside them. After that, they entered the house and distributed the drugs that Apache had stolen from a pharmacy. Finally, Apache, Outlaw, and Chirica took a few pictures of the two men lying in each other's arms.

So much for these "competent" soldiers.

Apache drove back to the pharmacy and intentionally tripped the alarm. Outlaw and Chirica disappeared into the shadows.

⟴

Two men from the neighborhood walked up behind Peanut. They said a few words into his ear and left.

Woods asked Peanut, "What was that all about?"

"Just an update on those two guys who were following you."

"What happened to them?"

"Not sure. Let's just say they put them someplace where they'll keep for a few days. After that, who knows what will happen to them. You guys don't have to worry about them anymore." Peanut's attention turned back the basketball game. He said to Woods, "Look at him out there. Tell me those guys wouldn't do anything for him."

"All of them look like real pros," said Woods. "I can see why you'd want to come here and watch them— seems like Max and Ebony have a special bond. What's up with those two?"

"When Max was a kid, he came down here by himself just 'cause he wanted to play ball. He literally got the crap beat outta him every day. But every day he came back for more. He turned into one of the toughest guys in these projects. When the fighting started, Ivory turned into a wild man. He could handle himself against three, four, even five guys. Yeah, he got beat up nearly every day, but the guys who picked the fight started to look just as bad.

"Eventually we all saw something in Ivory that the rest of us saw in ourselves. We saw the same emptiness. It's an emptiness where there's no pride in your past, and there's no future in your future.

"They stopped beating on him, let him hang around, and let him play some ball. But it wasn't until the best player his age took responsibility for him and convinced the other players and the gangbangers that Ivory was different. That

140

boy was Ebony. Ebony was by far the best player, and his declared friendship with Ivory—back then we called him Ivory for obvious reasons—was powerful. Those two were like brothers, and whenever they played together it was a beautiful sight. Most of the time they played against each other, and man there were some epic battles.

"Look at them out there. Ebony went on to play at Boston College, but he wasn't quite good enough for the NBA. He had no desire to go to Europe and play like a robot with a bunch of guys he didn't know."

Woods said, "How long are they going to play tonight?"

"They used to play all night. The "A" court had lights from the generators when Ebony and Ivory played. Those were the golden days on these courts. Life was different back then. It was better. You never know what will happen next out here now— too many gun-toting crazies running around here, wanting to be outlaws."

"What exactly is this place?" Woods said.

Peanut said, "One gang and one gang leader run this project. He's like the sheriff of a town. Nothing happens in these six buildings that he doesn't know about. He has to approve everything. For instance, he was the one that bought all the generators, and he's the one who determined who could use them. He has his hand in everything around here, and he takes something off the top from everyone. At the end of the day, it all works out well. The residents are absolutely safe from the law and the other gangs."

It wasn't much longer before Max and the rest of the players ended their game and walked their way. Woods stood up to greet them. Some of the players shook Woods's hand, without words but with a respect that said, if you're a friend of Ivory's, you're a friend of ours.

There was more bantering that preceded big farewell hugs and promises to come back soon. Max, Woods, and Peanut returned to the cab and headed back to what they knew as civilization.

Peanut drove them to an airport hotel, thanked them for their more than generous tip, and said good-bye.

"What do you think happened to those guys who were following us?" Woods asked Max,

"I have no idea, and I don't want to know. But I do know two things. They won't be bothering us again, and they deserve everything they got. Let's not forget what they tried to do to you at the Belfry."

Woods said, "It's been one crazy ... three crazy days for us. Let's get some sleep tonight and then catch the first plane we can get to San Francisco."

"Good idea. It was one great day, wasn't it? I'm really happy you could meet some of my friends."

"I agree, it was a great day, Max, or should I say, Ivory? It was a great day, and I felt privileged to meet your friends."

Apache called the Vero Beach police department and gave them an anonymous tip about a break-in at the address where they had left the men from The Order.

The police rushed to that address and found the stolen pharmaceuticals, then found the men and everything else.

They woke the "competent" men from The Order, cuffed them, and read them their rights. They marched their bare asses out of the house as Outlaw and Chirica recorded the comedy from a safe distance. They grinned at each other and chuckled with great satisfaction as they thought about their report back to Jackson and the rest of the boys.

Renegade, Cochise, and Geronimo stood in the lobby of the same hotel where Max and Woods had just checked in. They reported back to Jackson.

Jackson said, "Where are you? And what's going on?"

Renegade replied, "We had the very best plan figured out for those guys, but didn't have a chance to take care of business our way."

"Did you lose them? What's up with Woods and Max?"

"No, we didn't lose them, and we didn't have a chance to take them out. Let's just say we couldn't have scripted a better plan. Max led those guys to where he used to play basketball as a kid— the hood in Roxbury. Woods watched Max play several games with his old buddies while the men from The Order were dragged out of their cab. Within a few seconds, they were relieved of their weapons, their wallets, and their fancy shoes. A group of about fifteen black guys led them into one of the buildings, and I doubt those guys will be coming out of there anytime soon. Max and Woods just checked into the Marriot at the airport, and we assume they'll try to get a flight out tomorrow to San Francisco. We're checking in right now."

Jackson said, "Perfect. Well done, boys. The other crew has a good story of their own that you'll want to hear when you get back."

Chapter Twenty-Three

San Francisco

(Next day)

OUTSIDE THE BIRD'S-EYE DOUBLE DOORS PROTECTING ANTHONY HOLMES, his receptionist said again, "Mr. Holmes is not available for a meeting today. In fact, he is not even in the building."

Allen Woods smiled, looked up at his new friend, Max Tobin, then down at the receptionist and said, "We followed him into the building. We know he's here. Ring him again and tell him we're not leaving."

Max and Woods crossed the waiting area and sat down. The receptionist looked upset. She returned her attention to the papers on her desk.

The sound of elevator doors opening at the end of the long, wide hallway broke the silence. Three large, very fit-looking men stepped out and marched toward them like soldiers. One was dressed in a smartly tailored dark suit, and the other two were dressed down in cotton pants and dark, loose-fitting sport coats.

The man in the suit led the way. When the receptionist looked up, her eyes widened. Woods wondered how she would handle these brutes. Then thought, *these guys must be coming for us.*

Max and Woods stood to prepare for a confrontation. The three men walked right past them, without acknowledgment. The man in the suit yanked open the door without breaking his stride. The other two followed him into the office. The big wooden door slammed shut.

Woods and Max sat down. The receptionist blew out the air she had been holding in.

Loud, angry voices escaped through the door, but they couldn't make out the words. After a few minutes of argument, they lowered their voices.

The elevator door slid open again, and two tall, thin people marched directly toward the eye of the door. One of the two was a young lady with a very determined look on her face.

The young lady stopped at the receptionist's desk and said, "I want to see Mr. Holmes right now. I know he's been dodging our phone calls. We're not going to sit over there and wait for even one minute." She leaned in closer. "Now pick up that phone and tell Holmes we're here."

The receptionist picked up the phone and stabbed two numbers on the keypad. After a moment she said, "Excuse me, Mr. Holmes, but—"

They could all hear Holmes shout, "I told you not to disturb me!"

The trembling receptionist gave the young couple a helpless look, shrugged, and said, "I tried."

Woods took a closer look at the young lady's face, and it dawned on him.

He stood up and said, "Anna."

Anna turned an angry face at him and said, "How do you know who I am?" Her words were a demand more than a question.

Woods said, "My God, you look exactly like your mother."

The expression on her face changed to one of utter sadness. She seemed to be stunned by that one simple word— *Mother.*

She looked for help from the man next to her.

Anna's friend took a step toward Woods. "Look, our affairs are none of your concern. You can see that you've upset my friend for no apparent reason. I would appreciate it..." He stood taller, moved even closer, and lowered his voice. "I demand that you stay over there, mind your own business, and do not engage my girlfriend again."

Woods turned to Max and said, "Max, stand and meet your sister."

Chapter Twenty-Four

San Francisco

(Same day)

THE BIG MAN STOOD UP. ANNA THOUGHT HE LOOKED AS ASTONISHED AS she was.

The old man repeated, "Max, this is your sister, Anna, the woman I've been telling you about. Anna, this is your big brother, Max."

Anna didn't move. No one moved.

"My name is Allen Woods. I was very good friends of your parents, and I've been looking for you. I just found Max a few days ago, and he didn't know that he had any family either. It seems we're all here for the same reason—to talk to this Anthony Holmes fellow and find out what's been going on."

Anna stepped around Armando's side, looked up again at Max's face, and extended her right hand to shake his. Max reached out to accept her hand. They shook hands. With that simple touch, Anna felt it.

She felt family.

Anna flew into her brother's arms. She buried her face in his chest and started to cry. One of Max's hands cupped the back of her head. She felt him shudder.

They held each other for a long time.

Anna couldn't believe this was real.

The receptionist burst into tears.

Eventually, Max and Anna, brother and sister, stepped out of their embrace.

Anna stepped back and took another good look at her big brother. She studied the lines of his face, his eyes, eyebrows, his coloring, complexion, nose, mouth, and hair. She spoke softly and slowly, to no one in particular, "All ... this ... time."

She took a couple more steps backward. Her head shook back and forth, and her temper grew. With a loud voice, a shout, she repeated the exact same words, "All this time!"

Anna turned her attention to the barricade protecting Holmes, determined more than ever to get the answers she had been looking for her entire life. She approached the doors with a fury and pounded on the obstruction.

When no one answered, and with no worries of the consequences, she reached in the middle of the door, grasped the ancient doorknob, and turned the knob. The slight turn of the knob released the small metal latch that deceivingly secured the massive doors.

Twenty years of pent-up rage crashed directly through the eye of that door, and Armando, Max, and Woods followed their battle-ready leader with unanimous support.

Anna located the man who was clearly the banker in this group, stabbed her finger at his shiny round face, and said, "We want answers ... Now!" She didn't even glance at the three big men standing nearby.

Holmes cowered before her. Then he looked at one of the three men and said, "Jackson, take care of this."

Two of the men looked at Jackson, a man with hard, chiseled features. Jackson gave them a slight shake of his head. No. Then he tilted his head toward the big wooden doors. The two men left the room and closed the door behind them.

———⊰◦⊱———

After the doors closed, Anna scowled at Holmes who could only sit slumped over his desk. His face was pale and sweaty, and his hands trembled. He looked deflated. He took a furtive peek at the doors that opened on to the balcony. She knew what he was thinking ... *Taking the easy way out. The coward,* she thought and was about to say the same when the man named Jackson took a step to his right, blocking that escape route.

Holmes gave Jackson a pleading look.

Jackson shook his head. "This ends here."

———⊰◦⊱———

Jackson forced Holmes to disclose the Tobin family history and confess how his uncle had manipulated the Tobin children and their trust fund for the past twenty years. Holmes blamed his uncle for most of the decisions and downplayed his own role. Woods stepped in and detailed the specifics of the computer company, CTAG Pharm, and told them how Max and Anna's parents fit into the two companies.

Woods's explanation allowed Holmes's thoughts to wander in the opposite direction from the time when he first walked through the eye of the doors two years before. Instead of dreaming about the fantastic possibilities ahead, he reminded himself of the laws he had broken and the disgrace his family would be forced to endure. Holmes knew that Jackson wasn't aware of the hidden offshore accounts, but he was certain the bank's own compliance department, along with the Securities and Exchange Commission auditors, would uncover his scheme of skimming money off the trust and placing it into his private accounts.

He would be forced to explain himself in a court of law, and he would be held accountable for his greedy, illegal actions. Then, even worse, he pictured his family in the courtroom, listening to Cecelia on the witness stand. She'd be wearing one of her inappropriate, low-cut blouses, detailing every disgusting element of their sordid affair. Holmes felt what little strength he had left wane as the noose tightened.

Reed Jackson cleared his throat to rouse him from his trance. Holmes continued and eventually finished with the last file outlining the trust's assets. He looked up and around the room and said in a matter-of-fact voice, "Well, that's about it." He looked at Jackson for confirmation.

With no change in Jackson's hard look, he said, "Finish it."

Holmes winced. He looked at Anna and Max and then looked down as if talking directly to the top of the conference table.

He was having trouble getting the words out of his mouth, like a man trying to get out of his own skin. Jackson saw a beaten man with an invisible but heavy burden of shame bearing down on him.

Eventually, the words spilled out of Holmes's mouth. "There's another child," he said, his voice cracking, and he had to clear his throat.

"You have a younger sister living homeless in Munich, Germany. We've kept tabs on her for years. She apparently had a falling out with her foster family, who was set up and paid very well to care for her. She ran away months ago, and we believe she lives in a big city park, right in the center of Munich. But we haven't been able to locate her for weeks, despite our best efforts."

Jackson slid a phone in front of Holmes and said, "Call the CEO and tell him to come to your office with security."

Holmes complied.

Jackson pulled out a recording device that had documented everything Holmes said during the past couple of hours. He handed the tape to Max and pushed all the files toward Anna. He looked at Woods and then Armando's battered face and then closed his eyes in shame as he thought about how he was responsible for much of the pain these people had endured.

He looked back at Max and Anna and said, "You have been through so much over the last twenty years. The greed and corruption of this man, this bank, and in many ways myself, are inexcusable. There's no way to make up for what happened in the past, but now that you know your story—you have the opportunity to move forward with your lives.

"Please know that for the past few days, I have been protecting you from this man, and I will continue looking out for you from a distance." He turned his attention to Holmes. "I will make sure this bank and this man come completely clean and are held accountable for their actions." He took out one of his business cards and wrote his personal cell number on the back of it. He handed the card to Max and said, "If I can be of service in any way in the future, call me."

Half an hour later, Jackson met the CEO at the door, briefly explained the situation, waited for the security detail to arrive and then left the room. Shortly after, they escorted Holmes out of the office.

<hr />

The next several hours involved profound apologies from stunned bank officials and newly created and signed documents that turned the control of the TFT over to Max and Anna, under the watchful eyes of Allen Woods.

Later, Max, Woods, Anna, and Armando sat alone around the conference table. Some questions still needed to be answered.

"I've had flashbacks," Max said. "Sometimes images pop into my mind at random times with visions of our mom and what must have been memories of you, Anna. But I never knew for sure what was real and what was imagined. I was told from the beginning that I had no other family, so naturally I assumed the images were dreams."

Anna replied, "I know what you mean, but I think mine were all just hope and my imagination stealing visions from books or magazines about a mother or father."

Max added, "It's nice to know we have Mr. Woods with us now. He will be able to help fill in parts of what he knew about our parents and our childhood."

Anna said, "How can we really trust what he's telling us?" She looked at a surprised Allen Woods and then back at Max. "How do we know he's not just another business, just like this bank, that is only interested in our money?"

Max looked at Woods, who had a hurt look on his face. Max said, "Anna, he has pictures—pictures of himself with us and our mom and dad. He lived with us in California. He knew them when they were in college in Iowa City. The three of them were like family."

"Have you seen the pictures?" Anna said.

"No, but I trust him, and I have gotten to know him over the last few days. I believe everything he's told me about his connection with our parents and about the company he started with our father."

"That's another thing. Maybe he wanted to find you so he could get his hands on our money for this ailing CTAG Company."

"Anna! He's right here." All three of them looked at Woods, who was silent. He looked as though he was searching for the words to defend himself.

The silence continued until Max said, "Anna, CTAG is the name Mr. Woods gave the company—the company that he started on his own, with great personal and financial sacrifice. The letters stand for 'Cynthia Tobin's Amazing Grace.'"

All eyes went back to Anna as she digested the new information to see if it had an impact, if the words had penetrated her armor of suspicion.

Anna bowed her head and fell silent. She remained that way for what seemed like a long time. Finally, she stood up and walked around to the side of the table where Woods was sitting.

"Please stand up."

Woods looked at Max for direction.

Max tilted his head at Woods and smiled, as if to say, you better comply.

———◦◦◦———

Woods stood up next to Anna, and she put her arms around him. "I'm sorry, Mr. Woods. This is all coming at me so fast. I'm so sorry." Then she started to cry. It was clear that Woods was surprised. He wasn't sure what to do, so he continued to hold her. This was the first human touch he'd had since Cynthia Tobin gave him one of her motherly/daughterly hugs. That was almost twenty years ago.

An unexpected wave of emotion hit him. With a cracking voice he said, "Anna, your lovely mother was exceptionally amazing." He held on. She held on. Finally, they broke away.

Allen Woods thought this was all going to work out. He thought about how he had gotten to know Max during the past few days and about spending this short time with Anna. He felt good about the role he'd played in getting the Tobin children back together. He even wondered if they would take the baton and carry on with the business. He didn't want to lose touch with Max and Anna ever again. All this reminded him of Jeff, Cynthia, and the life the three of them had enjoyed together years before. He thought about his age and realized that this was the closest thing he'd ever have to a family of his own.

———◦◦◦———

Armando knew the pain Anna had suffered through the years and knew that even he would not have been able to totally mend the hole in her heart created by her isolated childhood. Just seeing her engage with Max for this short period of time gave him hope that she would truly be able to leave the past behind and begin to look forward to a happy future together.

———◦◦◦———

Max leaned back in his chair, laced his fingers behind his head, and thought about the last several days. He felt like a new man with an unbelievable weight lifted from his shoulders. A world of hope replaced the void when he looked at his sister shuffling through the paperwork in front of them.

———◦◦◦———

Anna's mind was still churning as she continued to leaf through the various files scattered in front of her. Her thoughts raced from one subject to another as she tried to sort out the web of lies that Richard and Anthony Holmes had created.

Her first childhood memory was of the loneliness she felt when she was just four years old. Someone dropped her off at a Catholic boarding school. She was scared of the nuns and everything else about that school. She remembered crying at bedtime every night in the dormitory when the lights went out. This went on for several weeks until another little girl braved breaking the strict rules. The girl walked across the dark dormitory and gave Anna a stuffed pink bunny rabbit. The little girl whispered, "Here, this will help." That little pink rabbit was Anna's lone possession. It was the only thing she could hold in her arms and love.

She remembered watching the other girls leave for Christmas break and the sadness associated with being "the one" with no family, with nowhere to go. She learned to shut down her emotions, shut out her friends, and never let anyone get close. If she would have known she had a brother, they could have been together and helped each other. If she had known the story of their parents, how good they were and how much they loved her, it all would have been so much better.

Then, something clicked in Anna's mind.

She slapped her hands on the big conference table, stood up, and with the eyes of authority, the eyes of a general, she looked straight at her big brother, and commanded, "We leave for Munich tonight!"

BOOK TWO

Chapter E
Munich, Germany
(Late that same night)

THE BLACK, BLACK NIGHT COVERED THE GIRL. SHE WOKE. DIDN'T MOVE. There was an unnatural noise. *Trust my instincts.* She stayed still and silent, and she listened.

She was bedded down in tall grass, a black hood covering her blond hair. She was wrapped in a blanket for warmth and camouflage.

Shhh ... listen ... quiet ... What was that noise? She checked her senses, time of day, and confirmed her grip on the knife. Her mind scrambled to determine the night's environment and her options. Listened again, then replayed the noise she had heard in her mind. *Did someone follow me? Has someone found me? Is this an accident? Maybe I'm wrong about the sound. Why would anyone be out here now?*

It was possible she had misinterpreted the noise. *Listen. Trust my instincts.* Silently, she moved into a crouched, ready position. She rearranged the dark hood over her head, the blanket, and the backpack slung over her left shoulder. Her body was poised in a starting position like a sprinter's at the line. Like a cat prepared to pounce.

She heard another noise. *Someone is here.* The sound came from her right side and behind her. *Don't move. No one can see me.*

Listen. Remember my escape paths. The path to the front: take five strides ahead, then left with four long, fast strides, jump over a fallen tree across the path, two quick steps, duck to miss a head-high tree branch. Then I have a flat path with plenty of turns where I can use my speed.

Listen. A rabbit wouldn't move. Don't give them anything. I'm smarter, and I'm faster. Wait.

She strained her ears, her nose, her deepest senses. Her heart pounded. *Slow down. I'm prepared. Listen.*

She identified the sounds of crickets, the wind in the trees, a lone bird, and faraway traffic. *Ignore them. Be still. Listen. Find the intruder.* The wind decreased. *Is that the smell of cigarette smoke?* That increased her alarm.

There it was—the muffled sound of a man's voice. *Who is it? Why are they out here? There has to be at least two.* A wave of fresh air swished the leaves in the trees. She waited. The breeze died. Another muffled human voice was closer. *The rabbit wouldn't move. Be smart.*

She looked at the sky to confirm the blanket of clouds was still there, blocking the moonlight. *The moon is no friend.*

A shoe scraped the dirt path. Now she knew exactly where they were. *Stay still, stay quiet, be smart.*

More talking. She could hear them, but couldn't make out the words. They sounded like men trying to be quiet. *They should walk right past me. My den is well hidden. There is no way they could spot me.* She could hear them walking closer.

An unexpected confidence pushed away her fear. She thought she could jump right at them to scare them and then easily disappear into the night. *Wouldn't that be something?*

She heard their voices again, but still couldn't make out the words. No wind. She could hear them clearly. They spoke with a distinct accent. *Same as Silvio's. Wait, they are close. Should be able to see them as they walked by.*

There they are. They held flashlights, shining their bright beams into the bushes. The lights danced around her. She didn't move.

It's okay. Stay still. If they spot me I will bolt. But wait. She thought about the escape route behind her, wished she were facing in that direction. *Next time, turn toward the sound. Much better escape potential.* Panic started to creep in, and her confidence waned as the powerful lights drew closer.

Be the rabbit. Give them nothing. Stay still. If their light gets through the bushes, they will see me. Be ready, readier! Stay still. Don't give them anything. Crouched, muscles strained, ready, always ready. *No way you can catch me when I go, even if I'm right in front of you, even with your bright flashlights.*

The men took two more slow steps and stopped on the path slightly in front of her. *Now I have to use the escape route behind me. Makes me slower because I have to turn around.* She replayed her rear escape route.

One lit a cigarette. They talked quietly. *Unmistakable same accent, but not Silvio. Same dark look, older, fatter, could never run me down. Have to hide farther from any path in the future. What are they saying? They could never hear me even if I did move. They're fat and stupid. Still, don't give them anything.*

They walked away. *Two stupid Silvios.* She watched them go. *Stay down. There could be more men. They have to be looking for me, but why?*

Wind rustled the leaves of the trees, masking their voices, and their lights dimmed with the increasing distance. They were gone, for now.

Her heart rate slowed. *There is evil in those men. Trust my instincts. Just like the beast, they won't stop with one attempt. These beasts will be back.*

It doesn't matter why. Why is not relevant. Why is wasted time. Focus on options. Focus on their next move. The beast wouldn't stop at a wedged door. These men will be better prepared next time. They must have been watching me today to know the direction I ran. They must have tried to follow me. My plan, speed, and knowledge of the park worked and saved me tonight. Next time might be different.

A dog! My God, what if they brought a dog. A dog would find me in an instant. A dog or dogs could outrun me easily. There are dogs everywhere in this park. Dogs wouldn't be out of place here, dogs would find me.

Those men are stupid. But don't underestimate the beasts. Find different solutions. They will come again.

She turned onto her side and let her muscles relax. Her mind raced with the advent of this new threat. *Just a few days until I'm eighteen, a few days until I can get a job and make a home outside the park. A few days is too long. I can feel their evil, the same evil that was in Silvio's eyes. They are coming.*

Try to get some rest. The girl felt safe right now, but this may be the last time. *Try to sleep. Tomorrow I'll figure this out.*

She thought about her foster home. *They told me I was alone. They told me I had no father and that my mother was a crack whore. They told me I would end up on the streets like my mother. I won't let that happen. This is just another test, another challenge. I'll manage this. A few days are all I need.*

I could go up to the north end of the park. They couldn't find me there. The days will go fast. I've been on my own for months. I can make it a little longer. I could leave this park and go somewhere else. I've been all over this city. I could find another park.

Stop, try to get some sleep, try to get some rest. Tomorrow I'll need my strength.

Noise! *What was that? Shhh!* The wind came up, the trees swished, and the first hint of the sun's morning light peeked over the horizon. *I must have fallen asleep. A nice rest. Good. It's still mostly dark. What was that noise? Listen. Be still. It was nothing. Try to get some more rest. Stay down a couple more hours. I'll need all my strength.*

They are coming.

Chapter Twenty-Five

Munich, Germany

(Same morning)

"GOOD MORNING. HOW DID YOU TWO SLEEP?" MAX ASKED ANNA AND Armando as he pulled up a chair to join them. They were sitting to one side of the big restaurant, just off the lobby of a hotel in Munich, Germany. They had stayed there the night before, after the long flight from San Francisco.

Anna looked up at him and said, "Why do you look so bright-eyed, and why are you so late?"

"Turns out, the bright-eyed look is all just heredity." Max couldn't help but chuckle to himself. He looked at his watch and said, "It's exactly eleven. I seem to remember when we checked in a few hours ago, you said to meet here at eleven, and here we are, little sis."

Armando said, "You two have known each other for twenty-four hours, and there is already some sibling bickering— reminds me of me and my sister."

Anna said, "Okay, boys. I'm outnumbered here. Let's start over. Good morning, Max Tobin, nice to see you on this fine morning. Please join us."

"Don't mind if I do, Anna Tobin! Did you guys order yet, and, by the way, what's your middle name?"

"We did order, and my middle name is Marie, but don't ask me why or where that name came from."

"Anna Marie. I like it—a very pretty name. It suits you." Max smiled at her. "Don't you agree, Armando?"

"I do agree, and we're both learning some new things today. I didn't know your middle name, either, but you are correct, Max. It's a beautiful name for my beautiful girlfriend."

"Wow, it's getting pretty deep in here. You two have known each for only twenty-four hours, and you're already acting like brothers."

Anna snickered and waved the waitress over.

The waitress looked at Max and said, "What can I get you?"

"I'll just take whatever those two ordered."

"You want two breakfasts?"

"Yes, please." Anna said, "Big brother has a big appetite, I see."

"I love breakfast, and we have a lot of work to do today. The idea you had about contacting Reed Jackson last night was a good one. I talked to him this morning. He told me about the other private investigative company Addison National Bank hired to look after our sister. He gave me the address of the foster family where she lived until recently and a report that says she's been seen in the English Garden. It's a big park, not far from here. I've been working all morning." He smiled at Anna.

"Ha, ha, a big appetite, and a big smarty pants too. I'm learning all kinds of things this morning." She winked at him. "Let's finish up here and pay a visit to the PI Company."

Max sat back in his chair and laced his fingers behind his head. "They're on their way here as we speak. I just got off the phone with a man named Herman Bock."

Their breakfasts came, and the conversation slowed as the three of them ate in silence. In a few minutes, Max was done with both his meals. "Wow," Anna said, "a fast eater, too. You continue to amaze me. I wonder what I'll learn next."

The young waitress returned to retrieve Max's empty plates. She gave him a wide, flirty smile and said in broken English, "Is there anything else I can get for you?" She paid no attention to Anna and Armando.

Max returned her smile. "No thank you, miss, not at this time. But don't go too far away."

The waitress blushed and then walked away. Anna said, "Oh, brother, you're something else."

"Hey, I'm just sitting here with my new family, minding my own business."

"Uh-huh." Anna smiled at both her men.

Armando looked across the room and said, "That could be our man over there. I'll go find out."

As Armando walked away, Max looked to Anna. "I really like Armando. I think he's a keeper. How close are you guys?"

"Big brother is smart, too. He *is* a keeper, my keeper, and we are very close."

"That's good to hear. It must be nice to have him back. The story you told me last night on the plane about his time in the swamp was terrible. Maybe there really is someone up there looking out for us, after all."

Armando returned with the man and introduced him as Herman Bock. He looked almost the exact opposite of the men from The Agency. He was a small, thin man with round spectacles and a weak handshake. He made minimal eye contact. He carried an overcoat, hat, and heavy leather briefcase. He reminded Max of a typical Cold War spy.

Bock sat down and got right down to business. "We were hired by Addison National Bank six years ago, and at that time we reported directly to Reed Jackson." His German accent was almost undetectable. "Mr. Jackson contacted me this morning and brought us up to date with what has transpired over the last couple of days concerning your—He looked at Anna and Max—situation during the last several years. Mr. Jackson made it clear that we will now serve in a support role for you in your attempt to find your sister."

He pulled a sheaf of papers from his briefcase and laid them in the middle of the table. "Before we initiate this relationship, I need you to sign these documents. They declare that our company had no prior knowledge of what Mr. Holmes's intentions were regarding your family and the irregularities at Addison National Bank. They also confirm that we were hired only to do observation." The man sounded more like an attorney. "I also want to assure you that we are at your disposal to help with your search."

Bock reached back into his briefcase and pulled out some files and a number of pictures. He spread the pictures out on the table. They were a mix of what looked like high school yearbook photos and enlarged photos from a hidden camera. The three of them shuffled through the photos. Armando, holding a picture of a girl in a track uniform, said, "Anna, this must have been how you looked when you were sixteen years old."

"Yeah, similar," said Anna as she leaned over to have a better look at the picture. "But I was never that pretty."

"Who is this?" Armando handed several zoomed-in long-shot photos to Mr. Bock.

"That is their sister," he said. "Her appearance has changed since she's been living in the woods of the English Garden. The English Garden is a large park just a few blocks from here. The park goes on for miles in both directions from here. It has many paths and roads." He sounded as if he were reading from a tourist brochure. "Your sister is an expert in navigating the park, and she is an exceptionally fast runner. Her daily routine starts early in the morning when she suddenly appears in different parts of the park, walking through the beer gardens looking for food in the garbage cans. She rarely finds something edible, but every once in a while she gets lucky. From there she goes to the public library, where she cleans up and spends a lot of time reading about current events and reading books written in English. She stays in the library until about two, then goes back to the park and sits on the edges, looking for abandoned food. She never talks to anyone. At dusk, she disappears into the woods and she is impossible to follow."

Anna said, "These pictures don't even look like the same girl, she is so thin. Why the hell hasn't someone stepped in to help her? How could you people let her live like this? What kind of people are you?" Anna's steel blue-eyes flashed at Bock.

"I'm sorry, Miss Tobin, but we were under specific orders from Mr. Holmes to never engage her. After she ran away from her foster home, Mr. Holmes ordered us to stop reporting to Reed Jackson and report directly to him. Because of her speed and intelligence, we couldn't keep up with her, so we would lose sight of her for days at a time. We haven't seen her anywhere in the park for a few days now. We petitioned Holmes for a larger budget so we could do a better job, but recently he did the exact opposite by cutting our budget in half."

Max said, "Mr. Bock, what do we know about the foster family and why she ran away from home? What could have been so bad in that home that she would rather live like this?" He slid one of the close-up pictures to Bock. It showed the girl digging into a trash receptacle. She had a gaunt face, short, ragged hair, and sunken eyes.

Bock said "We were able to access all the reports filed by her caseworker regarding her life with the Eichmann family. The reports indicated nothing wrong within the family unit. She lived with them from the time she was eighteen months old. The Eichmann's have a daughter almost the same age. But I agree with you. There must have been something very bad going on behind closed doors that she needed to escape. She was sent back to the Eichmann family once after a restaurant employee claimed she took away her job and turned her in to social services. In Munich, children are not allowed to replace an adult in the workforce without a signed petition from their guardians. She stayed in the Eichmann home for only a few days before she went back to live in the park. She will be eighteen years old soon, and I believe she will look for work at that time."

Anna said, "What kind of student was she? Didn't she have any friends from school who could help her?"

"She was an excellent student, the very top of her class. She didn't have any close friends. There was one girl who ran track with her and befriended her. She even went over to that friend's home a few times. We know the location of the house, and we hope she will go there. She—"

Armando pushed a picture across the table to Bock and said, "In this picture, she's talking and eating with a man sitting across a picnic table from her. That seems a little unusual based on how you described her life in the park. Is this a friend? Someone who she met with often?"

"This picture was taken—" Bock picked up the photo and turned it over —"just a couple of days ago. That man is Silvio Dzhabahl, a bad character in Munich's criminal underground. He and his cohorts are from Chechnya. There are thirty or forty of them roaming around our city creating all kinds of problems. They all look and dress like the typical east European gangster you see in this picture. These men are ruthless. They have absolutely no regard for human life. We consider this man and his associates as very dangerous men, especially as it concerns your sister. One of this group's criminal enterprises is kidnapping young girls, forcing them into drug addiction, and then turning them out in various places around Munich as prostitutes. Many of these young girls are sent to other countries in Europe. Your sister may have perceived him as a threat, or she may have been lured into his group to escape living homeless in the park. We simply do not know. But I have to make it clear. We don't have much time. If he gets to your sister, we may never find her."

Anna said, "We can't let that happen. We have to find her."

Bock said, "After Max talked with Reed Jackson this morning, Jackson requested that my company make finding your sister our highest priority. We will be working with you to find her as soon as possible."

Max reviewed this morning's conversation he had with Reed Jackson and said, "I told Jackson we would fund whatever it takes to make this happen."

Anna cried, "Well, what are you doing right now? Are your men looking for her right now?"

"Yes, ma'am," Bock replied. "We have four teams of two men in the park. We have additional teams on twenty-four-seven surveillance operations at Silvio's known locations. Jackson has ordered us to change our operation from surveillance to one of an operation rescue."

With that said, Bock stood up. "I will personally be leading another team that will continue looking in the park. We will be ready at a moment's notice to respond to any hint of hopeful activity throughout the city. I have Max's cell phone number, and I will call as soon as I have any news. We will find her."

Herman Bock shook everyone's hand and walked away, leaving Anna, Armando, and Max sitting together nearly speechless as they continued to look through the many photographs spread out on the table.

Anna said, "We just can't sit here and do nothing. I'm no good at looking at your phone and hoping it's going to ring."

"I agree," Max said. "I can go check out this Eichmann family and see what I can get out of them. Why don't you two pay a visit to her friend from school and see if she can give us anything?"

Anna nodded, looking at Armando for agreement. "That sounds good. We'll let you know what we find out."

Armando said, "Anna, you can handle that by yourself, and it will probably be even better if I'm not in the way. I'll go to the park and get a feeling for how it's laid out and try to figure out how a girl is able to survive there on her own." He looked at Anna with a hint of a smile. "I can use my unique swamp survival techniques to track her into the woods and free her from the evil Chechen enemy."

Max looked confused until Anna said, "Don't ask. Let's just say we're lucky to have 007 on our side."

Anna kissed Armando on the cheek and then sorted the photos. She handed the Eichmann file to Max and some of the most recent pictures to Armando. She kept the file with the information regarding her sister's high school friend and pushed the rest of the pictures into a stack.

Armando stood up and said, "We have to be very careful and take these Chechen men seriously. Anna, I don't want you to go into that park alone, especially with inquiries about your sister. If others believe your sister is more valuable than just a homeless street girl, it will be even more dangerous for her, and for you. In addition, we have to respect the warnings Bock just gave us about this group and assume all of us are in danger if these Chechens see us poking our nose into their business. This isn't America or the resort areas of Mexico. We have to be very, very careful."

"I agree," Max said. "Let's review. We know the professionals from the private security company are having trouble finding her, so we'll have to figure out a different, let's say out-of-the-box, plan to find her. If we just barge into the mix with no plan, as Armando noted, we could make matters worse for everyone."

"All good points," Anna said. "I think we can still split up this morning, though. I'll try to contact her high school friend, and Max can check out the Eichmann family without drawing any attention from the Chechens." She looked at Armando. "Armando, the park is where the danger is, so be on your toes and don't take any risks." She looked back to Max and said, "Give us the cell number for Mr. Bock so we can all contact him immediately if we see anything."

"Sounds good." Max and Armando said in unison.

Chapter Twenty-Six

Munich, Germany

(Same day)

INSIDE A DANK ABANDONED WAREHOUSE BUILDING JUST OUTSIDE OF CITY center, Silvio sat on a stack of wooden pallets behind a makeshift desk. There were two men on the other side of the desk pleading their case. "Boss, there was no way we could find her in that park. We had eyes on her, but just before dark she bolted off the park bench and sprinted into the woods. We tried to follow her but we couldn't keep up. That girl knows what she is doing. We walked the paths of the park all night looking for any hint of her, but didn't find nothing but road."

"He's right, boss. We're going to have to consider taking her during the day when we can get our hands on her."

Silvio stewed on his men's excuses as he sat back a little on the pallets. He looked again at his men, who both had an apologetic look on his face … waiting for their fate. A fate where men in this organization who failed were treated harshly, and these men had clearly failed.

Silvio looked at a group of men standing nearby, who were waiting to see what would happen next. He said, "Aslan." The two men sitting across from Silvio cringed when they heard that name. Aslan was Silvio's older brother. While Silvio was the brains of the gang, Aslan was the brawn. Everyone knew that he was a monster who would do anything for his younger brother. Aslan was one of the soldiers in this gang. Because he was in the trenches with the rest of the men, he was respected. Their father made the decision to let Silvio run the Munich operation. The two men who failed to find the girl knew that Alsan was the hammer that was responsible for handling the more violent assignments.

"I want you and your crew to take these two back to the park to find that girl and bring her back to me. I don't care how you do it. Just get it done. She is making fools out of all of us." Silvio looked at the two men in front of him.

"We will find her, boss," one of them said.

Chapter Twenty-Seven

Munich, Germany

(Same day)

THE GIRL SAT ON THE FLOOR IN THE CORNER OF THE CHURCH HALL. SHE wanted to be invisible. She wanted to be left alone. Her hood was up, and her head was down as people all around her ate their lunch. She could smell good food. She had to eat. It had been over two days since her last meal. She couldn't take a chance scavenging in the park after last night's encounter with the two "Silvios." The church was her last choice. A refuge, but it had too many rules and too many questions. If they thought she was a minor, they would contact the authorities.

Just as she was about to get up to stand in line, a young woman came over and sat down next to her, holding two plates of food. The young woman handed the girl a plate without saying a word. The girl's heart skipped a beat when she realized the plate was for her—full of food—without strings attached. She dug in.

I'm eating too fast. Slow down. Remember civilized manners. She had been on her own for so long she wondered if she'd lost the notion of decent human behavior. Last night she had tried to remember the last time she spoke out loud. It had been months. *Has my time in the park changed me? Can I go back? Have I been the rabbit too long?* The girl peeked from under her hood. *Are people looking at me? Can they see I'm off?*

I don't think I can go back. I can't speak! Terror gripped her when her throat seized up. Her lips wouldn't move. *What's happening?*

She took a proper-sized bite of potatoes and wondered if her appearance and mannerisms were disgusting. Did she look like the other wretches from the park? Her mind raced. *Slow down, you're okay, you can do this. I could stand*

171

and take my plate away from this lady. I could sit over there. She looked across the room at an empty table. *I could escape now before she—*

"Today's lunch tastes pretty good," the young woman said, not looking at her. "Tomorrow we're having meatloaf. That's my favorite." The girl's fear ebbed with those soft words and no probing questions. She tilted her head up and looked past the edges of her hood, like a turtle peeking out its shell to gauge the risk. She took another, more feminine, bite from the large plate, feeling a little closer to normal.

After a short period of comfortable silence, the young lady asked, "Would you watch my plate for me? I'll be right back."

The young lady smiled at her. She had a cheerful, round face and wide-set, sparkling eyes. She placed a half-eaten plate of food on the floor and walked away. The girl scanned the big room. The lady, her new friend, was doing some busy work in the kitchen. She took this opportunity to shovel in three big bites of food. The fried potatoes and onions tasted really good. She shoveled in two more bites.

Sister Elisa said to one of the older sisters, "Well, how am I doing?"

Looks to me like you're doing just fine. You can see she needs our help. This is your calling, Elisa. Think of her as a timid wild animal. No sudden movements. Let the Lord guide you. Your first mission is always your biggest challenge but the one you'll remember forever."

Sister Elisa placed more dinner rolls on a big tray. Her work was interrupted when she heard a commotion across the room. The girl, her new mission, was grappling with one of the volunteers. Elisa ran across the room to confront the situation.

She broke the grip the volunteer had on the girl's arm and said in a calm voice, "What's the problem here, Otto?"

Otto said, "This boy took two plates of food. You know the rules, Sister— one plate per person so everyone gets a share."

The girl held two empty plates. Her hood was up, and her head was head down.

"Thank you for your help, Otto, but this is my fault." She took the two plates from the girl. "I have a stomach ache, so I gave my plate to this girl and told her to eat the rest of my food because I didn't want it to go to waste."

The girl's head popped up when she heard those words.

Elisa still had half of a bag of rolls in her hand. She said, "Here" as she handed the bag to the girl. "Don't forget the rolls I promised you."

———◦◦◦———

The girl accepted the bag of rolls as she looked at the young lady's eyes. With that quick eye contact, she hoped the nice lady could see her appreciation. The girl tried to muster the courage to speak, but she couldn't. She ducked her head and walked toward the exit, hoping that no one would stop her.

"Remember, we have meatloaf tomorrow," Sister Elisa called to her. "Come back a little earlier if you can. You could help me in the kitchen. That would be fun."

———◦◦◦———

Sister Elisa returned to the kitchen. She looked into the soft, wrinkled face of her mentor. "Sister, I really messed up, and I don't know how it happened. The words just came out of my mouth. I couldn't stop the lies." Elisa waited, hoping for guidance.

"What are you talking about? Slow down and tell me everything."

"I just told two lies, to help my mission. I panicked and came to her defense." Elisa went on to explain the incident.

The elder Sister smiled at her. "Don't worry. Your intentions were good. You have to follow your instincts. You may have just saved that girl. But don't forget to mention this to Father at confession. He will give you wise guidance."

———◦◦◦———

The girl skipped down the steep steps at the front of the church and jogged across the six-lane boulevard to the safety of the English Garden.

One of Silvio's men saw her from a distance. He ran to the park entrance where she had entered. He was too late. The girl was lost in the crowd. There was no use in trying to guess where she went, so he documented the time of day and location.

He jaywalked through the traffic to the church and took the front steps two at a time. *What's going on in here?* He opened the heavy door to an empty church. Heard some noise in the back, so he walked through the church and found a roomy hall with dozens of people having lunch.

Free food. No wonder we haven't been able to find the little bitch.

Back outside, the man paced back and forth on the top step, waiting for his phone to connect. "I spotted her, boss, but didn't have a chance to grab her. You were right, she's clear up here in the north end. I saw her leave a church and run across the street into the park just a few minutes ago. The church serves lunch to what looks like all the homeless beggars in Munich."

Silvio said, "okay, good job. We'll be waiting for her tomorrow. Find Aslan and tell him what you saw. I want at least five men there when she crosses that street. Have the old van parked close by with the driver ready to pick you up when you grab her."

"I'm on it, boss. We'll run through it a couple of times this afternoon and give you an update when we get back tonight.

Chapter Twenty-Eight

Munich, Germany

(Same day)

Later that day Anna and Armando sat close to each other on the wooden plank seat of one of the picnic tables scattered around the beer garden in the English Garden, enjoying the warm breeze. People crowded the beer hall, talking, laughing, and drinking steins of cold beer. They had a few more hours of daylight.

Anna and Armando enjoyed each other's company after their full day apart. Their harmony was interrupted by the sight of Max carving his way through the throng, carrying three baskets of bratwursts and fries on a tray, along with large plastic cups of beer. Max placed the tray in the center of the table and distributed the baskets of food and the beers, then said, "Is there anything else I can get for you two?"

"No, this will do just fine ... for now," Anna replied with a smile.

Max said, "I hope you didn't start comparing notes without me.

"We did not. I'll start," said Anna as she reached for one of the food baskets. "I went to her high school friend's house and talked with her mother. Their house is in a nice suburban neighborhood, a typical middle-class home. There were a couple of younger children running around. It seemed like a very nice family atmosphere. Her mother gave me the address of the café where Lara works.

"I went to the café. It's a big, busy place. There were probably ten girls about the same age as Lara working. I was seated at a table where I could survey the entire restaurant. I picked Lara out easily because of the pictures we have. She is a lovely girl, and she had nothing but good things to say about our sister. Unfortunately, she had no clue about where she's been the last several months.

"I asked her about the foster family, but she didn't want to talk about that. She told me that she had been a foster child, too. She said that our sister was terrified of her foster father, but didn't go into detail. It turns out our sister was an exceptionally good student and a good athlete, but was very shy and didn't have any close friends." Lara told me, "I was probably her closest friend, but we were not close. I wanted to do more for her, but didn't really know what to do."

Anna took a sip of beer, then said, "I gave her my contact information and asked her to call me if she heard anything. Seems like a dead end there, so I decided to go to the library. That place is huge. There are reading rooms scattered all over the building and hundreds, maybe thousands, of people there. Bock told us she goes there every day, which is very good information, but finding anyone in that building will be tough." Anna looked at Max and said, "How did you do?"

"Not much to report. No one was home at the Eichmann house, but I wasn't sure what I would say even if someone was home. This was the place she escaped from, so the odds of them knowing where she is are slim. I waited at a bus stop across the street for quite a while, hoping to see some kind of activity. Eventually I gave up and went to a neighborhood pub for a late lunch. I asked the bartender if he knew Mr. Eichmann. He said he did, and he pointed him out to me. Eichmann was sitting at a table with a few other men. He looked like a disgusting pig, overweight, needed a shave and a haircut, and he was drinking heavily along with his friends. I couldn't imagine anyone having to live with that man. I waited for him to leave, followed him out of the pub, and engaged him by asking for directions. His personality was worse than his appearance. He acted as though he couldn't understand English. He just brushed me off. I walked with him for a while and kept asking him questions just to rattle him. He ended up ducking into another bar. I didn't know how to get through to this guy. I wanted to slap him down because of how he may have treated our sister. He won't be hard to locate if we ever need to find him again."

Armando said, "I wish I had some better news. I walked around the park and tried to understand how I would live here if I were homeless and looking for food the way we saw her scavenging in those pictures. The park is huge. Hundreds of people everywhere. I can see how it would be easy to stay hidden. I noticed a couple of what looked like homeless people. They had the same gray, thin face your sister has in those pictures. I also saw a couple of characters that looked like mafia types strolling around. They could have been men from the Chechen group, but it's hard to say. They weren't the man in the pictures."

He looked at Anna and said, "My time would be best spent here in the park. I can pretend to be one of the homeless and come at this from a different angle—something neither one of you could get away with. So … I'm planning to stay here all night."

Anna said, "No way. Where are you going to sleep?"

"I'll figure something out. It won't be a problem."

"Armando," Max said, "that's a generous offer, and I agree, it's also great strategy."

Anna shook her head. "I don't want you sleeping out here all by yourself. What are you going to do if there's some trouble?"

"Don't worry about me, Anna. I'll be just fine. Just think about your sister, who's on her own out there."

Max said, "He's right, Anna. This is our best shot. Armando is better equipped to handle this than we or Bock's men are. We'll have to find other ways where we can be just as effective."

Anna stared into the distance for a while. Finally, she looked at Armando and said, "How much charge do you have left your phone?"

Armando pulled out his phone. "I have enough to get me through the night."

Anna then looked at Max and said, "Max, will you please get us another beer? I want to talk to Armando."

"For sure … I can take a hint."

He loaded the tray and left. After a while he turned around and looked at them. Anna leaned her head against Armando's shoulder. This was the first time in Max's life when his sorrow wasn't for himself. He could see and feel the feelings they had for each other.

Max stood in the short beer line and thought about the carefree life he had left just a few days before. He thought about the basketball games with Ebony and his friends in Boston. He wondered about how his new friend, Allen Woods, was getting along. Then came thoughts about another sister, much like Anna, fighting for her life. She was alone and needed his help.

The significance of his task covered all his thoughts as he walked back to Anna and Armando. When he arrived, he found Anna alone and crying. He sat beside her, put his arm around her, and pulled her close. They watched Armando walk away, back into the swamp.

Max thought again about this man, Armando. How he had survived the brutal beating and the horrors of the swamp. Now he had offered to endanger himself to find their sister. Not his sister. A girl he'd never met.

With those thoughts in his head, Max said to Anna, "I think I'm in love with Armando, too." Anna managed to respond with a little smile. "Come on girl, he'll be okay. We have to get to work ourselves. Let's take a walk and develop a plan of our own. When we meet up with Armando tomorrow morning, I want to be able to report some good news. Hopefully, we'll find our sister by then, and the three of us can surprise him."

Anna got to her feet with what seemed like renewed strength and said, "You're right. Let's go see what we can find."

Max scanned the crowd again to see if he could spot Armando. No luck, but something caught his attention in a different direction. "Follow me. I think I see one of those Chechen gangsters."

Anna fought her way through the crowd, trying to keep up with Max. After they broke through the beer garden crowd, Anna said, "Where?"

"Just over my left shoulder."

"Move a little, I can't see over your giant shoulder." Max moved. "Yeah, I see them. Let's follow them and see where they go."

———◦◦◦———

Armando claimed a spot on the edge of one of the open areas just south of the beer garden. He noticed a homeless man wearing a faded Yankee's baseball cap sitting on the opposite side of the wide expanse of lawn, trying to be inconspicuous. As soon as the man spotted him, Armando sensed the competition beginning ... *Just sit back and see what happens next,* thought Armando.

Suddenly, unwelcome competition emerged from the bushes. He was a man of indeterminate age, scruffy from head to toe. This newcomer didn't waste any time. He brashly followed a group of three skateboarders, and he was close when one of them tossed a crumpled bag into a garbage can. He practically dove into the trashcan and rifled through the rubbish. Soon he came up for air, holding half a sandwich. Then turned to the vagrant wearing the baseball hat and made a wicked hissing noise. *Those two must know each other well.*

How could she live like this, with these crazies? I can't believe any girl could last one day out here. I bet she's sat right here several times over the last few months, fighting for a chance at a meal ... fighting against these wild, crazy animals. Armando thought she would be fairly safe during the daytime, when so many people were around, along with all the police officers he saw. *But what did she do at night?*

The air became cooler as the sun went down. He remembered what Herman Bock had told them at breakfast. *Just before the sun went down she would bolt off into the timber at a speed no one could match.*

I can see why. She ran for her life. I'll emulate her actions when the time comes.

———❖❖❖———

"Let's sit off to the side here and let those guys go," Anna whispered to Max. "I bet they're doing the same thing we are." They found an empty park bench.

Max said, "If they're doing the same thing we are, I, guess they haven't found her yet. But who knows what they're doing or even if they're part of the Chechen gang."

"I wish we had more to go on here," Anna said. "According to Mr. Bock, this is the time of day she disappears into the woods. Let's stay here until dark. Tomorrow morning we'll get up early and split up to monitor the beer gardens for any signs of her. We're meeting Armando at the Chinese Tower at ten for his update. It's right over there."

———❖❖❖———

NOW! Armando took off on one of the paths into the woods, trying to think the way she did. At first he kept up a pretty good pace but quickly tired. He angled off the path and leaned on a tree to catch his breath. He waited to see if anyone came behind him. *It's darker in the woods with the trees blocking what little light was left. What would she do now? I bet she would get to a place to sleep before it gets pitch black in here. I bet she has a place to go since she's lived here so long. What am I going to do?*

Armando got himself moving again, this time running at a little slower, more controlled pace. He jogged through the trees, looking for a place to hide for the night. He found no good spots. *I think I'll stop here for a minute or two and let things settle around me.*

After several minutes he took off again, heading deeper into the woods, away from the lights and sounds of civilization. This time he ran for a much longer time. *My leg doesn't feel so bad. Maybe I needed this exercise to get it working well again.*

I think I'm turned around in here, though. Not sure where I am. He stopped again, off the path, and this time he sat on the ground with his back against a large, old tree. Now he could hear the sounds of nature all around him—the wind in the trees, squirrels scurrying along the tree branches, birds and insects singing their songs. Armando listened harder and heard typical man-made noises such as traffic, a train, a church bell, and a siren off in the distance.

He stood again. He knew he was alone, but felt vulnerable to what he couldn't see ... felt as if he had given up his advantage. He sped off again.

I'm completely lost now ... must have gone three or four miles by now. Not sure why I keep running. It's like I'm trying to escape something. It's natural to feel like someone's watching, waiting for me to make a mistake. He picked up his pace. His eyes were more accustomed to the darkness now. He ran faster. *The next time I stop I'll stay there. Find a good spot.*

When he noticed a few fallen trees off to his right, he veered toward them and stopped. They would make good cover. He sat down low in the dead leaves and listened, waited for the natural night noises to start again. He took some comfort in this spot. *It's a warm night, and I'm warm from running, but I'll need a blanket to sleep on and a sweatshirt, preferably with a hood, for tomorrow.* He looked at his watch. *Nine. I've been on the run longer than I thought. Going to stay right here for the night. This isn't so bad—a lot better than the swamp.* He slid down a little lower.

Chapter AA

Munich, Germany

(Same day)

LARA PUT THE MOP AND BUCKET AWAY. HER DAY WAS ALMOST DONE. SHE patted the front pouch of her apron to confirm the thick bulge of tips she had accumulated throughout the day. She was in the process of putting her supplies away when the manager approached her to lend a hand with one of the heavier cans. He said, "Good work today. We were slammed pretty hard, and you really helped out. Go ahead and take off now, and I'll finish this up."

"Thanks, Mr. Fisher. I'll see you tomorrow."

She walked out the door into the dusk. Even though she was only a few blocks from her home, she hated walking home in the dark.

Her pink-striped, pleated skirt swung in time with her pigtails as she walked down the wide sidewalk. Her tongue slid over the front of her top teeth. She was glad that she had finally gotten her braces removed. When she stopped at the intersection to wait for the light to change, she noticed a smudge on one of her saddle shoes. She saw some kids she knew from school across the street and instinctually patted the tips in her apron pocket. She thought, *I should have put the money in my purse before I left ... seems like I'm always forgetting something.*

The light turned green, and she walked across the street. The cool breeze felt refreshing after being cooped up all day. The breeze lifted the front edge of her short uniform skirt. She patted it back in place.

Around the corner through an opening in the trees that lined the wide boulevard she saw what looked like a full moon rising. She jogged across another street where there was no traffic. Headlights glared behind her. She took a quick look over her shoulder and increased her pace. The vehicle was a black, windowless van. It cruised past her and stopped about half a block away.

Something felt wrong. Fear knotted her stomach. She slowed her pace and stopped. The passenger-side door of the van opened, and a man got out. *I have to get out of here. This isn't right.* She turned and started to walk in the opposite direction. The door of the van slammed shut, and it sounded like the van was moving in reverse. She bolted away and didn't look back.

A few seconds later, someone grabbed her arm. She tried to spin out of the man's grip, but couldn't break his painful hold. He pulled a black hood over her head. She screamed ... then screamed again. The van pulled up beside them, and the man flung her into it. Hands were all over her. She tried to pry them off. Blindly, she kicked in every direction screaming again and again. Someone grabbed her legs, her only weapon.

Oh, God. Help me! Stop! Let me go!

"You can't fight us, Lara," someone said in a soft voice.

They know my name! Nearly exhausted, she stopped struggling and tried to catch her breath. She yelled, "Here, take my tip money and let me go!"

The man said, "You have to understand that we own you now." His voice was calm, eerily calm. "You cannot fight us, so please stop, and we will stop."

She knew he was right. She went limp, and the hands came off her.

"See? Do as we say, and things will go much better for you. No one wants to hurt you. We are taking you to your new life."

What does he mean, my new life?

"You may think this is not fair, and you are correct. Life isn't fair, but it's how it's going to be for you from now on. Don't worry. You won't be alone."

She sat on the cold metal floor of the van, wishing she had pants on. Slowly, she surrendered to the voice. She tried to separate herself from everything that was happening to her. She pulled her skirt down as far as it would go, then put her hands over her face. The hood prevented her hands from offering even a small bit of comfort. She broke down and wept.

Chapter BB
Munich, Germany
(Same day)

L ARA DIDN'T SAY A WORD. IT WASN'T LONG UNTIL SHE WAS USHERED OUT of the van. She was led somewhere, and it felt as though she was tied to another person. She didn't want to know, she didn't want to touch. She heard people walking around, speaking in a foreign language. Closer to her, she heard the sounds of whimpering, sobbing. Other kidnapped girls? She wanted the hood off, but was terrified of what she would see. The hood smelled like vomit. It was made out of a thick cloth that gave her barely enough air to breath.

Finally, someone yanked it off. She squinted, even though the light in the room was dim. She looked left and right. *Girls, just like me.* Maybe twenty of them, all tied together. She was near the middle of the line. They were all sitting on the same small chairs with the same degree of horror in their eyes. Some of the girls had a bloody nose, blood on their blouse. The girl next to her had blood all over her face. They looked at each other. All the other girl could do was shake her head. She began to cry. Besides some whimpering sounds, the girls were quiet. She recognized one of the girls from school. Tears running down her face, the girl nodded at her. Lara couldn't hold back her own tears.

Lara looked around the large room. It was a warehouse of some kind. *What is this place, what do they want with us?* They were alone. Still, no one said a word.

A door opened and shut, echoing, on one side of the room. All the girls looked that way. Out of the darkness materialized an older man, with men following him. The man looked German. The other men looked like foreigners. They formed a half circle behind the German man, who stepped closer to the girls. He walked slowly down the line, inspecting each girl from head to toe. Eventually, he stopped right in front of Lara.

He spoke in that same soft voice she heard earlier in the back of the van. "Welcome home, girls. And make no mistake; this is your new home. Tomorrow your foster parents will receive a notice from the German government. The notice will tell them that you have run away. You will be labeled a 'runaway' in the eyes of the government. All your possessions and clothes will be taken from your old home and disposed of. You are eighteen years old, or will be soon. Your file will be quickly lost in the German government bureaucracy. Your host families will soon forget you and be given a new child. You are now the property of these men behind me. You work for them. You will make money for them by performing various sexual acts with strangers who pay for your services."

The man paced back and forth. "My name is Doctor. I work for these men, too. It is my job to keep you healthy so you can make money for them. Think of these men as your teachers. They will train you. You are no longer a schoolgirl. You are their property. They think of you the same way they think about a dog. Let's say a hunting dog. If a hunting dog works hard and pleases his master, the dog is rewarded with food and a good place to live. If the dog won't hunt or doesn't hunt well, the dog will be put down. It's not fair. It's just the way it is, and you and I cannot change this. When these men teach you, that is, tell you to do something, do it! If you do not obey them, you will be punished for your disobedience and end up doing it anyway. If you do well, you will be rewarded. After your three-week training period, you will either go uptown or to the docks. Either way you will be performing the same services to make money for your owners, your masters. They have paid good money for you, and they want a return on their investment. For those of you who do what you're told, act like you're enjoying yourself and try really hard, you will have a chance to go uptown, but you need to be very pretty and get an A-plus in your training. If you are not so pretty, you still have a chance to go uptown if you do some extra credit, let's say get an A–plus-plus. For those of you who don't perform well, you will go to the docks. Let me tell you, you do not want to go to the docks. Uptown you will have nice clothes and a very nice place to live. You might go to Vienna or London, and a special few will have a chance to go to America and live a luxurious life. At the docks, you will live in a building like this one, in a small cubical where you'll stay all day and all night serving man after man after man."

He walked to the end of the line and showed the first girl a large picture, then went to the next girl, then the next. When he got to Lara, she saw a picture of a girl who had been severely beaten, with blood and bruises all over her face and body.

After showing the picture to all the girls, he said, "This girl sat right where you are sitting now. She was told to do something by one of these men, and she hesitated. He took a metal pipe and beat her until all her teeth were knocked out. For the last year she has been down at the docks with her mouth full all day, making these men money. Her mouth is a big hit down there. Don't let this happen to you. Do what these men tell you to do when they tell you to do it. Make it seem as though you enjoy every second of it, or else you'll be down at the docks.

"Now, I want to give you a test," he said in that soft, slow voice. He approached the first girl in the line and said, "Do you want to go uptown or down to the docks?"

"Uptown."

He stepped to the next girl. "Uptown or the docks?"

"I just want to go home," she cried.

A man from the back ran up to her and punched and slapped her face over and over again until she passed out and dropped to the floor. There was blood everywhere.

The man rejoined his group. Doctor said, "She'll probably end up at the docks, because I won't be able to fix her face anytime soon. These men don't care. They need girls at the docks, too."

Doctor stood in front of the third girl. "Would you like to go uptown or to the docks?"

The girl replied, "Uptown."

When the doctor came to Lara, he said, "Uptown or the docks?"

Lara said, "Uptown."

The doctor then said, "Are you going to train really hard and act like you enjoy your training?"

Lara knew she couldn't hesitate. "Yes."

Doctor went down the line, asking each girl the same questions. They all gave him the same answers. He took a few steps back and said, "I am almost done with you for now. I won't have to see you again unless you end up like that girl." He pointed to the girl who had been beaten senseless. "Your training will start tomorrow. There is a shower in the back corner of the room where you can clean yourself up. You may untie yourselves tonight and sleep on the floor, but tomorrow morning when these lights go on, you'll have five minutes to get back in your seat and tie yourself to the girls next to you, just like you are now. You must clean yourself up really well. You must look pretty and have a nice smile on your face when your training begins. No talking to each other. There is nothing to say. This is the start of your new life, ladies. Your old life is gone forever. Please make your new life the best it can be."

He let that last thought sink in as he looked up and down the line of girls. Then he said, "Tomorrow, your training will start with the girls at each end." Doctor pointed to both ends of the line of girls. "One of these men will come in and give you a small glass of water. There will be a drug in the water that will relax you. It is no different than drinking a glass of wine. If you refuse to drink the water, I will be sent in with a syringe filled with a very strong drug. After that, for the rest of your very short life you will be hooked on that drug, and you will spend your time down at the docks."

Chapter Twenty-Nine

Munich, Germany

(Next morning)

MAX WOKE TO SOMEONE POUNDING ON HIS HOTEL DOOR. "HELLO?" "It's time to wake up, Max," Anna called through the closed door. "Meet me down in the coffee shop—pronto."

"I'll be right there. I, uh, was waiting for you."

"Uh-huh."

Max tried to rub the sleep out of his eyes before he walked into the coffee shop. There she was, dressed in running clothes, with her blonde hair pulled back in a ponytail. She sat alone with two cups of coffee on the small table. Max couldn't help but notice her long, crossed legs and clunky-looking running shoes. Anna's posture was straight and feminine. Max felt some pride with this sight of his sister. He joined her at the table.

"Thanks for the coffee, Anna. This is just what I needed. You look all ready to go. What are you thinking?"

"I'm planning on a long run through the park this morning." She was studying a tourist map of the English Gardens. "It should take me a couple of hours to get through these main trails. I suggest you concentrate on walking through these paths." She pointed to the narrower lines on the map. "You can take this map with you. Concentrate on this beer garden." She pointed to a place on the map. "I'll be around this other one at dawn, about a half hour. Stay on the move. Hopefully, we'll get lucky and spot her."

"Good plan, good plan. Then we'll meet Armando at ten and see how he got along last night."

"I thought we should also go to the big library and split up again there."

"That all sounds good. Let's get started." Max stood up and grabbed his coffee. "See you at ten. Good luck to both of us."

Anna headed for the door ahead of Max. She stopped, turned around, and ran into Max's arms. Surprised, Max almost spilled his coffee. He placed his free arm across Anna's shoulders.

"I don't know why I just did that. Sorry. I guess I'm just so happy we found each other and are in this together."

"I am, too, Anna. I am, too."

Armando stirred, felt a little sore. He slowly woke, remembering his current state of affairs. He looked at his watch. *Six, the sun will be up soon. I'll walk around to try to find out where I am. I guess I should scavenge for food in the trashcans so I look the part. Hopefully, I'll get lucky and run into her this morning. Not really keen on sleeping out here again tonight. Ten o'clock at the Chinese Tower.*

The girl woke, checked her senses. *A good night's rest.* She stayed down, was in a comfortable place, felt safe. She remembered the rolls in her backpack. *I can stay right here and have a nice breakfast.* She remembered the smiling face of the young lady at the church. *She must be a nun, but she wasn't dressed like one and didn't talk like one. She was so nice to me. I wonder why. I want to go back there to see her again. Maybe I'll go early like she asked. I could help, I could talk to her.* She reached into her backpack and pulled out a roll. It felt soft. She took a bite. It tasted fresh.

The girl heard an unnatural noise. *What was that?* It sounded like someone had yelled her name. More curious than alarmed, she slowly raised her head above the top of the log and saw a young woman with a long, quick stride running away from her on the main path, with her ponytail flopping back and forth. She put her head back down. *What's that all about? I'm sure I heard my name.*

She thought she heard it again. Popped her head up, but didn't see the runner this time … *too weird. I must have heard wrong.* She looked around again, sat up straight, and said in a soft voice, "Hello, it's me. I'm right over here." Surprised by her own actions, she quickly ducked back down. *There, I*

188

did it. I talked again. I can still talk. I can go back to the church today. I can talk to the girl. Just one day until my birthday. Maybe the lady will help me.

—————◆◇◆—————

"Yes, I met with them yesterday," Herman Bock said over the phone, "and they all seemed very concerned, as they should be. There may be a third party involved here. A group of Chechen mobsters seems to have taken an interest in the girl, and these guys are no good. They rolled into Munich a couple of years ago. Their brutal, deadly tactics have even the local crime syndicates on their toes and the police looking the other way. The police are either on the take or just unable to fight the battle. I hope we can find her before they do because we are not equipped for that battle. These Chechens are merciless, evil men. Every man we have is on this. We're doing all we can. We've spotted Chechens in the park looking for something."

After a long pause, Reed Jackson said, "Call me when you have anything. I mean anything." He ended the phone call. His mind raced, searching for answers.

Chapter CC
Munich, Germany
(Same day)

WHEN THE LIGHTS CAME ON, THE GIRLS SCRAMBLED TO GET BACK INTO their seats and tied together. Somehow Lara was able to get some sleep, and she had cleaned herself up pretty well. Other girls were frantic to get the bloodstains out of their clothes and wash the blood off their face and hair. No one had said a word the whole night. *The doctor was right,* Lara thought. *There was nothing to say. Somehow I have to figure out a way to survive.*

Lara waited. She knew they were coming.

Chapter Thirty

Munich, Germany

(Same day)

"There she is," Armando said to Max as he motioned Anna over to them. They were nearly alone this morning, a far cry from the crowds of yesterday evening around the beer garden. Anna sat down with them at the picnic table. "Hi, baby," Armando said. "Nice to see you." He kissed her. "Anything good to report?"

"No, no signs of anything." She cupped his jaw, looked at him closely, and plucked a leaf from his hair. "How are you doing? What happened last night?"

"I didn't see her last night, but I did see how the homeless live here. There are a lot of men fighting for any scraps they can get their hands on. I can't imagine how your sister survived here for this long all by herself. The men she's competing with are probably all hardened criminals who have mental problems. They scare the hell out me every time I try to connect with one. I talked to one of them this morning and showed him the picture. He spoke a little English, so he was able to tell me that he'd seen her in the northern end of the park. I was planning to go there now, but I need to do some shopping along the way in case I have to spend another night out here. A blanket and a hoodie will make the night way more tolerable."

Anna said, "I ran all over the northern area this morning. It's a nice place for a run, but there's not much there."

Max said, "I had a couple sightings of what may have been the Chechen gang this morning, plus a couple more who I'm sure were Bock's men … seems like the only people in the park this morning are all on the same page."

Anna said, "I never saw any hint of either group up there." She looked at Armando and said, "Before you go, let's check in with Bock, tell him what we know, and see if he has anything to report."

"Okay, sounds good."

Bock picked up on the first ring, and Anna filled him in. He cautioned her again about the Chechens, but had nothing to give her.

Armando kissed Anna, traded phones, and walked away. Max broke Anna's daze, saying, "Come on, let's head up to this section." He pointed to a place on the map.

Geronimo sat next to Cochise on the airliner. "Jackson is really dug in on this one," Geronimo said. "We haven't had time to put together a plan, and we won't have any weapons when we get there."

Cochise said, "Now is not the time to second-guess Jackson. You know as well as anyone, we owe these people."

"You're right. I just have a bad vibe with this one. Let's get our game on. We land soon."

"Are you guys all set to go?" Silvio asked the crew that was loading the van in front of the warehouse.

Aslan replied, "I'm going to let these guys take care of this one. Seems like an easy grab and stash. We just got a call confirming the girl entered the church, the same door she came out of yesterday. There's a collection problem down on the dock that needs my attention right now. I should be able to get it all straightened out and get back here about the same time these guys pull in with your newest project."

Silvio looked at the others. "You got this? I don't want any surprises."

"We got it, boss. In a couple of hours that girl will be on her knees in front of you asking what you want next." The other men snickered. Silvio had to crack a smile himself.

"Okay, better get gone. Call me when the package is tied up."

The girl stood in the church kitchen with a trash can in front of her, a big bowl holding a few unpeeled potatoes on her left, and a bowl full of peeled potatoes on her right.

She was peeling potatoes. She was helping out. She had a smile on her face, and her hood was down.

Elisa drew close. "How's it going here?" She looked down at the almost empty bowl and said, "Looks like you're getting along just fine. Does your hand hurt from all that peeling?"

"Not too bad," the girl replied, feeling pleased with her accomplishment and her communication skills. "Are you going to cook all these today?"

"We serve over a hundred meals every day, so we always make a lot of everything. When you're done here, you can help me put the meatloaf in pans." Elisa walked away, looking for and receiving a nod of approval from her elder Sister.

Max and Anna decided take a break from their search. "Grab us a table?" Max asked Anna. "I'll get lunch."

Anna chose a table on one side of an open picnic area. On the other side was an active beer garden. She scanned the surrounding area. There was a family spread out on a large blanket in the middle of the lawn, enjoying their lunch. The young children ran around while their parents kept a protective eye on them. She noticed a young couple, hand in hand, sitting off to the side on one of the park benches, and then noticed what she thought was one of the homeless men Armando had described earlier. He looked creepy, and he seemed to be talking to himself. Just then, a group of bicyclers rolled by with a leader shouting instructions to them.

Max plopped down beside her. "How does this look? Not sure what you take on your burger." Max looked around. "This is a great place. We can see all over of the park from here. I bet you and I used to run around on this lawn when we were kids. Allen Woods told me that our mother would bring us here nearly every day. Interesting how it all comes back around to where we started."

Anna looked back to the family on their blanket and wondered if that was how they looked. "What else did Mr. Woods tell you?"

"He said our dad worked all the time and that our mother was the very best mother and the very best person possible. I think he really loved her and Dad. They were—we were—like a small family. When we find our sister, the three of us have to hang out with Mr. Woods for a while. He's an old man without any family. Just like us. We were his family. He lived with us, helping out, feeding you, and teaching me to walk. He's a really great guy who needs us."

"I'm with you. That all sounds good. First things first, though.

Hey, do you think that's a couple more of the Chechen guys over there?" Anna tipped her head slightly toward them.

"Could be … let's follow them. They're heading in the direction of the library, and that's our next stop anyway.

Armando walked out of a store and ran across the wide street to the first trashcan he saw. He ripped the packaging off the blanket and sweatshirt and then stuffed them into his new backpack. He continued walking along the sidewalk just outside the park. There was a high, stonewall on the edge of the park's property. One of the entrances to the park was a couple of blocks ahead.

The girl said her good-byes to Elisa and some of the other sisters. She walked through the big, heavy front door and down the steep stairs of the church. Her hood was still down, and a smile was on her face as she thought about the new friends she had made. The girl wove through the six lanes of traffic, and then she heard someone from the church call out to her. Standing on the sidewalk across the street, she looked back to see Elisa on the top step. "Come back tonight about six. I have some things we can do."

Feeling totally delighted, the girl smiled at her and yelled, "I will. Thank you!"

Just then the girl heard someone down the street call her name. She turned and saw a tall, thin man with a slight limp running her way, waving at her and yelling, "Sophie! Sophie!" The girl looked back at Elisa on the steps for some kind of direction. Instinctively, the girl turned and walked away from the man.

He shouted, "Sophie, please wait. I'm a friend of your sister and brother. Sophie stopped in her tracks. She turned around to take another look at the man, who was now very close. "I'm here to help you. Please wait a second and talk to me."

Sophie heard movement behind her. A bag whipped down over her head, someone wrapped their strong arms around her and picked her up.

Armando saw what was happening. He raced toward them and attacked the man holding Sophie. Someone across the street screamed as he fought for Sophie's freedom. Within a second a black van pulled beside the fight, and two men jumped out. Sophie was kicking and screaming, trying to escape the big man's grasp. Two men from the van were on Armando quickly. He was forced to break away from the man who had Sophie. The first one came right at him, but Armando hit him hard on the side of his head with his fist.

The big man who had Sophie was dragging her to the van.

Armando couldn't let them put her in the van. He went for the big man's head, and from behind got one arm around his neck. He had a strong arm-bar hold across the man's throat. The Chechen was forced to release Sophie.

Armando saw Sophie rip the bag off her head. She fought like mad with one of the men and escaped his grasp. She ran away, but then she turned back to help the stranger who had just helped her.

Armando yelled, "Run, Sophie, run!" away." He heard more screaming from across the street. It was even louder now.

Armando stayed on the back of the man and tightened his grip. He watched Sophie escape the man's grip and run away. Two different men ran toward Sophie from the park entrance.

She was cornered. Armando hung on tight, and he could feel his man's strength waning. *When this one goes down, I can go to help Sophie. I just have to keep her away from that van.*

The Chechen spun around and crashed Armando against the side of the van. The screams from the street came closer. Armando felt a sharp pain jolt through his back and neck, but he held on. Then Max came out of nowhere, sprinting to the middle of the three men surrounding Sophie. Max tore into them like a caged animal. The Chechen men flew all over the place. Max threw one of them over a parked car into traffic. Tires screeched just before a car hit the man in the road.

More screams, closer now, and the blare of car horns. Vehicles crashed into one another. Armando hung on to his man. He could see Sophie running farther away, right at Anna. Armando's man went limp, and Armando let him drop to the sidewalk. He turned to help Max, but he was hit from behind and lost his balance. He fell to his knees.

Max landed a clean shot on one of the men. He knocked the Chechen out cold. The last thing Armando saw was Anna grabbing Sophie and Max running his way.

Then darkness. A bag pulled over his head. Two men threw him into the van. Everything was black. Armando struggled, but to no avail. In an instant, tape secured his arms and legs, and the van raced away.

Max nearly caught the van. He heard more screams, and he ran back to Sophie and Anna. The two men still there fled in the other direction. Max caught one of them and turned him around like a rag doll. The man had no defense as Max hit his face five or six times with pinpoint accuracy. The man fell unconscious.

Elisa ran to Sophie and Anna. Max dragged the fallen man on the sidewalk back toward them. He felt out of control. *Like I'm twelve years old again fighting for a spot on the basketball court.* Max released the Chechen he was dragging and noticed another Chechen lying motionless in the street.

A bystander timidly approached him and said, "The police are on their way." The man pointed to twenty or so onlookers. "We all saw what they tried to do."

With her arm around Sophie, Anna called Max over. "Max, this really is Sophie."

Suddenly, Max remembered Armando. He took several quick steps past the girls and raced back to the place where the van had been. But realized that it was too late.

He stopped and turned around to see that the three girls looked as afraid of him as they were of the Chechens.

He tried to calm himself, to figure out what had just happened, and then he realized that Anna didn't see, she didn't know.

Max couldn't come up with the words. "What?" she yelled at him.

He returned to the girls and said, "They have Armando."

"What do you mean? Where's Armando?"

"Just before I ran away from you, I saw one of the men we were following take a call, and in an instant both men took off running. You were off to the side, looking at something. I had to follow them. I yelled to you, but I had to stay up with the men. When I rounded the corner over there"—Max pointed at the entrance to the park, "I saw three men grab Sophie, so I fought them to free her. Then I noticed Armando up there a ways." Max pointed in the other direction and said, "He was fighting two men next to a van. I ran for him, but was too late. They threw him into the van and raced away. You saw the rest."

Elisa said, "I saw the whole thing, and that's exactly what happened. I was screaming the whole time. Those men were trying to kidnap this girl when another man ran to save her. He fought off two men, and she was able to get the bag off her head and get away."

"Who are you two?" asked Sophie in a soft voice.

Anna looked at Sophie. "We are your sister and brother, and we have been looking for you."

Max said, "The man who came to your rescue is Armando. He is Anna's, your sister's, boyfriend."

"You are my sister? You are my brother? How? I don't have any ... I don't ... ."

Anna replied first. "It's true, Sophie. We're your family." Anna pulled her close.

Eliza lifted her face to the sky and mumbled a few words as several police cars rushed to the scene, blaring their two-note, hi-lo sirens. They roped off the area.

Max said to Anna, "Call Bock now. We don't have time for this. We have to find Armando."

Anna let go of Sophie and quickly retrieved her phone.

The police had a man in custody. There was a paramedic team working on the Chechen in the street. The police who surrounded them were taking statements from the bystanders.

———◦◦◦———

A few hours ago I was sleeping under a log, all alone in this world, without an ounce of hope. Now I have a brother, a sister, and a friend. Sophie kept her thoughts to herself as she looked around at the chaos. She wasn't sure what would happen next.

Anna said to Max as she put her phone away, "Bock is close, and he's on his way." She turned to Sophie. "We'll explain everything to you soon. Max and I found out about each other only a few days ago. We have been frantic to find you." Anna pulled Sophie into her arms. "Everything is going to be alright. We are here and are going to take care of you."

A Munich city police officer joined them and started asking questions in the German language. Sophie remained silent. Elisa stepped in and gave a complete explanation to the officer.

Max said to Elisa, "Tell them about Armando."

"They said they already have that information from talking to the witnesses."

"Tell them the men are Chechen mobsters, and they were trying to take Sophie when Armando stepped in."

Elisa had just started with the explanation when Herman Bock ducked under the crime scene tape surrounding them. He flashed his ID to the officer in charge and began talking to him in German.

Anna said to Sophie, "Are you okay? Do you understand that we're here and won't ever leave you? You are safe now."

Sophie just looked at Anna's face, without speaking.

Bock said to Max and Anna, "The police have a good idea about what happened here. They may want an explanation from you later. One of the bystanders was able to get the plate number of the van. The police have already run the number and got nothing. As I told you two days ago, I have a team at two locations where the Chechens are known to congregate. The police have put out an all-points dispatch to the entire Munich police department regarding the black van. That's our best hope right now, but if we don't get something really soon, that lead will be worthless."

Bock said, "Why don't you take her back to your hotel." He motioned to and spoke in German to the officer in charge, then said to Max, "They'll assign two officers to stay with you at the hotel until we get this figured out."

Chapter DD
Munich, Germany
(Same day)

THE GIRLS SAT IN SILENCE, TIED TO EACH OTHER IN THEIR CHAIRS FOR hours. When Lara heard a door open, all the girls sat up straight. Two men walked toward them, each one holding a glass half full of a clear liquid. One of the men gave the drink to the first girl in line, and the other man gave it to the girl at the other end of the line. Both girls drank the contents of the plastic cup.

The men watched the girls swallow the liquid and then left the room through the same door they had entered.

The girl that Lara knew looked at her and scrunched her shoulders up, as if to say, *What should we do?* She looked back at her, but didn't respond to her with any expression. A few minutes later, the girls at both ends of the line started to act a little funny. They looked around, giggling as if they didn't have a care in the world. They were still giggling when the same two men returned, again carrying a small cup of liquid. The men walked over to the girls sitting next to the giggling girls. They watched them drink the liquid. The men then untied the first girls at each end of the line and walked them out of the room. The rest of the girls just sat there in silence. Lara expected to hear screams.

How am I going to do this? What are they going to do to me? Lara thought everyone there must be wondering the same thing.

About ten minutes later two different men came in and escorted the first girls back to their seat. They gave the third girls in line a cup of their evil potion and then put their hand out to the girls on happy juice in the number-two positions.

The happy girls accepted the men's hands as if they were being asked to dance. The men escorted the number-two girls out the door.

201

They don't look too bad, Lara thought as she observed the first girls sitting in their chair. They weren't the giggly girls who had left. They didn't look beaten up. *They looked different than before, though. I guess we will all change. We all want to stay alive and stay away from the docks. I'll have to do what they tell me.*

Soon the door opened again, and the men escorted the number twos back to their seat. The men gave the girls in the fourth seat their drink and politely escorted the giggling number three girls out of the room. The girl Lara knew was in the number five seat. She looked terrified. Lara met her gaze and tried to give her some reassurance without saying a word. *This is getting close. Stay alive, stay away from the docks. I don't have a choice. None of us do.*

Chapter Thirty-One

Munich, Germany

(Same day)

ARMANDO WOKE. HE WAS TAPED TO A CHAIR. *I MUST HAVE PASSED OUT FROM that last blow.* The hood was still over his head. The wet burlap reeked of sweat and desperation. He tasted the blood leaking from his nose. He felt weak from the beating they gave him. He heard men talking but couldn't understand a word.

His back and ribs hurt—a painful reminder of his time in the swamp. His tongue surveyed the inside of his mouth. *My teeth are all there. Good.*

What's next? What are they going to do to me next? He twisted his wrists to challenge the bindings. *No slack. No options. It was a good run. My life was good.* Armando thought about his parents and sister. Then about the first time he saw Anna on the dance floor in that small bar in La Crucecita. He pictured her hourglass silhouette sauntering away from their bliss the first morning they were back together on their boat. In spite of his situation, he smiled when he remembered her dazzling smile when she turned to him with those big blue eyes. *Is this Okay?* she had asked him as she held up a small bikini. What a sight. What an amazing sight. The thoughts of her soft touch and their love-making eased his pain. *Anna now has Max and Sophie in her life. She won't be alone. Yeah,* he said to himself, *I'd do it all again.*

His smile died when he heard a man yelling, again in the language he couldn't understand.

<hr>

"There were six of you there," Silvio said with an angry voice. "Khizir is in the hospital, Sulim is in jail, the girl escaped, and you bring me back this guy. What the fuck happened? Why did you bring him here? What are we going to do with him?"

"Boss, he knew her name. He called out to her, and we found this picture in his pocket." He handed the picture Armando had of Sophie to Silvio. Silvio looked at the picture. "His driver's license is from Mexico. He had plenty of money and credit cards in his wallet. Not what you'd expect from a guy that looks like he's one of the park's beggars."

"What about that other guy, the guy that took care of you pussies all by himself? I knew that Aslan should have been on this one."

"We have no idea who that other guy was. He was bigger and stronger than even Aslan, and it was like he was on drugs or something. He looked crazy, like he was fighting for his own life, not just helping some street girl."

"This was supposed to be easy. You say ten to twenty people saw you throw this guy in the van. That's a big problem. With that many witnesses, the police won't look the other way this time. They'll have to do something.

Silvio paced around the empty warehouse, talking to himself, while ten or twelve of his men watched him. They all looked very nervous.

"We'll wait until Aslan gets back," Silvio said. "And give him a chance at this guy. We'll see what he can get out of him before we put him down."

Silvio walked to Armando and slapped him on the side of the head. "The clock is ticking for you, sport," he said in English. "Aslan is on his way. You better figure out how to talk before he starts in on you … tic, tic, tic."

Chapter EE
Munich, Germany
[Same day)

TWO MEN WALKED INTO THE ROOM ESCORTING THE NUMBER THREE-SEAT girls. They gave the girls in the number-five seats the drink and then moved on to the smiling girls in the number four seats. Lara watched her friend drink her drink. *What an orderly way to say good-bye to my innocence,* she thought. She counted three more girls between her and her fate.

Chapter Thirty-Two

Munich, Germany

(Same day)

"SOPHIE, WHAT ARE YOU THINKING ABOUT?" ASKED ANNA, WITH MAX at her side. The four of them sat around a small, round table in Anna's hotel room.

Sophie looked down at the table, feeling unsure about how to move forward with this change in her life, with these new people, these Americans. *I'm an American, not a German. My mother wasn't a crack whore. She was a good mother who would have loved me. My father was a good man. All this time I've been living someone else's lie. But Max and Anna have been, too. They came for me as soon as they knew. Armando saved me from that van, saved me from Silvio.*

Sophie looked at Elisa for comfort, then back at Anna and Max. "I don't know what to say except that I still can't believe it's all true—for the first time in my life." She looked up to Anna, with tears, to make sure Anna saw her sincerity. "For the first time in my life, I don't feel afraid. There is no way I could possibly explain that horror." She slowly lowered her head to catch her breath, wanting to put her hood up. *It's happening again.* She was having trouble getting her words out.

"This morning … " She looked at Anna. "I saw you running in the park. I heard you call my name. I peeked over a dead tree as you ran past me and softly said out loud, 'I am here.' That was the first time I'd spoken out loud in months. I thought I was crazy, like the crazy men in the park who want to hurt me."

Sophie couldn't hold back the years of fear and loneliness any longer. She buried her face in her hands and just let go. The release of emotion she felt overwhelmed her. She couldn't catch her breath. Her thin, dirty face was smeared with tears and snot.

"I'm so sorry!" she cried. She looked at Anna again with a distorted face that only family should see. "Please don't mistake my silence for anything other than confusion and surprise. She took a deep breath. "This is … the happiest day of my life." She grabbed Max's hand, then Anna's.

Anna took Max's hand, closing the circle. They sat that way for some time, saying nothing.

Finally, Sophie said, "What about your friend Armando?" They released their hands.

"I don't know." Max replied, "But we have to do something. Call Bock again, Anna. See what those guys are doing."

She made the call, talked to Bock for a few minutes, and then looked angry. She started to throw her phone across the room, but held her fire. "They haven't done a damn thing. According to Bock, the police are absolutely no help. He said his men have been calling all their underground contacts, but no one has any information about where the Chechens are holed up. They—"

A loud knock on the door interrupted her tantrum. Max showed the girls the palm of his and walked to the door. He bent down and looked through the peephole, then opened the door.

Reed Jackson and two of his men walked in. The two other men stood silently off to the side. Jackson said, "I talked to Herman Bock yesterday. He said he doesn't have a good feeling about how things are going over here, so we decided to leave right away. It's a good thing we did. Bock filled me in. We don't have much time."

He looked at Sophie, whose face was still wet and red, "You must be Sophie. Nice to see you've been found and you're safe, but Armando is in deep trouble. We have to find him right now. I don't think we can rely on anyone else but the people in this room to accomplish that." Jackson looked at Sophie again. "I can see you're upset, but we'll have to deal with that later. Do you have any clue about where these guys may have taken Armando, any little clue at all?"

"I do not. I've been approached by a man named Silvio a couple of times, but it was always in the park. I know men just like him have been trying to find me the last few days."

Jackson looked at Elisa, sitting quietly off to the side. "Who is that?"

Elisa said, "I'm a nun and a friend of Sophie."

Jackson looked back at Max and Anna. "When was the last time you talked with Armando?"

Anna replied, "We met him this morning at the Chinese Tower in the park. He spent all of last night in the park, by himself, looking for Sophie. We know that he talked to one of the homeless men in the park. We traded phones, and he was planning to go to the north end of the park today after he bought a blanket and sweatshirt. We believe it was totally by accident that he spotted Sophie this afternoon."

Max said, "We've noticed there are Chechen men working in pairs. They're easy to pick out of a crowd because they look and dress alike."

Jackson said, "Go back. What's this about the phone?"

"He has my phone because his phone was almost out of juice," Anna replied.

Jackson motioned to his men. "We can locate him by using your phone. We'll go get him."

Jackson stopped just before walking out the door and looked back at Elisa. "Better start praying, Sister."

Chapter FF

Munich, Germany

(Same day)

LARA HEARD THE DOOR OPEN AGAIN AND WATCHED THE SAME ROUTINE work its way closer to her place in line. One of the men had just offered his hand to her happy friend when a commotion started in a different part of the building.

The men talked to each other in their strange language. Another man ran into the room and yelled something. One of the captors looked at the girls and said, "Tie yourselves back up and keep your mouths shut!" The men ran out of the room and slammed the door behind them.

Chapter Thirty-Three

Munich, Germany

(Same day)

ARMANDO HEARD A DOOR OPEN, AND SEVERAL MORE MEN WALKED INTO the room. Their muffled talk soon turned into a shouting match, but he still couldn't understand a word.

——◊◊◊——

Aslan marched through the door with two more men. Silvio told him what had happened earlier in the day. Aslan scowled at the hooded Armando. Silvio explained that their captive was from Mexico. They had beaten him until he passed out, but he still would only speak Spanish.

Aslan said to Silvio, "Why don't you call Ramon? He speaks Spanish. He's at the club right now. But what do you hope to get out of him anyway? He looks like one of the park's bums."

"Hey, talk to these guys about why they brought him here. That wasn't my idea. But he did have a picture of the girl in his pocket, so there's some connection."

Aslan just glared at him.

Silvio didn't say another word. He pulled out his phone and called the club.

——◊◊◊——

Jackson, Geronimo, and Cochise walked away from their car. They were one block from where the GPS tracker had located Anna's phone. It was still light out, but they couldn't wait. Jackson thought that every second counted. He couldn't think of any reason for the Chechen mobsters to let Armando live. Jackson and his men quickly walked around the outside of the one-story building. The place looked deserted. Chains secured the front door, and the windows were boarded up. In back of the building, off the alley, they found a loading dock where the black van was parked, along with several other vehicles.

The men from The Agency had no weapons and no plan, but they had their advanced training. Jackson knew their training was worth twenty men with weapons, especially mobsters, who thought they were tough guys.

Jackson gave Geronimo and Cochise quick instructions in the back alley. His men jogged to the front of the building. Jackson waited exactly three minutes and then marched directly through the back door, without knocking and without hesitation.

He walked past several surprised-looking men. Armando was on the other side of the open warehouse. Jackson nodded to the Chechens, acting like someone who was supposed to be there. He reached Armando, took out a knife from his back pocket, and cut the tape off Armando's wrists and ankles. He lifted the hood off Armando's blood-caked head to find a terrified-looking man. Jackson could see he had suffered a brutal beating. Jackson leaned close to Armando and whispered, "It's me, Jackson. Are you okay? I came to get you out of here. Don't get off this chair until I tell you to."

Armando nodded.

Jackson turned around and calmly put his knife back into his pocket. One of the men whispered something to another man. That man got up and walked away, to the front of the building. There were now ten men in the room. They all took a few steps toward Jackson.

Jackson looked at the man who had given the orders and recognized him from the pictures Bock sent him. He said in a calm voice, "I came here to get my man. I don't want any trouble. I couldn't care less who you are or what you do. I understand there was a mix-up earlier today and my man got caught in the middle."

Silvio looked at Jackson and took a step toward him. "He's not your man now. He caused us some problems. Someone's gotta pay."

Jackson met Silvio's gaze. "I didn't come here to negotiate."

Silvio laughed and then nodded to three of his men. They rushed at Jackson.

Jackson landed a quick hard jab on the chin of the first Chechen, knocking him flat on his back. Then the other two came in at the same time. Jackson ducked under a roundhouse swing from one of the men, and side-kicked him in the ass. Spinning and staying low, he threw out a leg and swept the third man's feet from under him. The third man crashed down onto his back next to the first man, at the same time the second man crashed into some metal barrels.

Silvio motioned for his other men to stand down.

Jackson looked at Silvio and said, "That man you sent for your weapons isn't coming back."

In their native language Silvio said to Aslan, "Who is this guy?"

Aslan swaggered a few steps away and picked up a four-foot piece of metal pipe. The other men followed his lead.

Silvio's men spread out in a half circle in front of Jackson. Silvio grimaced at Jackson and said in English, "I repeat, he's our package."

Jackson stood his ground in a ready position. He eyed each of the thugs and said, "Come and get him."

The Chechen men looked at one another and waited for Silvio's next order.

Jackson said, "Any weapon you use on me will be used on you. No one here is badly hurt yet." Jackson nodded at Armando and said, "He is of no value to you. We're going to walk out of here. I'll be out of your life forever."

Silvio said to Aslan, "What do you think?"

Aslan replied, "This whole thing started with a skinny street girl. We have twenty of them just like her back in the room."

"But we paid extra for this one. We'll have to …"

Jackson turned to Armando and said, "Follow me."

Armando stood up, got his balance, and grabbed his wallet and other valuables off the crate next to him.

Silvio and Aslan were still talking when Jackson took his first steps straight into the teeth of the group with Armando on his heels. He took slow, deliberate steps, ready for action at any moment. The half-circle of Chechen men parted to let them through. Jackson pulled Armando in front of him, and they headed straight to the door.

Just before Jackson closed the door behind them, he looked at Silvio and said, "This ends here."

Chapter Thirty-Four

Munich, Germany

(Same day)

Cochise downshifted to slow their Audi S6 as they approached the intersection. He took a quick look in both directions. No traffic. He floored the gas pedal and raced to the next intersection, where he turned left and roared off again. Soon the speedometer needle edged past 100 kilometers an hour. Cochise hurtled through stop signs for the next three blocks. Then he braked and downshifted and squealed into a right-hand turn.

Jackson and Armando sat in the backseat, trying to stay on their side of the seat as the centrifugal force of the turns tugged them from one side to the other.

Jackson looked through the back window to see if any vehicles were following them. He saw none. "Okay, I think we're good," he said. "Drive normally for a few blocks, and find a place to pull off the road where we can monitor what's going on behind us. We'll wait for Geronimo's report."

Cochise slowed the car as they entered a commercial section. He scanned both sides of the street. He turned the Audi into a corner drugstore parking lot and quickly backed it into a parking place where they could see the traffic and where they had escape routes in two directions. He left the vehicle running while the three of them surveyed the field of view in front of them.

Armando looked at Jackson and said, "What the hell happened back there? I can't believe they just let us walk right out of there. You're Jackson, from the bank in San Francisco—right?"

"Yes, I'm Reed Jackson, and we got lucky back there. Are you sure you're alright?"

"Yeah, I think so. Those guys beat me unconscious, trying to get me to talk. I've been through a lot worse ... not that long ago. I was sure they planned to kill me. Still can't believe we walked out of there."

Cochise looked at them in the rearview mirror. "What *did* happen back there?"

Armando told Cochise all about it.

Cochise chuckled and said, "Yeah, I think I know what you're talking about. Me and the other guys have seen it before, we call what you saw 'Jackson's crystal-clear persuasion.' He chuckled again.

Jackson said to Armando, "We'll get you back to the hotel and back to your friends as soon as we get the all-clear from Geronimo. Thanks to you, everyone is safe and all together, but they're really worried about you. We heard the story. You saved Sophie from those guys the way you stepped in." Cochise added, "We'll call that Armando's crystal-clear rescue." He chuckled once more.

Armando said, "The last thing I saw was Max beating the crap out of three or four of those guys, and Anna jumped in and grabbed Sophie. You're sure everyone is okay?"

Jackson said, "Yes, they are. Do you want to call them now or surprise them when we get back?"

"I better call them, and tell them we're on our way." He tried to use Anna's phone, but found he was shaking too much to operate the small buttons. He struggled to make his hands work the simple machine. Jackson could see he was having problems, so he placed his hands over the phone and said, "I got this. It's going to take you a while after what you've been through. I have Max's number in my phone."

Armando resisted a little, but Jackson came back in with some more of his crystal clear persuasion, "It's okay. There's no shame in letting yourself come down a little." He looked into Armando's eyes and went on, "This hero stuff isn't all it's cracked up to be."

Jackson was just about to make the call when his phone vibrated, showing an incoming message.

Jackson said, "Geronimo says no one followed us. They're loading up a bunch of stuff from the building into their trucks." Jackson spoke to himself as he texted Geronimo: "Video their actions and follow them." He nodded at Cochise. Cochise put the S6 into first gear, and the vehicle rolled into the street.

Jackson called Max and handed the phone to Armando. Armando waited, and then said, "Max, it's me, Armando. I'm safe. Reed Jackson got me out of there in one piece, and we're on our way back—should be just a few minutes away." Armando heard a scream in the background, and Max said, "That was Anna. She appears to be happy to hear you're safe, but now she's crying for some reason. Good to hear you're okay. See you soon."

Chapter GG

Munich, Germany

(Same day)

TIME TICKED WAY. LARA SAT QUIETLY IN HER SEAT. SHE COULD HEAR LOUD voices coming from the rooms surrounding them. *What was happening? Maybe the police have come to rescue us.*

One of the men came through the door and said in broken German, "We have change of plan. We leave soon. Keep mouths shut."

Please let there be police outside.

Chapter HH
Munich, Germany
(Same day)

T HE GIRLS HAD BARELY ENOUGH ROOM IN THE TRUCK TO STAND. THEY were jostled back and forth in the dark confines as they rumbled through the streets.

Finally, they stopped, and the door on the back of the truck rolled up. They all squinted in the bright sunlight. Before them stood a warehouse that looked deserted. Their captors quickly unloaded boxes and moving equipment from another truck and carted it all into the building.

The girls were still tied together. They walked down a ramp from the back of their truck and were led into the warehouse. One of the men opened the door of a semi-trailer without wheels, which sat off to one side of the big, open building. Men herded the girls into the trailer and slammed the door. Lara heard the scraping of metal on metal as the latch locked them inside. It was pitch black in there. She was cold. All girls were cold. They huddled, they were terrified and shaking with fear of the door opening again.

I wish I had my jeans on. Now what? Most of the girls were crying again. *Who can blame them?* Still, no one said a word. There was nothing to say. The girls were accepting their fate. Lara had questions, but there weren't any good answers. All answers ended with her new life—a life of survival and obedience. Survival was her priority, obedience was her key. *Survival meant doing what they tell me to do. Be prepared when it's my turn, no hesitation. I have to do what they tell me. I don't have a choice. This is my new life. I don't want to end up down at the docks.* Lara cringed. *I have to get an A-plus. I have to accept my role when they come for me.* The girl she was tied to on her right was crying hysterically. *Time to grow up.*

Chapter Thirty-Five

Munich, Germany
(Same day)

Tʜᴇ ᴡᴀʀᴍ ᴡᴀᴛᴇʀ ꜰᴇʟᴛ ɢᴏᴏᴅ ᴛᴏ Aʀᴍᴀɴᴅᴏ. *I had two days of blood and grime on me. Better lather up again.* The jet sprays from the shower hurt in the same places the soap stung. *Hard to tell which wounds were new and which ones were from the swamp.*

He looked down at his bruised and cut arms, body, and legs. *That's about as good as I can do for now.* Armando closed his eyes and put his head back under the warm water. The solitude in the cozy confines of the shower felt even better. Knowing that all this might finally be behind them was beyond description.

"Everything okay in there?" Anna said, waking Armando from his thoughts.

"Yep, all finished up in here and good as new." Armando turned off the water and slid the shower curtain aside. There stood his lovely Anna, but she wasn't alone. Beside her was a short, elderly man holding a black duffle bag. "This is Dr. Schmidt, the hotel doctor. He's going to check you out to make sure you don't need to go to the hospital."

Armando growled a little and said, "Alright, but at least hand me a towel."

Anna snickered and said, "I'll leave you two boys alone." She walked out of the bathroom and closed the door behind her.

Max said, "How's our man doing?"

"Not too bad, considering how he looked when he went in there. The doctor will patch him up."

Jackson and Cochise sat at the small kitchenette table at one side of the room. Sophie and Elisa sat on the couch, and Max was sprawled on one of the living room chairs. Max said to Anna, "Well, little sister, now what?"

"I guess we should go back to the States as soon as Armando is able."

"I've been trying to figure out what your best options are going forward," Jackson said. "Since I know the most about all of you, I'm in a unique position to offer some ideas and make a plan for a way you can start your new lives together."

Anna said, "Great. We're open to hearing any suggestions you have."

"Good," Jackson said, "But, let's wait for Armando to join us.

Eventually, Armando came out of the bathroom, wearing only shorts and twenty to thirty different-sized white wound dressings on his face and body. Max and Cochise eyed each other and snickered at the way he looked. The doctor followed him out of the bathroom and said, "I had to put stitches in several of his wounds. They will need to be taken out after seven days. I don't even want to know what this man has been through, but he needs a lot of healing time. I've left some dressings and antiseptic cream. The dressings should be changed every day. He's going to heal up fine if he takes it easy for a couple of weeks. If you need anything else, contact the front desk. They know how to get in touch of me." The doctor headed to the door.

Jackson stopped him and put a wad of bills into his hand. "We appreciate your help, but we don't want anyone else knowing our business. You follow?"

"Of course," the doctor replied, and then left the room. Jackson closed the door behind him.

"Now that we're all here," Jackson said, "I want to begin by emphasizing that we are all still in a great deal of danger. So don't let your guard down for one minute until we get out of Munich."

"Read you loud and clear," Max said.

"I have an option that you may want to consider. First of all, the four of you need to get out of town as soon as possible, but before you can do that, Sophie has to have a passport." He looked at Sophie and said, "Do you have your passport with you, or is it at the foster house?"

Sophie replied, "I don't have a passport, but I'm pretty sure they have my birth certificate."

"So that's where we need to start. I have some contacts at the U.S. Consulate General here in Munich. I'll go there first thing in the morning. The four of you can go as a group to the Eichmann house and get Sophie's birth certificate. We'll need that to get her a passport. Are you okay with that, Sophie?"

"I'd love to show up there with my family so those people know I do belong somewhere."

"Great. We'll get going first thing in the morning. Max, you call Allen Woods and bring him up to speed on Sophie and ask him if the four of you can spend some time with him. He can tell you everything he knows about your parents. I know quite a bit about Woods, and I can tell you he's in a class by himself."

Max said, "That's a great idea, Mr. Jackson. I'll call him after we're done here."

"Perfect. In the meantime, Cochise will go relieve Geronimo. We're going to keep our eyes on the Chechen gang until we leave."

Jackson's phone vibrated and he picked it up. "It's a message from Geronimo." "He wants us to watch a video of what's going on." Jackson looked at Anna and said, "Do you mind if I forward this text to you so we can see the video on your iPad?"

"Sure." She retrieved her iPad and sat down between Cochise and Jackson.

The video showed the Chechen mobsters carrying computers, furniture, and several heavy trunks that took two big men to lift from the same warehouse where they had held Armando prisoner. At least twenty men loaded everything into one of their big trucks. Then a man led a group of about twenty girls, all tied together, from the warehouse and shoved them into a small box truck with no windows.

Jackson, Cochise, and Anna didn't say a word as the second video started. This video showed a warehouse in a different location, where the Chechens unloaded the trucks, including the girls, who were tied together. Something bothered Anna that she couldn't put her finger on. It wasn't anything specific, but there was something in those videos that disturbed her even more than the sight of what the mobsters had done to Armando or the sight of the young girls.

When the video finished playing, Jackson turned his attention to the rest of the group. "There's another piece of this puzzle we need to tell you about. When we rescued Armando, we discovered a group of young girls held captive in one of the rooms of the warehouse. We can assume Sophie would have been in that room if you all hadn't saved her. This creates a dilemma for us. Can we just walk away from this atrocity? These Chechens men are a small part of a worldwide sex trade operation. This is their business.

"We have to ask ourselves, are we obligated to save the world every time we witness a wrongdoing? If we get involved in their business, there will be serious consequences. If they link any incursion into their business operation to any of us, we all will need a place to hide. According Herman Bock, the Chechen mobsters have the Munich police department under their thumb. So I'm not sure we can count on any help from them. Tomorrow, I'll review our options with the appropriate officials at the American Consulate, and we'll continue to monitor the Chechens.

"I suggest the four of you, or the five of you if Elisa takes part, stay in the hotel tonight and have dinner together. Maybe buy Sophie some new clothes and spoil her the way a big brother and sister should. We'll meet here again tomorrow morning. By then you should have had enough time to consider my suggestions, and we'll decide how we want to proceed."

Max said, "That sounds good, Mr. Jackson. Thanks again for all your help." Then he turned his attention to Cochise and said, "We haven't been properly introduced to you. What's your name?"

Cochise smiled, looked at Jackson, and then at Max again. "My friends call me Cochise. But you guys can call me … Cochise." He gave everyone a mischievous grin.

Max laughed and held out his hand. "I'm Max Tobin, nice to meet you. Do you guys want to join us for dinner?"

Jackson replied, "Thanks, but no. We have some things to do." He and Cochise took off.

———※———

As Jackson pulled out his room card he said to Cochise, "Before you go we need to figure out what we're going to do about those girls." He opened the door and motioned for Cochise to go in first. Jackson said, "What are your thoughts?"

Cochise replied, "Geronimo and I saw the girls sitting in a line of chairs, tied up to each other. They looked really young and terrified. We probably could have gotten them out of there pretty easy. We only saw four or five men in that front area of the building. The two we took care of went down easy."

"There were at least twelve men where I was," Jackson said. "Maybe more like fifteen. If we save these girls, they'll find twenty more just like them. We know this is a worldwide problem. We can't be responsible for every crime we see." Jackson walked to the window. "If we open that can of worms, we'll never get that lid back on it. There are too many variables. Too many things can go wrong. We'd have to have eyes in the back of our heads for the rest of our lives if one of their men goes down. You know damn well they're all related to each other one way or another. These people's lives are based on revenge. They'll find out who we are, including the Tobin clan, and even the score. There's no way we want that responsibility." Jackson shook his head.

"We know the police are on the take, so no help there. I could talk to an Interpol connection I have tomorrow when I go to the Consulate, but we both know they won't do anything without a week's worth of fighting the courts for a warrant. Have to assume these gangsters have eyes and ears all over the court system. They'd be tipped off and long gone before we had a chance to do anything."

Cochise said, "I hear ya, boss."

Jackson said, "It would be just plain stupid for us to get involved any more than we are now. Those girls aren't our problem. They're not our clients. Bad shit happens to good people all the time. If their own police won't step in, why should we?"

Cochise had worked with Jackson for a long time. Despite Jackson's logical thinking, he knew how this conversation was going to end. He said, "You want me to call in some of our other guys, or are you going to do that?"

"I'll call them. Go spell Geronimo. This doesn't mean we're doing anything, though."

Cochise smiled and said, "I'm on it."

Before Cochise got out the door, Jackson said, "Contact me if you need anything. I'll see you in a few hours. I'll figure out something."

"I know you will, boss."

Chapter Thirty-Six

Munich, Germany

(Same day)

ELISA WAS CONCERNED ABOUT SOPHIE, BUT SHE COULD SEE SHE WAS IN good hands now. She wasn't sure if she should get any deeper into their affairs. Her sisters had warned her about getting too close to people during a mission.

She looked at Sophie and said, "It's time for me to get back to the church. I have a lot of duties there, and my sisters are probably worried about me."

Sophie said, "When will I see you again?"

Elisa, wanting to distance herself from her first successful mission, replied, "You know where I'll be … stop in anytime … you know I can always use your help." Before she left, she said good-bye to Anna, Max, and Armando. "Good luck. I'll be praying for you."

―――◦◦◦――

The four left in the room sat down at the small table. "It's so nice to have you with us, Sophie," Max said. "I won't feel like a third wheel around these two." He looked at Armando across the table. "I have to say, brotha, you look like shit. You should try to go a week or two without—"

Anna kicked him under the table. "Ouch! He knows I'm kidding—just trying to lighten things up."

Anna said to Sophie, "How well do you know Elisa?"

"I just met her a couple of days ago. She was nice to me."

Max and I met only a few days ago in San Francisco. That's when we found out about our parents. The bank that managed our trust fund had been intentionally keeping us apart so they could maintain control of our money. We put a halt to that scam. Max and I don't know much about each other, but we know one thing—we'll never be alone again, and that includes you, Sophie."

Sophie took both of Anna's hands in her own and smiled at her.

Armando said to Max, "What do you think about that Allen Woods guy?"

"Who is Allen Woods?" Sophie said.

"He was a friend of our parents a long time ago," Max replied. He told her the story of Woods's relationship with their parents. Max said, "When Mr. Woods discovered what the bank was doing to us, he started to look for us. About a week ago he found me and told me our story. We believe the bank hired men to kill him, just like they tried to kill Armando."

Then Max turned to Armando. "I agree with Mr. Jackson. We should reach out to Mr. Woods in California. He should be part of our family, and that would be a good place for us to get to know each other." Max looked at Anna and said, "Why don't you help Sophie get cleaned up then take her down to one of the clothing stores in the lobby and buy her some new clothes to wear to dinner. We'll meet you later in the hotel restaurant. Get dressed, Armando. We'll belly up to the bar and wait for these two."

"Good idea. He grinned at Anna and Sophie. "You girls have fun."

Chapter Thirty-Seven

Munich, Germany

(Same day)

AFTER A FEW DAYS, STEFAN HAD ALMOST FORGOTTEN ABOUT THAT CRAZY night in the bar, about seeing his good friends and drinking too much, and about the incident in the men's room.

He and his partner were on their way to a club that had called to report a disturbance. The dispatcher had told them a group of adolescents there wouldn't leave. When they arrived, the woman who had called ran up to Stefan's partner and said, "They just ran out the back door." Just as Stefan and his partner started to head in that direction, the woman clamped onto Stefan's arm and said, "Will you stay with me?" Stefan looked at his partner for help. He grinned at Stefan and took off toward the back of the club.

The woman dropped her flustered expression and handed Stefan an envelope. "My boss wants to talk to you in that booth right over there at midnight tonight." She pointed to a booth with a large, round, dimly lit sconce on the wall behind the booth. Stefan looked at the woman. She said, "Be there at midnight, or you will regret it." She walked away.

Stefan looked at the envelope. He didn't want to open it. *I should just put it on the table, unopened, and walk away. What's in here? Wait. I know what's in it.*

Chapter II
Munich, Germany
(The same day)

THE GIRLS HAD BEEN LEFT ALONE FOR HOURS WITHOUT FOOD AND WATER. One of the girls whispered, "I can't hold it any longer," and then everyone's seal broke. It was dark in there, and they didn't want to take the chance of sitting in the filth. So they stood, said nothing, smelled their own waste, and shook with fear.

Occasionally, they heard a commotion outside the confines of their metal cell. At first they were terrified someone would open the door. Later, Lara thought, *I hope someone will open the door, take me out of here, and do what they want with me. What a terrible thought ... I just want to get out of here. What if they just leave us in here to die? Why did they move us in such a hurry? If they left us here, no one would know.*

Chapter Thirty-Eight

Munich, Germany

(Just after midnight, the next day)

A T MIDNIGHT SILVIO SAW STEFAN WALK THROUGH THE FRONT DOOR OF the club wearing civilian clothes that were soaking wet. "That downpour must have caught him unprepared," Silvio said to Aslan. "He probably didn't want to be late. Look at him, he's upset. He looks scared. Let me handle this."

No objection from Aslan. His job didn't involve talking. Ramon sat on the other side of Silvio. He said, "That's my cue. I'll leave you guys to it."

Stefan looked dazed as he tried to stand up a little taller to find the round, lit sconce. He had his hands in his pockets and his head down as he approached.

Silvio and Aslan were in the middle of a whispered conversation. They didn't look up or acknowledge Stefan. He stood there waiting for a while, and then said, "You guys want to talk to me?"

Silvio kept talking to Aslan for a few seconds more, then slowly looked up and said, "Stefan Jaeger, sergeant in the Munich police department, father of a young boy, and husband to a beautiful wife. What did you think of the pictures? Did you know that girl is fifteen years old?"

Stefan looked even more upset. "What do you guys want?" He put the envelope on the table.

"That's all yours," Silvio said.

"I don't want the pictures or the money." Stefan pushed the envelope toward Silvio. "Why are you doing this? It was a set up. Nothing happened, and you guys know it."

Silvio said, "Hey, that wasn't my dick in her hand."

Stefan closed his eyes and hung his head.

"Stefan, your life is going to change. You should consider the rest of your life as your new life. You should understand that I now own you. If you want to keep those pictures out of sight, you will do what I say, when I say it. If you hesitate or don't comply in any way, those pictures will surface. And when you go home to try and explain yourself, you will go home to an empty house. Your wife will make money for me in Poland, Turkey, or maybe Hong Kong. Your son will be doing the same thing, but in a different location. And your father … He will take a bullet in the head—fired by one of your good friends, who we also own. If you think this isn't fair, you are right. But it is your new life."

Stefan didn't say a word. The blood drained from his face.

Silvio knew he had him. He knew he owned him. He handed Stefan some pictures of a woman on all fours on what looked like a coffee table. An older Asian man was giving it to her from behind. A group of men stood around them, waiting for their turn. Stefan recognized the woman. She was one of his co-worker's ex-wife.

Silvio said, "Lynnette didn't divorce Rinehart as you were told. Rinehart hesitated when we called him. Now his wife makes money for me doing strange things with strange men, very strange men. His two young daughters are next in line if Rinehart hesitates again. They're pretty. We may take them anyway."

Silvio could see Stefan's mind racing as he continued to look at the pictures of Lynette. He said, "Your wife is much prettier, and young boys are a big hit in some places. Remember, Stefan, from now on you will do what we say, without hesitation. Do you understand me? Do you want to see pictures of your wife on a table like that in Taiwan?"

Stefan said he understood.

"Very good. Now I'm going to give you a test. If one of my men calls your mobile number and asks you for information about an investigation, or asks you to go to the airport and pick up a package, or asks you to put a bullet in some politician's head, what will you say?"

"I'll say tell me more."

"Perfect. I'm glad we have an understanding. I know we'll be good partners. Now pick up that envelope. Spend that money on your beautiful family. We'll be in touch."

Stefan picked up the envelope, turned around, and walked away.

Stefan walked out of the club and into the rain. After several blocks of brisk walking, he jogged across a dark street, opened the back door of a nondescript black sedan, and slid into the backseat. He said, "Did you get it?"

The man sitting next to him replied, "Yes, we did, and we have confirmation the video was a success, as well. Nice job. Your dad will be proud of you."

Stefan knew from the start that the Chechens must have had someone on the inside, because how else would they have known he was planning to meet his friends that night for his birthday? They waited for him. Since he knew there were enemies behind the gate, he said nothing to any of the Munich police. Instead, he went straight to his uncle at the BKA. The BKA had been trying to get something on these Chechen mobsters for over a year, but only found dead ends and dead bodies. The sting tonight had been set up perfectly and pulled off with true German efficiency.

Chapter Thirty-Nine

Munich, Germany

(The next morning)

MAX GOT OUT OF THE FRONT SEAT OF THE BLACK MERCEDES TAXI. ANNA, Armando, and Sophie slid out of the backseat. The four of them stood in a line looking at Sophie's secondary school. Sophie said, "Thanks for letting me have one last look at this place before we go get my birth certificate."

They looked through a chain-link fence at the redbrick building and its two clock towers, which rose about twenty feet above the top of the roof. It looked like a prison. The clock towers looked like guard towers.

Sophie said, "This would have been my final year, a time of passage for me and other kids my age."

Noises came from inside the building, indicating that school was in session. Anna looked at Sophie, trying to understand her thoughts while Sophie gazed ahead.

Anna said, "Any good memories for you in there?"

"No … just memories. I never really felt like I belonged here. I did have one friend, though. She and I had a couple of classes together, and we were both on the track team. She was always really nice to me."

"Was that Lara?" Anna said. "I met her a couple of days ago at the diner where she works. We were hoping she could help us find you. She seemed like a really nice girl."

Sophie smiled. "You met her? She lives with a foster family, too."

Then it hit Anna. *Was that Lara in the video? I didn't get that good of a look, but the uniform, it was the uniform. Don't say anything. When we get back, I'll watch the video again.*

Sophie turned and said, "Let's go. The Eichmann house is only four or five blocks this way." She led the way.

Sophie's walk home from school took her through a residential neighborhood, except for when she had to cross a busier street that had commercial buildings on both sides. As they approached the intersection, Sophie stopped and looked ahead. Her actions caught the attention of everyone. Two men were having a heated argument. Anna thought Sophie looked like an experienced hunter who sensed danger.

Armando noticed that, too. "Hey, that looks like one of those Chechens who was beating on me."

"Yes," Sophie said. "He's the man who approached me first in the park."

Max said, "That's our man Eichmann he's fighting with. I'm going to take care of both of them right now."

Max started forward. Sophie grabbed his arm. "No, Max, not now—don't give them anything." *Be the rabbit.* "We have the advantage. Let's stay out of sight and see what happens next."

The four of them moved off the sidewalk and watched as the two men continued their argument. Silvio poked Eichmann's chest a couple of times to make a point.

Armando said, "Did you get any of that, Sophie?"

"They're arguing about money, but I didn't catch any of the details. I can't believe those two know each other. I wonder what those beasts are up to."

Silvio got into a car that raced away, and Eichmann slithered into a pub. Sophie said, "Come on, the house is just a couple of more blocks."

Max said, "Are you sure you don't want me to go in there and confront that man?"

"No, thanks—I never want to see him again. This whole place really creeps me out."

After they had walked two blocks, Sophie stopped and pointed. "There's the house. Not sure how we should do this, though."

They all looked at her.

"Let me think a minute. Mrs. Eichmann should be home. I'll go up to the door alone. You guys stand over there so you can hear how she treats me. I'll try to get her to talk in English so you can understand what she says. Then

I want you to come up the stairs to the porch, and I'll introduce you. This will be good."

Sophie rang the bell, and a few seconds later Mrs. Eichmann opened the door. She looked stunned when she realized it was Sophie standing in front of her. Sophie's appearance was quite a bit different, but eventually it sunk in. She yelled at Sophie in German, "What are you doing here? Are you looking for trouble?

Casually, Sophie replied in English. "No, Mrs. Eichmann, I don't want any trouble. I just wanted you to meet my brother and sister. Anna approached first, then Max with his towering presence. They walked up the stairs together.

"Well, well, this is quite a surprise," Mrs. Eichmann said in a different tone of voice. "We've been worried sick about you, Sophie. You gave us quite a fright running off like that."

Anna stepped up to her. "We came here to get her personal effects, specifically her birth certificate."

"Of course, anything I can do to help Sophie. We didn't know Sophie had any family."

Max said, "Neither did Sophie until yesterday."

Mrs. Eichmann said, "Well, I'll have to call my husband to see if that's okay, because he is her social services officer, and there may be more to this than I know."

Anna looked at Sophie. "Your social services officer—did you know that?"

"No, I never knew he was also my SS officer."

Mrs. Eichmann smirked at them. "Oh, yes. And he also happens to be the supervisor for the entire city of Munich's foster family program. He is an important man, and he has the law on his side. He is at work right now. I'll call him, and he'll have the police here in a matter of minutes."

Armando walked up the steps and onto the porch and stood in front of the woman.

"Listen, lady, we didn't come here to negotiate. Sophie turned eighteen today. She is no longer the ward of the state. We know as well as you do that your husband has been taking money from both the social services department and from Addison National Bank & Trust in San Francisco. That's a clear violation of several laws. We don't give a damn about your business. We came here to get Sophie's birth certificate. Now go get it, and we'll be out of your lives forever."

Mrs. Eichmann stared at him, slack-jawed.

"Now," Armando shouted.

She huffed at him and bustled away.

"Where did that come from?" said Anna. "Nice work, Captain."

"I got that from Reed Jackson—except he took control of fifteen mobsters, not just one old lady."

A minute or two later, Mrs. Eichmann came back with the birth certificate. She handed it to Armando and said, "So who are you?"

"It doesn't matter. *You* don't matter."

The four of them walked back the way they came.

Anna said to Sophie, "Are you okay? How do you think that went?"

Sophie gave her a big grin. "It went perfect. Thank you so much for helping me. I'll be glad to get all this behind me."

Max pulled out his phone. "Got it—okay, see you soon." He put his phone away. "That was Jackson. He wants to meet back at the hotel for an update." Max looked at Sophie as they approached the intersection. He jerked a thumb at the bar where they had seen Eichmann. "You sure you don't want Armando and me to go in there and give that pig a little Tobin family introduction?"

Sophie laughed and said, "That would be a wonderful thing to see, and I would like to know how he knows Silvio, but I'd rather just get away from all of this."

Max said, "Alright, little sister ... your call." He looked at Armando and said, "*Vamanos!*" as he opened the front door of the taxi.

Chapter JJ
Munich, Germany
(The same day)

THEY TOOK THE GIRLS' PHONES, WATCHES, AND JEWELRY. THE GIRLS HAD nothing—nothing but black space filled with terror. *This must be their plan, to leave us in this tomb and break us down even further,* Lara thought. *But we're all there already! We'll do anything to get out of here.* No food or water. No light. Not a sound from anyone. The criers had given up hours before.

The twenty girls stood in line against one wall. Several of them had fallen to their knees into puddles of urine. *They must have lost all their strength. We'll all be there soon.*

With that last thought, something snapped. Everyone has a limit, a final straw. What snapped wasn't Lara's will. It was the exact opposite. She had had enough. She figured that half the girls were sitting in waste and knew she wasn't far behind. *I'm not going to live my life like this. I refuse to serve those animals,* she yelled to herself.

She reached down to untie the thick twine that tied her to the girls on both sides of her. One was standing. The other had been down for hours. Neither of them had the fortitude to resist or question her actions. Lara felt her way to the other side of the dark trailer. She touched the floor. It was gritty but dry. *If I'm going to die in here, at least it will be on my own terms.* She sat on the cold, metal floor. *I wish I had my jeans on.*

She fell asleep.

Not sure for how long. Seemed like a minute. The metal lever scraped against the catch. She thought about standing and returning to her spot. *Fuck those guys! I'm not doing this.* She remained seated.

When the door opened, light poured into the pungent tomb. The girls looked terrified, desperate. No one moved. One of the girls tried to stand, but didn't have the strength, and she fell down again.

Two men spoke their strange language while waving their hands in front of their face, trying to fan the stench away. They looked at the girls in the line and then eyed Lara. She looked right back at them without fear. *I don't care what happens to me.*

One of the men said, "Lara?" Lara nodded, "Come with us," he said in German. "Boss wants you cleaned up."

Lara stood up. *Anything to get out of here.* She walked out of the trailer, her knees feeling weak, and into the open area of the warehouse. They closed the door and the metal latch screamed as she walked away.

Chapter Forty

Munich, Germany

(The same day)

ANNA USED HER KEY CARD TO OPEN THEIR HOTEL ROOM DOOR. SHE AND Sophie walked into the room. She went straight for her iPad and searched for the videos Jackson had sent her yesterday. She found them, then looked at Sophie and said, "Come over here and look at this with me."

Sophie sat next to Anna at the kitchenette table. Max and Armando walked over and stood behind them. Anna started the video. Sophie said, "Is this the video Jackson's men sent to him?"

"Yes. They shot it from pretty far away, but look closely."

Sophie said, "That looks like a few of the men I saw in the park." The men were loading equipment into their trucks.

Anna said, "Keep watching." A few moments later they watched a line of girls all tied together being led to a small box truck. The girls walked up a ramp into the truck.

Sophie said, "Can you play that again and zoom in a little?"

Anna enlarged the picture, and they all watched the video again.

"Hold it," said Sophie. "That's my friend Lara." She pointed at the screen.

"That's what I thought," said Anna. "It didn't hit me until you told us that Lara was a foster child, too."

Armando said, "That must be the connection between Eichmann and Silvio."

Max said, "Silvio must pay Eichmann for the foster girls. He probably paid Eichmann for you."

The four of them jumped when they heard a loud knock on the door. Max peered through the peephole and opened the door. In walked Jackson with five of his men. The five men from The Agency walked over to one side of the room.

"I've brought in some reinforcements," Jackson said. "Did you get the birth certificate?"

"Yes."

"Good. We'll be able to get a fast-track visa from the embassy soon. The visa and temporary passport will allow Sophie to leave Germany and get into the United States. We'll figure out the rest of the details after we get her stateside."

"I talked with Allen Woods," Max said, "and he's prepared for us. Turns out he's been living in our parents' old house, where Anna and I lived as children. The home is big enough for all of us."

"Perfect," said Jackson. "Now we have to decide what to do about the girls we saw in the video. I was also able to meet with some agents from the BKA, which is equivalent to our FBI. They were very interested in helping us and agreed we should not involve the Munich police. Unfortunately, German laws are very specific about what the BKA can and cannot do. For one thing, they can't make an arrest. This separation of authority is because the Gestapo had too much power over German citizens and government officials back in the Nazi days. Bock was a BKA agent before he went into the private sector. I asked him to follow up with his connections. He's on his way here to give us a report. Hopefully, we'll be able to hand this problem off to them and stay completely out of the Chechen's business."

Anna said to Jackson, "We have some additional information that's very important."

"What've you got?"

Someone knocked on the door. After checking the peephole, Max let Herman Bock in. Jackson said, "Glad to see you, Bock. You're just in time. Anna was about to give us some information that might be important to you." Jackson looked at Anna. "Go ahead."

"We discovered several bits of information that separately mean very little, but when put together reveal a plot that involves the kidnapped girls and Sophie. Number one, we were able to get Sophie's birth certificate from Mrs. Eichmann. She let it slip that her husband is the director of the whole foster family program in Munich. Number two, we saw Mr. Eichmann and Silvio arguing about something that involved money. Number three, Sophie confirmed that one of the kidnapped girls in the video is her friend, who is also a foster child. We believe Eichmann has been selling these foster girls to Silvio."

Sophie added, "When foster children disappear, no one knows about it or cares."

Bock said, "That's an interesting theory and probably very accurate."

Jackson said to Anna, "Set up your iPad again. I want my men and Bock to see what we're dealing with."

All the men stood behind Anna as the video played. Anna pointed to the screen. "That's Lara, Sophie's friend." Lara was easy to identify because of her pigtails and pink-and-white striped dress. Anna pointed to another girl. "Sophie knows she's from a foster family, too."

Jackson said to Bock, "We have them under surveillance. With the new information about Sophie's friend in the mix, we need to take care of this now."

Bock said, "Are all of you sure you want to get involved in this? My advice is to take Sophie and get out of here. Go back to America where you belong, away from these mobsters. My contacts in the BKA tell me that the Chechens are part of a worldwide sex-trafficking ring." He pointed at the dormant iPad. "Those twenty girls won't make any difference."

"We can't just walk away from them," Jackson said.

"Okay, but there's no easy solution for this. Here's what you're dealing with. We know with one hundred percent certainty the Munich police department is compromised. They will be no help and could actually be working against us. However, we have caught a break. A man named Stefan Jeager is a brave young police officer who has been working undercover with the BKA. The Chechens used their typical method of intimidation, threats, and blackmail on him, but he didn't fold. He went directly to the BKA. However, the BKA cannot arrest anyone. They have to work with local authorities because of German law. So our hands were tied until Stefan's information came to light. Based on information obtained by Stefan, the BKA was able to bring Interpol into the mix. Interpol is an international organization. They stay away from military or political unrest, and only concern themselves with crimes against humanity. With proof that the Chechens work in more than country, they can get involved. This case is a perfect fit for them. That all sounds good, but nothing will happen until we can get a warrant allowing us to enter the warehouse. The video you have is enough to get a warrant issued, but that could take weeks."

Everyone looked at Jackson. He was staring at the floor. After a long minute, he lifted his head and said to Geronimo, "When would be the best time to hit them, a time when they're the most vulnerable?"

"Early in the morning, right about now—those guys stay up late and sleep in."

Jackson looked down again, as if the answer was written on the floor. After a few seconds, he looked at Bock and said, "We're going to take the lead on this and go in there first to get those girls. You have Interpol and the BKA waiting outside. When we bring the girls out, the authorities will get eyewitness reports from them. That will be more than enough proof for them to act without a search warrant."

Jackson then looked at Geronimo. "Call Cochise and tell him we're on the way. Have him move in and get a closer look at what's going on inside that building. Stay on the phone with him the whole time and begin to formulate a plan of rescue."

Jackson looked back at Bock and said, "Will you be able to get them on board? You have one hour. Look at your watch and mark the exact time. One hour from now, at ten o'clock, those girls will be walking out of that warehouse."

Bock said, "You don't have any firepower. If you wait a little, I can get you what we have."

"All we need are two roles of duct tape. We'll serve those Chechens to you on a platter,"

Chapter KK

Munich, Germany

(The same day)

A s Lara followed the men, she surveyed the warehouse, looking for an opportunity to escape and for something to use as a weapon so she could fight a good last fight. She saw a bunch of men sleeping on cots. On the other side of the room chairs were lined up, just like those at the other warehouse. She followed the two men until one of the men stopped and pointed through a doorway with no door. "Go in there and clean up. There's a shower with soap and towels. Clean your dress the best you can and put your hair back up like it was. Boss likes that look. You're a lucky girl."

Lara looked at both men and without saying a word walked into the makeshift bathroom. The shower was filthy. It had no curtains or walls, just a showerhead hanging over a dirty drain. She looked around to find a towel, then turned back to see the two men, plus a third one, watching her.

Suck it up, she said to herself. *I have to get through this. At least I can get a drink of water.*

She took off her dress, bra, and panties. She wouldn't acknowledge the men's presence. She took out her hair ties and placed them where she could find them again, then stepped under the falling water. It was freezing. She rinsed herself off and reached for her panties to wash them. One of the men appeared next to her. He took her panties and bra and said, "You won't be needing these." He handed her the dress. She took it and with the bar soap washed the stained areas and then threw it over the back of a chair. They were still watching her. She stepped back under the cold water. Shivering, she found the soap and began washing herself.

She thought, *their boss is going to be in for a surprise. I'll figure out something. I guess my new life will be very short.*

Chapter Forty-One

Munich, Germany

(The same day)

JACKSON AND HIS MEN HUDDLED TWO BLOCKS FROM THE WAREHOUSE. Geronimo said, "I was able to get a good visual of what's going on inside. There are twelve men sleeping on cots and three more men roaming around. I saw them lead a girl out of a semi-trailer and into another room. I couldn't see what was in the other room, but the three men stood just outside the room and watched something. Next to this room are stairs that lead up to what looks like an office-type room with a couple of windows looking out into the big open warehouse. We have to assume there are more men up there."

Renegade said, "The video showed seventeen men, so there has to be at least two more somewhere."

Jackson digested that information. "Bock's men won't be here for anther half hour. This mission should be over quick. We'll wait here a little longer."

Chapter LL

Munich, Germany

(The same day)

L ARA TURNED OFF THE WATER AND REACHED FOR THE TOWEL. ONE OF the men came at her with evil intentions written all over his face. *This isn't the way I thought this would go.* She held the towel up in front of herself as he came closer. She looked around. *No weapons.* He held up her dress. "Hurry up. Get your hair back up and this dress back on. The boss is getting anxious."

Lara complied.

The man led Lara up some rickety wooden steps and knocked on the door at the top of the steps. He then opened the door, shoved her inside, and left, closing the door behind him. Lara faced two men. She wanted to cry, but wouldn't give them the satisfaction. One of the men looked like a giant, hairy monster. He leaned against a wall, off to the side. The other man sat behind a desk, like a businessman.

The man behind the desk said, "My name is Silvio, and this is my brother, Aslan. Welcome to our office, and welcome to your new life. Your foster father sold you to us. Do not feel ashamed. It was all part of a plan that you had no control of. You must remember that you no longer have any options, and you have nowhere else to go. This is your new home, and we are your new family. We want to take care of you, Lara. Aslan and I have picked you to be our special girl, and we will train you accordingly. Don't worry, we like different things. He stood up and walked around to the front of the desk and picked up a small plastic cup of what looked like water and handed it to Lara. He said, "Here, this will help us get off on the right foot."

She took the cup from him, thinking—*do not drink this!* She put the cup to her lips, tilted her head back, and pretended to drink the liquid. When she tilted her head forward she let the contents drain from her mouth back into the cup. She had noticed a trashcan sitting off to the side. She took a few steps and dropped the cup into it.

"Now come over and have a seat," Silvio said. "I have a story to tell you." He dragged a chair to the middle of the room.

I only have a few minutes before I need to start acting the part.

"Do you feel okay, Lara? You don't have anything to be afraid of. We are going to take good care you, protect you, provide a nice life for you. All we ask in return is that you take care of us. Your parents didn't want you. Your foster parents didn't want you. But we want you. We want to make you happy. This is a natural progression for you, from a girl into a woman. We're here to help you with that transition."

Lara noticed a pen on the desk. *That's going into his eye when I have the chance.* Lara smiled at that thought. *Perfect timing for the ruse.*

"There, that's a girl. It's nice to see you smile. You are so pretty."

Smile again, giggle. Lara giggled. Aslan stepped toward her. *Giggle again.* He put his hand on her shoulder. *A test. Don't cringe.* Lara leaned her head against the giant man's hand. Aslan said something in their language to Silvio, walked into a different room next to the office, and closed the door.

Silvio said, "Aslan will give us some privacy for a few minutes, and then I'll leave you two alone. This will be fun."

Lara shrugged her shoulders, *I have to get to that pen.* She stood up and walked to the desk with her back to Silvio.

Silvio approached her and unzipped the back of her dress. She leaned forward and seized the pen.

Silvio said, "Not so fast. Let's go a little slower." He slipped the straps of her dress off her shoulders. She tightened her grip on the pen. Then the door banged open. She didn't move.

Silvio said in English, "You again." Then he yelled, "Aslan!"

Lara turned around. A man who looked like an American stood there. Aslan came flying through the door of the connecting room and launched himself at the man. The man stopped him with a high kick to his chest and a straight punch to the nose. All of this happening in two seconds. Then he buried the knuckles of his fist into the meat of the monster's throat, Aslan's face turned white. He gasped for a breath. The man got Aslan in a headlock and snapped his neck. Like a puppet without strings, the giant's massive body crumpled to the floor.

Wide-eyed, Silvio threw his hands into the air, stepped back, and cried, "Stop! You can't come in here and do this. I have my rights. This country is a democracy."

"I'll give you the same rights you gave these girls," the man said in a deep voice.

He sounds American.

Then he said to Lara, "Turn away."

She did. She heard a short scuffle, then the same neck-cracking sound.

Someone walked up behind her. She was too terrified to turn around. She gripped the pen, ready to attack.

"It's okay, Lara," the American said. He zipped up the back of her dress "Your friend Sophie sent me to rescue you."

Lara turned around and looked up at him. *Sophie? Rescue?* She tried to understand what had just happened, saw the two dead Chechens on the floor, dropped the pen, and lowered her head with relief.

The American said, "The other girls are safe, too. Did they hurt you?"

"No, you got here just in the nick of time."

"Good. Let's get out of here."

Chapter Forty-Two

Munich, Germany

(The same day)

A<small>T 10:01 A.M. STEFAN YEAGER AND HIS UNCLE STOOD BEHIND THE CHECH-</small>en's warehouse. At least ten unmarked BKA cars were parked nearby. A minute before, the cars had rushed onto the scene at the same time and from every direction. Stefan and his uncle watched the organized chaos play out in front of them. Agents herded a group of Chechen mobsters out the back door of the warehouse, all of them with their hands duck-taped behind their back. They were silent and docile, and they all hung their head. The agents loaded them into a box truck that acted as a paddy wagon.

A group of about twenty young girls huddled nearby, surrounded by BKA agents and women from social services.

Stefan's uncle said, "No press. This is going too well. These guys have completely taken this city hostage for the last couple of years. Now, today, it all comes to an end? A storybook ending that you may never see again. Take note, Stefan. This is a good day for Germany."

Stefan remembered the pictures of Lynette and hoped Rinehart could get his family back. *But how could it ever be the same? At least his daughters were saved. And the girls here have been saved.*

He noticed the young girls watching the mobsters walk up the ramp into the truck. *How many other young girls are out there in the same trouble? How many other families have been torn apart? The Chechens are exceptionally professional. I was fortunate. I had an option that Rinehart didn't have.* Stefan said to his uncle, "Will this take care of it?"

"What you did was heroic, and the plan worked because of the American, Reed Jackson. But don't think this will end now. Today was a great victory, worthy of celebration, but the fight will go on. These men will be replaced, and so will those girls. Our duty is to keep all this shit out of Munich."

Something caught his uncle's eye. "That must be him." He pointed to the back entrance of the warehouse.

Out walked a young girl dressed in a pink-and-white-striped waitress outfit. A big man with broad, square shoulders followed her.

Stefan said, "That's Jackson? I heard he was a U.S. Navy SEAL."

"He was, along with the rest of his crew. Herman Bock told me they didn't want any weapons today. All they wanted was two rolls of duct tape. He gave us a one-hour notice, and one hour to the minute his men walked those girls out of that warehouse. He said he wanted us to take the credit."

They watched the girl in the pink-and-white dress run to the group of girls, and they watched Jackson locate Herman Bock. Jackson and Bock talked for a minute, and then Bock pointed to Stefan and his uncle. The American squared his shoulders and marched up the slight incline to where they stood.

He stopped in front of them. "I had a little trouble in there," he said to Stefan's uncle. "You'll find two dead in the office upstairs. It was two against one, and I had to save the girl. It was self-defense. You follow?"

"I understand. We've been fighting these guys for a couple of years. Thank you for what you did today. We appreciate your service."

Jackson turned to walk away. Stefan's uncle said, "Before you leave I want to introduce you to my nephew. He went undercover to learn about their specific methods of operation."

Jackson turned back and said, "You must be Stefan Jeager. I heard what you did and how you did it. Well done. It's an honor to work with you."

Stefan almost fell over. *He knew my name.* This man was like a god to him and all the other Germans on the site. Jackson shook his hand.

Stefan said, "Thank you, sir."

Jackson said to his uncle, "I'd find a place for this young man in your unit if I was you."

"I've already started that process."

Jackson shook his uncle's hand, then turned and walked away.

Chapter Forty-Three

Somewhere over the Atlantic Ocean
(The next day)

ANNA DROPPED INTO THE SEAT NEXT TO MAX. SHE DIDN'T SAY A WORD. They watched Reed Jackson, holding a beer and wearing the first smile they had ever seen on his face. His men surrounded him. Armando was right in the middle of the group. Cochise told the men about Armando's short time in the backseat of the Audi S6 after Jackson walked him out of the warehouse.

Cochise said, "I wish I could have seen the look on your face when Jackson pulled that hood off your head."

Everyone laughed.

Jackson said, "He was beat up bad, but looked like he was ready for whatever was coming next. He's one tough hombre." Jackson slapped Armando on the back.

Armando bent over and cringed with pain. The men's expression turned to one of concern. "Ha, got you!" Armando said. They all cracked up.

Anna and Max smiled.

Sophie sat next to Allen Woods on the other side of the aisle, facing forward. She was listening intently to Woods talking about something. *Probably something about her parents*, Anna thought.

Anna said to Max, "Your friend Mr. Woods really came through with this private jet for our ride home. I can see that you were right about him all along. Do you think we'll actually get through all of this and live a somewhat normal life?

Max laced his fingers behind his head. "I'm not sure about the normal life part, but we'll figure out something. By the way, I've been meaning to ask you, have you ever been to the Señor Frog's bar in Playa del—

261

Cochise rushed up to them and said, "Anna, give me your iPad. You have to see the video of the night you and Armando were in Vero Beach. Two men were following you. They were hired by Addison National to take out our buddy Armando. Apache, Outlaw, and Chirica were there to protect you guys. You gotta see what they did to them." Holding the iPad, he sat down on the floor next to Anna. Armando and several Agency men hovered over the screen.

Cochise said to Max, "We also have some good stuff on those guys who followed you and Mr. Woods to that basketball court in Boston. You guys are gonna crack up."

Everyone laughed while the videos played. Woods explained to Sophie what the frenzy was all about.

Anna noticed Jackson standing away from the group. His smile was gone. He had a serious look on his face when he turned and walked to the back of the cabin and sat down.

BOOK THREE

Chapter AAA
Monte Carlo
(Two days later)

I CHECKED MY LOOK IN THE MIRROR. BRUSHED SOME HAIR AWAY FROM MY face and moistened my lips. I turned my head back and forth, examining my face. No marks at all from the most recent plastic surgery. *Nice*. Even in this light.

All nineteen years of my life I've tried to look and sound American. Mother's genes helped. She's a beautiful runway model. Luckily, I got her slender build, long legs, and a great rack. Father was quite a bit older. He was a good-looking man but had that hard, masculine look. I got his olive complexion and his thick, dark hair. But that beak of a nose was my cross to bear. Not any longer. It's been fixed. And it wasn't so bad hanging out in Switzerland with mother for the surgery and three-month recovery.

I smiled to confirm my perfect, white teeth. The smile reminded me that I could turn on the charm anytime and conquer anyone. I nodded, checked my look one more time, then walked out of the ladies' room wearing new five-inch Gianvito Rossi alligator stilettos.

The luxury suite was crowded. It was a perfect setting for me to saunter around the tables scattered around the big room.

On my left was a giant wall of glass. The world-famous Monte Carlo Formula 1 race raged on below. The glass wall protected us from the deafening sounds. Pedestrian spectators had to sit outside, where they belonged.

I held my head high. Everyone in the room watched me glide between the tables.

Mother's golden rule, and part of my training: *If you are looking at them, they're not looking at you.*

My gaze was ahead, off in the distance. Suddenly, I stopped midstride and turned to look through the windows. *Wait for it.*

There it was. Heads turned to find what had caught my eye. Proof they were watching me.

The windows framed the Monte Carlo marina, which was just beyond the racetrack. It was full of huge yachts docked in rows, side by side.

That's where father wanted to be, but he didn't have that kind of wealth. Yet.

"Poor man wants to be rich. Rich man wants to be king. King ain't satisfied till he rules everything." Words written by my favorite American rock star. They reminded me of father.

I continued my trek across the room to my family's table. I couldn't have cared less where I was or who else was in the room.

Father stood and pulled a chair back for me, next to my mother, my mother who looked like my sister. We smiled.

Amazing what a rich man could acquire for his third wife. Wife number four is probably in this room somewhere.

Mother and I knew her days were numbered. We hoped that she wouldn't suffer the same mysterious disappearance that wife number two had. Mother was in a much better position, though, because I turned out. Father loved me, unlike those two pussies sitting next to me at our table. My two half-brothers from father's second marriage were next to a pair of middle-aged couples that were either friends or political contacts. *Didn't know. Didn't care.*

My back was to the wall of glass and the race, but I could see it on the wide-screen TVs scattered throughout the room. I picked up my place-setting knife and tilted it so I could casually look at the reflection to see what the people behind me were doing. Mother noticed, and she smiled.

The night before, we had attended a private party and gambled in the opulent casino. *It was mad.*

That morning, we had been with all the beautiful people in pit row before the race. *That was just okay.* Mother knew all the cool celebs. We'd VIP with them later that night at the victory party.

I was completely bored. Father commanded everyone's attention at the table with words I didn't care to hear.

Mother was just as stuck and just as bored. We smiled at each other in silent agreement about our hostage situation. She not only looked like my sister, we acted like sisters.

I saw some activity in a back corner of the room. A couple of father's henchmen looked disturbed. One of them walked up behind father and interrupted his monologue. *Something was going on.*

He bent down and whispered into father's ear.

Father looked up at him and said, "You're sure?" The bodyguard nodded yes.

The couples sitting at our table knew it was a time to look away. They talked among themselves.

Father turned to us and said, "Silvio and Aslan were killed yesterday." He bowed his head; I'd never seen him hurt like that.

Silvio and Aslan were my half-brothers from father's first marriage. Father loved Silvio and Aslan because they were just like him—strong, handsome, and confidant. They both worked the business. The proper fellows next to me were the exact opposite.

Mother covered father's hand with hers. He pushed it away.

He said to us, "This is something we'll have to square. Someone's gotta pay."

I could see his head was spinning. I knew he'd develop a plan to take violent revenge to honor his sons.

Father looked at his dandy sons sitting next to me. His face was a mask of disappointment and disapproval.

Then he looked at me and said, "Milaana, I want you to suit up for this one."

I smiled and nodded and said to myself, *Finally!*

Chapter BBB
Red Square, Moscow, Russia
(One week later)

THE CAB DROPPED ME OFF ON THE EDGE OF RED SQUARE. I HADN'T BEEN to Moscow since I was ten years old, and I wanted to stroll around the big plaza again before meeting Father at the hotel. The buildings that encircled the square hadn't changed a bit. I'd bet nothing ever changed here.

It was nice to get away from the traffic and stretch my legs on the square. It was bigger than I remembered. I weaved my way through the mass of random, uninteresting bureaucrats and tourists. Significant historic events had played out on these worn bricks. I should have known more about those events. *Maybe I'll do some research before dinner.*

It was end of May. There was still a winter chill in the air. It must be cold here all the time. *That wind.* The click-clack noise of my suitcase rolling behind me started to annoy me. *I should have had the driver take my bag to the hotel.* These high heels weren't meant for walking on these old bricks. My feet hurt, but that was no problem I learned a long time ago to fight through the pain.

All these people ... Where do they come from, what are they doing? I remembered when I was little, thinking there were men lurking in the crowd who were spies on dangerous missions. It still seemed that way, and the men still wore the same stupid hats. I wished Mother were with me. It would have been more fun with her stories floating on the edges of our observations. She had met father somewhere around here. *I bet that's a good story, hopefully one I'll never hear. Some things are better left unsaid.*

Mother stayed back at our place in Baku, where it was warm, where the sky was blue, and where there were beautiful people. Father wanted me to make this trip by myself. I felt like I was being handed off, as if Mother had relinquished both my training and me to Father. The cold, gray day was probably a foreshadowing of how things would change for me. I was sure father would introduce me to some of his associates that night at dinner. They wouldn't be beautiful, but they were part of the business. I wasn't sure what to expect. I just knew from Father's statement in Monte Carlo that I was part of the plan going forward. That was okay. I was ready to see what was behind the curtain. Father never talked about his business with Mother or me. We had no idea what he and his men did. We assumed they didn't operate within the boundaries of the law, but in Russia those boundaries were hazy. As long as you had the government's blessing, there were no laws.

When Silvio and Aslan came home for holidays, it was exciting. I wanted to be in the room with them. To know what they talked about—to know why they celebrated. I knew that Father wanted me to be part of his revenge plan. Not sure what that meant, but I knew I couldn't hesitate when my time came. Father would not tolerate any show of weakness. My blood was his blood. I knew I could do whatever he asked, whatever it took.

I remembered the way to the Metropol. It was just a couple of blocks away. There was a Four Seasons and a Ritz right here, but no, Father liked that ancient Russian landmark. He was a loyal Russian. Loyalty, something that was completely lost to my generation.

It would be cool to see that old hotel again, though. I remembered running all over that place when I was little. I bet it hadn't changed a bit.

What was that? Something wasn't right. There was a man pretending not to look at me. He wasn't creeping on me like most middle-aged men do. He was watching me.

I had to confirm my hunch. It was easy for anyone to see these heels weren't meant for the bricks. I stopped and squatted down to adjust the back of one of my shoes. Then I looked into the flat buckle on my suitcase, using it as a mirror.

He was there. No doubt he was following me.

The hotel should be right over there. I had to make it to the flat sidewalk, and then make a beeline to the front door. I played it cool, didn't overdo it, and made my way to the front door. Before I went in, I stopped and took my phone out of my purse. I pretended I'd gotten a call, pretended to talk. I turned nonchalantly and looked right at the man as I talked into the phone. I got a good look at him. I would remember his face.

Why was he following me?

Chapter Forty-three

A bellman came out of the hotel and took my suitcase. Another one opened the door. I walked into the grand hotel. Head high, back straight, my feet no longer hurting. This was where it would all begin.

Chapter CCC
Chaliapin Bar, Metropol Hotel, Moscow, Russia
(Five hours later)

W*HERE IS HE?* I HATED WALKING INTO A ROOM WITHOUT KNOWING EX-actly where I was going. I looked around at the beautifully finished marble, tile, antique furniture, and those chandeliers. I guessed the Ritz didn't have a room like this.

There he was. His broad back and thick, black hair were hard to miss. I crossed the room to the long bar that supported my father's elbows.

"Is this seat taken?"

Father jumped to his feet. "Milaana. There you are. You look so beautiful. Let me see you." He held me at arm's length, and then pulled me into a bear hug. "The dress fits perfect. I knew it would look great on you."

"How did you know my size? It does fit nicely."

"There are a lot of things you don't know about me. Properly sizing a beautiful woman is just one example."

I wasn't sure how I should react to that, but I smiled and sat on the open stool next to him. He slid his stool close to me. The tender behind the bar was waiting for instructions. Father said, "She'll have a champagne cocktail, and I'll have another." Father pushed his empty tumbler forward.

The bartender said, "You got it, Mr. Dzhabahl."

"Ah, I can see you've been here before," I said.

Father replied, "This place is my home away from home. I always stay here when I'm in Moscow. I brought you and your brothers here a few times years ago."

"Yes, but I don't remember this room or the opulence of this place. It's pretty cool. So, your note said we're dining here tonight."

"Yes, we will be meeting a few of my associates in the Restaurant Savva. They should be there now. I want to be a little late so your entrance is properly highlighted."

"Hmmm. Who are our dinner guests, and where do I fit in?"

"Two of the men work for me. The other two are connected to the Federation. You'll be able to tell who's who when we get there."

"Will the man who was following me today be there?"

Father looked surprised. "You saw him? He's GRU and a real professional. You made him. That's interesting. You must be a natural. Anyway, my men were following him and watching out for you."

"Why would anyone follow me?"

"I guess the word is out that Aslan and Silvio are gone. They must think I've brought you here for a reason."

"Who?"

"The Russian Federation. I partner with them. Putin is a cagey animal. He trusts no one. For now, we have a good relationship because I'm loyal, and I make money. Those are the only two things he cares about. But he's always on edge, and our partnership can change on a dime. His meddling in my affairs is just something we have to put up with. Tonight is all for show. Just enjoy the dinner, be mysterious, and follow my lead. Tomorrow morning we leave for Munich to find out who was responsible for your brothers' death. We're holding a man who will give us the answers. That's when our real work will begin."

We walked into the restaurant. This space was even grander than the bar. I had father's arm. Everyone looked at us. I felt like they saw a hooker on father's arm, not his daughter. The four men all stood at the same time, when we approached the table.

One of them said, "Demir." He shook Father's hand. "This must be Milaana." He released Father's hand and gave me a restrained hug and a peck on both cheeks. I smiled.

Father said, "This is Mr. Petrov and Mr. Fedorov, and you know Ivan and Grigory."

I smiled again and tried to avoid another embrace. Two waiters held chairs for us on the other side of the table. As we took our seats all the men's eyes were on me. Creeping.

The maître di' hovered nearby. Father yelled, "Bring us a bottle of Mamont vodka, two bottles of Taittinger Brut Reserve, and ten ounces of your Beluga caviar. Let's get this party started!" His voice was loud enough for everyone in the room to hear.

Father owned the table and the room. I was a complement, just like his suit and voice. The dinner dragged on. Most of the talk centered on American politics and how Putin had them under his thumb. I wondered what waited for me in Munich. I recalled Father's words, *holding a man who will give us answers.* I guess I'll have to wait to see what happens. I hoped these two gorillas wouldn't be going with us. Wished Silvio and Aslan were here.

The four men at our table started to disgust me. I played my part, supported Father with brief, perfectly timed comments, and kept my mouth shut most of the time. I considered different ways to excuse myself when the gazes from the men started to linger a little too long.

Heads turned and all conversation stopped when six stunning young ladies, clearly professionals, walked into the room. They stationed themselves at the bar on one side of the room and ordered drinks. All the men at our table, including Father, sat up straighter and gawked at them. Father looked like one of Pavlov's dogs. He was just as disgusting as his four friends.

This looked like a setup to me. I was sure Father had ordered them up, just as he did the caviar. I pretended not to notice the drunken fools' reaction and stood up. "Gentlemen, it's been a pleasure dining with you this evening. I'm going to leave you men to your business now." I kissed Father's cheek and walked away before anyone had a chance to give me a farewell grope.

Without taking my eyes off the front door, I noticed the working girls giggling with one another at my expense. I also spotted the man who had followed me earlier in the day sitting at a table with another man.

I was taken by surprise when a different man slipped into my elevator just before the doors closed. He didn't say a word. I couldn't get a good look at him because he was standing too close to me. My heart raced. Who was he? Did he have something to do with Father's business, or the Federation? I pushed the number-five button. He reached across me, nearly touching me, and pushed number six. I was not prepared. I'll never let this happen again. The ride took forever. What would I do if he got off on my floor?

When the elevator bell finally sounded, I looked up. Fifth floor. The door slid open, and I walked out and down the hall. My heart still pounded. I couldn't hear the man or the elevator. The doors hadn't shut. I kept walking. I put the card in the door and looked back. He was holding the doors, watching me.

He said, "Good night, Miss Dzhabahl."

I bolted inside and chained the door. My heart threatened to explode. Was there someone in my room? I need to be better prepared in the future. I turned on all the lights and checked the bathroom and closets, then under the bed. I confirmed that the balcony door was locked. I slid one of the chairs to the door and wedged its back under the door handle. I looked around again. My mind raced.

He must be one of Father's men. Had to be. I'll find out tomorrow.

What have I got myself involved in? This was just day one. Maybe I'm not the gangster that I thought I was. I better call Mother.

Chapter DDD

In a small plane

(The next morning)

I YELLED AT FATHER, "I NEVER KNEW THESE SMALL PLANES WERE SO NOISY. How much longer?" I could tell he was hung over. Who knew what went on last night after I left. The two gorillas were sound asleep with their mouths wide open in seats looking directly back at father and me. It was a small plane.

Father didn't answer me. He was awake, but just ignored my question. He probably thought I was a whiny little kid asking about when our vacation would start. I had to remind myself that we were not on vacation. Something bad was going to happen in Munich.

A black SUV waited for us as the plane taxied over to the private transport gate.

I could tell that Father didn't want to talk to me with Ivan and Grigory around. No one said a word.

Half an hour later, the SUV pulled up in front of a hotel, and we all got out. Father told his men to meet us in the lobby at two. That was four hours later. I assumed they all wanted to nap. The two men walked away. Father secured his overnight bag and gave me a cold look. Like a man I didn't know. "Be in the lobby at two. And change your clothes. We're not going to a fucking brunch." He looked as if he was ready to hit me. I let him walk away without any rebuttal.

I better go shopping for a gangster outfit while the tough guys take their nap.

A few hours later, the four of us were back in the SUV. Father said to his men, "When we're done here today, I want you two to stay here to get this operation back on track. Make sure this guy Ramon is up to the task." Father pulled a fat wad of euros out of his pocket and handed it to Ivan. "Here, spend what you need. I'm sure it will be at least two weeks."

We walked into the warehouse, where the men waiting snapped to attention. Father yelled at all of them. They stood in a line with their head down, taking their punishment. Father slapped one of them. Then he slapped another big man, and that man fell to one knee. Father looked like an animal. He walked over to who must be Ramon and talked to him I couldn't hear what they said. Ramon pointed to a door at the side of the warehouse. Father nodded to Ivan, Grigory, and me. We followed him through the door.

Inside the room there was a man sitting in a chair with his hands and ankles tied to the chair. His face had been beaten to a pulp. The man looked up at us. It must have been hard for him to see anything, because his eyes were nearly swollen shut.

Father walked over in front of the man. He didn't say a word, just stood there. He slowly pulled on leather gloves. The man tried to keep his head up, but couldn't.

Father lifted his chin and said to the man, "You are going to tell me who killed my sons."

The man tried to open his eyes. Father slapped him hard across the face, almost knocking him and the chair to the floor. I tried not to shudder. Father signaled Ivan. Ivan was a big man in his mid-thirties. He looked like Aslan, a hairy monster of a man. Ivan sauntered over to the man and yanked his head up from behind. There was an ice pick stuck in a nearby table. Father jerked it free and walked back in front of the man.

He said, "I'm going to ask you a question. If you answer the question quickly and I believe what you say, I won't use this spike. Do you understand?"

Ivan cranked the man's head up and down to indicate his answer was yes.

Father asked, "Do you know who killed my sons?" The man didn't answer. Down came the ice pick into the man's hand. He shrieked and struggled to catch his breath.

Father asked again, "Do you know who killed my sons?"

"Yes, yes, I know."

"Who?"

"It was an American."

Down came the ice pick into the other hand. Another shriek. The man sucked air and sobbed.

Father yelled, "I didn't ask you his nationality. Next time I will stab your arm."

"His name is Reed Jackson. He … he runs a private security company out of San Francisco. He was hired by a bank and by an American family to find one of the family's young girls. He was rescuing the girl when he met up with your sons. I can give you names and addresses of everyone involved."

"What was your role in this?"

"My firm was hired by the bank to observe the girl. She was living as a homeless person in the park. We didn't know that she had any family."

"Why did the bank care about this girl?"

"Not sure, but I suspect her family has money that is somehow tied to the bank."

"Are you telling me that one guy, this Reed Jackson, took on, and killed, both Silvio and Aslan?"

"I wasn't there. But that's what I heard."

Father flung the ice pick against the wall and screamed with rage. Then he gathered himself and strode away from the man. He told Ramon to get the names and addresses of Jackson and the girl from the man.

He looked at me. "You're coming with me."

We were silent in the backseat of the SUV. I hoped he had calmed down. I couldn't wait to get out of there and back to Baku and my mother.

"There's a lot going on right now," Father said in a calm voice, "and I'm going to need your help figuring it all out." He closed the plastic window between the driver and the backseat. "I want you to get close to Ivan. I think he could be working with some of my enemies to take away my power. I don't know if it's the Federation or someone else. I want you to get him to open up to you, see if he's still loyal to me."

"How do you expect me to do that?"

"You use that sweet ass of yours."

"You want me to bed down with Ivan?"

Father slapped me across the face. It almost knocked me out. *My nose. My nose.* There was blood on my hand. I started to cry.

He lifted his hand again, but stopped. "It's time you start pulling your weight in this family. I don't want to hear any excuses. I want results. The sooner you get me the answers I need, the sooner you'll get Ivan's prick out of your mouth."

The SUV stopped in front of the hotel, and father got out. "I gave Ivan some money. You'll have to get what you need from him. Call me when you know something. I don't want to hear from you until then."

Chapter Forty-Four

San Francisco – Lloyds House

(Two weeks later)

THE ROOM WAS FILLED WITH THIRTY SOMBER-LOOKING BUSINESSMEN, who were all dressed in suits and ties. They sat in folding chairs lined up in orderly rows, like pews in a church. In the front of the room, a man stood behind a podium with a gavel in his right hand. In the back of the room, behind the rows of seated men, were Anna and Armando, holding hands. Max was next to them with an arm across Sophie's shoulders. The four of them were dressed in tee shirts, shorts, and flip-flops. Sophie and Anna's shorts and flip-flops matched. Sophie held up a paddle with the number twenty-two written on one side, bouncing on her tiptoes. The man at the podium cried, "SOLD!" and pointed to Sophie.

Sophie screamed and jumped into Max's arms. All the men turned in their chairs to look at her. Anna and Armando joined them for a group hug.

Chapter Forty-Five

San Francisco

(Two days later)

REED JACKSON'S OFFICE WAS NOT IN DANGER OF SOMEONE DESCRIBING the square room as warm or elegant. It contained nothing that didn't have a specific use. Three metal filing cabinets stood on one side of the room. Behind the medium-size metal desk was a narrow, wood-laminated table under a bare window.

Between the table and the desk sat Reed Jackson. His computer was on the left side of his desk. Cochise and Geronimo sat on metal chairs in front of him. Jackson squinted his eyes as he looked at a calendar and a schedule on the computer screen. Still looking at the screen, he said, "Things don't look too bad going forward." He scrolled down the page. "I've been concerned about how to keep everyone working." He clicked the mouse a couple of times to close the file and then looked up at his men. "Hopefully, this afternoon's meeting will be a good one for us. After that trouble at YouTube headquarters, all the social media companies are having to rethink their campus security."

Jackson pushed himself away from the desk. "This afternoon we'll meet with the head of security at TekTwitt headquarters. I worked with him on a couple of ops in the Philippines several years ago. Cochise, you may remember him—Bart Buster."

Cochise said, "Yeah. He was the one with the long hair."

"That's him. Like all of us, he's changed over the years, and now he has a good gig at TekTwitt. The board of directors has allocated additional funds for his department so they can stay on top of security issues. He knows our expertise, and he wants to bring us in as consultants. This could be a new side business for us. I'll offer to review their current processes and make suggestions for enhanced protection. I'm also going to suggest a training program for his employees that will be an ongoing revenue source and some easy money for us. I think we'll be able to sell this model to other corporations in the Valley. We'll need to make a good professional first impres—"

Jackson's cell phone vibrated and danced on the metal desktop. He picked it up and looked at the number. It was an international phone number. "I better take this."

"This is Jackson."

"This is Stefan Yeager, with the Munich Police Department. We met a couple of weeks ago at a warehouse when we rounded up a group of Chechen men."

"Yes, I met you and your uncle. What's up?"

"My uncle wanted me to call and give you a heads-up. Herman Bock went missing a few days ago. Earlier today, parts of his body were found floating in the river. It looked like he was tortured before they killed him."

"So that roundup didn't put those guys out of business."

"It may have slowed them down, but the stink here still lingers."

"Thanks for the call. I'll keep your number in case we see any action over here."

"Let me know if we can help."

Jackson placed his phone on the tidy desk and told his men what had happened. "We have to assume he gave the Tobin children and us up. They'll come here soon. We'll go to Woods's house after our meeting at TekTwitt. We have to alert them."

Cochise and Geronimo stayed silent. He could feel their eyes on him as they waited to hear his plan. "There's a barbershop around the corner. You guys go there. I'll call ahead for you. Get a short haircut and a close shave. Then go home and put on a suit. Meet me back here at one. We have to look the part for this afternoon's meeting."

Cochise said, "We got it, boss. You probably won't recognize us."

After they left, Jackson thought, *I knew this was coming, but not so soon. They won't stop until they take their revenge. This is one of the few times I'm glad that I've never had a wife or family. They would be the first ones on their list. The Tobin kids are just as much my responsibility. I have to figure out a way to protect them and end this. At least they all live here and are together now.*

Chapter Forty-Six

San Francisco – Allen Woods's house
(Later that day)

ANNA AND SOPHIE LAY NEXT TO EACH OTHER ON A DOUBLE CHAISE LONGUE beside the pool. They wore matching yellow bikinis and held tall, cool drinks. Fleetwood Mac songs filled the backyard as they gazed at the turquoise water in the pool.

Armando's head popped up through the surface. He treaded water, shook his head, and wiped the water from his eyes. Then looked at the two girls.

"You were close that time," Sophie yelled above the music. "You just need to get up a little higher. Try it again."

Armando dog-paddled to the side of the pool, climbed the ladder, and padded back toward the diving board. He noticed movement in the privacy hedges. Sophie called to him, "You'll nail it this time." He flashed a smile at the girls and kept walking. Something else caught his eye again, this time near the gate. Feeling concerned, he walked past the board to the corner of the yard.

"Where are you going?" Anna yelled over the music.

He showed them the flat of his hand to keep them silent.

Anna and Sophie sat up in their chair. Anna watched Armando creep up to the gate. He grabbed the door handle and yanked it open. Three men walked into the backyard. Armando looked surprised. Then he shook one of the men's hands. Anna relaxed when she saw the man smile. When the four of them turned toward her, Anna recognized Reed Jackson.

"Look who I found," said Armando as they approached her.

Jackson said over the music, "We rang the bell and knocked. We heard the music, so we walked around to the back."

Anna said, "We're so glad you're here."

Sophie turned down the volume on the boom box. Anna took a closer look at the other two men and recognized them. "Hey, I know you guys. You clean up well. What's with this new look?"

Cochise said, "We were out trying to drum up some new business for the firm. Jackson came up with a great idea that looks like it's going to be a really good thing for us."

Jackson dropped his smile and said, "We have some news that we need to talk with you about." Jackson looked around the yard. "Is Max here?"

"No," Anna replied, "he's been going to the office with Mr. Woods the last few days. They usually get home about seven. We've just been hanging out here watching Armando try to do flips off the diving board. We have some news for you, too. We're all moving."

Jackson said, "Moving? Where? What's going on?"

"Sophie bought a five hundred-acre estate that includes over two hundred acres of vineyards and a small cattle ranch. The compound has a huge mansion type of villa and seven small houses. It's down by Paso Robles, a couple of hours from here."

Sophie said, "I didn't buy it. We bought it at an auction a few days ago."

"What're you going to do there?" Jackson said.

Anna said, "It all started when Addison National tried to buy us off so we wouldn't press charges against the bank. They told us that the Holmes family estate was to be sold to fund the payoff. So we drove down there the same day to check it out, and we fell in love with the place. The next day was the auction, and Sophie made the winning bid. When the men from Addison National explained how our funds would be disbursed from our trust to pay for the estate, I told them we're going to take the estate instead of putting them all in jail. We couldn't believe it, but they agreed. Now we're landowners. It all happened really fast. We figured that we have to do something with our lives other than hanging out at the pool all day."

"That all sounds good," Jackson said. "We came here today because we have some bad news. Herman Bock was found dead a few days ago. The Munich police called this morning to warn us. Bock was tortured before he died, so he probably gave us up. We have to assume the Chechen men are responsible for this. I think they'll come here to take revenge."

Anna said, "Revenge for what?"

"There's probably no one thing, but any time their business gets interrupted, things can get ugly. Max injured a couple of their men, and there was some trouble when we went in and freed Sophie's friend. Two of them were killed, and several men in their crew will be in jail for a long time. They will turn their eye-for-an-eye retaliation on us. We can take care of ourselves, but you all are in real danger, especially Sophie, because she's how it all started. I warned you the decision to interfere in their business would be dangerous. These men are professional killers, and they will be coming."

Anna said, "What are we supposed to do? Call the police?"

"I've already called my connections at the local police as well as my contacts in the FBI. But they can't provide twenty-four-hour protection without a creditable threat. Even if they did have the manpower, you would still be in grave danger. You saw how easy it was for us to find you through the fence. If we had been the Chechens, you would have heard three muffled pops, and Max would've come home to a bloody mess. Moving away is probably a good thing. Tell me more about the estate."

Armando said, "Basically, they own the top of a mountain. At least that's what the locals call it. It's actually a big hill. There's only one road going up the hill, and the compound is about halfway up, right in the middle of the vineyards and pastureland. The place looks like something in a movie. It's really beautiful."

"This could work out perfectly," said Jackson. "I know that area. The Chechen men we saw in Munich would stick out in that small town and on the narrow roads. I suggest you get down there as soon as you can."

Sophie said, "We're already packed. We're planning to go there in the morning."

Anna said, "It's clear that we still need your help. Can we hire you again to protect us?"

"Of course. We're in this together until we find a solution." Jackson held out his hand and said, "We formalize all our contracts with a handshake." He shook Anna's, Sophie's, and Armando's hand to seal the deal and then said, "I'll leave Cochise and Geronimo here with you tonight. You can fill in Max and Mr. Woods when they get home." He looked at Armando. "Text me the address of the estate. I'll leave now for Paso Robles and recon the area. I'll come up with a plan, and we'll all leave first thing in the morning."

Chapter EEE
San Francisco – Fairmont Hotel
(That evening)

I NEED TO WAIT HERE JUST A LITTLE LONGER, I SAID TO MYSELF AS I STOOD JUST outside the entrance to the hotel restaurant. *Father said these Americans have been too smart for prostitutes. Even the best ones couldn't get close. He thought our mother/daughter routine should work. Okay, now.* I stepped into the restaurant and looked around, pretending to look for Mother. She stood and waved me over, just as we had planned. She looked spectacular in her formfitting dress. Everyone stared at her. Now it was my turn. I waved back and sashayed to her table. She greeted me with a hug and two cheek kisses. We laughed and waved our hands for effect, then sat down. I peeked over mother's shoulder and spotted them. They were watching us.

Mother said, "This is our last night. We have to finish it tonight. What are we going to do if our plan doesn't work? Did you get the second room?"

"Yes, on the same floor, just three doors down."

"Did you leave it unlocked?"

"Yes. Now don't worry so much. You're driving me crazy."

A waiter interrupted us with his long, boring recital of the night's menu.

While the waiter droned on I thought. *Our plan better work. I can't go back to Father empty-handed. I have no idea what he'd do to me. Worse yet, what he'd do to Mother. I still can't believe how he's changed. I've gone from his precious little princess to a prostitute/assassin with one slap of his hand.*

We placed our orders, and the waiter left. "Here they come," I whispered to Mother.

"Good evening, ladies. You both look amazing tonight. Is there any chance you'd be up for some dancing later tonight?" One of the businessmen asked.

Mother said, "I don't know. We had a busy shopping day today. Not sure if dancing with you studs is in the cards again tonight."

The other man said, "We saw you come back this afternoon with your hands full of packages. It must have been a good day."

I winked at them and said, "I bet you'd like to see what we bought." They both smiled. I said, "I tell you what. After we finish our dinner, we'll go over to the club. If there's a chilled bottle of Dom Perignon waiting for us, I can promise you at least one dance. Now you boys run along." I winked at them again. Mother winked, and we giggled. The American men hustled away like good little boys should.

After dinner we walked into the lounge and spotted the two men sitting in a booth against the wall. Mother and I waved to them and headed for the dance floor. We looked good. Everyone in the club was looking at us. The Americans came out to join us on the dance floor. We ignored them, and then Mother said, "We're not ready for you guys yet. Now go back over there, sit down, and make sure the champagne is cold." I smiled at them and put my hands on Mother's shoulder from behind. Then smiled again. I said, "We want you to watch us dance for a while. We'll be ready for you soon." The Americans did what they were told.

We stayed on the dance floor for another song and then walked hand in hand to the table. Mother said, "How did you like our dancing?"

"We loved it."

"Are you ready for us?" I asked with a smile. "Is the champagne cold? Go ahead and pop the cork."

"Yes, please sit down," One of the men said as he scooted over to make room on the leather seat.

Mother looked at me for confirmation and then said, "That's a good idea. You guys are so much fun."

We sat with them, laughed at their corny wit, and flirted like pros before I said, "I have an idea."

They looked at me with their mouth open. I whispered into Mother's ear. She whispered back and shook her head no. I whispered again, this time loud enough for the men to hear, "Come on, this is our last night." I looked at the men and said, "We're going up to our suite and dance some more. If you guys want to watch us, grab another bottle and meet us in suite seven forty-four. Maybe we'll model some of the things we bought today for you."

Five minutes later there was a knock on our door. We let them in and continued to dance with each other. I heard the cork pop and then felt hands on my hips from behind. I shook my ass and saw mother dancing with the other man. He moved in on her, his hands all over her. To slow things down, I led my man to them, and we switched dance partners.

Mother and I flipped off our heels. I said to the men, "Take off your shoes." They obeyed. We took off our jewelry and put it with our heels on a table. They took off their watches. Mother said, "Shirts, too." They obeyed. I said, "You two must work out. You look good."

We danced. Mother and I stripped down to our bra and underwear. They took off their pants. We took off our bras and put them with our clothes and jewelry. We danced together. They came close. I put my hand up to stop them and said, "It's your turn," looking at their shorts. "Get yourselves ready." They stripped down and stepped toward us to dance. They were at full attention. We let them get close. Mother and I backed away and danced with each other. Mother said to them, "You guys go sit down on the edge of the bed and get ready for us." They looked at each other.

I said, "Go on, watch us dance, get yourself ready, and we'll come in and finish you off." They obeyed and sat on the edge of the bed.

Mother said, "Okay, boys, close your eyes." I repeated, "Close your eyes! We want to surprise you with who gets whom." They closed their eyes.

Mother and I fled the room after we grabbed our clothes and my phone, which had captured our beguiling soiree. We ran out the door and down the hall to the vacant room we had waiting.

The next morning I woke to a loud knock on our door. It was still early. I ignored it. Mother didn't move. The annoying noise came again. I slid out of bed, stepped over to the door, and looked through the peephole. It was one of Father's men. I said through the door, "What do you want?"

"He sent me to get you. You're done here. You have an hour to get ready and say your good-byes. Don't keep him waiting."

"Why say good-bye?"

"You're leaving. Your mother has to wait here. He'll meet her later, and they'll fly back together."

An hour later a bellman opened the back door of a limo for me, and I got in. Father was waiting for me.

"Nice work last night, Melaana. The video was perfect. It even looked like they were enjoying each other's company. Couldn't have turned out better. We needed this win. The director will be pleased."

"I want to stay with Mother. We haven't seen each other since Monte Carlo."

"I know, I'm sorry, but I need you to suit up again right away. When this one is done, I promise you'll get a long vacation with your mother."

Come on! That's what he said after I finished at Munich. Now what's he want me to do? Hold your tongue.

Father said, "I need you to settle the score with the crew that killed Aslan and Silvio. They're just south of here on a mountaintop vineyard. I sent some good men down there to take care of this, but they failed. The plan is for you to get hired as a field worker who is interested in an internship through the local college. I realize this one will take a few months because of how secluded and private the family is. The driver will take you down to San Luis Obispo. There is a university there that specializes in viticulture. Your story is that you want to be part of the internship program, but came too late to get accepted for the current semester. The Tobin family is advertising for field workers, and you'll pretend to see this as a way to learn the business while you wait for an opening in the internship program. The driver will drop you off at the campus. You'll have to figure out how to get up to their vineyard and get hired."

Father handed me a large envelope and said, "Your new bio is in here, along with a passport and driver's license. Your name is Mandy Miller. There's a phone in there, too. Don't give your number to anyone, because the registration is not in your name. Just use it to report back to me, and you can call your mother, too. But don't call anyone else. I've packed a bag for you with clothes that a farm worker would have. You'll have to be patient to get close to this family. Sophie is the one we want taken out. She's the one who started all this. She's an easy target and the family member who will be missed the most. When you're done, we'll have a big celebration. You got it?"

"I guess so."

"Okay, off you go. Read your bio and the information on the Tobin family several times on your ride down there. Then give it back to the driver. He'll dispose of it. Good luck. Call me in a couple of weeks."

Chapter Forty-Seven

Highway 101 South, California

(Two months later)

ALLEN WOODS SAT IN THE PASSENGER SEAT NEXT TO MAX. THEY HAD finally broken away from the after-work San Francisco traffic on their way down to the Tobin estate near Paso Robles. Woods felt irritated. The music had gone on long enough, so he turned the radio off. He said, "There, isn't that a lot better?"

Max laughed. "This reminds me of the first time we drove together, when we fled from the Belfry. That seems like a long time ago."

"You're right about that. Things have changed quite a bit for us since then. I hear that the crew in Paso has really been working hard. How are they coming along with the restoration work on the old winery?"

"Really well. We'll be able to check it out tomorrow. Two weeks ago they moved the new tanks and equipment into the building. The rest of the place looks like a small city. They're building more homes for the workers and a day-care center for the working families. They're even talking about building a small school. It turns out Armando is quite a farmer. He works side by side with the rest of the workers in the fields. It will be interesting to see if they can get the winery up and running in time for this year's harvest."

"How do they even know what they're doing?"

"They're getting technical advice from Cal Poly, the university down in San Luis Obispo. The college is teaming up with them as an off-site, hands-on teaching opportunity for the students interested in their wine and viticulture program. Anna and Sophie are working together on that project. It will be pretty cool when we start making our own wine."

Woods asked, "Has anyone heard what happened to Anthony Holmes after he was arrested?

Max said, "He's in the state pen. Reed Jackson said he'll get what he deserves."

"What did Jackson mean?"

Max smirked. "It turns out that Holmes agreed to a plea deal so he and his family wouldn't have to go through the rigors of a jury trial. Holmes' attorney negotiated a twenty-month prison term, but his deal didn't specify the location. At the sentencing, the men from The Order detailed to the judge how Holmes wanted you and Armando killed to keep the bank's secret safe. The judge couldn't change the term on his sentence, but he did change the location where Holmes would serve his time. Jackson said that Holmes is doing hard time, and he will be treated exactly the same way Sophie and the rest of the foster girls would have been treated by those Chechen's mobsters if we hadn't got them out of there. According to Jackson, Holmes will get what he deserves for turning his back on Sophie when she needed help."

Woods grimaced a little. "Well, justice can be served in various ways, I guess. What's the latest with the Chechens?"

"Jackson has two of his men living on the compound at all times. They rotate the guys in, and Jackson pops in every once in a while. Armando has all the field workers in the valley keeping their eyes open for any gangster-type men lurking around."

"Didn't they identify a couple of them a few weeks ago? What happened to them?"

"Jackson made their lives miserable without even engaging them. Their rental cars mysteriously got flat tires, their luggage was stolen, they lost their billfolds, and they got in a couple of fights and ended up in jail. They were given wrong directions at every turn, and they were followed day and night. With the help of Armando's army, Jackson stayed two steps ahead of the gangsters. They eventually gave up and went away. Jackson said they'll be back, though, but with a different strategy. He's just like you, Mr. Woods. He never takes a break. The girls are going to be so surprised when they see you get out of the car. They'll have you for a whole week."

"Hey, I never said anything about all week. What am I going to do all day?"

"Don't worry. Anna will keep you busy. She's asked me if you could help her with some of the business decisions she's been trying to make. And Sophie needs some new blood around there. Jackson won't let her off the estate, so she gets a little stir-crazy. It's easy to feel like a third wheel around Anna and Armando. She will be thrilled you're going to hang out with her. I'll call you every day with updates, and you can give me instructions as needed. It's just one week. It will be good for you."

Chapter Forty-Eight

United States Penitentiary, Atwater, California
(Same day)

H E HEARD A SQUEAK FROM ABOVE. DID JEFE SHIFT HIS WEIGHT, OR WAS it another round? Holmes lay still. He shouted to himself, *Go back to sleep! Please go back to sleep!* Their cell was eight feet wide, twelve feet long, and nine feet high. Of its 864 cubic feet, not one square inch belonged to Anthony Holmes. Jefe owned the room, and he owned Holmes too.

Holmes had learned this quickly. There was no point in resisting Jefe the beast. Jefe was his cellmate, a thick, massive giant compared to Holmes. The first night, Holmes put up a fight, but Jefe got what he wanted and Holmes couldn't see, walk, or talk the next day. Jefe told Holmes, "I own you. It's not fair, but it's your new life. I want you to call me Jefe, Spanish for the boss— your boss." Any remote thought Holmes' had of standing up to Jefe vanished.

That was two months ago. Holmes never forgot Jefe's words. "You got two choices, little man—do as I say and take good care of your owner; don't hesitate and act like you enjoy what I give you—or take your beatings in here and take your chances on the outside without my protection." Holmes had twelve to eighteen months left. Twelve to eighteen left to wonder if a squeak from above was a shift of Jefe's weight or the start of round two.

Uncle Richard had said, "Do the time. It will go fast, and I'll get you back on your feet when you get out." Holmes tried to stay focused on what his life would be like after he was released. He figured Cecelia would be waiting, even though he hadn't heard from her yet. Uncle Richard would honor his commitment to take care of him after his time was up, and he still had a small piece of the bank coming to him after his father passed. Soon, he hoped.

A simple, quiet life with Cecelia was possible, not what he had planned just a few months before, but it could be a nice life. *We'll sell the jewelry I bought*

299

her. She said she didn't need it. I wish she would answer my calls. I wish I had never hired those traitors from The Order. The plea deal those bastards made to save their own asses got me transferred from a country club prison to this hellhole.

The springs screeched from above. Holmes knew that sound well. It was an intentional move. Jefe was coming.

Holmes forced his mind to replay his future—Cecelia, Uncle Richard, inheritance. Jefe climbed down from his bunk. "Time to take your medicine little man."

Cecilia, Uncle Richard, inher ...

Chapter FFF

Paso Robles, The Outpost

(The next day)

"WHERE ARE YOU?" MOTHER ASKED.

"I'm sitting in back of the Outpost, eating my lunch and calling you, just like I've done every other Saturday. Where are you?"

"I'm back in Moscow."

"What's he having you do now?"

"I don't want to talk about it. When can you come back?"

"It's still not going very well here. I spend every day in the fields with the Hispanic workers. Everyone thinks I'm Hispanic, including me. I speak Spanish, my hands are callused, and I haven't looked in a mirror for weeks. After work, I'm so tired, that I go straight to the bunkhouse and sleep with the other workers. I haven't been able to get close to any one of them except Armando. He works with us in the fields, but he's all work. He doesn't see me any differently than any of the other workers. He's a good man who only has eyes for Anna. I can't blame him. She's a real knockout."

"He's not the one you're supposed to get anyway."

"I know. Sophie never comes out to the fields. Sometimes she plays around with the sheep and other livestock, so I volunteered to shovel their shit onto a wagon and then spread it out in the vineyard. I've been shoveling shit for a week and haven't seen her once."

"Well, hang in there, and try to figure something out. I need you. Your father is getting worse and worse.

"Okay. I'll do what I can. I'll call you again in a week."

"Where are you?" asked Father.

"I'm sitting behind the Outpost on a picnic table, eating my lunch and talking with you, just like I do every Saturday."

"How are you able to get away like that?"

"I'm the only field worker who can drive, so I get to come here once a week to pick up supplies."

"How's it going? I thought you would be done by now."

"I'm doing the best I can. I work in the fields all day, and I sleep in the bunkhouse at night. I haven't had an opportunity to go up to the big house where they live. It's close to two kilometers from the bunkhouse, and they have security all over the place. The security men live with them. I don't have a weapon, and I have to figure out a way to do this without getting caught. I can report that I volunteered to shovel cattle manure as a way to see Sophie. I've been shoveling shit around the stables for a week, and haven't seen her once."

"I know you're doing your best. Is there any way you can use your special talents to get close to Max or Armando?"

"Armando is untouchable. Max goes fishing every Sunday morning by himself when he's here. Two weeks ago I went to the lake before him, and I know he was watching me. I'll try again tomorrow. He came in last night with some old guy that everyone seemed excited to see."

"Then get Max on your good side. That may be your way in."

"But I look like a field hand. The clothes you bought for me don't exactly show off my curves. I haven't had a decent bath or shower since I've been here. Max brings home a different California girl every week, and believe me; they're all dressed for the part. I'll see what I can do. I'll call you next week."

I ended the call and put my phone on the table. *That man doesn't care one thing about me. I'm just another one of his soldiers. He made me whore myself out to that disgusting Ivan. I'll never get that out of my mind. Then he made me team up with Mother to ruin those men in San Francisco. I'm glad we figured out a way to get what he wanted without having to prostitute ourselves again. I'm sure he wouldn't have cared one bit if the video showed one of those men raping me, just as long as he got his blackmail evidence. Who knows what he's making Mother do now or what's in store for me after I'm done here.*

Chapter Forty-Nine

The Tobin Compound

(The next day, early morning)

Max saw Apache making his rounds beyond the driveway and gave him a good-morning wave. He put his fishing pole and a white five-gallon plastic bucket into the back of an old pickup truck. He spotted Juan, the foreman in charge of all the field workers, down by the bunkhouse with a cup of coffee in his hand. He waved to him, pulled his bucket out of the pickup, pointed to it, and gave Juan a thumbs-up signal. Juan shook his head no and returned Max's smile. Juan let Max use his truck on Sunday mornings to go fishing, but he teased Max when all he ever brought back was that empty bucket.

The rest of the compound was still, except for an easy breeze rustling the live oak leaves. It was still a little too early for the birds to start their morning ruckus. Max looked to the east and thought he had at least an hour before the sun peeked over the top of the hills. He put the old truck in neutral and let it coast downhill, away from the estate house, on a dirt road that ran between the bunkhouse and the stable. The truck slowly and quietly bounced down the road, not disturbing anyone who was still asleep.

The dirt road meandered through the pasture and a wooded area to a remote lake. Max knew there had to be some big bass in that lake, but hadn't caught one yet.

Maybe today would be the day I show Juan a bucket filled with fish. Maybe this morning I'll get lucky and surprise him. Maybe this morning I'll get lucky and see that girl swimming in the lake again. Who is she? Where does she come from? If she's there again, I better talk to her this time.

Max stopped the pickup at his usual spot. He got out, grabbed his pole and bucket, and walked through the brush. The sun was still on the other side of the ridge, but there was enough light for him to see everything well. He heard the sound of water splashing. *She must be here.* He stopped and peeked through the bushes. *I bet she's not wearing anything.* Max walked through the brush and pretended not to notice her. He knew she saw him. He fiddled with some tackle on the end of his line and kept his head down.

"Excuse me, but I was here first."

The girl was treading water not far from him. Max stood up, and gave her his patented smile, hoping for a nice conversation. He said, "Good morning. Have you seen any fish swimming around in there?"

"No. Hopefully, I scared them all away. Who are you? This is private land. There is no public fishing allowed here. Armando runs this place. Does he know you're on his land?"

"Oh. I'm sorry. Armando is a friend of mine, and he said it was okay if I fished here. I didn't mean to bother anyone, just wanted to try to catch some fish."

She swam to the shore and walked out of the lake with nothing on but shimmery drops of water. Max looked down, but had to look up again. She stopped in front of him and said, "A gentleman would hand me that towel over there."

Max found the towel, picked it up, and brought it back to her.

She said, "I'm done here. You can have the place all to yourself." She smiled.

Man, she is absolutely beautiful.

She wrapped the towel around herself and said, "Brrr, it's cold out here." She stood in front of Max, waiting, then said, "Do you mind if I put my clothes on?"

"No. Sorry." He stepped out of her way and looked at the lake. "I won't look."

She laughed. "I think you already did."

"So how do you know Armando?"

"I work for him. I'm in the fields with him all day. This is a good place for me to get away from everything for a little while."

"You don't look like a field worker."

"I'm trying to get into the internship program at Cal Poly, but got here a little late for this semester. I needed a job, so this is working out great. Hopefully, everything will fall into place in a few weeks when the new term starts."

"How's it going for you here, working with Armando and everything?"

"He's great. Everyone is great. My best friend is a man named Juan. He reminds me of my grandfather." She picked up her wet towel. "Well, I'm off. Good luck with your fishing."

"You can stay here and keep me company."

"Not today. I have to get back and clean out the stables this morning. Maybe I'll see you here another time. Do me favor, next time honk your horn when you come over the rise. On second thought, don't bother. This was kinda fun. She smiled again.

Max extended his hand. "I'm Max. You made my day today."

"I'm Mandy. I'll take that as a compliment. Good-bye Max."

Max let his eyes take a walk all over her as she sauntered away.

Chapter GGG
Paso Robles, behind the Outpost
(Two weeks later)

MELAANA SAID TO HER MOTHER, "I DON'T KNOW IF HE'S GOING FISHING tomorrow. He came in last night with another blond bombshell. They all look alike, the exact opposite of what I look like. You should see him. I can't believe I'm saying this, but I think I'm falling for him. And, no, I still haven't met Sophie. But I'm still shoveling, loading, and spreading manure every day. No one else wants the job. I've become the boss, Juan's favorite. Did I tell you he reminds me of Grandpa?"

"Yes, you told me several times."

"The fields are looking really good. We finished the canopy management last week, so the rows in the field look nice and neat. This week we've been thinning the crop. It's called 'green harvesting.' It involves identifying bunches of grapes that aren't perfect, that don't fit in with the rest of the grapes. Once they're identified, we cut them off so the rest of the family of grapes will be stronger. Juan has taught me how to cut the bad bunches and keep the good ones. He trusts my judgment. Some of the red grapes are just now starting to change color. The pigment development is called 'veraison.' It's all very interesting."

"I never thought I'd hear you talk like this. It sounds like you're starting to like it there. I wish you could get back here. Your father isn't the same when you're not around."

"What's he making you do now?"

"I don't want to talk about it. Just do what you can to come back to me."

I ended the call, then called father. "Nothing new to report here. Next week I'll join the group of college interns coming in from Cal Poly for their working semester. I'll be learning more of the wine-making side of the business.

It should give me better access to Sophie. They're coming right along with the rebuild of the winery. I should get some time in there with Sophie and Anna."

"What's your take on why my men said they couldn't get the job done?"

"I believe what they told you is true. It's like we're on an island here, and those guys would stick out like two African men hanging around that small town where you grew up. I have to go now. They're expecting these supplies, and I have some shit to shovel."

A few hours later I was loading the manure cart behind the stables when I saw Sophie in with the lambs. *Now's my chance.* I fell down under the cart and screamed, "Help! Help!" For some reason the cart rolled back a little, and I screamed again. Sophie ran through the mud and looked under the cart. I said, "Here, grab my hand. I hurt my leg." Sophie reached for my muddy hand. *I could pull her in here now and smother her in the mud. It would be easy, and I could figure out a way to explain what happened. Grab her.*

Sophie took hold of both my muddy hands. The cart moved again. Sophie pulled, and I pulled back. Sophie's grip slipped because of my muddy hands and she fell back into the mud. Several other workers ran up to us. They pulled me out, and I fell into the mud right next to Sophie. We looked at each other and started to laugh. The concerned workers said, "*Esta bien,* Mandy?"

"*Si, si, esta bien. Gracias.*"

We looked at each other and began laughing again. The workers shook their head and walked away.

I finally said, "Thanks for saving me. Sorry you got all muddy." I flicked some mud off my fingers at her.

She squealed and laughed again. "Are you alright? How's your leg?"

I pulled my jeans up to look at my leg. "It looks okay. I slipped in the mud and got stuck under the cart. Then the cart moved, and I panicked. I shouldn't have yelled."

No. I'm glad you did. I don't think I've ever laughed that hard. What are you doing here anyway?"

"I just finished loading the cart with manure, and now I have to spread it in the vineyard."

"Can I help?"

"You don't want any part of this job. It's disgusting."

"Come on. I'm bored. I'll help you."

That's a surprise. The princess got her hands dirty. Maybe I can still end this today. We'll be all alone out in the vineyard.

An hour later I drove the tractor back to the compound, with Sophie in the back wagon. Armando was talking with Juan and the workers who pulled me out from under the cart. *This isn't good.* I stopped the tractor and turned around to see Sophie standing there, dirty as one of the pigs, with a huge smile on her face. I said, "Okay, this is your stop. Thanks for your help, but you better get cleaned up before I get in trouble."

"I want you to come up to the house for dinner tonight."

"Me? Dinner? I can't go up there."

"Why not?"

"I have more chores to get done, and it wouldn't be right. That's your home, and besides, I don't have anything to wear."

"Wait. There's Armando." Sophie yelled, "Armando! Come here." When Armando walked up to us, Sophie said, "Can Mandy join us for dinner tonight? She says she has too much work to do."

Armando looked at both of us in our muddy state and smiled. "It's alright with me, but you better clear everything with Juan."

"Come on, Mandy, please. You're my only friend. Max brought back another girl. Armando has Anna, and the rest of the guys have their wives. You have to say yes."

I looked at Armando again for confirmation, and he nodded yes. "Okay. I'll ask Juan."

Sophie jumped up and down and then hugged me. Come up as soon as you can. You can shower in one of the guest rooms, and we'll get you dressed. You can easily fit in my clothes."

Perfect. This will be easier than I thought.

Chapter HHH

Tobin Compound, inside the winery

(One week later)

ANNA LED JUAN INTO THE ROOM. A GROUP OF TEN STUDENTS SAT ON ONE side of the room. The new interns and I waited for our class to begin. Juan stood silent next to Anna. His appearance wasn't imposing. He was probably five feet, five inches tall, and he had a slight hitch in his step that I had never noticed in the fields. His salt-and-pepper hair was thick, but it needed to be trimmed. His thin, black mustache was a pleasing contrast to his nut-brown skin. He looked like the kind of man who would not be comfortable in front of a group of people—the kind of man who belonged in the vineyards.

A worn brown belt held the faded dungarees on his hips. His holey tee shirt and torn flannel shirt were probably older than any of the students in the room.

Anna introduced him to the class. She looked like a giant compared to Juan, but in the vineyards, he looked ten feet tall. The respect he had there lifted him above mere mortal status. He belonged in the vineyards, was as much a part of the vines as the grapes themselves. The vines seemed to recognize him, trust him, and wait for his instructions, as did the field workers. The rocky soil called him its friend, because he never applied toxic chemicals that poisoned the earth. Mother Nature encouraged the fog to roll in every morning to cover the vines and nourish them in appreciation of Juan's gentle touch. She trusted him. She was his partner.

Anna told us about how Juan had been born in the labor camp and how he had worked in these fields under his father's supervision. Twenty-five years ago he became the foreman. She said that no one knew this land and how to grow grapes better than Juan did. He bowed his head and shuffled his feet, obviously uncomfortable with her praise. He was a sweet, humble soul. He became even more uncomfortable after Anna left him alone in front of the class.

He looked surprised to be there. His hands shook. Seconds ticked away. We waited. As he stood there looking at his feet, I felt pity for this man who was so out of place. *Don't make him do this!* I screamed to myself. He kept his head down and walked to the door. *Good, he's leaving the room. He's going to where he belongs.* I wanted to go with him, to support him. *I will.* I stood to follow him outside.

But Juan stopped at a table at the side of the room and picked up a full bottle of wine with one hand and an empty bottle with his other hand. He walked back in front of us.

His head was still down. But then he looked up and said, "This bottle of wine was produced from grapes harvested from our fields five years ago."

I was surprised to hear him sound so confident.

"The wine in this bottle tells the story of what happened in the vineyards that year. It's the history of a record-breaking hot, dry growing season that included invasions of different pests that wanted what we wanted. They wanted to devour the plant for their own selfish needs. The taste, color, and aroma of the liquid in this bottle tell a story of how we pruned the vines the winter before. How we thinned the correct vine shoots and later dropped small bunches of grapes so only the best fruit would hang. How we discovered the invasion of the leafhopper and mite colonies early enough to let the cover crops grow high and bloom to attract parasitic wasps to defend our plants. That year the sun was extra hot. There wasn't a cloud in the sky all summer, so we doubled the time we normally spend on canopy management to shade the tender fruit. That year, not one grape was harvested before midnight or after five o'clock in the morning. We worked by the moonlight, like madmen fighting time, the dark, and the wasps to bring in the crop. The grapes that made this wine were completely different than any grapes before or after, and the wine in this bottle tells their story."

He looked at his feet again. Then with renewed vigor, he lifted the full bottle of wine into the air and said, "The wine in this bottle is the best wine ever produced in the history of the world, and it's not because of the science or chemistry you learn in those books. It's not because some winemaker mixed up some magic blend."

Juan pointed out the door and said, "Great wine is made in the *field!*"

He held up the empty bottle. "This bottle is empty. What are we going to put in this bottle?" How will this season test our knowledge, our skills, and our stamina? We don't know, but I am worried. I am always worried. This spring we escaped disaster because the early hot weather cunningly provoked the sap in the roots to rise into the vines. It was too early. If we had had a late frost, we would have been in big trouble. We were lucky."

A couple of students behind me whispered to each other. I turned around and gave them a look that could kill. They shut up.

Juan said, "The forecast looks good for the next few days, but do not let your guard down. We have a lot of work to do. Tomorrow I will take you into the fields and teach you how to make great wine. You must always remember, great wine is made in the *field!*"

I wanted to clap for my friend. I could not have been more proud of what kind of a man he was and what a great presentation he had made. He still belonged outside where the dirt was his friend, the breeze called his name, and the vines knew his touch.

What have I gotten myself into? I thought. *A few months ago I was the toast of Europe. Mother and I were on a level all by ourselves. Now I spend most of my time on my knees in the dirt, wondering why I'm here, wondering how this place and these people have changed me. I'm not sure I like what I've become.*

Chapter III

Paso Robles, The Outpost

(Later that day)

I DOWNSHIFTED THE OLD PICKUP AND PULLED INTO THE OUTPOST PARKING lot. But I couldn't park in my usual place. There were probably forty parked motorcycles scattered around the lot. I'd never seen this before. *Good, it looks like they're all on the bar side of the building.*

I walked up the steps to the provisions side of the building. Two disgusting looking men dressed in leather and chains sat in rocking chairs on the wide front porch. One of them said, "Why don't you come over here and show us what's underneath those overalls, sweetie?"

"Fuck off," I said and walked right past them. They laughed at me. I loaded the truck with the week's supplies without incident and went behind the building to eat my lunch and to call mother.

"Yes, I'm having dinner with them again tonight," I told Mother.

"Where are you with Max?"

"He's still bringing a different girl down every weekend, but he flirts with me. I can tell his eyes follow me wherever I go. I wish I could be alone with him. You should see him. But I have to completely ignore him. He asked me again to go fishing. I scolded him for even asking me when he's there with one of his dates. I don't know, maybe I'm just not his type. If I were, he wouldn't be bringing a different blonde down here every week. We're going to be dropping more fruit this week. Juan has me teaching the new interns. He keeps waiting for something to go wrong, because this has been a perfect year so far."

"You really do like being there."

"Yeah, I think I do. Why don't you come here for a visit?"

"I wish I could, but things aren't going well here."

"Why?"

"I think your father is going to put me out to his business partners. He has those young prostitutes hanging all over him, even when we go out together. The other night he made me join them in bed. I have to figure a way out of this. But if I ever told him no, I don't think you would see me again."

"Hang in there. I'll talk to him. You could— Hey, what are you doing? I'm sitting here!"

"What's going on?" Mother asked.

"Some men are giving me a hard time. I need to move. Hold on."

There were four of them. One of the filthy bikers grabbed my phone. "Give it back!"

The man said, "You'll get it back when we leave."

"Well, then leave."

Behind me, another man put his hands on my shoulders and said, "We'll leave when we're done with you. Looks like you're all alone back here, sweetie. You want to tell me to fuck off again? Go ahead."

I could tell this was no joke. These guys were serious.

"We're going to carry you over there behind those trees and do what we want, one at a time. If you're a good girl, you'll come out of this with no black eyes or cuts on your pretty face. If you're not a good girl, we'll still get what we want, but your friends won't recognize you for months." He grabbed my hair and pulled me up off the seat. I screamed. He clapped his hand over my mouth, and another man lifted my feet. They carried me toward the trees. I couldn't twist myself loose. *Oh, God! This is going to happen!*

"Sorry to interrupt you boys, but I heard the young lady say she wasn't interested," a voice came from behind us.

The bikers stopped and turned around. A man I had never seen before stood there by himself. He said, "Now put her down and be on your way."

One of the bikers said, "Buddy, you just stepped into a bucket of snakes."

———◦◦◦———

(Later that evening, Tobin dinner table)

"In a split second the stranger's fist erupted from his side and caught that biker square on his chin," I told them. "The biker fell flat on his back and didn't move. Another guy went after the man, and the biker who was holding my feet dropped them and took a knife out of his pocket. The stranger punched the first one square on the chin, and then his foot flew up and landed under the chin of the man with the knife. I thought his head was going to pop off. Both men fell down at the same time and didn't move. The fourth biker dropped me and pulled out his knife. The stranger told me to move away. I did. The stranger took a step toward the biker and said, "Run." That guy ran like a scared little girl through the trees and down the hill. The stranger asked if I was okay and helped me find my phone. Then he walked me to the truck and said he would wait there to make sure no one followed me. I don't know what would have happened to me if he hadn't stepped in.

Sophie said, "Who was he? Did you ask his name?"

"No, he was just concerned with how I was."

Armando said, "Did he have a deep, calm voice?"

"I guess so. You could tell he was in charge."

Armando said, "I think I know who it was." He looked at Cochise. "Sounds like some of Jackson's crystal clear persuasion to me."

Cochise grinned. "It does to me, too."

Armando said, "Where is he?" just as Jackson walked in.

"Where is who?" Jackson said.

"Hey, boss," Cochise said, "do you recognize this girl?"

Jackson looked at me. "Yeah, we met earlier today." He put his finger up to his lips, signifying, shhh. Then said to me, "Nice to see you again." He looked at Cochise and said, "I'm going to run down the backside of the mountain. I want to check how well the motion detectors work in the dark. Give me about twenty minutes to get down there, and then go check the monitors. We'll see if they pick up my movements as I come up through the brush."

(Later that night)

Sophie and I sat alone on the back patio, watching flames dance in the fire pit. I asked Sophie, "So who is that Jackson guy, and why is there such tight security around here?"

Sophie replied, "It's a long story, but here's the short version."

She told me everything that had happened to them, from the days in Munich to their move to the compound.

"What a horrible story. I had no idea there was such evil out there. Thank heaven for Jackson. He is a real hero."

"Yes he is. But this isn't the end of the story. The Chechens want revenge. We spotted two of the mobsters in town a few weeks ago, but Jackson figured out a way to get them to leave without them knowing we were on to them. We think they're still coming, and that's why I never leave the estate. I'm so glad I have you for a friend, Mandy. It's nice having someone I can talk with."

Later that night I walked down to the bunkhouse in the dark and thought about Sophie's story. I imagined Father's henchmen raping Sophie and her friends. I remembered how Jackson saved me from those bikers, men who were men probably just like my brothers. I thought about what Father was putting Mother through, and then I felt Father's slap on my face. What kind of man is he? What will he make me do the rest of my life?

The moon was up, and its soft light covered the hills and trees. I meandered down the hill, still thinking about my friend Sophie. I thought about how bad I wanted Max, but I know that will never happen.

I had to make a choice. I reminded myself about what will happen to mother and then conversely, I reminded myself of the life I was destined to live.

Those thoughts weighed me down. I sat down on the bare ground that sloped away from the Tobin family home to review my choices and to appreciate the moon's gift a little longer. The long shadows that were created from the bright moon seemed to come alive as I contemplated my options.

After a few minutes, it all became clear to me. *There is only one way out of this. I don't have a choice—I start tomorrow.*

Chapter JJJ
Behind the Outpost, Paso Robles
(One week later)

I CALLED MOTHER FROM MY PICNIC TABLE BEHIND THE OUTPOST AT MY usual time. "Keep your calendar open for the last weekend of September. I'm going to have this wrapped up here soon, and we'll be celebrating in Sochi at the next Formula 1 race. Just like we did in Monte Carlo. I'm making father set it up as a reward for my mission accomplished."

"That's just a couple of weeks away. How will you manage that?"

"I don't even want to think about it, much less talk about it. But I don't have a choice. This is the only way you and I have a chance to move forward. I haven't finalized everything with Father yet, but I'll call him right after I talk with you. My plan is for all three of us to meet in Sochi. After the weekend, you and I will fly back to Baku."

"Are you sure you can do it?" Are you sure you will be able to get away when it's done?

"Don't worry, I have a good plan. How's Father been treating you?"

We're in Moscow. Something is going on here that has him on edge. I wouldn't be surprised if he brings you in on it. I'm not sure my services are enough to keep everyone happy."

———

"Hello, Father. I have a plan for ending this soon, but I want you to agree to a few things."

"Let's hear your plan first."

"Okay. We will start harvesting the grapes soon. After the grapes are picked they will be crushed into juice. The juice will be poured into very large wooden vats, where yeast will turn the grape's sugar into alcohol. This fermentation

319

process takes about two weeks. My plan is to get Sophie next to a full tank, slit her throat over the red wine, and then wrap a log chain around her body. She'll lay at the bottom of the vat unnoticed until they drain the tank. There won't be any mess to clean up because I'll do it right over the big tank. I have the knife and chain waiting. They won't find her for at least two weeks. By that time I'll be long gone. But when they do find her, they'll know it was us. It will tear them apart."

"How will you get her alone?"

"That's no problem. I eat supper with her every night. We hang out by ourselves and go down to the winery to check on things after supper when no one is there. It should take less than ten minutes, with no noise and no mess."

"That is a good plan. You have this figured out well."

"I'm glad you approve. I need your help with a couple of things. Number one, get me a ticket for a flight out of the Oakland airport on Saturday, two weeks from today. That's the closest airport. Instead of coming here to The Outpost that morning, I'll drive straight to the airport. Number two, the Formula 1 race in Sochi is two weeks from tomorrow. I want to celebrate with you and Mother there, like we did in Monte Carlo when this whole thing started. While I'm there, you can take care of some business. Then I want to fly back to Baku with Mother for a couple of weeks before my next assignment."

"I think that will work. I was planning to do some entertaining in Sochi anyway. I'll send the ticket to your email account. You should know that your mother and I aren't like we were before."

"I know. You can bring your girls. Mother and I can share a room in Sochi. But I want you to promise me some time alone with you. We need to talk about how I can take on more responsibility. We need to start thinking globally. America is where the big money is. These people are clueless, and this democracy is open for business. I have a plan for what we should do to take advantage of it."

"What's your plan?"

"I want to tell you in person while we drink a nice glass of Russian vodka."

"Alright—you have a deal. I'll see you in a couple of weeks. I will want to hear about how it all went down."

Chapter Fifty

The Tobin Compound, Paso Robles

(Later that evening at the Tobin family dinner table)

THE DINING ROOM IN THE ESTATE HOME WAS HUGE. THE LONG TABLE IN the center of the room was surrounded with armoires, buffets, china cabinets, and servers hustling the salad plates off the table and refilling the water and wine glasses.

Sophie said to everyone at the table, "Mandy and I have an idea. We want to have a big picnic when we're done with this year's harvest and invite everyone. We want it to be in the pasture, under the live oaks.

"Great idea, girls," Max said. "We'll do it up right and have a lot of fun."

Armando stood up to get everyone's attention and said, "We agree, but you guys would be stealing our thunder."

"What do you mean?" Sophie said.

He looked down at Anna, smiled, and took her hand. "Anna and I have a couple of announcements to make that fit right in with your picnic idea. She and I are getting married, and we wanted"

Sophie screamed, jumped up, and ran around the table to hug Anna and Armando. Everyone else clapped their hands.

Armando said, "We want to have the ceremony after the wine barrels are tucked away in the caves." He looked at Sophie and Mandy. "And, like you two, we wanted to have a big outdoor picnic for the reception and invite everyone."

Mandy raised her glass of wine and said, "Great minds think alike—to Anna and Armando, congratulations."

Everyone at the table clinked glasses. The sound of muted applause came from the kitchen.

"You said you have a couple of announcements, so what's the other one?" Sophie said.

Armando took Anna's hand again and was about to speak when Anna shouted, "We're going to have a baby!"

Sophie screamed again and ran around the table. Anna stood up, and they embraced, both of them crying and smiling at the same time. Sophie pulled Armando into their hug, and then Max joined them and gathered everyone into the circle of his long, strong arms. Anna cried, "Our baby is due in March!" Sophie screamed once more. When Mandy came forward, Max pulled her into the huddle.

After a few minutes, everyone was back in their seat, carrying on animated conversations and making toasts. All the server's faces wore a wide smile.

Mandy surprised everyone by saying, "I need to tell you all some news. My mother has asked me to come home for a few days. Her father isn't doing well. She needs some support, and she wants me to spend some time with him. I was hoping to leave in a couple of weeks. It will only be for a few days. She looked at Armando. "Do you think that would be okay? I've already cleared it with Juan."

Armando said, "Of course that's okay. Take as much time as you need."

Sophie said, "I'm sorry to hear about your grandpa. Do you want me to come with you?"

Mandy looked at her and said, "Thanks, Sophie, but unfortunately, this is something I have to do by myself."

Chapter KKK

Sochi International Airport, Russia

(Two weeks later)

THE TIME GETTING THROUGH CUSTOMS WAS PAINFULLY SLOW. THE ONLY upside was I didn't have to wait for my luggage, because I just had a small carry-on. Mother said she'd be waiting for me at the baggage claim area. When I first noticed her, it hit me. I'd missed her more than I thought, and I had made the right decision. She saw me and ran up for an embrace. I could tell she had missed me just as much. I said, "Let's go. Get me out of here and back to civilization. Where are we staying? Father better have put us up somewhere nice."

"He did. We're at the Sochi Park Hotel. It's where all the action is—close to the beach, the Olympic Village, and the racetrack. We have a great room."

The drive away from the airport reminded me of home. Sochi is a beautiful part of Russia, but it's still littered with dull gray buildings and many hopeless faces of those living in poverty.

Chapter Fifty-One

The Tobin Compound, Paso Robles
(The same time, the same day, early morning)

ARMANDO SAID TO ANNA, "HOW DO YOU FEEL THIS MORNING? ANY BETter?"

Anna sat at the breakfast table next to Armando with a small glass of juice in the middle of her place setting. Armando covered her hand with his.

She replied, "Not so good again this morning. How could something so small and sweet make me feel so bad? I'll be okay. This is the last week of the first trimester. Hopefully, I'll feel better soon. Where's Sophie? Have you seen her yet this morning?"

"I haven't, but I'm sure she'll be down soon."

Maria came in with a plate of eggs and bacon for Armando and a bowl of oatmeal for Anna. Armando said, "Maria, have you seen Sophie this morning?"

"No, Mr. Ruiz, I haven't."

"Did she get any food from the kitchen last night?

"I'm sorry, Mr. Ruiz, but I wasn't in the kitchen last night. I could find out for you."

"No, thanks. She'll turn up."

Chapter LLL

Sochi Park Hotel, Sochi, Russia

(Same day, early afternoon)

MOTHER AND I WALKED INTO THE SOCHI PARK HOTEL LOBBY. EVERYONE there was dressed up. I was still wearing my grubby work clothes, so I felt completely out of place. I said to Mother, "Did you remember to bring me some decent clothes? I need to spend some time in the spa to get my game back on."

"Yes, I brought everything you need. You'll be as good as new before tonight's festivities. Let's go straight to our room."

"You go ahead. I have to use the bathroom. I'll meet you up there in just a minute."

"Okay, but hurry up. I want to hear how you got the job done and got out of there without getting caught."

Chapter Fifty-Two

Tobin Compound, Paso Robles

(The same day)

ARMANDO PUSHED HIS CLEAN PLATE AWAY AND DRANK THE LAST OF HIS coffee. He noticed that Anna had barely touched her oatmeal. "Why don't you take it easy today? They can take care of things without you for one day.

"They probably can, but this is the most crucial time of the year. We still have tons of grapes coming in, and we have to get them in the fermentation tanks as quickly as possible to preserve their freshness."

"I know, I know. But you should at least eat something."

She waved a hand to dismiss that subject and said, "You know what? I haven't seen Sophie since Mandy left. She must be holed up in her room. Or maybe she's already down at the winery. Will you call down there, Maria, and ask if anyone has seen her?"

"Yes, of course, Miss Anna."

Armando said, "What are the experts from Cal Poly saying about the grapes that have come in?"

"They love what they see. The viniculture specialist told me that he has never seen a better crop."

"Good to hear. I'll pass that on to Juan. He'll be pleased."

Maria returned and said, "Sorry to interrupt, but nobody at the winery has seen Sophie this morning."

Armando said to Anna, "Well, I better get out to the fields and see how this morning is starting out." He stood up, then bent down and kissed Anna. "At least take a couple of bites before you go. You both need some nourishment."

A piercing scream, then another, and then another scream came from the kitchen. Max ran into the dining room as though someone was chasing him. Armando instinctively moved in front of Anna.

Chapter MMM
Sochi Park Hotel, Sochi Russia
(Same day, early afternoon)

I WATCHED MOTHER WALK AWAY AND LOOKED AROUND THE LOBBY. I DIDN'T know what I was looking for. If he was there, he'd have to be the one to find me. I sat down on one of the upholstered benches against the wall, pulled out my phone, and scanned the room. A man walked my way. He must be the one. He sat down next to me and said, "Melaana?"

As I pretended to talk into my phone, I said, "You must be Stefan Yeager." I looked away.

He replied, "Yes, I am. Reed Jackson told me a lot about you. You are a brave young lady."

"I'm not sure about that. Do you have something for me?"

He said, "Yes, it's in this water bottle. I will leave it behind." He looked at his phone. , "There is a small vial inside with a dropper. Two or three drops on his skin or in a drink are all you need. You should have brought clear nail polish. Cover your fingers with it before you administer the toxic liquid. Flush the vial down a toilet, then wash your hands thoroughly."

I nodded.

He stood and walked away. I continued to pretend to talk into my phone, put the water bottle in my purse, and walked in the opposite direction.

Chapter Fifty-Three

Tobin Compound, Paso Robles

(The same day, the same time)

AFTER MAX CRASHED THROUGH THE KITCHEN DOOR, HE LOOKED AT ANNA and said, "That sister of yours—"

Sophie came flying though the same door holding a white five-gallon bucket. She yelled at Anna and Armando, "Don't believe a word he says. I caught this fish myself. He's never even caught one fish." She showed them a big fish flopping around in the bucket.

Max said, "I walked away to take a leak. She grabbed my pole and caught my fish."

"Not your fish. This is *my* fish," Sophie yelled as the fish jumped out of the bucket and onto Anna's feet. She and Sophie screamed again.

Chapter NNN

Tobin Compound, Paso Robles

(Two months later)

THE AFTERNOON SKY WAS THE MOST BEAUTIFUL COLOR OF BLUE I'D EVER seen. Small, popcorn-white clouds dotted the sky. The gentle breeze was just enough to offset the warm rays of the sun. Today was the perfect day for Anna and Armando's wedding. Mother and I sat in the back row of wooden chairs on the right side of the aisle. Mother had a twinkle in her eyes—something I thought she had lost forever. Juan and his wife sat across the aisle from us. He noticed I was looking at him and smiled.

His smile reminded me about how he had taken me under his wing from the very first day. I suppose he saw something in me that only a parent could. It occurred to me how the process of "green harvesting"—cutting the bad bunches of grapes off the vine so the rest of the family could grow stronger— applied to my family. My father was a bad bunch. Either he had to go or we did.

Three of the field workers played a soft melody on their guitars. I clutched Mother's hand and reminded myself that asking Reed Jackson for help was the best thing I've ever done. His plan to make it look like a typical Federation assassination was brilliant. Everyone, including Mother, believed that Father had been betrayed, and none of the local authorities cared. Only Jackson, that nice German policeman, and I know the truth.

The music picked up, signifying the start of the ceremony. Mother looked even more excited now. Max and Sophie started the procession, holding hands as they marched down the aisle. Sophie looked at me and smiled. Max gave me a wink. I looked back. Standing tall and holding Allen Woods's arm, Anna slowly stepped forward with a beautiful grace and a small baby bump.

Mother said, "Who is that man?"

"He was the one who helped get Max, Anna, and Sophie back together. He was a close friend of their parents."

Max stood next to Armando with pride written all over his face as he watched Anna approached them. Armando's face was full of emotion. Mr. Woods delivered Anna. The priest encircled the lasso of wildflowers that Sophie and I had made earlier in the day over their heads so as to make a figure eight. Sophie helped the priest from the side.

They recited their vows. The priest lifted the lasso. Armando kissed his bride. Anna and Armando walked back down the aisle under a shower of wildflower petals.

The sun was below the hills of the western horizon but still above the Pacific Ocean. I had noticed before that the last ten minutes of hidden sunlight changed the sky to a dark blue and gave everything else a golden sheen. The Christmas lights we had stranded from the sprawling live oaks twinkled above the tables of wedding guests, who had finished their dessert and were on their way to the dance floor.

I sat alone at our table and watched the activity of the wedding celebration. Max's heartfelt speech before dinner ended with, "I was thrilled to find out I had a sister and then even more so when we found Sophie. Today I welcome my brother. Sophie and I are here to support Anna and Armando, and we hope one day that we will find the same happiness." Sophie finished her short speech by saying, "Every day for the last year has been better than the day before, and today is by far the best one of all."

The dance floor was filled with good people with a smile on their face. Juan and his wife were right in the middle of the crowd. Max's friend Tom Riley from Scotland swayed with his wife, Rose. Anna and Armando looked so good together. *Where's Mother?* Max, Sophie, and Sophie's friend Lara pulled anyone without a partner into the chaos.

That's when I heard them. I knew they were coming, but I didn't think it would be this soon. *I'm just going to sit back here. I should be okay here out of the way. I hope I don't get hurt.* The screaming started right on cue. *Where's Mother? She'll be trampled.* The dance floor emptied in a flash while some of the workers herded the steers away from the party and back down the hill. Within a few minutes the music, the laughter, and the dancing started again.

Cochise and the other men from The Agency danced with their wives, joining in the fun. Sophie danced with Armando's cousin. *That's an interesting development.* He was another tall, dark, and striking young man, who reminded me of Armando. She was smiling ear to ear. It was nice to see.

Then Max appeared in front of me with his hand out and said, "Will you dance with me?"

I looked up to see his handsome face as he waited for my reply. I realized for the first time that he hadn't brought one of his blonde friends with him. I smiled at him, thinking, *Finally.* Then I leaned back a little in my chair, folded my arms, and said, "Where are your girlfriends tonight?"

Still holding his hand out, he replied, "I don't have any girlfriends. I came for you."

I placed my hand in his and smiled the biggest, most uncontrolled, natural smile I'd ever shown anyone. Again I said to myself, *Finally.*

Song after song we danced, touched, talked, and laughed right in the middle of the celebration. I'd never felt so happy.

When the music slowed, Max pulled me close. I rested my head on his chest. Here I was, in the middle of this splendor with a feeling of belonging, of family, and of love. I pressed my body against Max, and he responded. Then I spotted Mother. She was on the dance floor, captured in Reed Jackson's arms. My eyes brimmed with tears. My heart swelled with the warm flush of an emotion that I'd never known.

I couldn't go on. Something inside made me stop and back away from Max. He looked down and brushed away my tears. My knees went weak. He picked me up as though I was a feather and cradled me in his arms. I surrendered to his strength as he carried me away.

Finally.

ACKNOWLEDGMENT

Thank you to Paul Thayer, my editor. He is a true professional and teacher. Thank you to my friends who gave me encouragement and suggestions. Thank you to Jesse and Abby for inspiration, and to Julie Ann, my research assistant.